A LIKEABLE WOMAN

Also by May Cobb

Big Woods
The Hunting Wives
My Summer Darlings

A LIKEABLE WOMAN

♦ ♦ ♦

MAY COBB

BERKLEY | NEW YORK

BERKLEY
An imprint of Penguin Random House LLC
penguinrandomhouse.com

Library of Congress Cataloging-in-Publication Data

Names: Cobb, May, 1973- author.
Title: A likeable woman / May Cobb.
Description: New York : Berkley, [2023]
Identifiers: LCCN 2022049264 (print) | LCCN 2022049265 (ebook) |
ISBN 9780593546796 (hardcover) | ISBN 9780593546819 (ebook)
Classification: LCC PS3603.O225554 L55 2023 (print) |
LCC PS3603.O225554 (ebook) | DDC 813/.6—dc23
LC record available at https://lccn.loc.gov/2022049264
LC ebook record available at https://lccn.loc.gov/2022049265

Printed in the United States of America
1st Printing

Book design by Elke Sigal

This is a work of fiction. Names, characters, places, and incidents either are the product of the author's imagination or are used fictitiously, and any resemblance to actual persons, living or dead, business establishments, events, or locales is entirely coincidental.

This one's for Liz, my incredible mother, who taught me from a very young age that it's best to aspire to be an unlikeable woman.

A LIKEABLE WOMAN

PROLOGUE

It's night. Nearly eleven and pitch-black on the street.

Elsewhere in the neighborhood, streetlights cast golden pools of light across the pavement, but not down here on the edge of the circle, near the entrance to the woods.

I can barely see my shaking hand in front of my face, but it's so cold out, my breath clouds white in front of me. And other than the wind, which rattles through the tops of the pines, it's quiet.

And dark. So dark.

Good. She can't see me.

But I can see her. Through the chain link, which is strangled by vines that should have been weeded a long time ago. She probably thinks it looks so cool.

Through the silver net of fencing, I see the white wooden shed. The light is on inside; she's sitting at the table. My blood boils at the sight of her. Her hair draped around her, her face made up like a whore's.

She thinks she can get away with anything. Well, she's about to learn that I'm putting an end to all that tonight.

1

KIRA

Midmorning sunlight winks through the glass-slat windows, but I'm still lying in bed, the black paper invitation shouting at me from across the room. It's sitting upright, resting atop a stack of junk mail on my wooden café table, where it's been since Friday evening after I retrieved it from the mailbox.

> *20 years and still going strong!*
>
> *We'd be delighted if you'd join us,*
> *Chad & Genevieve Greer,*
> *as we re–tie the knot with a*
> *Vow Renewal Ceremony*
>
> *Saturday, October 15th, at 6 p.m.*
> *The Walters's Farm*
> *7328 Evergreen Road*
> *Longview, Texas*
>
> *Please RSVP by September 15th*

The envelope it came in—black on the outside, bloodred on the inside—is gashed open, the tiny RSVP card peeking out like the tip of a cat's tongue.

I can't pull it out yet and mark "Attending" or "Not attending" because I can't decide.

Of course Genevieve wants to throw herself a bash. She's always been attention seeking, and from the group text I've been ignoring since Friday night, it's clear that it's not just the ceremony itself but a weekend full of eye-rolling events she has planned for us.

Friday night at the bowling alley, kids welcome. Saturday morning ladies' brunch at The Farm (no doubt some farm-to-table BS), followed by crafts of some sort (WTF, are we five years old?), ending with a spa day complete with manis and pedis and a wine tasting.

The guys, of course, get to do the fun stuff on Saturday—canoeing, archery, and duck hunting. Chased with a private uncorking of a local distillery's batch of bourbon made exclusively for the occasion.

I'm certain the entire event will be just a giant Band-Aid on what has, from all accounts, been a very nasty marriage. But it's not just the spectacle that's making the pit of dread in my stomach expand. It's the prospect of having to go home again. A place I fled over twenty years ago, after I lost her. Mom.

I've returned only the one time, for my father's funeral.

All eyes were on me the entire day, to see if I would shatter. I'm the fragile one, the potentially unstable one. *Just like her mother,* they shout-whispered. And also, I'm the only one who believes my mother was murdered, that she didn't die by her own hand.

I've put acres of auburn desert land between me and East Texas, moving as far west as I could without plunging into the Pacific. But every so often—especially for events like these—East Texas tugs at me, threatening to yank me back to its pine-soaked atmosphere and engulf me. Just reading the invitation has landed me in bed for virtually the entire weekend.

Especially because of the venue: The Farm. The last place anyone saw her alive.

She wandered into the woods. She'd been having one of her spells, they said. Sadie. Always quick to tears. Hysterical. They glanced up from the bonfire and saw the shock of her platinum hair, her russet-colored fox-fur coat, before she slipped into the forest.

Now I'm up, pacing the thinly carpeted length of my six-hundred-square-foot apartment in the Hollywood Hills. I make a pass by the invitation, wanting to snatch it and shred it into tiny pieces, but instead I continue on into the galley kitchen, where I open the fridge and drag out a paper carton of pad Thai. I eat it cold from the container as I lean against the counter.

When I opened the mail on Friday evening after work and my cell started exploding with the group texts from my childhood friends—Genevieve being more frenemy than friend—I ordered four servings of pad Thai and three bowls of coconut and mushroom soup, knowing I'd be moored at home for days.

I sat, parked at my tiny café table, staring at the invitation, swirling the steaming noodles around on a plate, forcing myself to eat small forkfuls.

And I texted Jack. Jack Sherman, my childhood best friend and former crush. We were each other's first kiss, four years old and zipped up inside his Incredible Hulk sleeping bag. An odd kiss where our teeth knocked together. We only ever text now to wish each other a happy birthday—his on October tenth, mine August third—and I took this as an excuse to check in. Pathetic, really, since he's been blissfully married for a decade now and has a real life, unlike me. He's a neurosurgeon at Johns Hopkins and has a three-year-old son.

Me: Umm . . . You guys going?

Jack: Umm . . . Hi! And hell no 😊.

A sinking feeling spread over me. Even though I didn't want to return home, the chance of seeing Jack again after all this time cast butterflies across my chest.

A few seconds later, the three dots started leaping again, letting me know he was writing more.

Jack: Why? Are you?

Me: Don't know yet. Probably not.

Jack: Well, Melanie's going. I told her she could have a girls' weekend, but she's pissed. Wants me there with her. I'm just . . . not really like those guys anymore, y'know? And I can't imagine you want to go either?

This was the most we had texted in years, and my pulse jangled in my neck, my face flush from this new contact with him. I could hear his voice across the line, as if he were speaking in my ear. That rich oaky voice, which was never bent with the twang of the region but always sounded sonorous and kind. And yes, sexy.

Also, Jack was the one who came to my side the night they found her. When I was shaking, when I wouldn't let anyone else near me, he asked my father if he could see me. I remember him standing in the doorway to my bedroom, his fifteen-year-old bulk filling the space. A silhouette of strength leaning against the frame. I was in bed, buried under my floral-printed bedspread, eyes bloated from wailing.

He'd been at an out-of-town football game that night, a few hours away. He was a second-string running back, usually sitting on the bench—sports were never his forte; he only played football because the rest of his friends were doing the same—and he told me he'd come as soon as he'd gotten off the bus and heard the news.

He crossed the room, slid into bed, and roped his strong arms around me.

"You're not alone, you're not alone," he whispered in his soothing voice, over and over again, as more hot tears gushed out of me. Somehow, he knew those were the very words I needed to hear then, because my mom and I had been simpatico. Best friends. Tethered by our artistic souls—misunderstood by Katie, my older and more sensible sister; and my cold-faced father, Richard. We had existed in a kind of bubble, and Katie had been part of it at first, but then she grew out of it, drifted away from us.

I'd spend bottomless hours in Mom's art shed as a little girl, our knees touching as she guided wax over cotton sheets for her batiks while I moved globs of paint around on poster board. I can still hear her voice in my head, sometimes singsongy, sometimes frantic, sharing things with me she probably shouldn't have been. Always followed by a "Don't mention that to your father, Kira."

She named me Kira after Olivia Newton John's character in *Xanadu*, one of her favorite films. She'd seen it at the drive-in years before I was born and loved the music, the mythology, the story of nine muses who cross back and forth between time. When it finally came out on VHS, she made me watch it over and over with her.

After I couldn't stomach any more pad Thai, I peeled the plastic lid off the soup as I considered how to respond to Jack. I knew what he meant by *And I can't imagine you want to go either.* He was referring to Mom, but I didn't want to get into that with him, to prick at that old wound again, so I dodged the subject.

Me: I need time to figure it out. But I was thinking about it.

Jack: Well, I'll only go if you go, so let me know.

I sent back a simple thumbs-up emoji and placed my cell face-down, cradling my chin in my hands.

I woke early this morning, before the birds started their chirping and when the sky was still a deep indigo, and dragged my laptop into the bed. I emailed in sick to work. I sat there, cross-legged in bed, my laptop baking my thighs, looking at flights, before slamming it shut without booking anything.

I shouldn't go. I shouldn't put myself through all that, but as pitiful as it sounds, I want to see Jack. I want to see myself reflected in his face, the strong girl I was once was, his neighborhood friend who he admired. *I'll only go if you go.* Sounds like he wants to see me, too. And now I have to decide if it's worth it. My vision blurs around the edges when I think about facing the others—Genevieve, Katie, not to mention Jack's wife, Melanie—and also returning to The Farm.

I refold the carton of pad Thai, shove it back in the fridge. Drag myself the few steps back to bed, where I wilt under the covers and feel myself sinking back down into sleep.

2

KIRA

It must be past noon, because the garbage men are here; I'm yanked from sleep to the sound of the windowpanes rattling as the trucks rumble past.

The air inside in the apartment is hot and still. These old-timey windows—which have a dozen glass slats on them that you hand-crank open—are great for maximizing air flow, but wretched for noise control.

I can hear the twist of a key in a neighbor's lock or the fumes of an argument from the couple in the house across the street if they're out on their front lawn. And on trash day, the tiny panes practically flutter as the hulking vehicles squeeze along the tiny streets.

Usually, I'll open the windows and the smell of jasmine will float through the room, but today I leave them shut. The Santa Ana winds are already gusting from the east, carrying the scorched-earth heat of the desert with them, so I lie under my sheet, damp with sweat, my studio now a tinderbox.

My cell starts to chime, small pops of sound that cause my anxiety to surge with each ping, and I glance at the sender.

My grandmother.

A second text lands right on top of the first.

Insistent dinging.

It's *so* like her not to give me a chance to respond before launching another round at me.

But I don't swipe and clear them; I let them rest for now. She'd be able to tell from the "Read" notification if I checked them, and then my window of time for replying would slam shut.

I've thought about changing that in settings—making it so she can't tell if I've seen her texts or not—but she would notice, and then we'd have to have a guilt trip–induced discussion about why I'm trying to avoid her. Not worth it.

Ah, my grandmother. Granny Foster. Still in control of me all these years later, even though there are fifteen hundred miles between us.

Some of it has to do with the money. She established a trust fund for me when I was little, and when I turned eighteen, I was eligible to start drawing off it.

I never have. I consider it blood money. Hush money. Granny is the one who has gaslit me the most over the years about Mom, ushering me off to boarding school right after she died so I would quit asking questions, quit being such a hassle for my father. I was a basket case, erratic, and all the other labels she was able to get her shrink to slap on me.

I *was* a basket case, but who wouldn't be?

So I leave the money untouched. I don't even open up my statements anymore; I just drop them in a file. It's not like it's enough to quit my dead-end job over, but I could probably do something nice for myself with it, like upgrade apartments or take a year off and focus on my art. I haven't touched my paintbrushes in years now. They just languish on the top shelf of my closet, throwing shades of guilt at me each time I reach up there for a hat or a bag. They rest next to Mom's batiks—which I haven't touched since shortly after her death; I can't bear to.

Anything to do with art has gone mute in my life. I haven't really painted in earnest since college. Pathetic. But without the structure of classes, and faced with the harsh reality that most painters don't make a living from their art right out of the gate, I chose the safe route, taking dependable office jobs. I wouldn't allow myself to touch Gran's money then, and I still won't. To do so would feel like I'm going along with their narrative, being complicit in their lies.

I loved my apartment when I first moved in over two decades ago. The off-white stucco exterior, hugged by walls of fuchsia bougainvillea. The spindly grapefruit tree out back, always pregnant with fruit, its peach-colored orbs rolling on the floor of the quaint parking lot.

I live on Cheremoya Avenue in Beachwood Canyon, a winding street that sits right underneath the Hollywood sign.

Moving here felt so exotic, so different from home, with its ranch-style houses and forested land. If I step out onto my playing card–size balcony and crane my neck just right, I have a sweeping view of the canyon below me—more stucco homes lining twisting streets that rise and fall and switch back so sharply that it almost feels Mediterranean.

I love it still, but when Granny showed up about ten years ago, uninvited and unannounced, when she crossed my threshold she proclaimed, "Oh my, Kira, you have sunk so low."

The industrial carpet with its edges frayed from my vacuum, the settling cracks and peeling plaster in the dining area, the absence of a dishwasher, the lack of AC on one of a handful of blistering days when we have a heat wave, like today: all of these made Granny's hit list, which she ticked off to me over dinner that night, and then I started to view my abode through her judgmental lens.

If Granny had her way, I'd be living back in East Texas, married to a good local boy with connections, floating from room to room in a white-carpeted house while a nanny attended to my babies. She thinks I deserve more than what I have now.

I don't want those things, but she's not wrong. My life is a glacier—frozen, unmoving. I'm thirty-eight. Still single with no end in sight. I'm lonely most of the time, except when I have the occasional dinner with my small group of friends, who are really just acquaintances. Hate my job. Wish like hell I'd stuck with my sole passion—painting—instead of letting it wither away after college. Every year I swear I'm going to dig in, spend the weekends creating new work, update my portfolio, and drop into galleries to show them my stuff, but every year I fail to do so. I just can't find the drive, even though it's all I really want to do. The only time I've felt truly alive was when I was creating, but it's as if there's an invisible shroud wrapped around me, weighing me down.

It's what Sadie and I shared; it was our connection. And though I continued to paint in college after her death, as a way of holding on to her, with her gone now over two decades, that part of me still feels lost.

When Granny arrived here for her one and only visit, I heard a horn blasting and peered outside. I was greeted by a black stretch limo containing Granny, her window lowered, waving a white-gloved hand at me. The driver came around and opened her door; she was wearing an Hermès scarf on her head and oversized sunglasses, and she did an honest-to-goodness visual sweep of the street, as if she were scouting for paparazzi lying in wait.

She stayed only the one night, at the Beverly Hills Hotel, and whisked me down the hill to dinner at Musso & Frank, where she flirted endlessly with our middle-aged waiter, a plump, boyishly handsome man with silver hair.

I wasn't surprised when he flirted back, all but ignoring me.

I'm used to being invisible around Granny. Her tongue is ruthlessly witty and biting. And yes, she's attractive, with high cheekbones and steel-blue eyes, her silver hair luminous and perfectly coiffed, hanging just above her chin line. But more than that, she radiates power, and she's always dressed to kill—her slender frame usually swishing inside a silk Prada trench, with snappy trousers and pointed flats in every shade. Old money can buy you those things.

I roll onto my back and lift the phone to my face, swiping open the first text.

Granny: You got the invite, right? And you're coming?

I place the warm cell on my chest, exhaling a jagged sigh. I swipe and read the second text.

Granny: I really think you should.

That text is followed by the shoulder-shrug emoji.

I simply text back No. A burning spot of indignation spears my chest as I hit send. Even though I'm actually considering it, I want to cut her off, make this decision on my own.

Although she's never returned to Los Angeles since that brief visit, which she refers to as her "wellness check," Granny's presence still floods my life. Usually in the form of terse, handwritten letters that are folded around my childhood friends' wedding announcements from the local paper

Granny typically includes commentary on them, such as, "She's one of the last ones. A pity she's found someone finally and you still haven't."

Her perfume, White Shoulders, permeates the air around her letters, and it's as if she's in the room with me, giving her head a quick shake of disapproval.

I'm hoping my text has shut her down, but no, two more surf into my cell before the screen even darkens again.

Granny: I think it's time you come home. I have something of your mother's. Something she was keeping in secret, and it's time you found out about it.

Sigh. I'm not falling for her bait. She's trying to reel me back home because she wants to see me again, but I want nothing to do with that. She's lying. But before I can call her bluff, another text lands. Reading it knocks the breath out of me.

Granny: And Kira, I think you're right about your mother, about how she died.

3

SADIE

It happened again last night. At the dinner party. I caught Mike staring at me, his hooded, kind eyes sheepish over the edge of his sherry glass, sneaking a glance while Bertie carried forth, her harsh laughter barking out of her like an excited seal.

My cheeks flamed and heat pooled in my stomach under his stare, but I quickly dropped my gaze from his, worried the others might notice.

Bertie.

But especially Richard.

I waited for my moment, until after I'd cleared all the platters from the dinner table and everyone was clumped in groups in our sunken living room, half-mooned around the various glass ashtrays I'd set out just before the guests arrived.

The air swirled with cigarette smoke, a nicotine stratus cloud hovering over our heads, and Mike rose and headed down the back hallway toward the guest bath.

I took it as a signal and his timing was perfect: Richard was knee-to-knee with Ty Henderson, both men gnawing on cigars, and Bertie, once again, was holding forth to a clique of women on the sofa. Even though she's new to town—or perhaps because of the fact that she's new—all of my friends are captivated by her.

Swiping a near-empty champagne flute from an end table, I

beelined to the kitchen under the guise of tidying up. No one seemed to notice my exit. The clamor from the living room hummed through the paneled wall, giving me a sense of invisibility, so I rounded the corner and waited in the dimly lit hall for Mike to finish up in the bathroom.

Our home looks like a set design from a 1970s film; it's badly in need of updating, but we can't afford it. Richard's mother, Granny Foster, has offered, of course, to foot the bill, but Richard doesn't want to be beholden to her any more than we already are. And neither do I. Plus, I still like it. The gold chintz wallpaper with bamboo shoots in the dining room. The shiny penny-colored parquet floors. The candy-yellow cabinetry in the kitchen. It reminds me of my twenties, when we had this house built; I'm still in denial that I've just turned forty. I never thought my life would turn out this way.

When Mike exited the bathroom, he froze in place when he saw me, his eyes crinkling into a smile. Like me, Mike's not a smoker; I could smell the sharp tang of soap on his hands and his full, dark brown beard carried the scent of oaky aftershave.

I guess I should clarify. I *do* indulge, but I'm not a pack-a-day smoker like everyone else. I'll have one only when I'm really worked up and also when I'm all by myself. Although Richard enjoys his cigars, he doesn't like me smoking, so I do it in secret.

I've been doing a lot of things in secret lately.

"I was just picking up some things in my daughter's room," I said to Mike, my neck turning crimson at the lie. "They're at their friends' for the night and I—"

He leaned against the wall, a smile playing on his lips as if he knew I was lying, as if he knew *he* was the reason for my being back here. He loosened the tie around his neck, a boyish move that made my crush on him surge even more, and I could've kissed him then; I wanted to, but instead, I just stood there like a dipshit, my hands twisting around each other like trapped birds.

"Oh?" Mike said, his voice rich and deep.

He took a step toward me. Something about the way he looks at me makes me feel like he's really seeing me.

"Well *there* you are." Bertie's voice rushed down the hall at us, half-indignant, half-playful, as if Mike were a child caught with a fist in the cookie jar.

Could she tell there were sparks crackling between us? It's not like I left a lipstick print on his collar, but still, she stepped over to him, encircled his waist with her arm, lassoing him into her.

"I was just taking Mike a hand towel; I forgot to stock the bathroom before the party. Silly me!" My voice came out shaky and shrill, and there I was, sliding into my usual posture of self-deprecation. I don't know why I do that, only that it seems to keep things smooth, seems to disarm folks. And it always works on Richard.

"Well, thank you for looking after him, Sadie." She fumbled my name around in her mouth as if she'd forgotten it but remembered it at the last second. "And thank you, dear, for just everything." The expression in her eyes was unreadable behind her cat-eye glasses, and even though her words were drawn out with warmth, I detected a pinprick of jealousy from her, laced with condescension.

"Everything," she continued, stretching out the *ev-er-y* until it contained more syllables than one would think is possible, "has been marvelous tonight: the food, the drinks, the company. Ev-er-y-thing."

Mike looked slightly embarrassed by her over-the-top declarations, but nodded when she twisted her neck toward him, expecting him to concur.

She tapped the face of her silver Rolex with a powder-pink

fingernail. "We should be going, we have an early day tomorrow, remember?"

Mike nodded and they moved down the hall together, Bertie whispering something in his ear before erupting into her barking laugh again.

I didn't even want to have the stupid dinner party—we'd just had one a few months before—but Granny Foster had insisted, and Richard is desperately trying to score more clients, so I pretended to be overjoyed at the prospect of hosting, even though I was screaming inside.

But as much as I dislike parties, throwing them is also a reprieve from Richard's temper, which has been too much to bear lately. I'll do nearly anything to keep him happy. Plus, a house filled with people means he has to be on his best behavior, so even though the chore of cleaning up from the aftermath is exhausting—I can barely keep the house picked up when it's just Richard and the girls leaving their messes—the thought of blocking out several hours of time without having to walk on eggshells around him sounded divine to me.

And Granny Foster and Hilda, her longtime housekeeper, do most of the cooking. They arrive with the dishes premade—beef Wellington, potatoes au gratin, a leafy salad—and Hilda sets about warming them in the oven, squinting around at my messy kitchen with a pinched look of distaste on her face.

I swear that woman has it out for me.

Granny Foster wants everyone to think I've prepared the spread—"It's the impression, dear"—so she and Hilda slink out the back door just before the guests arrive.

I'm only in charge of the relish tray, which amounts to nothing more than peeling open and draining a can of black olives, then arranging them on a platter with pickled asparagus, grapes, and a cheese ball I made the night before. I studded it with crab meat and jalapenos, then rolled it on a cookie sheet dusted with Ritz crackers, before wrapping it in cellophane and popping it in the fridge.

And for this party, in particular, as much as I might have dreaded it, I was thrilled at the prospect of seeing Mike again.

Even though we just had those few stolen moments, my stomach has been in a pinch all day thinking about his eyes on me, how he moved toward me in the hallway. I'd been practically skipping around the house earlier, refilling the dishwasher, ironing the table linens, and emptying the ashtrays while Richard stayed cemented on the sofa in a martini-hangover haze, eyes trained on the television, watching college football, unaware (or, at least, I hoped) that my attitude had nothing to do with him and everything to do with Mike.

4

KIRA

I'm parked at a small crescent-shaped table at an upscale airport trattoria inside LAX. Though it's just ten in the morning, they're already serving pizza, and I'm grateful; airport breakfasts make me squeamish.

The nutty, bitter aroma of freshly brewed espresso mingles with the charred-dough smell from the pizza oven, and for a moment, I'm excited, as if I'm on my way to someplace exotic, like Europe. As if I won't be boarding my plane soon, hurtling toward Texas.

After I received Granny's last text, I laid in bed for an hour, my abdomen contracting, stomach clenching and unclenching.

And then I called Jack. I assumed it would roll to voice mail because he'd most likely be busy at the hospital, but surprisingly, he answered on the second ring.

"Kira Foster. The one and only," he greeted me, his voice warm butter in my ear. But all around him, a wave of tinny noises. "Hang on, I'll step outside."

The sound of birds chirping soon filled the line and Jack exhaled. "In the courtyard now."

"Is this a busy time? I mean, I know it is. Are you sure you can—"

"It's not every day that your old friend calls. And yeah, I'm actually finished with my rounds and need a break. How *are* you?"

It was a simple question, but the genuine affection in his voice made my eyes sting with tears.

"I'm . . . good?" I said, curving the word into a question, as if my state of being were up for debate. It was. "How are you guys? How's Aiden?"

"Good, too. I mean, it's becoming more challenging with him. I'm sure you've seen Melanie's updates on Facebook." I had.

Aiden was diagnosed with autism six months ago, and while Melanie doesn't flood the social media airwaves with their private family life, she has thrown up a few cryptic posts that hint at how hard their life has become.

"Yes. I'm so sorry I haven't been in touch about that, I—" My voice cracked with emotion.

"Please. If I know you, you were respecting our privacy, and I respect *that* more than anything else."

He was right. When I first saw her post—a photo of a golden-locked Aiden sitting cross-legged on what appeared to be their back patio, eyes downcast and cheeks pink from the sun—with the simple caption: "It's what we suspected. Aiden has been formally diagnosed with ASD," my first instinct had been to get in touch, by either texting or calling.

But the longer I'd waited, debating the right words to say to Jack, the more increasingly odd it felt to reach out. Especially since we *don't* chat, haven't chatted in years. It did feel like I would have been intruding on what seemed like a very delicate situation.

"Well, I'm always here, Jack, I mean it. And I hope he's okay. He's *so* cute," I added, going for chipper.

"He's a champ. And you know I'm on it, tracking down the best care."

"Of course you are."

Jack had always been on it, an actual Eagle Scout. I remember him, when I was seven and he was eight, cradling a wounded baby bird, then nursing it back to health by building a straw nest for it in a cardboard box, which he kept in the shade in his backyard.

"But that's not why you're calling," Jack said. A lightness had crept into his voice and I felt my shoulders relax. "You're calling about more pressing things, like are we going to this rodeo of a vow renewal party, or not. Am I right?" His playful tone almost bordered on flirty and I felt a zap of heat my neck.

"Umm, yes. Guilty. I'm actually going, and wanted to see if you'd really be up for it."

A long pause.

"Kira, do you really think that's a good idea?" His voice was now serious, weighed down by notes of concern. My throat tightened; tears were threatening.

He'd been witness to the explosive aftermath of my mother's death. My deteriorating mental state, my otherwise easygoing nature blunted by the sharp grief of a sudden death. The war I'd waged against my father and Katie, my campaign of proclaiming Mom's innocence in her own death. And finally my expulsion, by Granny, to the posh boarding school in Dallas. Hockaday.

Jack had been the only one who would listen to my jagged, bottomless rants about how my mother would never have killed herself, how it all had to have been a huge mistake, how somebody must have had it out for her. We'd sit in the bottom of the creek bed of our neighborhood for hours, the earth cracked, sunbaked, and thirsty for rain, and he would just listen. Nodding appropriately. His strong jaw set, his hands on his knees, fingers steepled together.

"I know I've said I'd never go back. And believe me, I'm not going because of Genevieve's marital bliss parade. Or to see the old crew; those girls are horrendous. But, Jack, Granny texted me something a little while ago."

I recounted for him her texts, word for word. And my reaction to them. Disbelief. Anger.

"I don't know if she's just playing me or if she really does have something of Mom's and has truly changed her mind about how she died, but I have to go and find out."

"Well," he said, solemnly. "This is . . . a *lot*. Kira, I can't imagine how you must be feeling.

"I didn't honestly think you'd go through with attending the party, so I just signed up to be on call that weekend. But obviously I'm coming now. I can't let you face this alone."

I felt a swell of tenderness for him then, so strong I had to clamp my lips shut so I wouldn't gush out *I love you.*

"Really?" I managed, my voice thick with feeling.

"Absolutely."

"God, thank you, Jack!"

"Of course. And actually, why don't you set your arrival time at DFW to match ours? Melanie and I would be happy to give you a lift to town from there, catch up."

The mention of Melanie startled me back to reality; it was as though I had forgotten all about her and was making plans to spend a weekend away with Jack.

So now I'm sitting here, nibbling on the last bites of pizza—crispy arugula dotted with goat cheese—while I wait for boarding to be called. It's mid-October and the Santa Anas have returned, making the atmosphere volcanic. I'm anxious to get out of here, to have a change of scenery—even though it's just for the weekend.

I finally texted Granny back a few weeks ago to let her know I was coming, but firmly drew boundaries. I would be staying with her for only one night—Friday—then I'd move to the cabins at the Walters's Farm Saturday. I would be arriving in time for an early dinner Friday, but leaving Longview promptly at dawn on Sunday morning.

I've got to be on the defensive around my grandmother; I'm getting in and out of there fast.

5

KIRA

I'm waiting in the baggage terminal at Dallas Fort Worth Airport, sheets of hot wind slapping my back every time the sliding glass doors open.

It's mid-October, but sometimes fall doesn't arrive in Texas until Halloween. I've packed hot-weather clothes, but because a cold snap is forecast for tomorrow, I've also tossed in my puffer jacket, a knit sweater, and boots.

My flight was due to arrive ten minutes after Jack and Melanie's, but he texted me a little while ago to say that theirs is delayed by half an hour, so I'm sitting on a low bench, watching suitcases tumble from the mouth of the baggage carousel.

I send Katie a simple Landed! text. She replies with the thumbs-up emoji. Typically cool and short.

Before I popped my RSVP in the mail last week, I called Katie. We haven't talked over the phone in years—there have been only the obligatory texts: for her kids' birthdays, holidays, etc.

But I knew I needed to let her know ASAP that I was coming back before she heard it from someone else, and simply texting her felt too casual for something this big.

When she answered the phone, she sounded annoyed, just as she has for the past twenty plus years. Longer than that, actually. She had been annoyed with both Mom and me ever since she turned thirteen. That age was when the curtain dropped for her on any closeness or warmth she'd shown either of us.

Blame it on hormones, blame it on the fact that she had outgrown Mom's eccentricities—whatever the reason, she'd drifted away from us.

I've often wondered if part of the closeness between Mom and me was because we looked so similar. When I was a little girl, my hair was the same blinding shade of platinum as hers. And we both wore it down to our waists, our curls frizzed by the damp East Texas heat.

My hair has now faded to a darker blond—dishwater blond they call it, such an unflattering term—but when Mom's started to dull, she turned to the box and kept hers bleached.

"Women should be allowed to do whatever they want with their hair or their bodies," she once told me while taking a slow drag off her cigarette. A habit she'd kept secret from everyone but me. "We have it hard enough in this world." Her glass-green eyes were focused on guiding the wax across her latest batik while her lips worked the cigarette.

I was twelve and didn't fully grasp what she was getting at, but I nodded as if I understood exactly what she meant. I couldn't let on that I was in the dark, wanting to feel relevant and like her confidante. So I learned to nod in the right places, learned to keep certain things just between us. Like the smoking and, later, the feminist content of the batiks she was making for a museum show she was supposed to have; a show that was on the books but never happened because she died right before it.

I sensed early on that there was one version of Sadie in the shed with me: the real version, or what she referred to as "the transparent self," a term taken from a book by the same title that she became obsessed with in my teenage years—and the Sadie she showed my father and sister and the rest of the neighborhood.

There was the housewife who made us grilled cheese sandwiches for dinner and kept her trap shut about anything edgy or controversial, then the Sadie who would talk to me in a stream of consciousness, unguarded, her mask down.

I loved being in the shed with her, loved working next to her, the smell of simmering wax mingling with the sharp scent of the acrylics and oil paints she bought for me.

Batiking was far too complex; she tried to teach me the technique, but I had no patience for it, so eventually she set up a little desk in the corner, creating for me a workspace all my own, complete with an old easel she'd picked up at a yard sale.

I can remember my first real painting, the one that went beyond just smearing paint on canvas or poster board. I was six. Sadie and I sat elbow to elbow at her art table, her long hair tickling my forearm as she instructed me on technique. How to layer colors together, how to move the brush across the thick ivory page. Once we finished creating a rainbow of color—teals and ruby reds and cerulean blues—she had me paint over that with a coat of white. Then, with her thin hand over mine, we guided a sharp tool across the overlaid paint, and with it drew an elaborate underwater scene of mermaids, turtles, fish, and oceanic plants. It was as if I were in a trance. She left my side, left me to it, and resumed her own work. The brilliant colors underneath bled through and I was awed by the results.

"See, it's like my batiks but a bit easier," she said, giving me a light nudge with her elbow. She clicked her tongue in admiration of my handiwork and hung it on the wall. I was hooked from that moment on. But wanting to copy her style as closely as I could, I soon moved on to collage—the medium I would use all through college—using found objects and trinkets of nature we collected on our long, meandering walks through the woods together.

Back then, when we were still young, Katie would wander into the shed with her sketch pad and join us. She'd sit on the red beanbag chair and sketch a portrait of Mom at work on her batiks. She was actually pretty talented, and Mom encouraged her, praised her, but she would get fidgety after a while and head inside to play Barbies or go around the corner to meet up with friends.

By the time puberty hit, Katie had abandoned Mom's art shed altogether, sneaking in only to use Mom's new typewriter for school assignments, rolling her eyes at us if we happened to be in there, engrossed in our projects. We learned to tiptoe around her, cut a wide berth.

Katie favors our father, her hair a deep shade of chestnut, luscious and shiny, her skin tone olive, and her eyes a toffee brown. Dad's hair turned silver early, but they shared the same tanned coloring, and when Katie turned on Mom and me, she also adopted our father's frosty disposition.

When she hit her teens and we lost her, the secrets started. Katie's new clique of catty friends. The string of boyfriends, each relationship more tortured than the last. Her embarrassment and never-masked repulsion toward Mom.

She'd been like a different person before that—open and affectionate and prone to making me laugh. I remember, when I was six and Katie was eight, riding in the back seat of Mom's cherry-red Oldsmobile while Katie rode shotgun, both of us headed to elementary school, with the windows lowered and Mom blasting Donna Summer's "Bad Girls" from her eight-track. The trio of us shimmying in our seats, singing along with Donna.

We knew Mom was different then, that not everybody's mother carpooled them to school while blaring disco. But unlike Katie, I never stopped thinking Mom was cool.

After she died, and I became unhinged, Katie pulled even further away from me. She was angry that I wouldn't fall in line with the family consensus that Mom had killed herself. Our relationship has been on razor-thin ice ever since.

The few times I tried to call her to mend things, she never failed to take a shot at Mom. *You make her into a saint, but believe me, she wasn't. There are things you don't know.*

There was a period after Mom died, and I was away at boarding school, when Katie spiraled. I heard a little bit about it from Gran, but mostly all the nitty-gritty came from Meredith, my one real friend from back home other than Jack.

Katie started drinking more. Staying out later. Broke it off for a spell with Ethan Hayes, the coolest guy she'd ever been with. Fell in with a sketchier crowd. One night she and a few guys even broke into the high school and vandalized the locker banks, spray-painting profanities and denting the metal with hammers. Gran even let it slip that Katie got caught shoplifting a designer handbag at the mall and that Gran and her old money had to come to her rescue.

I was worried about her then and tried to call, but every time she heard my voice on the other end, she'd sigh and snap at me; she's always been a genius at shutting me down. And after a while, I stopped checking on her.

After college, she returned to Longview and married Ethan. He's tall, good-looking, with sandy-blond hair and beach-water-blue eyes, and like Katie, he had a bit of a wild side in high school—though he never got into the trouble that she got into—but he still has a chill boyish vibe to him.

They have two daughters, Eva and Shelby, eight and five, respectively, who call me Aunt Kira but will most likely not recognize me if I'm lucky enough to see them. We've only ever seen each other via FaceTime, and very few FaceTimes at that.

"They'll be at the thingy Friday night—the bowling alley—so

you should see them there," Katie said when I called her. Making it clear that she was not inviting me over to their home.

If she was shocked that I was coming back, she didn't show it. She only sounded disinterested. When she first answered and I told her my plans, all she said was, "Okay, cool. I wasn't going to hit all the events, but I'll try since you're coming."

I sat on the other end of the line, anxiety needling my chest, on the verge of apologizing for returning, for being me.

Now I flick my eyes to the bank of monitors displaying the various flight statuses and see that Jack's plane has landed. Sweat pricks my armpits; suddenly, I'm overly aware of my appearance, smoothing down my shirt, fluffing up my hair, glossing my lips with my berry-tinted lip balm. I can't believe I'm about to see him, and Melanie, after all these years.

My cell chimes. I dig it out of my bag, assuming it's Jack or even Katie, but it's from an anonymous number. And when I swipe and read the message, the blood drains from my face and my mouth goes dry as paper.

You're making a very big mistake. You'll be sorry.

6

SADIE

Granny Foster tried to warn me years ago; I see that now.

It was the spring before our wedding. I can picture the day, ocean clear in my mind. The air in East Texas was saccharin sweet, the afternoon soggy with humidity, and all of us were gathered on her chartreuse lawn at one of her sumptuous high teas; the powder-white iron tables were laden with petit fours, finger sandwiches filled with chicken salad with the crusts cut off and the edges crimped down, and a selection of candied fruits.

This was before the girls were born, of course, so it was just Richard and me along with a gaggle of Granny's friends who'd never met me but wanted to before the wedding.

I don't know anyone else in East Texas who has high teas other than Granny Foster—most people sip sweet iced tea here. After the tea-and-sandwich service, she started in on the champagne.

When she'd downed enough glasses, she waved me over to the soaring pecan tree under the guise of wanting to show off the bounty of nuts that clung to the tree—hard forest-green shells that drop to the ground in the fall. But when I crossed the spongy lawn, she hooked her fingers into my shoulder and pulled me in tight, as though she didn't want the others to hear her.

"Richard has always been a good boy; he just has." Her breath smelled of alcohol and mints.

I had no idea why she was telling me this. Even though he could be chilly, detached even, he'd never been anything but kind to me.

Until recently.

"But Richard's father, Richard II, he—" Here Granny paused, her slender frame seeming to tense with what she was about to share. "Well, there's no delicate way to say this: he had a temper."

I studied her face just then in the dappled afternoon sunlight—her jaw-length silver hair that was done weekly at the local salon, her crystal-blue eyes, and her cheeks, which were beginning to hollow—and I could picture the turquoise cloud of a bruise on one.

I'd never met Richard II. He'd died five years before I met my Richard, but he looms large over all of us, his portrait done in oil paint hanging in the oak-paneled hall at Granny's estate.

Even in the flattering painting—he's dressed in a white shirt and deep navy-blue suit, hand resting on the back of an armchair like he's the picture of paternal love—there's a hardness to his features. Jaw squared, brown eyes almost squinting, though he's obviously trying for his best smile but not quite getting there.

He was a deeds lawyer, working mostly in oil and gas leases, and in his fifty-two years on Earth, he amassed an insane amount of wealth, which Granny now controls.

Richard has never spoken fondly of his father; he actually won't discuss him much with me those times when I've tried to probe, but has hinted over the years by dropping things into an otherwise unrelated conversation about how mean his father was, how cold, how hands-off.

It's one of the reasons Richard has tried to separate himself from Granny, and her fortune, altogether. Why he bucked against going to law school and partnering with Richard II, why he struck out on his own and created the small investment firm. Oh, to be clear, Granny still controls us. Mainly because we *do* lean on her when we have to—especially now that Richard's business is so shaky—and I think this only fuels his frustration.

I can hear someone now saying, "There were signs," but other than that awkward conversation with Granny on the lawn that day, which left my stomach in a twisted knot, there weren't any signs. Not in the beginning anyway. And that's all Granny said to me—*he had a temper.* She wouldn't discuss it any further, and I've never felt comfortable dredging it back up. And at that point, Richard had been nothing but gentle with me and, by her accounts, a docile son, so I'm not saying she was warning me about *him*, per se, but rather alerting me that the streak was there. Latent, but liable to spring forth given the right set of circumstances. Maybe Old Man Richard had started out one way with her, too, but had wound up—through age, through the pressure that comes from maintaining wealth—a nasty man.

The first time I saw Richard's temper—just a flash of it—was when Katie was ten and you were eight. The bad oil deals had just started then. Richard, and by default his clients, were getting swindled by a crooked wildcatter. Richard came home one Friday evening from the country club, where'd he'd been golfing all day with prospective clients—none of whom, mind you, would turn into actual clients—and when I questioned the wisdom of continuing to fork over the ungodly membership fee each month, he flung the remote control across the room, splintering the wood-paneled wall in the den.

That nick is still there, but there have been so many others since then: a hail-shaped pock in the Sheetrock in the laundry room formed by his fist; the gaping hole in the wall of the garage where he kicked it one day, leaving a crater that looks like the outline of a shark's mouth; and the crescent-shaped scar on my forearm from his fingernail. Marks of his rage.

I can't really blame him for that last one, though. I pushed every button known to man that evening and was threatening to leave in the middle of the night and go out to a bar, go walking, go *wherever* the hell to get away from him, and he yanked me back inside the house. Had me calm down and insisted I take one of my pills.

But still. If things don't get better moneywise, and if I don't keep myself in line, keep my desire in check, I worry about what he's capable of. About what he'll do next.

7

KIRA

My cell lolls in my hand; I can't decide whether or not I want to continue holding it.

You're making a very big mistake. You'll be sorry.

I blink, reread the message in case I'm missing something, misreading it. I know I'm not. Blood thrums in my temples. What in the actual fuck? I probably *am* making a huge mistake coming back here, but who is this anonymous person and why are they sending me this? I can't decide if it's a warning or threat, but dread slithers over me, causing my vision to swim.

Before giving it too much thought, I tap out a reply:

Who is this?

I press send before I lose my nerve. Maybe it *is* just a wrong number. Maybe the sender themselves made a very big mistake. But it seems too coincidental—the text hitting my phone so soon after my arrival in Texas.

Whoever is sending this must know I'm coming home.

The only person in Longview, other than Gran, who has reached out to me—the hot second she retrieved my RSVP from her mailbox, no doubt—was Genevieve herself.

Genevieve: SO thrilled you're coming!!! Everyone here is buzzing about it!!

Me: Yep! See you soon.

Genevieve: So, no plus-one?

I cringed at Genevieve's question. The world hates unmarried women. At best, we're a nuisance, a problem to be solved, and at worst, we're a threat. I ignored her cloying question. Obviously, if there *were* a plus-one, I'd be bringing them home with me. I could picture her lips curling into a smile as she typed that one out. She and her equally obnoxious mother, Bertie, have perfected the art of the thinly masked insult.

I honestly wish she didn't have access to me via text. Hearing that everyone was buzzing about me coming home set my teeth on edge. Like I'm a spectacle to behold, the crazy girl who lost her shit when her mom died. But thinking of her text now, it doesn't annoy me; instead, it chills me: everyone back home knows I'm coming, so the text could be from literally anyone.

Genevieve and I were friendly growing up, but it was out of neighborhood convenience; we were never truly friends. I left Longview for a reason, would prefer to have all this behind me, but Genevieve and her ilk still think they own me. And more than anything else, they want to know if my life is as exciting as it seems on social media; of course, they're hoping that's it not.

It sure as shit isn't, but that's the vibe I give off on Instagram. I don't post that much, but when I do, it's carefully curated: a selfie of me at the beach in Malibu, foamy ocean and palm trees framed in the background; casual mentions of me at awards ceremonies (every so often our firm gets a stack of tickets and I once posted a selfie with Keanu Reeves because he's a client, and our nicest one at that).

. . .

I stare at my phone's screen, willing a response to appear. A quick, embarrassed "Sorry, wrong number!" reply. But the screen remains blank. I toss it in my bag, wipe my sweaty palms on my linen shorts, hoping that the whole "watched pot never boils" adage will apply here.

Also, Jack, Melanie, and Aiden will be descending the escalator soon, so I need to pull it together.

I hear them before I see them. A loud, grunting noise followed by ear-splitting shrieks. I glance up and spot Melanie at the top of the escalator, clutching a writhing Aiden in her arms. Jack is on the step behind her, his body laden with carry-on bags.

I draw in a long breath. He's as handsome as ever. His coal-black hair still thick and styled like a print model's—short and molded with product. His chiseled high cheekbones, those chocolate-brown eyes. Oh, those eyes.

He's wearing a crisp oxford shirt, cuffed just below the elbows. I'm gaping at him when he spies me. I stand and wave, and he flashes me his signature high-wattage smile.

Melanie spies me as well and grins, even though Aiden is still twisting in her arms. She's a looker, too. Tall and leggy with sleek brown hair that she wears past her shoulders. I feel a prick of embarrassment watching her descend in her designer outfit—shorts that look like they cost a thousand dollars and a billowy blouse that flatters her Pilates-sculpted frame.

When they reach the bottom, Aiden lurches away from Melanie, grabbing the rubber handrails, which guide him to the ground. Obviously flustered, she tries to move him out of the way, but he's now on his back on the floor at the escalator's exit, causing a logjam behind them. He continues his shrieking, even louder now, a staccato, high-pitched squeal that sounds like a dolphin in distress. I can feel the whole room flinch with each screech. His blond curls are slick with sweat and he's bucking his hips and kicking his feet at Melanie's hands as she tries to move him.

Jack, though, slides around Melanie, shrugs his bags off, and manages to slide Aiden out of the way of the ballooning crowd behind them.

I freeze in place, wanting to help but not knowing if I should intervene. Melanie's face is twisted in exasperation, and she stands there, hand parked on a hip, a heavy air of defeat dragging her features down.

Aiden begins slamming the back of his head on the floor. I wince each time he smashes it, my stomach twining into a cord. His honey-colored cherub face has now turned to stone, his little jaw clenched, eyes fixed into space as though he's no longer present.

A sharp "Stop it, honey" escapes from Melanie's mouth, but Jack waves her off, shoots her a look. He's kneeling now in front of Aiden, eyes averted from the boy's face, one hand cradling the back of Aiden's head while the other serves as a barrier between Aiden's kicks and Jack's face.

I've heard all about Autism and meltdowns, but I've never witnessed one up close like this; it's absolutely heart shattering. I feel for Melanie, I feel for Jack, and I certainly feel for little Aiden, who looks like he's out of this world, consumed with what seems like frustration, fear, and anxiety.

He continues to slam his head into Jack's hand, and manages to get a good kick at Jack's left eye before Jack's able to twist his head away. He's grunting and thrashing and there's a slow train of rubberneckers moving past, their faces full of disdain and disapproval, as if Aiden is just another brat throwing a tantrum because he can't get his way. Because his parents won't control him. After what feels like half an hour but is in actuality five minutes, the head banging stops and Aiden allows Jack to lift him to his chest, resting his little head on his daddy's shoulder.

I'm in awe of (but not surprised by) my old friend's ability to keep calm in this situation, to de-escalate Aiden's outburst with precision and grace.

Jack lifts his chin toward me, and I walk over to greet them.

"Heeeey!" Melanie says, leaning down to give me one of those hugs that are all air and arms, no meeting of the chests, no real sincerity. I catch a whiff of booze floating off of her.

"Hey, Mel," I say, trying for breezy.

She's a year in between me and Katie, so I was never that close to her growing up, but she was always around, a bland and neutral presence, friends with my friends and friends with Katie's friends, but not with either of us.

"Kira," Jack says, pulling me into a three-way hug with him and Aiden. I nestle in closely but am careful to give Aiden enough space.

Jack smells the same way he always has—crisp and clean with tangy notes of tangerine (he must use the same shampoo as he did when we were teens)—and my heart bangs in my chest at the very nearness of him.

"Aiden, this is your aunt Kira," Jack says softly in his ear.

Aiden appraises me with a sidelong glance, but then buries his face again—splotchy with red from crying—into Jack's chest.

"Long flight," Jack says, cocking his head to one side.

"You guys are amazing. Seriously," I say to both him and Melanie. "And Aiden is a doll!"

Melanie exhales, blowing her bangs toward the ceiling, giving a tiny shake of her head. She looks at me as if I'm insane for saying all that.

Jack just beams at me. "Twenty plus years, Kira. And you look the same." He's always been good at changing the subject.

Jack takes my hand, gives it a squeeze, and continues holding it. I feel my cheeks burn at his show of affection, and I flick a nervous glance to Melanie, to see if she's watching. She is. But she seems totally unfazed by the fact that Jack is holding my hand in his. I'm not sure whether to be offended or relieved. Does this mean she doesn't see me as a threat? That she can't imagine he would be attracted to me? Or has he never shown anything to her other than our friendship?

Even though there was more.

After that first kiss, there was another, a furtive one when we were fourteen. In the deep end of Jack's pool during a neighborhood birthday party for him. I had never stopped crushing on him, but it felt unrequited. Until that night. After all the parents left us teens to ourselves, Randall Sparks, the neighborhood bully and tough kid, snuck in a case of grape-flavored wine coolers. We all got tipsy off the sticky-tasting booze, and while all the teens were gathered on the steps of the shallow end, drinking and smoking, I decided to float on my back toward the diving board, wanting to be alone under the deep shade of a canopy of oaks that blotted out the moonlight.

To my surprise, Jack joined me after a few minutes, winding his legs through mine, lacing his arms around my waist. I stared at him as if to ask if he was joking, my breath shallow and quick, but he just stared back, fixing me in a trance with those velvet eyes of his. I inched my head forward and kissed him. This time it wasn't awkward; we made out for a few sizzling seconds before unlatching ourselves so the others wouldn't see us. I instinctively knew that Jack wouldn't want that, wouldn't want them catcalling at us from across the pool.

When I passed him in the hallway at school the next day, he nodded and said, "Hey," as usual, as if the kiss had never happened. And I certainly wasn't going to bring it up. We'd been best friends for so long, and as much as I wanted to be his girlfriend, I didn't want to mess up our friendship. I always assumed my feelings were one-sided, anyway, and chalked our kiss up to us both being tipsy. I was just thrilled that it had happened at all.

I wasn't as good-looking, or as smart, or as popular as Jack, who always had girls chasing him. He did nothing to make me feel this way; I just sort of assumed he was out of my league, but I still nursed a secret fantasy that once we got older, and maybe once we left Longview, we'd wind up together.

But after Mom died and I got whisked away, we never had our chance.

Now Aiden starts to fidget in Jack's arms, so my old friend finally releases my hand and strokes Aiden's head. From inside my bag, my cell dings. I wanted to tell Jack all about the creepy text and get his take, but now is not the time. With Aiden arching his back and starting to shriek again, we walk quickly toward the rental car kiosk.

8

KIRA

Aiden is finally buckled in his car seat. The rental is a brand-new Honda Pilot, black with a tan leather interior and tinted windows, the new-car scent so strong I nearly choke on it. It came with a child's seat, but as soon as we approached the vehicle and Jack opened the back door, Aiden started thrashing his body around in Jack's arms.

"I told you we should've brought his own car seat," Melanie seethed to her husband under her breath. He ignored her.

They each took turns wrestling Aiden's writhing body into the seat, an adult on either side, one blocking his kicks and blows while the other struggled to snap the buckles shut.

I stood there, helpless, my legs wobbling like Jell-O.

Finally, they clicked him into place and he mellowed.

They circle to the back of the SUV and Melanie aims the key remote at the hatch, opening it. While Jack loads their luggage, she digs in her sage-colored Kate Spade bag, clawing around until she retrieves an amber prescription bottle. She twists off the lid and rattles a rectangular pill into her palm.

"Mommy's little helper," she says to me with a tight grin.

"Xanax is the pharmaceutical name," Jack jokes, leaning over to peck her on the forehead.

I can't blame her; I'd probably be checking out, too.

She tosses the keys to Jack.

"Guess I'll be driving," he says.

I wait to see where I should sit, having assumed that I'd be up front and one of them would ride with Aiden, but Melanie strides to the front passenger seat and swings her leonine frame inside.

Jack looks at me, seemingly embarrassed. No doubt he would've offered me shotgun if Melanie had been the driver. I don't care so much about riding in the back seat; I just hope Aiden won't mind my presence.

I slide in as gently as I can, careful to keep my movements calm and peaceful. Aiden eyes me through a screen of his sun-kissed curls, then twists his attention to his dad when Jack fires up an iPad.

"Hope you like *Mickey Mouse Clubhouse*," Jack says to me, grinning, eyebrows lifted as if in apology.

"It's aces," I say, smiling back at him, giving him the thumbs-up.

Nestled in my seat and zooming down the highway, I finally retrieve my cell from my purse to check the text.

It isn't from the anonymous texter; it's a chain of messages from Granny, each one more urgent than the last:

Have you arrived?

Let me know when you've landed and are on the way.

Hilda needs to know when exactly to have dinner served.

Kira, text me.

Ninety miles still sit between Granny and me, but I can feel the sting of her presence, like a torch on the back of my neck. I text back a quick:

Landed and en route. ETA hour and a half.

The base of my skull throbs with a dull headache. It could be the prospect of seeing Granny soon, it could be the cloud of new-car scent that's still stinging my nose, or it might be the fact that I still haven't heard back from the nameless texter.

Feeling both tense and drained, I slump back in my seat, letting my posture droop. Jack eyes me in the rearview and shoots me a wink, as though he can pick up on my discomfort. Again, I wonder if Melanie is bothered by his attention to me, but I see her reflected in the glass of the passenger-side window, fingers dancing over her cell in what is most likely a text-a-thon. From the seat beside me, Aiden's plump hands grasp the tablet as Mickey Mouse trills away.

An hour dissolves as we drive over flat, lifeless prairie land, the scenery drab and colorless save for the occasional jade pasture dotted with cattle. Aiden starts to squirm in his seat, then starts chant-screeching, "Snack, snack."

When we near a gas station, Jack exits, easing into a parking spot next to the gas pump.

"I'll feed him," he says to Melanie, who now has her cell clasped to the side of her face. She's recounting the horror show at the airport with Aiden, doing her best, it seems, to speak softly, but every so often a barking laugh escapes her. She's looped on the pill and appears oblivious to what Jack's saying to her.

Jack hops out, opens Aiden's door, and hands him a small bag of opened Goldfish. I feel a stab of pity for my old friend, having to man the whole ship by himself while she chatters away.

"I'm gonna top her off," he says to me, chin pointing to the pump.

I want to get out of the car, chat with him while he fills the gas tank, but I'm afraid to disrupt the delicate balance with Aiden.

"Yeah, she *is*. Same as she always was." Melanie has lowered her voice but my attention is pricked—I feel like since she's all but whispering, she's definitely talking about me. "It's all a bit . . ." She hesitates, as if finding the right zinger to attach to the next part of her sentence. ". . . *much*." More laughter sprays from her nose, a hideous whining sound.

Is she talking about me? My neck is scorching with heat and I feel like my body is all of a sudden too big for my clothes. I want to kick the back of her seat, remind her I am sitting here. With her son. But maybe I'm being paranoid; maybe she's talking about someone else entirely. It sure doesn't feel that way, though.

"Mmm . . . sounds good, girl. I am *ready* for a draaank." She's slipped back into her old East Texas accent and may even be talking to Genevieve herself. She ends the call, flips her visor down, and checks herself out in the mirror, as if unaware that I can see her primping, combing her hair with her fingers.

Jack opens Aiden's door once more and retrieves the now-empty bag of Goldfish, replacing it with a juice box.

"How we doin'?" he asks me over the top of Aiden's head, his lips curving into a grin.

"Right as rain," I chirp. He keeps staring at me, his eyes scrunched in a smile. My stomach clenches with longing and I find myself wondering if he and Melanie still have sex. They've been married ten years or so now. I don't want to be thinking like this, but I can't help it. She's certainly drop-dead gorgeous, so I wouldn't doubt it, but there's a palpable current of resentment coursing between them.

And, as I do nearly every time I visualize having sex, I think of Jack pressed up against me, hands lifting off my shirt, mouth roving over me. We never did make it past that kiss as fourteen-year-olds, and I've been with a few other men since, but nothing comes close to my fantasy of Jack.

That cheesy country song from the '80s, "Lonely Women Make Good Lovers," floats through my mind. Sadie used to belt it out sometimes when she'd been drinking, and I wickedly think that I'd like the chance to try that theory out on Jack.

But when Jack takes his seat again, he places his hand on her bare knee, all but answering my question and instantly deflating my mood.

The highway starts to dip and crest, and trees begin to thicken on the side of the road. This signals we're about to enter what's known as the Pine Curtain, the dense, lush pine forest of East Texas, where Longview is located.

The late-afternoon sun, glaring just moments before, slides behind the fringe of the tall, lanky pines, scattering the light so that the highway is feathered with shadows.

Over the jubilant sound of *Mickey Mouse Clubhouse*, Melanie's phone chirps. Again, she cradles it in her hands, fingers flying over the screen, a curtain of her glossy hair hitting her lap as she's bent over, texting.

My own phone begins to buzz and ding in my purse, and I yank it out, assuming it's Granny yet again.

It's not.

It's from the same anonymous number. Hands shaking, I swipe and open it. A grainy image fills the screen.

It's a short, jagged video, like a GIF, of a walking path through a thick stand of pines. The video plays on a loop, and at the very end of it, the trail opens to a clearing that holds two ponds, side by side, a steep ridge between them. Surrounding the ponds is another thick ring of trees.

I recognize it at once—it's the Walters's Farm. But the way it's filmed—the woods darkened as if at dusk, the footage gritty and coarse—doesn't suggest a welcoming. This is a warning. A menacing message.

I gasp. Melanie doesn't notice because she's still enraptured with her texting, and she and Jack most likely can't hear me over Aiden's iPad, anyway. I glance at him in the rearview, but he's got his eyes forward, navigating us deeper into that forest-cloaked countryside.

9

KIRA

As I stare at the text, every hair on the back of my neck stands up.

Someone doesn't want me coming home; they're clearly trying to frighten me, keep me away. What the hell? And who is fucking with me?

Who has access to the Walters's Farm other than Genevieve and her family? Who could nab that footage? And why? Lord knows I don't have any true friends left in Longview, only family. But I also don't feel like I have active enemies. Could this have something to do with what Granny allegedly has of Mom's? Not that I'm even convinced she actually *has* something, but if she does, how could someone else have found out about it before me, especially since Granny said it's a secret?

Meredith, the one girl from our neighborhood who I was actually close to, has, unfortunately, declined to come home. She and her family moved back to England our junior year of high school, so it's not exactly convenient for her to fly in for this.

We've stayed in touch casually via Facebook over the years, but our true closeness shriveled up after I left for boarding school.

Because the Longview rumor mill is as strong as ever, Meredith has kept me up on the gossip over the years, like the details of Genevieve and Chad's marriage-on-the-rocks. Meredith likes to stay out of the fray as much as I do, but she still talks to folks back home. Not me, though; I *had* to get away, and have, for the most part, cut ties.

She pinged me on Facebook right after she got Genevieve's invitation.

Meredith: You're not going, are you?

Me: Actually, I am.

Meredith: Wuuut? You said you'd never go back . . .

I kept my reasons close to the vest, replying only that I needed to go see Gran. Unlike Jack, she was doe-eyed in the wake of Sadie's death. She'd always been fairly sheltered and didn't know how to respond to my spiraling, so she'd sit tongue-tied on the other end of the line, until I learned to stop bringing it up altogether.

Meredith lived three houses down from me. She was shy and brainy, her Bambi-brown eyes always conveying shock at the rest of our circle's hijinks. We gravitated to each other at six years old, when she moved to the States, spending summer days forming red-clay fairy huts on the squishy forest floor, our fingers threading together as we shaped the slick domes. Meredith's family was in the same financial stratum as my own—middle class, inching toward upper-middle—but neither of our positions was as well-off or secure as those of the other girls in our group.

We stayed bonded through our adolescence, clinging to the sovereignty of each other's level-headedness while everyone else spun jarringly into puberty: first kisses rocketing into other salacious firsts, spilling out of windows on weekend nights and not returning home until dawn, sneaking nips of tequila in the school cafeteria. Meredith and I went along with some of the shenanigans; we were peer-pressured into smoking Marlboro Lights and doing keg stands, but we always pulled back from the edge, two solid bookends anchoring our wilder friends' behavior.

Other than Jack, I'll have no real ally in Longview this weekend. He's the only one who truly understands what I lost when I lost Sadie. I'm dying to get him alone, to show him these ominous texts.

I do a quick, cursory search of how to trace texts that are anonymous.

Scouring the different articles, I learn that if someone is using a burner phone—especially one they bought incognito, without having to show ID—then it can't be traced by the police. Great.

My tongue thick in my mouth, I twist the lid off my sparkling water and take a mouthful. The bubbles singe through the pastiness, scorching the back of my throat as they surf down. Drawing in a smooth breath, trying to soothe my crackling nerves, I study the image again. Plumy pine needles sway against the breeze, their amber color turned a bruised black by the darkening sky. A shiver sizzles through me. The Farm. I can't believe I'm going back and have agreed to stay there Saturday night. What was I thinking?

But Chad and Genevieve have expanded the once-rustic property, constructing rows of minimalist-yet-lavish cabins on either side of the main house for guests. And it's not as if there are ride shares in Longview. To get through the vow renewal Saturday evening, I know I'll need to be lubed on booze, forget about trying to figure out how to safely get home to Granny's. Also, Jack let it slip via text that he and Melanie are planning on staying there Saturday night as well; I'll want to be around him as much as possible.

When the Walterses first arrived in Longview from Dallas—almost a year to the day before Mom died—The Farm was our teenage playground. On weekends, we'd spend languorous days sunning at the same ponds that are in the unnerving footage.

One was stocked with catfish and lined with cattails. A gnarled fence of weeds and wild blackberry vines laced its rim, so the only access to its clouded water was a rickety fishing pier whose wooden slats were so warped they looked like a row of crooked teeth.

The other pond, its water a sharper blue, was for canoeing and swimming. When our Coppertone-slathered bodies became broiled from lying on the silty shore, we'd slide the rust-colored canoes into the pond, paddling out to the middle, where the natural cool spring gurgled. We'd capsize the canoes, treading in the warm water while the spring cooled the soles of our feet.

We'd chatter about our boyfriends (not me; I never had one) or boys we liked. I never talked about Jack, though. I didn't have to. Every one of the girls—Genevieve, Courtney, Meredith, and Rachel—knew I had a long-standing crush on him and that he was off-limits to them.

Genevieve's mother, Bertie, would haul out trays of food: grilled hot dogs with their flesh scorched to perfection, juicy hamburgers gooey with Velveeta, all the toppings laid out in colorful plastic bowls. Icy pitchers of pink lemonade with sprigs of mint floating on the surface. A Pinterest mother before such a thing ever existed.

"Your mom rules," willowy Courtney said once while wiping ketchup off her lip with the back of her hand.

"No, she's spying on us," Genevieve hissed once Bertie vanished back into the pines.

Bertie is tall and broad-shouldered, while Genevieve is short, but they share the same pug nose and barking laugh, an emery-board scrape against the eardrums. Neither is particularly attractive, but Genevieve is busty—"talented," as Katie used to say, motioning with a sweeping gesture across her chest—and for that fact alone, she always had a boyfriend in play. Like her mom, she possesses a certain aggressive charm that hooks you, makes you want to be around her, please her. That guy-catching quality has always eluded me, and even when we were teens, envy used to sear through me when I'd watch Genevieve with a boyfriend, his arms laced around her back, her face upturned toward his, her body language begging for him to take care of her.

On weekend nights, we'd secretly gather back at The Farm for bonfires and keg parties. Though I always suspected Bertie was aware of them, she just couldn't openly condone them. Sometimes there would be as many as fifty teens out there in the woods, from all grades, including Katie and her friends, Melanie, and also Jack. Foamy beer sloshed around in Solo cups while couples paired off and trekked down the wooded path to the ponds so they could shed their clothes and skinny-dip.

The cabin—that existed then but has since been demolished to make way for Genevieve and Chad's million-dollar home—was forbidden during these parties. I imagine Bertie didn't want a teen getting knocked up on one of the musty-smelling mattresses at her weekend home.

The Farm itself was also off-limits during the handful of weekends a year when the adults would congregate there for cookouts and bonfires. It was during one of these evenings, a bone-chillingly cold night in late October, that Mom spent some of her final hours out there. I've tried to conjure up what went on that night based on what I was told, but the details are few and slippery.

A sparkling bonfire. A weenie roast. Mom in one of her moods, hysterical and close to tears all night. Raised voices between Mom and Dad. Her exploding with emotion and fading into the forest line. Him leaving her to it, shrugging to his friends. Mom snaking through the woods, sneaking to the back door of the cabin. Lifting the keys off the wooden bar, driving herself home alone.

Dad finding her later in the shed, unresponsive.

It's been over twenty years, so when I think of that night, the tears don't leak like they used to; they're tucked behind a fortress. Like right now, there's just a closing up of my throat, a tightening in my vocal cords, a warning to move on with my thoughts before the sobs threaten to form, turning into a riptide.

Jack eases us past the city limits sign and it feels as though a barbell has been dropped into my stomach. I'm home. There's no hopping on the next flight to get me out of here, to undo my decision to return.

We're still on the outskirts, the drive a blur of strip malls, big-box chains that have crept up since I was here last. As we inch toward the older heart of Longview, the streets are buckled from the cycle of spring rains chased by summer heat, the sidewalks enclosed by slender pines, their garnet-colored bark the predominant hue of my childhood. Red bark, scarlet dirt, iron ore–colored creeks. Sadie always used that shade in her batiks, blending red and orange dye to get the right tone, the one closest to the color found in nature. All of her batiks—at least on the face of them—were an homage to the natural beauty of East Texas, and being back here feels unreal, ethereal. As if I could reach out the car window and touch her.

Jack veers off the main road, taking a roundabout way to Granny's, so that we pass by our old neighborhood, a latticework of residential streets with one-level ranch-style homes and two-story mini mansions. When we fly by our old street sign, Warwick Circle, Jack finds my eyes in the rearview, holds my gaze with a meaningful stare. The pressure builds in my gut, then spreads up to my torso; I can barely breathe. I glance away, look over at Jack's little boy. Aiden's eyes are closed even though Mickey Mouse still dances on the screen, his tiny chest rising and falling with dreamy breaths. Watching him steadies my own breath, making it easier to take in more oxygen, reset the sense of trepidation lurking all around me.

10

SADIE

My first inkling that marrying your father might've been a mistake came about a year into our marriage. I was twenty-three; this was a few years before your sister was born.

You have to understand that in my time, we married young, too young, before you even knew if you were truly compatible with the person. There was none of this living together for a few years first to see, just usually a string of dates, and maybe, if you were lucky, a courtship that stretched several months at the longest before the pressure to tie the knot became unbearable.

We lasted three months before we decided to get hitched. I'll go into that later, but for now, I want to tell you how precisely your father revealed his true colors. The moment that slapped me into reality, letting me know what married life—beyond the passionate honeymoon—would really look like.

It was a Wednesday, and he had actually been in a playful mood that morning. Sleeping in with me, delaying going into the office. I made us a stack of pancakes for breakfast. I remember this because, as you well know, my first pancake always turns out a mess—undercooked on the inside, no matter what I do—so this day I tried my hand at making silver-dollar pancakes and they came out perfect. Golden, crispy at the edges, with just enough firmness inside.

We lingered at the breakfast table over coffee, midmorning

light splashing through the back patio door and casting Richard in a warm glow as he read the morning paper.

The phone rang, interrupting our golden morning. It was Ty Henderson, one of the men in the neighborhood whom your father had been trying to score as a client.

Richard answered, and I could sense him tensing up from across the room. "Sure thing, buddy, we'll see y'all tonight." He glanced up at me, gave me an apologetic smile.

"Ty and Nancy will be around for dinner tonight. Seven o'clock. Sorry to spring this on you but I didn't think he'd really come."

Even though this was before things got rocky with us money-wise, your father could still get edgy about business stuff. I attribute this to the enormous pressure he felt from his own father, and from the other men in the neighborhood—of feeling like he had to live up to their standards.

"No problem," I said as I cleared the table, setting the dishes in the sink to wash later. "I'll just run out and get something to cook."

Your father had switched over to work mode and was stuffing his briefcase with things, hurriedly heading for the door. "Just . . ." He paused. "Just make sure it turns out good. Tonight is important."

The back of my neck tensed at this—I've never been a huge talent in the kitchen—but I nodded, smiled.

I decided to go all in, hopping on my bike and pedaling to the library. I checked out one of Julia Child's cookbooks, then stopped at the supermarket, selecting all the different ingredients I would need.

Back at home, I fastened an apron around my waist, put on ABBA, and began preparing a feast in the kitchen. I wanted it to be special, wanted to please your father, wanted to continue the good thing we'd had going that morning.

Most of all, I wanted to make him proud, make him look good in front of our guests.

I prepared a sweet potato soufflé; a cold soup called vichyssoise with heavy cream, leeks, and potato; and an elaborate salad with homemade dressing, all from her recipes. For the main course, I did a chicken fried steak. Then, for dessert, I made Julia's chocolate mousse.

I rested for only a few minutes after cooking the entire day, then showered, did my hair and makeup, made sure to wear my best party dress. By the time your father got home from working late, the table was set, the martinis were ready to be shaken and served, and my stomach buzzed with anticipation.

After the Hendersons arrived and we finished our first round of cocktails, I pulled dinner out of the oven and began setting it out on the counter to serve.

"Smells good in there!" Nancy said brightly.

But your father stormed into the kitchen, his expression a twisted mask of exasperation. "What, what is all this . . . mess?" he asked, scanning the row of dishes.

He lowered his voice so our guests couldn't hear, tugged me by the wrist into him. His breath smelled like gin and cigars. His face was red. "Don't ever play with the food again."

My heartbeat thudded in my throat. "But I was just experimenting; I wanted to do something different, something special—"

"Just steak and potatoes from now on. The usual stuff. You're just looking for attention. You think you're so interesting, but you're an embarrassment."

As he stepped away from the kitchen, his form blurred; my vision had clouded with anger first, then humiliation. It was the first time I felt ashamed of being who I am.

11

KIRA

We make the final turn that will lead us to Granny's, onto a blacktop road that ribbons out toward the opposite edge of town and spills into her neighborhood, Kingston Acres, a sprawling collection of wooded estates.

Jack flicks another glance my way, then lifts his eyebrows as if to say, *Here we go.* I shift in my seat, steeling myself for the reunion with Granny. My palms grow damp from angst as I claw through my bag for my solo tube of lipstick. Granny is always going on about appearances, so I swipe the dark blush shade across my lips, fluff the roots of my hair with my fingertips.

Jack noses the SUV into her drive, a long meandering path of impeccable concrete that sweeps over her property, the end of which climbs a sharp hill, where her house rests. She's on three acres, half in the front, half in the back, all of it thickly carpeted with forest-green St. Augustine grass so pristinely kept that it perpetually resembles a fresh buzz cut, its sides edged and the top shorn.

Dotting the land is an orchard of archaic pecan trees, their leafy tops snaking together, forming a net of shade. One of my favorite memories from when I was a young girl is strolling the property with Katie and Granny, harvesting freshly dropped pecans. After our wooden baskets were filled, we three would sit out back in Granny's courtyard, shelling and sipping cold Dr Pepper from glass bottles while sneaking bites of the buttery-tasting nuts.

"Don't let Hilda catch you," Granny would joke, "or she'll hide us."

Hilda, her housekeeper, would periodically emerge outside from the French doors, wordless and austere, then remove the bowls of shelled pecans as if snatching a book of matches away from a youngster. She'd later fill hand-size pie crusts with a mixture of pecans, eggs, butter, and sugar to make pecan tassies so Granny could serve them at the weekly bridge games she hosted. This was in the golden days, when my childhood was backlit with love and security, before things got rocky between Mom and Dad, before Dad's temper acted as a blowtorch, singeing our home life.

"Nice place," Melanie says from the front seat, the first words she's spoken to me since we left the airport.

"Yeah, thanks; I guess it really is," I reply dumbly.

Granny's house is massive and airy—done in the style of a French country manor—with yellow stucco exterior walls the color of drawn butter, the roof made up of layered slate shingles whose gray-blue sheen looks like the ocean twinkling at night. The windows are fringed with wooden shutters, and a pair of potted fir trees flanks the front entryway.

But no one ever enters the house through there, so I tell Jack to keep inching up the hill to the portico that leads to the side door. His fingers thrum on the leather steering wheel, as if he's as nervous as I am. He shifts into park.

Melanie cranes her head around the seat and addresses me again. "See ya tonight, Kira." Her voice is sludgy, likely from the pill.

"Thanks for the ride!" I say with too much forced cheer.

Jack and I climb out, the silky East Texas air bathing my skin, cradling me like a hug.

At the back of the SUV, Jack squeezes the key remote; the hatch springs open. He lifts out my carry-on, leans down to give me a one-armed hug, pecks my cheek.

"Don't worry, I'll get a meal in her," he says, angling his head toward the car. "She'll sober up before tonight."

I'm not worried about Melanie, but I do feel bad that he's embarrassed by her.

I bat my palm in front of me. "I get it," I say, referring to Aiden, who's still dozing, without actually having to bring his name up.

Jack smiles but points his gaze to the side of me; he clearly doesn't want to discuss his child right now.

"Hope it goes well in there," he says. He knows what a drama queen Granny is; everyone in town does. "And I hope she hands over what she's promised."

My stomach is warm butter over his concern and our eyes meet as the sun plunges behind the tree-speckled horizon, turning the sky burnt orange.

"Thank you, Jack. See you guys soon."

I hear the click of the back door and then, to my horror, I spy Granny, her angular figure gliding toward us, a shark cutting through the wake.

Every muscle in my body tenses at the sight of her approaching us; I was hoping to bid Jack goodbye without her prying interference.

"Jaaaaack," she drawls, her voice maple rich.

"Mrs. Foster," he chirps. "So very pleasant to see you after all these years!" He leans down, kisses both of her cheeks.

She actually blushes, draws her hand to her chest, and I simultaneously blush for her.

Her eyes carve out the air in front of us, taking in the scene with Aiden and Melanie still in the car.

"That must be your wife," Granny says, nosy as ever.

"Yes, sorry she can't say hello, she's in there with my son, who's napping. Otherwise—"

"Well . . ." Granny waves a hand in front of her, a top note of distaste lingering in her *well*. Why must the elderly always insist on proper introductions and everyone socializing?

If Jack has picked up on her tone, he doesn't show it.

"Well, hi, Granny," I say, passive-aggressively calling her out for not greeting me first.

"Oh, forgive me, Kira darling, I forgot all about you when I saw dear Jack here, handsome as ever." Bile rises in my esophagus; I choke it down.

Granny is now folding me into a hug, her body brittle against my own. She smells of her customary White Shoulders perfume tinged with alcohol, most likely Beefeater. Her summertime cocktail of choice is a gin and tonic, garnished with a lime wedge and two jarred cherries.

She draws back, fingers still curled around my hand, sweeping her gaze over me, head to toe. Her mouth is a thin line. If aversion had an expression, it would be her face right now. I can already read her mind—she can't believe I've dressed so casually in front of Jack, with my shorts and simple blouse.

Granny herself is decked out as usual. Silver hair glinting against the blazing sunset, subdued, classy makeup covering every pore. She's dressed in the fashion of the day: a long skirt, shredded around the edges, with leggings underneath, her narrow feet in leather ballerina flats. Her top is a black knit, shredded as well, and a single dazzling diamond dangles from a silver chain around her bone china–thin neck. She could be dressed to go to the Met in New York City or the symphony instead of just greeting her long-estranged granddaughter.

She slowly shakes her head, still taking me in. I can't tell if it's a trick of the filtering sunlight or not, but it looks as though her eyes are glassy, like she's fighting off tears.

"It has been *too* long, Kira." Another head shake, her voice softer this time. "Too long."

It's then that I can see her age. Eighty-three. She's slimmer, and the skin around her eyes is etched with even more wrinkles. But more than any of that, what I notice is, where as she used to stand straight, her figure is now slightly stooped, a puppet whose master has slackened the strings. I feel a swell of emotion for her and want to pull her back into a hug, but of course I restrain myself.

"Jack, thanks so much for the lift," I say to him, then pivot back to Granny. "Granny, he needs to get going."

After a farewell embrace, Jack finally extricates himself from her and coasts away from us in the Honda Pilot. I watch as the SUV vanishes back down the drive, my stomach sinking as my only link to normality evaporates.

"It would have been nice to have met his wife," Granny says, her voice in my ear like scissors cutting paper. She stares longingly after the SUV as well. "I know you still have *feelings* for him. It's obvious."

Shit. Is it? I actually bite down on the tip of my tongue to stop myself from responding, from taking her bait.

The sun continues to droop behind the skyline, summoning the evening song of the cicadas, whose buzzing swells with each passing minute. Out of the corner of my eye, I feel a presence, and turn toward the portico.

Hilda is standing in the open doorway, watching us. A shudder quakes over me and I instinctively cross my arms over my chest, hugging myself at the sight of her.

She looks the same as she did when I was a teen. Sure, she's aged, but she always looked old, with her stark white hair yanked into a taut bun at the base of her neck. She's not unattractive at all, but her face is severe, her mouth lined with rivulets of distaste.

Mom complained about her a lot to me in the shed as we worked on our various art projects. How Hilda made her feel inferior, like a lesser mother. *Negligent* was the word Mom used a lot in her rambling monologues about her.

"But I don't give a hairy rat's ass," Mom would hiss to herself while stirring her bubbling pot of wax, "*what* that woman thinks of me."

Although it was clear that she did.

And I always felt it, too, the glare of Hilda's disapproval of Mom and, by extension, us. She would mutter about our wild hair, how we needed a visit to the beauty shop, how it would be nice to see ribbons in our hair, and Katie and me in little dresses instead of the faded denim overalls we chose to wear. She'd also drop comments about how much candy—Starbursts and Jolly Ranchers—we liked to consume, remarking about how back home—I never knew exactly where *home* was, just some cold, vague Nordic place—the children there "wouldn't be having sweets all the time like this." She referred to home a lot, about how it was always better, the superior, docile children there playing in the woods all the time, not disrupting the adults, which is basically what we, too, were always doing. Crazy bitch.

And I feel it right now, all over again. Hilda's glowering aura, the way she can darken particles in the air between us. Her steely eyes on me, unsmiling and harsh. She crosses the driveway to me, and instead of offering a hug, collects my carry-on bag and backpack and gives me a brisk nod.

"Kira." She says it in her rough accent. Not a greeting, just an acknowledgment of my existence.

"Hello, Hilda," I offer, but stop myself from saying anything else. I have this tendency to try and warm up every interaction, smooth things over, but I'm not here to be nice. I came home to find out the truth, finally, about Mom.

I follow her through the door, Granny trailing behind us. We step into the darkened foyer that leads to the kitchen, which is glaring in its brightness. Clear glass globes hang from the ceiling, beaming light across acres of white quartz countertops. When I was here last, the kitchen was still in its original state: all dark cabinetry and iron light fixtures—a very medieval chateau look. But now, it's something from the pages of a design magazine. The homey smell of roasting chicken infuses the air and my stomach grumbles, longing for non-airport food.

I continue following Hilda.

"I'll show you to your room," she spits out at me over her shoulder.

When we exit the kitchen, I see the rest of the house is exactly as it was when I left here. A mixture of oak paneling and plaster walls with flickering sconces. Cream-colored soapstone floors as smooth as suede underfoot. Arching molded ceilings with glittering chandeliers, and Granny's collection of high-end antiques. It still holds its original splendor—something I used to be awed by—but since I've been in the mansions of some Hollywood A-listers, Granny's house feels a bit shopworn to me with its unused rooms filled with classic yet outdated furnishings.

"We had the kitchen done, as you can tell," Hilda says, as if reading my thoughts, "because that's where we spend most of our time. But we are leaving the rest as is. For now, at least."

My nerves rattle at this disclosure. What does she mean by *for now, at least*?

I turn to ask Granny, but she's no longer behind me. Again, as if reading my mind, Hilda says, "Your grandmother's not feeling well this evening. She's gone to her room to rest before dinner."

I glance down the long hall that leads to Granny's wing; I want to holler after her to come back right this second, to give me what I came all this way for. But she extinguishes the light in her room, clicks the door shut.

A hint of a grin plays on Hilda's face, as if she and Granny have won the first battle in some unspoken chess match, and I'm startled when she plants a bony hand on my shoulder and twists me in the direction of the opposite wing, which houses the guest rooms.

The halls in Granny's house have always felt dusky, dimly lit by the scroll-shaped wall sconces, and as I track the back of Hilda's form down the lengthy passageway, my chest tightens; I feel a shift, an unbalancing of power. Being back here, I no longer have the upper hand that comes from withholding my presence from all the way in California. Alarm bells sound in my mind and I want to flee. But I'm trapped. I don't even have a getaway car. And I'm certain that Granny may very well continue to fuck with me. She didn't show any signs of feeling unwell when she was outside just now, licking her chops over Jack.

She's stalling, and the suffocating thought that my every move in this house has already been choreographed by her and Hilda makes me want to scream.

12

KIRA

Hilda leads me into what's known as the Blue Room, named after its color scheme. The walls are plaster white, but the room is trimmed in shades of blue: the cream-colored floral bedspread dotted with periwinkles, the window dressed with a white-and-sapphire curtain made of brocade so thickly layered it resembles a wedding gown, and the thin mat of baby-blue carpet that covers the floor.

I've often wondered if Granny was wishing for grandsons when she had this room done up, a few years before Katie was born.

Placing my bags on the silk-upholstered fainting couch, Hilda heaves a sharp sigh.

"I'll ring you when supper's ready."

Of course Granny has her chime an actual dinner bell—she always has—and the brisk shake Hilda gives it makes its trill more like a fire alarm than a pleasant-sounding peal.

I'm grateful when she takes her exit and I click the door shut, sinking onto the fainting couch next to my luggage. The last beams of sunlight sputter through the dense drapes, drenching the room in an even deeper shade of blue, and a sinking feeling washes over me, as if I'm pinned to the cushions, unable to move my limbs.

I can't shake the feeling that it was a mistake to come here—like the anonymous texter warned. That I've fallen right into

Granny's trap, whatever that may be. Maybe she just wants to see me after all this time, but I swear to god, if she doesn't cough up the goods, I'm going to lose my shit.

Like the rest of the house—except for the stylishly remodeled kitchen—the Blue Room has remained seemingly untouched, unchanged since I was here as a teen. It still smells of talcum powder and furniture polish, the scents I once associated with security. This room, with its four-poster bed that Katie and I used to share, and dainty framed watercolors of zoo animals dotting the walls, used to be a sanctuary for us, an orderly space where we were free from Dad and Mom's bickering.

When we were still little, we'd drag our Barbies out from the shoebox under the bed and play dress-up with them, fighting over Granny's costume jewelry, strands of fake pearls and snap-on earrings.

And as we got a little older—around the time Dad's temper started to roil—we'd lie on our backs in bed, gazing up as the shadows from the pecan tree combed the plaster ceiling, and strategize about acting better at home. Keeping our rooms tidier, arguing less, whatever, to try and make things easier on Mom and Dad. This was usually on a Saturday night, when they would go out to a party or a local bar. We'd have a meal with Granny and Hilda, usually a pot roast with root vegetables, and after *The Love Boat* and *Fantasy Island* aired, Granny would usher us into our satin nightgowns and then into bed, even though the sun was still drooping in the sky.

In the mornings, Hilda would lay out a sumptuous breakfast. Fresh cantaloupe, sliced in wedges, arranged on a platter, with honey drizzled over it. Crispy clumps of bacon resting on greasy paper towels, and creamy scrambled eggs steaming on our plates. Even the Raisin Bran cereal's presentation was elevated, served in

Granny's fine china bowls, the milk, frosty from the fridge, waiting to be poured from a tiny silver pitcher.

By our teenage years, we stopped sleeping over at Granny's altogether, having outgrown the need for a sitter. Instead, she'd beckon us over for a monthly Sunday dinner, dangling our allowances over our heads until we showed.

Dusk has now settled over the room, and I walk to the bedside table, switch on the Oriental lamp. The bed has been turned down, like a fine hotel's, and I resist the urge to climb under the comforter and hide there for the rest of my time in town. Instead, I sit on the edge and draw in a series of steady, calming breaths, something I learned in the few yoga classes I took in Santa Monica before I discarded them. Nothing resembling self-care ever seems to stick with me for very long.

Though this room holds the glow of happy memories, it also holds my grief, and I feel myself sliding back into it. This is the place where I fell apart in the days after Mom's death, before the family doctor slipped me into a floating state of numbness with a script of Valium.

The sun would rise on the east side of the house, washing Granny's library and living room in tree-filtered light. Noises of life would clink outside my door: Hilda's loafers tonguing the soapstone floor, the bleating sound of Granny's rotary phone echoing down the halls, the jangle of dishes being stacked into the sink.

The four-poster bed became my fort, and I rarely left it, never bothering to part the curtains, marking time only by the slow parade of meals Hilda would deposit on a lacquered tray just outside the door. Under the hypnotic layer of Valium, it seemed as if I existed in a world of murmured voices. Namely, Granny's. Daily, she'd park herself at the foot of my bed, dressed snappily as if she were heading to a boardroom, pressing her plum-colored nails into my ankle to get my attention.

You need to snap out of this. To stop this nonsense. Your mother is dead and I'm sorry for that, but there's no bringing her back. She killed herself, Kira, and the sooner you accept that, the better off we'll all be.

And I'd want to, at times. Snap out of it. Be released from the gauze of sedatives. To accept that maybe Mom had been a bit unstable, perhaps more so than I thought, and that's why Dad found her slumped in the art shed, curled in on herself, a loosely coiled tentacle on the dirt floor.

But other times, especially first thing in the morning when I'd awaken, mouth desert-parched from the drugs, I'd feel the sharp pain of Mom's absence all over again.

No. She had *not* sat next to me the day before, cross-legged on the floor of the shed, blond hair shaggy and crystal-green eyes sparkling with hope, peeling back a stack of the batiks she had selected for her upcoming show, and killed herself the next day.

She'd been giddy that afternoon, her voice almost squeaking, like that of a small child who's just inhaled helium, as she asked me to approve the titles she had given her batiks.

Magnolia Tears: a pearl-white cluster of petals dripping with rust-colored drops; at closer inspection, a woman's face is half-sheltered in the blossom. *Caddo Lake*: a murky swamp surrounded by towering cypress trees, their trunks in the shape of the female form.

And what she considered her masterpiece, *Scarab Beetle*: the insect, but with human vibes, its upper leg pointed skyward like someone flashing the peace sign at a Beatles concert. Each had a deeper meaning, usually tied to mythology that Mom would teach me—the magnolia blossom represented fertility; the cypress-tree women depicted the way in which women are rooted, trapped by their geography; and the scarab beetle, she explained to me during a lively discourse, had been considered a sacred insect in ancient Egypt, a powerful portent of metamorphosis, a topic Mom was endlessly fixated on.

Of course, this was all kept secret from Dad. And Katie. She thought Dad would be mortified if he knew what she was up to, what she would soon show the whole town; she just assumed Katie would laugh at her.

When she started batiking, she used to make benign stuff like bedspreads. I loved them—their starbursts of color, their vibrancy—loved the fact that no other kids had anything like ours.

But later, as she began experimenting more and finding her voice, she wove radical feminist themes into her work. I was fascinated as I watched her, her bony hands guiding the metal tools across the sheet. The way in which she mixed the colors. But, again, I had no patience for it myself.

Collaging was my way of doing something parallel to Sadie. With my easel set up in the corner, Sadie also taught me the basics of painting still life.

But even while she was schooling me on the fundamentals, she was pushing me beyond them. On the wall above her worktable, she had a row of different quotes she'd written out and tacked up. Her favorite, the one she used to quote the most, was from Edvard Munch: "You should not paint the chair, but only what someone has felt about it."

She was teaching me to paint, yes, but she was really teaching me a way to think, a way to be in the world. Another quote I used to gaze at on the wall and wonder about was a play on a line from Gertrude Stein: "When you get there, there is no there there."

This is part of the reason I chose collage in college. After having a few courses in feminist studies under my belt, instead of pine needles and leaves, I'd use clippings from the headlines and make those the backdrops to my abstract paintings. It felt like a continuation of my work with Mom.

Some headlines:

WOMAN GONE MISSING WITHOUT A TRACE

A WOMAN IS ABUSED EVERY FIFTEEN SECONDS

WOMEN SHOULDN'T WALK ALONE AT NIGHT

Pretty hardcore stuff, now that I think back, but at the time I was just using what Sadie called my "creative unconscious" to guide me through my work. And she was what all my unconscious was consumed with.

She was big on intuition and claimed that all art came not from its creator but rather *through* them. "We can all be in touch with the muse if we just allow ourselves," she'd say with a shake of her wild hair, batiking tool in hand. "You don't need to plan it all out, just go with it, let yourself be led."

As a five-year-old sitting cross-legged at her feet, it made little sense, but later, when I was a teenager, it slowly became my way of being.

No way this vibrant woman who breathed so much life into everything around her had robbed herself, and Katie and me, of her own existence.

I became so stubbornly set in my stance that Granny's will finally shattered one day, and the back of her bony hand struck me across the cheek.

"Goddammit, Kira. You've left me no choice."

It didn't hurt. I was too zoned out on drugs to feel the sting. A giggle of shock actually bubbled up in my throat and escaped before I could stop it, which only enraged her even more, her normally composed face contorting into a crimson snarl.

I didn't care; I was relieved. Relieved she'd given up on trying to convert me to the story line that Mom had offed herself. Relieved that a few days later I was riding in the back of her cavernous Cadillac, seats as plump as inflatable rafts, gliding down the highway away from Longview and onward to boarding school.

At college, University of North Texas—a small state school north of Dallas—I had no friends, but I liked it that way. I was still deep in the jaws of grief and couldn't relate to the doe-eyed, blissed-out experiences of other students. In order to both keep me happily away from Longview and keep an eye on me, Gran arranged for me to live in the carriage house of an oil-rich family she and Grandad knew. It was perfect. Completely private. I had my own ivy-walled entrance to the backyard, and the little cottage above a renovated garage was ensconced behind a thick screen of shrubs. I rarely crossed paths with the elderly couple who lived there.

I spent most of my hours in the Art Department's studio, anyway, lost in the flow state that Sadie had taught me. And I no longer needed the pills to cope. While I created, the outside world dimmed and my inner world throbbed with vitality, emotion. My pieces were all about my connection to Mom, trying to memorialize her, trying even to possibly resurrect her.

I won a gold ribbon for my piece called *Silence*, which featured text from newspapers about a mother who had vanished without a trace, overlaid above a silhouette of a woman's face, her features shrouded by woolly hair.

"You really ought to consider this as a career," Samantha Parker, my professor, told me. She had summoned me to her office, and as we sat in her cramped but sunlit space, she tried to encourage me to become a professional painter. Her hazel eyes were warm as she ran her fingers along her flaxen-colored braids, coaxing me.

"I have a friend at Parsons School of Design in New York," she said in her no-nonsense way. "I am happy to reach out to her. Not many students possess the raw talent that you do, Kira. You really should consider making this your path."

Even though I kept my private life hidden, it came up with professors I admired and trusted, like Samantha, because Sadie haunted my work. Just bits and pieces. Not my theory that she had been murdered, but that she'd died too young and had been an artist herself.

"Getting out of Texas might do you some good," she added before our conversation ended that day.

I knew then, in my senior year of college, that I did in fact want to leave the state, but when I looked up Manhattan, I was too overwhelmed by the skyscrapers and busyness of the place. By all the people crammed on sidewalks. I swerved my compass west, started looking for entry-level office jobs in Los Angeles. With its open skies and coastal vistas, it seemed like a good segue, a palate cleanser from East Texas. And I knew there would be plenty of arts colleges out there, too. Ones that I swore I would look into, but never did.

My kaleidoscopic thoughts are pierced by the jarring sound of Hilda clanging the dinner bell. I've been slouched on the edge of the bed, my mind spinning, my fingers working the cuff of my shorts like a worry stone, but I jerk to attention as a rod of anxiety lasers through my chest. I smooth down the top of my crinkled shorts, draw in a few slow breaths again, and steel myself for face-to-face time with Granny.

13

KIRA

The long hallway is even darker now without the setting sun splashing light in from the other rooms; I trail it toward the formal dining room, my stomach growling and popping from the alluring aroma of roasted chicken. But before I reach it, Hilda's form glides out from the library, catching me off guard, sending adrenaline zinging through my veins. I shoot her my best what-the-hell look.

"She's *waiting* for you in here." She emphasizes *waiting* with a tone of impatience that suggests I haven't been the one waiting on Granny while she rested.

I step into the library and it's as grand as I remember. Floor-to-ceiling mahogany shelves line one wall, packed with Gran's impressive collection of first editions. Agatha Christie, Gustav Flaubert, the Brontë sisters, as well as Grandad's first editions of the Hardy Boys. Gran majored in English lit in college, a fact she likes to wedge into nearly every conversation, and reading is most likely still one of her favorite pastimes. While Katie and I would whiz through the house on Sunday mornings, playing chase in the tunnels of halls, Gran would cozy up on her love seat, a chenille blanket swirled around her, her nose in a book while sipping café au lait the color of gulf sand.

The flooring in the library is glazed Spanish tile, sun-dried-tomato red; my sandals thwack against the stone as I enter. A sparkling pool of windows lines the back wall, peering out over the rolling lawn. The library has always been Gran's domain, the gilded hub from which she conducts her business. The antique rolltop appears to still be in use with a rose-gold Mac notebook resting on its surface. When I was old enough to understand exactly what her "work" was, I deduced that it amounted to slitting open the conveyor belt of envelopes that arrived daily with gas-and-oil-lease royalty checks. Hilda helps, or used to help, with this, too, feeding tax stubs into the archaic fax machine, filing Gran's portfolio statements, even placing the odd phone call.

Their relationship has always been, from my viewpoint, one of dysfunction and suffocating codependence. Namely, Gran's dependence on Hilda, who has lived with Gran ever since Grandad died, in a mother-in-law suite in a far-flung wing at the rear of the house. Hilda is clearly the servant, attending to Gran's every need—snapping fresh sheets on the beds, preparing all their meals—but on occasion, she's also the boss, with her sharp tongue and rigid rules, the only person I've ever seen Gran cower before. It's a strange, fraught, edgy dynamic that can feel extremely uncomfortable to be around.

A pair of tufted armchairs is positioned in front of the windows and Gran is reclined in one, sipping a gin and tonic from a highball glass. She looks resplendent, her skin glowing under the cocoon of light cast by the brass floor lamp, a black shawl draped dramatically over her outfit. Seeing her sitting there, expectantly, as if waiting for a date, makes me feel the slightest bit sorry for her. But she looks so radiant just now that I'm not sure I'm buying Hilda's earlier line about Gran not feeling well.

"Here, Kira, sit," she says, motioning for me to take the seat across from her.

My stomach tightens and groans. "Gran, I'm starving after the flight. Can we just—"

Clearly having none of it, she speaks over me. "You know I always have cocktail hour before supper." Her hand swats in the direction of the seat I'm supposed to take.

I cross the room and plop into the chair. It's nearly eight o'clock. The event at the bowling alley starts in half an hour. I honestly don't care if I'm late, but my nerves are ragged and I don't want to sit and chitchat with her. I want what she's promised to give me. It's why I'm here.

"What can Hilda fix you?"

"I'll have one of those, too, please," I say to Hilda, who's already marching back toward the kitchen.

Gran lifts her glass to her lips, takes a sip. Crunches on ice. "You know, I caught a glimpse of Jack's wife in the car while they were here. Looks like a bit of a tart if you ask me."

"I didn't."

Gran snorts. "Well," she says, sweeping her gaze over me, mentally picking apart my attire once again. I'm sure of it. "Maybe we can go shopping while you're here?"

"You know I'm not going to have time for that. But don't worry, I'll be changing into something nicer for the thingy tonight."

Hilda arrives at my side, places the drink at my elbow. I can hear the hiss of the cocktail, which mists on my hand as I clasp it. I've always loved Gran's gin and tonics: the piney, bitter taste of gin cut with the tang of tonic, the glass jammed with ice, doused with lime juice. And Gran's secret ingredient, a splash of cherry syrup, strained from the Maraschino jar, and two cherries speared with a cocktail sword balancing on the lip.

"Thank you, Hilda," I say.

I get a sharp nod before she takes her leave.

Because I'm ravenous, I pluck the cherry-laden sword from the glass and chomp on the cherries, which ooze sweetness into my mouth.

"To our reunion." Gran raises her glass, clinks it against mine. "I can't tell you how nice it is to see you after all this time, Kira."

Again that glassy look in her eyes, like she's on the verge of tears.

I soften inside; can't help it. "It's nice to see you, too, Gran." The cocktail fizzes in my throat as it goes down, coating my near-empty stomach. "You didn't want to invite Katie here tonight?"

A dark look crosses her face, something like sadness, but more charged. "Your sister never comes to see me. So no, I wanted some alone time with you."

This revelation runs counter to what I've always envisioned in my head: Katie and the girls gathering at Gran's for lunch on Sundays, Katie and Ethan depositing the girls here for a sleepover on weekend nights, like we used to have when we were little.

"Never?" I take another icy sip.

"I mean, she drops by twice a month. So no, not *never*. But it's usually when they're on this side of town, on the way to someplace else, as if they're just crossing a visit with me off the list."

She doesn't say it, but it lingers in the air between us. *As if Katie is doing the bare minimum to remain in my will.*

"Do the girls ever spend the night?" I feel a slight twinge of shame for asking this, for betraying Katie by digging, but again, I also do feel a bit sorry for Gran.

She shakes her head. "Heavens no. She and Ethan are . . ." She squints her eyes like she's searching for the right words. "What do you call it these days? Helicopter parents. No, Katie would never leave them out of her sight with me around."

I nod. "Sorry, Gran."

I don't disagree with my sister's decision to shield the girls; I'd probably do the same. No telling what wicked thoughts Gran would fill their heads with. But still. It hits me that she's here, moored in the house, all alone with Hilda, day after day. Guilt starts to trickle over me for never coming home, for not staying in better touch, but then I catch sight of a framed photo of Dad, Mom, Katie, and me, resting on the hunched top of Gran's rolltop.

It was taken on an Easter Sunday. Katie and I are in our lacy yellow bonnets, Mom and Dad behind us, hands resting on our shoulders. Mom had pressed her hair straight that day, making an effort, no doubt, to appear polished for their biannual appearance at Gran's church (Christmas Eve being the other occasion), and I think of how Mom used to try and fold herself into Gran's expectations of her. And Dad's. And Hilda's. Always failing. The rest of the time letting her hair run shaggy and free, letting her throaty laughter blanket the room.

Gran's texts bubble to the surface.

I have something of your mother's. Something she was keeping in secret . . . I think you're right about your mother, about how she died.

"Listen, I'm home because of your texts, I—"

"Oh?"

Gran had been staring out the window. She swivels her face to me, expression puzzled, as if she's just developed Alzheimer's. An almost imperceptible shake of her head.

A surge of frustration rises up in the back of my throat.

"Gran, I—"

"You seeing anyone special out there?"

A clatter of noise from the next room, the dining room, makes us both jump. The sound of Hilda plunking plates on the wooden table, laying the place settings.

I pitch my voice louder. "Gran, I'm here because you said you have something of Mom's, something secret, and I need—"

"Shh." She flicks her eyes to the far wall, the wall adjoining the dining room. Fret clouds her face, as if she doesn't want Hilda to hear what we're saying.

The clanging has grown quieter; Hilda may very well be eavesdropping.

"Tomorrow. At breakfast," Gran says, her voice low, her gaze trained back on the windows, the inky silhouette of her pecan trees shifting in the night breeze.

"But I'm not *staying* for breakfast; I'm due out at The Farm for an early brunch. I—"

"You will if you want what I have," she says under her breath, almost to herself.

Anger spreads across my chest, and I want to throttle her. I want to storm around this library and fling every cabinet open, searching for what she has of Mom's.

"If you don't tell me right now what it is," I say, my voice low but strong, like faraway thunder, "after I leave tomorrow, you'll never hear from me again."

Gran flinches slightly as if I've struck her. Shakes her head. Then lifts her gunpowder-blue eyes to mine.

"It's something she was writing."

"Like a letter? Or—"

But Hilda swoops into the room, a flour-spattered apron lashed around her waist like a tourniquet. "Dinner is *ready*." Her words whistle through clenched teeth; it almost sounds like a threat.

14

KIRA

Hilda steers her wine-colored Buick out of Granny's drive and onto the blacktop road. It's 9:15. I'm late; Jack pinged me a little while ago.

Jack: Err, you still coming?

Me: Be there soon! Sorry I'm late!

Jack: Could you hurry? It's brutal here. 😊

After dinner, I escaped Gran's as quickly as I could, rinsing my face in the bathroom sink, changing into jeans and a fresh top, before climbing into Hilda's sanitized car. A box of Kleenex rests on the console between us, but other than that, the inside is immaculate, devoid of personality, save for the disturbingly soft murmurs of sound coming from the easy-listening station the radio's tuned to. *Of course* she listens to this kind of music. Psycho.

She curves the car along the winding road, which at night resembles a black water moccasin rippling across the surface of a lake. Our drive is wordless and I'm grateful; I almost feel anesthetized as we drift through the deep, velvety forest.

Dinner was a wordless affair, too, with me seated across the table from Gran and Hilda. Throughout the meal Gran kept her head bowed over her plate as if in prayer, her attention seemingly focused on carving tiny bites of chicken off the leg quarter with her butter knife. Either she genuinely wasn't feeling well or she was soused from cocktail hour. Or she was rattled by our confrontation. Probably all three. I can't believe she has something Mom wrote. How long has she been hiding this? I guess since Mom died. And what *is* it? My first fleeting thought was a suicide note, because if she left a letter behind, she must've known she was going to die. But no. Mom didn't kill herself; I know that, and Gran has told me that whatever it is, it makes Gran believe that Mom was murdered. Maybe it's a letter of another kind. Something written out of fear or desperation. I shift in my seat, squirm with the discomfort of not yet having it in my hands.

Like Gran, Hilda also remained tight-lipped throughout the meal, save for some razor-pointed questions: Did I still like my apartment? Did I still have my same job? And did I like it? When I answered yes, yes, and yes, she replied with a lilted statement: "Well, that's good, that's good," as if my stability or well-being had ever been in doubt.

We reach the bowling alley, and the parking lot is packed, a jigsaw puzzle of Suburbans and minivans. Hilda pulls right up to the entrance and I feel silly being dropped off by her, solo and childless, as if I'm back in middle school being dropped off by my parents to a dance.

She thrums her fingers on the steering wheel as neon bleeds through the windshield. The signage, **THE OIL BOWL**, blinks on and off like a turn signal. I suck in a steady breath and open the car door.

"See you later," Hilda says.

I hope not, I think to myself, but say nothing, waving bye instead.

I googled the Oil Bowl back in Los Angeles. A young couple—originally from Longview but fresh from living in Brooklyn for the past decade—returned home and refurbished the old bowling alley of my childhood, transforming it into a hipster spot. Their menu lists items like deconstructed Frito pie—whatever the hell that means—vegan s'mores, and craft beer and cocktails.

The automatic glass doors part and I enter. The place is churning with people, and anxiety needles my stomach. A giant disco ball hangs above the lanes, tossing sparkles of light across the space as Prince's "Raspberry Beret" thumps through the air. Candy-colored bowling balls clack together on the racks, and a slender, brightly lit bar spans the back of the room.

My eyes immediately light on Jack, who stands about a half foot taller than the group of men encircling him at a far lane. He wears a smile and appears to be holding forth, midstory, the others' eyes trained on him.

Jack has always been one of them, but also not one of them at all. He's always been too classy, too smart for their clannish prep-boy ways. Even when he would hang out with them in high school, he'd still maintain an air of autonomy.

During weekend parties at the Walters's Farm, for instance, he would allow himself to drink some, but not get sloshed like the others, who'd then get up to antics he'd never partake in: pawing at girls who weren't interested; racing back into town to start a fight with the boys from the rival high school, a mainly lower-middle-class lot; toilet-papering random people's homes for fun.

Jack knew he was destined for something else, meant for something other than going to a state college only to return and get trapped back in the orbit of this small town, inheriting work through "connections," instead of seeking a life path based on one's passion.

I recognize most of the men, and a snicker creeps out of me as I take in their attire. Unlike Jack, who is dressed in a white button-down with designer jeans—looking very urban—the others are wearing the local uniform of polo shirts with khakis that are cinched around their bulging waists by braided leather belts.

Along the farthest wall, a few lanes over from Jack, I spy Katie with Ethan and the girls, chatting with a few of her friends. Including Melanie. Not that Katie and Melanie were ever close, but they share mutual friends.

My stomach spins. She turns her head and I think she sees me, too; her eyes squint in my direction, and I give a quick wave. But she slowly turns her head back to the group, a curtain of dark hair spilling over her shoulder. My mouth goes dry as embarrassment spreads over me like a rash. *Did I just get dissed in front of everyone by my sister?* Surely not. She *is* clear across the cavernous room. And we haven't seen each other in years; she genuinely might not have realized that it's me. But still, I can't shake the thought that she clocked me and purposefully ignored me.

Genevieve, Courtney, and Rachel are in the lane adjacent to Katie's, and I swear I can hear Genevieve's sandpaper laughter from all the way over here. Next to her, her mother, Bertie, hovers over a cluster of hyperactive children.

I glance back at Jack, willing him to notice me, but he's fishing a ruby-red ball from the rack, stepping up to take his turn.

I'm definitely not prepared to stride alone across the room to Katie, so I drift to the bar to order a drink. A few twentysomethings perch on bar stools, sipping tawny-colored pints of beer, but other than that, the action is all at the lanes.

A lone guy stands at the far end of the bar, leaning against the gleaming wood. I wade toward him, wanting to get as close to Jack as possible without having to actually approach him since he's tangled up with the group. As I draw closer, I notice that the guy is staring at me. Like he knows me. I don't recognize him at all. He's probably married to someone I don't know very well.

I stop about four barstools down from him, lean into the bar.

"Kira?" His voice floats over to me, sonorous yet shaky around the edges, as if he's nervous.

I twist toward him. He's tall, his taut body stuffed inside a graphic tee and faded jeans. Blond bangs frame his lettuce-green eyes, a dimple pooling on one side of his smile. Attractive enough for heat to flame my face, but my body also registers danger. There's something slightly off-kilter about him. Something jittery, like his eyes are lit from behind.

He obviously knows me, but I still can't place him.

He stretches out his arm, extends his hand. "Randy."

Southerner that I am, I accept it and we shake, my mind still grasping for recognition. "I'm sorry, but—"

Jittery laughter barks out of him. "Don't be. I wouldn't recognize me, either, if I didn't know any better. And you knew me as Randall."

A beat. My mind clicking into place. Randall Sparks.

Oh my god. We lock eyes and of course it's him. And *of course* I wouldn't have recognized him. He looks vastly different from the lanky, sandy-blond bully who used to terrorize the neighborhood. Skin mottled with acne, limp hair licking his shoulders. Dirty clothes. A perma-scowl screwed on his face.

The man standing before me gleams. Skin tanned and smooth as shea butter, clothes flattering and crisp. Glossy smile.

"You're not even trying to hide your shock," he says, teasing.

My neck burns with shame. "Sorry, you're just so . . ."

"Different?" he offers, auto-filling my thoughts for me.

"Yes," I admit. But I don't add the extra adjective I'm thinking: *hot*.

"That's what getting out of Longview for a few years will do for ya." His hands clasp his cocktail, rattle the ice in the glass. "I'm sorry, can I get you a drink?"

"Sure!" I say brightly, trying to further mask my disorientation.

He signals to the bartender, a young, bearded guy in a trucker hat whom I peg as the owner. "What can I get y'all?"

"Another vodka tonic for me and whatever she's having."

"Umm . . ." I trace my finger down the plastic menu. "The Bowling Bock for me." I'm sold by the clever name and am craving something softer than a cocktail.

"So where did you go?" I ask Randall.

"Vegas. A couple of years ago. Best time of my life. Moved back about a year ago."

"Why'd you leave if you liked it so much?" The question tumbles out before I realize that it might sound both nosy and judgy.

He jerks a shoulder up in a shrug. "Cost of living and all that. Plus my little girl is here. But I needed a break from my ex for a second."

The bartender places my beer on a paper coaster in front of me and I'm glad for the distraction; I don't really want to get all personal with Randall at the moment. My nerves are tweaking from being in such close proximity to Katie—not to mention everyone else from the past—and small talk is about all I'm game for. Plus Randall is giving off the vibe like he wants to unload and unload a lot.

"To us both getting out of here!" I raise my beer in front of my nose, tip it toward his glass. He smiles, nods, and clinks his drink against mine.

The beer goes down smooth—rich and thick with notes of toffee that coat the back of my throat.

"I heard you were coming in from LA for this." Randall takes a long, wincing pull off his vodka tonic.

"You did?" I ask, surprise peppering my voice. I'm surprised he knows where I live, not that he heard I was coming back; Genevieve had made it clear when she texted me that everyone here knew.

He punches me softly on the shoulder with his fist. "Don't look so spooked! I live here. Word gets around."

His eyes are dancing again, electric green and skittish. I wonder for a sec if he's on something, but decide it's likely just nerves. He's probably even more nervous to be here than I am. Even though he was always part of the group, due to the fact he lived in our neighborhood, he was cast to the outer crust, simultaneously shunned but also kept part of things because of his willingness to pull pranks and take dares from the guys, and later because of his ability to procure a fake ID and keep us supplied with a steady flow of alcohol.

I look at him with different eyes and soften at what I interpret as flirtation. It's been a while—years, in fact—since anyone has flirted with me. And three years since my last date. Pathetic. I had finally talked my closest friend, Li, into checking out a popular dive bar with me in Silver Lake. The promise of a jukebox stocked with country and western classics, a floor coated with sawdust, and Lone Star beer served in metal ice buckets beckoned me. Not so much because I was homesick for Longview per se, just missing Texas and its open skies and easygoing attitude.

We drank an uncharacteristically huge amount of beer, Li was pulled more than once on the dance floor to two-step with handsome strangers, and by the end of the night, as I was veering toward the bar, I met Carter.

Shockingly handsome for someone ostensibly interested in me. Honey-brown hair and hazel eyes. Plain white T with cuffed jeans. A rockabilly vibe. He had this endearing habit of wadding up the napkins that served as coasters, as if he was nervous, his neck flushing as I asked him about himself. Grew up in Kansas, now working for a tech company in Culver City. Homesick for a simpler life. Finally, someone seemingly normal in a town of dizzying personalities.

Later, back at my apartment, we both lay in bed topless, making out, while his finger slid between the waist of my jeans and my stomach, tracing back and forth. I shuddered.

"What's your biggest fantasy?" he breathed into my ear.

Every nerve bristled. Huh? Even though I was half-naked with him, that question felt way too intimate to be asking on a first date. "Uh . . . kind of personal, don't you think?" I giggled.

A guffaw.

"Well, what's yours?" I asked, turning the tables back to him.

"Mmm . . . being naked in front other people."

Record scratch.

"You mean, like, with me, now?"

"Mmm . . . no, I mean, like in front of people. I guess you could say I'm an exhibitionist." A coy chuckle.

Recoiling, I shifted away from him, bunching the covers up over my breasts. For fuck's sake. I knew he was too good to be true. Of course, there had to be something up with him.

After that, I sort of closed up shop. Became even more walled off than ever. Radiated don't-even-look-at-me vibes. I wasn't what any man in Los Angeles was looking for, unless they had serious baggage, like Carter.

So having someone familiar paying attention to me—even if it was icky Randall Sparks from the neighborhood—feels good for a change.

"I guess word *does* get around. It's just . . . I'm bad at keeping up with people from here, so I'm always surprised when anyone knows anything about me," I say to Randall.

Not untrue, but not strictly true, either; I'm just trying not to look like such a freak.

"That's pretty fancy, you living out in Los Angeles. It must be so fun to be around all that."

Sigh. I inwardly cringe, regret misleading everyone here with my posts.

"It's great, but honestly, it's not all it's cracked up to be—"

I'm in the midst of answering Randall when I feel a presence creeping up behind me. Hot and solid.

"Randall." Jack's voice scuds over my shoulder.

Randall dips his chin. "Jack." His energy has jumped up in frequency again and I can sense the hum of his nerves like static electricity.

The men shake hands. Cordial but cold. And before I know what's happening, Jack's hand is pressing on the small of my back, guiding me away from the bar.

"I know you want to see your sister," he says to me, but loudly enough for Randall to hear.

"See ya around, man," he says to Randall.

I glance over my shoulder and see that Randall's once-sunny expression has plunged. I feel bad about my sudden departure, hoping I didn't come off as rude. I flash him a grin and his lips lift into a smile. Good.

But as happy as I was shooting the shit with him, I'm even happier to be back with Jack. Relieved to be in his sheltering presence, as solid as an oak.

Plus, I can't wait to find the right moment to show him the ominous texts and see what he thinks. Someone in this town doesn't want me here, and I can't help wondering if they're here tonight.

"Escaped the guys as quickly as I could. Sorry to leave you hanging—"

"It's fine. I just can't believe that's *Randall*, can you? I mean, he seems to have changed so much—"

A snort puffs out of Jack.

"What?" I ask, craning my face so I can see his.

Eyebrows knitted, he gives a quick shake of his head. "Uh, hate to burst your bubble, but that guy's bad news. Still."

Burst my bubble? Could Jack tell that we were casually flirting? The thought thrills me because that means he noticed the lightness between Randall and me, and he seems almost jealous.

"Really?" I don't want to let it go just yet.

"Trust me. I'll fill you in later."

We reach the end of the bar, where Jack's feet pause. He turns to me, eyes flecked with concern. "So, you ready?"

We're about ten feet away from Katie's group. In the half hour since I've arrived, the noise level has reached a louder, buzzier pitch, the sound a companion to my walloping heart.

"Not really," I reply. Katie's earlier possible diss of me is still crawling over my skin like a sunburn.

Jack's hand is still on my back as we approach their area. To onlookers who might not know any better, Jack and I could appear to be a couple, with his arm roped behind me, guiding me toward the group. I don't hate it at all, but I wonder again what Melanie thinks. She's too engrossed in chatting with the other girls to notice, though, fingers twined around the stem of a wineglass, hip cocked to one side as she nods alternately to Katie and Gina, Katie's closest friend from high school.

My stomach quakes with unease. Katie is turned to the side, her profile sleek and polished, her tall figure framed glamorously in a white peasant dress.

Melanie notices us first, eyes even hazier than they were in the car. She doesn't break the conversation, merely leans toward Jack, strings an arm around his waist and tugs him to her, claiming him, her property.

I feel Katie's eyes on me before I see them. Searing and probing. I shift my gaze off Melanie and onto Katie. Her eyes are glassy, like Melanie's. I can't tell if it's because she's been drinking or if she's emotional over my presence. A lump forms in my throat like rising bread and I close the space between us, looping my arms around her and claiming her as my own, like Melanie has just done with Jack.

I'm too choked up for words, so instead of talking, I squeeze her harder, trying to pull her into a tighter hug, but she only leans her top half toward me, keeping space between us, patting my back with a flattened palm. A hug you might offer an acquaintance, not a long-estranged sister.

But when we pull back, there are tears dancing in her eyes, which she quickly flicks away, so I guess she's just the same old Katie. Inwardly churning but outwardly not one to show emotion or warmth.

"Girls!" she says too loudly, her voice gravely with emotion, "come and meet your aunt Kira."

"Whaaat? How has she not met them yet?" Gina asks, referring to me in third person as if I'm not standing right here. I've never liked Gina, have always held her partly responsible for Katie's withdrawal from us in high school.

Katie ignores the question as Eva and Shelby scramble over to her side. Eva, the eight-year-old, is Katie's twin. Glossy brown hair and copper skin. She eyes me with wonder laced with a bit of suspicion.

"Mom says you live next to Disneyland!" she squeals, pulling on Katie's side and looking up at her.

Does she? Does this mean that maybe she'd actually bring them out to visit me one day?

"That's right, I do," I say, crouching down so that I'm at eye level with them. "And you must be Shelby," I say to the little blond-headed girl who has her arms wrapped around Katie's legs. She lifts her face to mine and nods slowly.

It strikes me (and not for the first time) how even with the wider age gap, Eva and Shelby remind me of me and Katie. She must be confronted with this, too, on a regular basis.

I wonder if she misses me. Even though I'm choked with emotion at seeing her and at meeting my nieces for the first time, I can honestly say I don't miss her. I don't miss her sharp edges, her anger, her volcanic fury at me since Mom died.

I miss the Katie of our childhood, all lightness and love, not the Katie standing here before me. She's already turned from me, in fact, chatting up Melanie again as Shelby churns between her legs. So no, it's clear she doesn't really miss me, either.

I glance around for Ethan, desperate to sink into his easygoing vibe, but he's been absorbed by the gang of preps that Jack was just hanging out with.

It's weird having my reunion with Katie be so public, and again, I'm stung that she didn't at least offer to come to Gran's last night to see me. All eyes are on me, including Jack's, and I feel like I'm acting on a stage: the errant sister returning home. The crazy one who fled long ago. I can feel the prick of Gina's eyes invading my thoughts, trying to read me, so I train my expression into a happy one, even though my cheek muscles want to rebel and slouch into a grimace.

But before I can continue to marinate in my discomfort, Genevieve is on us, a bad witch swooping in without a broom.

"Kiiiira!" she squeals, and my ears splinter. "How have you been?"

She looks the same as she did in high school, just a bit thicker, her round face doused in heavier makeup. She wears a black V-neck blouse that plunges just enough to expose a shot of cleavage, a pleasing crevice between her full breasts. The skin of her neckline and chest is glowing, flawless, and I wonder which local tanning salon she hit this afternoon for her spray-on.

"I'm fine!" I say with too much forced cheer in my voice.

As if beckoned from the underworld, both Courtney and Rachel appear on either side of Genevieve, all gossip thirsty with hungry eyes.

Those two have always been unbearable at best, but once Genevieve moved to town, she only amplified their bitchiest tendencies even more.

I can remember Genevieve's first slumber party, how Genevieve talked Courtney and Rachel into prank calling Cindy Turner, one of the nerdiest girls in our class and a late bloomer.

"Ask her why she hasn't gotten her pubic hair yet," Genevieve ordered, snickering behind her hand, as Rachel and Courtney cradled the phone between their shoulders.

They could be vicious together. Cruel. Cindy stayed home from school the next week because of their bullying.

Courtney, ash blond, her nose splattered with caramel-colored freckles, bends down and wraps us all in a group hug.

"Girl, it's been forever!" she trills. Out of the three of them, I've always disliked her least.

She's spoiled and ridiculously shallow like Rachel and Genevieve, but unlike Rachel, who has forever been downright nasty, Courtney's always possessed a fragile innocence about her, a lack of awareness of any world outside her cotton-padded bubble of privilege. An endearing, if at times maddening, obliviousness and gullibility. As a daddy's girl with one of the wealthiest fathers in town, Courtney never had to think for herself, never had to define herself as anything other than a happy little rich girl. Which led her to going along with whatever meanness Genevieve wanted to pull.

"I know!" My voice cracks again with too much pretend giddiness.

"Hey, Kira," Rachel growls, a look of annoyance tugging on her otherwise attractive face. I don't take it personally; Rachel is permanently moody and pissed off at everyone, her raven-colored hair perfectly matching her bitchy mood. She's a little rich girl, too, but her father abandoned her and her mom for a Jazzercise teacher, leaving them stranded in their outsize Tudor-style mansion, branding young Rachel with the scarlet letter that comes from being raised in what our neighbors would call a "broken home."

I study their three faces, which loom out at me. Their skin is threaded with age lines, which even their concealer can't mask, but other than that, they look the same as the last time I saw them at Dad's funeral. Pampered, well-heeled, sparkling.

As I rinsed my face in the powder room at Gran's, I examined my looks. Mousy dirty-blond hair, but with some bounce, skin still clear; I could still pass for late twenties. I felt decent about myself.

But standing here now, the absence of wrinkles doesn't make me feel more attractive than them; it makes me feel less so. Like I don't belong, like I'm a pariah. Those wrinkles are a badge of parenthood, earned through years of the kind of sleep deprivation only children can give you.

My insides burn with self-awareness. And as if on cue, Genevieve's young boys stampede over to us while racing each other on the way to a Ms. Pac-Man machine.

"Isn't this *so* fun?" Genevieve squeaks. "We figured it would be best since everyone has littles."

No, everyone fucking doesn't have littles, I want to say, but just nod dumbly instead.

"Saw ya talking to Randall," Genevieve says, her eyes sparkling with mirth.

"Yeah, for a sec."

"Kind of turned out to be a hottie," Courtney shout-whispers.

"I just *had* to invite him," Genevieve says with the same tone of morbid pity she used to adopt in high school when referring to her missionary work in Houston. *On Saturdays, we would volunteer at street corners and pass out sandwiches to the less fortunate.*

My phone buzzes at my hip. I slip it out of my pocket. It's Jack.

Jack: Told ya it was brutal in here.

I feel the heat of his stare on me and glance up. Sure enough, he's looking right at me, a smirk oozing across his face, but we both drop our gazes before we're busted by the group. I close my phone and put it away.

So, as I was saying," Genevieve hammers on, "I just *had* to invite him. I mean, he's been hanging around *forever* and after what happened with him and his wife, I just *had* to." Her face shimmers with a grin. She doesn't feel bad about whatever it was that happened with this wife; she's trying to bait me into gossiping with her.

And because I *am* curious, I bite. "What happened?"

"Well," she says, tucking a lock of product-molded hair behind an ear, "rumor has it that his ex, Brianna, ran around on him. And Randall, well, he lost his shit." She's all but licking her lips, eyes darting over to Randall, who still sits alone under a beam of light at the bar. "Think he got rough with her. Lost custody of his daughter for a time."

Genevieve dips her head inches closer to me. "Just thought you should know, well, because . . ." She bores her eyes into mine but lets her words trail off. She doesn't need to finish her sentence. I know what she's trying to impart: *Because you were over there talking to him. Even if he's single and the only guy here paying you any mind, don't do it. Don't mess with him; he's got issues.*

This intel does make alarm bells ring in my head. Randall seemed all grown-up, evolved, but to hear bad things from Jack, and now this, I should probably be more guarded around him. But still, if he's all that bad, why did she invite him? He's probably just a victim of the Longview rumor mill.

"Got it," I say, enunciating each word slowly to let her know how atrocious she sounds for gossiping.

A snort escapes her crinkled-up nose. "Just warnin' ya, Kira." And then her expression shifts, from barely masked glee to something like horror. "Shit, Mom's coming over."

A firm clap on my shoulder makes me jump.

"Kira Foster!" Genevieve's mother shouts as I twist around.

Sigh. Bertie Walters. She still domineers over us, in height as well as personality, her thickly eye-shadowed eyes peering over silver-framed glasses that ride the end of her nose.

"How *are* you, honey?" she asks, as if there's something fundamentally wrong with me.

"Just fine, Mrs. Walters," I say, my mouth straining into yet another fake smile.

"I am so happy to *hear* that!" She clamps her hand on my shoulder, fixes her gaze with mock concern. "I'm actually surprised you came! But I know it means *so* much to Gen to have you here!" There is so much loaded in her words, my chest tightens under her scrutiny.

"Happy to be here," I say, aiming for neutral.

"I mean, how have you *really* been?" She squeezes my shoulder as if she can pump more info out of me this way. "I mean, after your *mother* . . ." A quick shake of her head, like she's swallowed something bitter.

I hold her gaze but stay silent, letting her bumble over herself.

"I mean, I wouldn't blame you for not wanting to come back all this time. Such a tragedy—"

"Mother," Genevieve hisses. Even Genevieve knows better than to go there.

"Well how is your *grandmother*?" Bertie pivots like a master. "Last I heard she was doing well, still living in that big ole house with the housekeeper!"

Even though I can't stand Hilda, I bristle at Bertie's snide commentary about Gran. Sweat beads on my skin and the air around me seems to contract, making me feel claustrophobic.

My hip vibrates again and I slide my phone out of my pocket.

Jack: Let's gtf outta here. Specifically, let's get YOU out of here.

I don't dare look at him, not with Bertie's eyes drilling down on me. I gnaw my bottom lip, text back.

Me: Is that even possible?

Jack: Yep.

Me: How?

Jack: Melanie's good and liquored. She won't care, trust me. I told her I was over this scene, and that it was hard on you.

Again, I chafe at the thought that Melanie doesn't care, that I don't raise even the smallest prick of jealousy.

I glance up to locate Katie, who's drifted over to the guys' group; she's pinned under Ethan's arm. Jack must be watching me because he hits me right back with a text.

Jack: We're gonna have all weekend with these people. Let's bolt while we can. Meet me outside. We can go to Dusty's. I gotta get out of here.

Dusty's is a beer joint in the strip mall next door. I feel guilty for hitting the road already, but why? Katie couldn't care less. I don't want to hang out with Genevieve and the girls, and I can't take being around Bertie for one second longer.

Me: Deal.

I slip my cell back in my pocket, bite down my smile. "It's been nice catching up, but I need to hit the ladies' room," I say to Bertie.

A nearly inaudible chortle whispers out of her. "Of course, *dear.*"

She fans her hand out in front of her and gestures toward the restrooms, as if she's an air traffic controller guiding a plane down the runway. Her mouth is now a tight line, her dark eyes simmering with disdain.

"We'll have plenty of time to chat later," she adds, her voice as cold as a steel blade.

15

KIRA

I study my face again in the restroom mirror. Madonna's "Papa Don't Preach" pulsates through the wall, which is perfect; I'm in here primping like a preteen before I meet Jack.

I smooth my hair down one way. Then the other. Neither looks great, so I tousle it instead. Fuck it, it'll have to do. I don't have long, ropy, thick hair like Melanie and Katie; mine is baby fine—a thin sheet of silk—and once again, I feel like an adolescent compared to my peers.

The door thumps open and Madonna's guttural plea to her papa—"So pleeease"—bleeds into the room.

It's Katie.

When she sees my reflection in the mirror, she brakes in place, as if she doesn't want to be all alone in here with me. She quickly covers her face with a smile.

"Sister," she purrs, her voice syrupy with booze.

She stands next to me at the row of sinks.

"I hope you don't mind, but I'm actually gonna head next door to Dusty's for a bit. With Jack," I say back to her reflection.

Her eyes go wide. "Oh my god; you *still* have a crush on him!"

"Sssshhh! I do *not*!"

"Oh my god, you *do*!" Her voice is helium light.

"No, it's just, he *is* my oldest friend and I can't take this scene anymore."

"Don't blame you. Believe me, I have to fucking live here."

A knife in my spleen. That used to be one of the things we'd argue about, long distance over the phone. How Katie was the one who stayed behind, looking after Dad, being the responsible one, while I was allowed to go away and fall apart.

"I don't know how you do it. Honestly," I say turning to her, so we're no longer speaking through the mirror.

She shakes her head, her glossy hair shimmering around her face, signaling that she wants to move on in the conversation. "You gonna be at the brunch tomorrow?"

"Yes!" I say with so much glee that my cheeks feel like they're going to split.

"Well, we'll just have to power through with mimosas." She bumps her hip against mine. Then stumbles in her wedge sandals.

I feel a melting in my chest; Katie is being nice to me for a change. It could just be the liquor, but I grab her into the hug she robbed me of earlier.

She squeezes my waist for a sec, then pulls back. "Okay, okay, don't get all sloppy on me," she says, her eyes twinkling into a grin.

Digging in her bag, she plucks out a tube of lipstick. "Here, trust me. And you can just keep it."

"Ha! Do I look that bad?"

"God no, you look terrific. Just thought this would look good on you. Ya know, for your date with Jack and all." Followed by another jab to my side with her hip.

I drag the lipstick over my mouth—a creamy shade of rhubarb—and Katie's right: it does suit me.

"Thanks!"

"Behave yourself." She winks and exits the bathroom.

16

SADIE

I liked the neighborhood at first, enjoyed having a group of friends nearby to get together with. And the very earliest days with your father were a time of discovery for me. When we got engaged, the contractor began building our new home here, and I threw myself headlong into decorating it, stopping by the local art gallery, picking out pieces, and meeting with the interior designer to select wallpapers, furniture, flooring.

This was before our money problems started, so things were still rosy for a while. Having grown up with modest means, this was a new world to me, a way to fill my time, to fulfill my creative side.

I told myself I'd go back and finish my art degree at the community college, but for now, I was happy to be in Longview, happy to leave that part of my life behind for a while, because I was still grieving over my parents' sudden deaths and needed a break from that painful chapter.

But something shifted after I had your sister. Nowadays they call it postpartum depression, but back then there was no name for it. Only sleepless nights and a gnawing, persistent sense that doom was lurking just around the corner.

It didn't help that your sister was colicky. And Richard—lubed on whiskeys or martinis—managed to sleep through her cries, but

I'd be up all hours, walking the floor, cradling her in my arms, trying to soothe her.

As he'd be getting dressed to leave for work the next morning, I'd sometimes plead with him to stay with us just a little longer; I felt so frayed, so unsettled, so overwhelmed.

He rarely would, though, offering his mother's help instead. I'd sometimes accept it, but having her in the house usually just put me more on edge.

After Katie turned six months old, though, everything shifted. She stopped spitting up her formula, began sleeping through the night. The colic was magically gone.

Fortified by sleep, I felt my sanity return and I actually felt contented—not fearful that disaster was lying in wait for us or that I'd mess something up when I was alone with her. She was adorable, her tawny brown eyes sparking with life and wonder.

One Saturday morning I even convinced your father to take the three of us to the art supply store so I could buy paints. I remember us strolling Katie through the aisles while she napped, passing by the brushes and bottles of colors, feeling alive in a way I hadn't in months.

I loaded up the basket with everything I could think of, and once we got home I had your father park the car at the curb so I could clear some clutter out of the garage to make a space to paint.

To his credit, he silently left me to it while he looked after Katie as she rocked in the mechanical swing.

During the week, while your father worked, I would head out to the garage and paint during your sister's naptime. It gave me energy, gave me my life back, to be out there creating. And it made the rest of my day with her even more joy filled. I could be more present, having tended to that side of myself that had become so lost.

And to your father's delight, our sex life—which had flamed

out after childbirth—returned. Because of that, he saw the value in my art, even if he didn't necessarily want to discuss my paintings or even look at them.

Which was fine with me; the garage was my domain and being out there by myself made me feel whole again. I didn't need him in that part of my life at all. I wanted to keep it to myself completely—that is, until you came along.

I did share my art with Sally, of course. But the rest of the women in our neighborhood? Are they my soul sisters? No, they aren't. Only Sally. Her presence has always been comforting and grounding and I can tell her just about anything. She's never shocked or judging things that come flying out of my mouth.

The other women, though, are another story. While it was exciting to have an instant group of friends to hang out with, I quickly learned when to keep my trap shut.

Like having any kind of life for myself outside of the house.

I realized that they were all "model" housewives who fell in line with how their husbands wanted them to behave. To be clear, I have nothing against a woman staying home and raising her children, cooking the meals, cleaning. What I have a problem with is the fact that back then, for the most part, the world had an issue with women having any other ambition outside of that.

And how ambition can somehow make a woman less likeable in the eyes of society, especially if she chooses herself sometimes over her family or decides to keep a career and juggle it with motherhood.

An example: I remember being at one of Sally's happy hours one afternoon. That was a real perk of the neighborhood: having a bunch of new moms together in close proximity. We would stroll our carriages up to Sally's on Wednesdays at three in the afternoon and sit in her backyard on large picnic blankets, our babies at our sides, lapping up the fresh air and bright sunshine. Sally would mix us all different kinds of cocktails—whiskey sours, her famous margaritas, and on the one day I'm thinking of, grasshoppers.

It felt wonderful to be able to pass Katie around to the different women, who'd bounce her on their knees, and I did the same with their babies. Then we would all walk home, pushing our little ones in their strollers, our skin sun-kissed, our minds blissed out from the booze.

On this particular day, though, I remember sitting cross-legged on the lawn next to Caroline Matthews. I had spoken to her only a handful of times—she always seemed frosty and uptight. But after a few grasshoppers, which went down like candy, I felt myself opening up to her questions, which, in hindsight, were trap doors.

How do you like the neighborhood?

How do you like being a new mommy?

I stretched my legs out, leaned back. Sally was across the yard, under a shade tree, giving Katie her bottle so I could have a break and sip my cocktail, let my hair down for a sec.

I answered Caroline honestly. I confided in her that I was starting to think seriously about going back to school to finish my art degree. About how much I missed being in the classroom, being stimulated in that way, and did she know how that felt?

She let out a quick, sharp laugh, shook her head as if I were being ridiculous.

But you're a mom now. We're not in school anymore.

I can still remember the wicked smile that spread across her face as we chatted; I instantly batted a hand in front of me as if to agree with her.

What I was really trying to do was make her forget that I had even said that. If that was her reaction, most of the other women would probably feel the same way (except for Sally), and I certainly didn't need her gossiping about me.

I changed the subject to things I knew would interest her:

cooking, decorating the house, which store in town sold the best dresses.

It didn't work.

That Saturday evening, after I got Katie down for the night, I poured your father a bourbon. He had been quiet all night, and I didn't know why, but it felt like it must have been work related.

One sip in, though, he set down his drink, told me we needed to talk.

"What's this I hear about you wanting to go back to school?"

I nearly choked on my bourbon, my throat burning with rage at Caroline.

"Darrell Matthews seems to have heard from his wife that that's what you want. You know he's in my Friday night poker group. Imagine how silly I felt when he blurted that out in front of everyone last night. Said I needed to keep an eye on you."

Tears stinging my eyes, I took a huge swallow of my bourbon. Fucking Caroline. She couldn't *wait* to get home and spew my secret to her husband. She probably blabbed it to the whole neighborhood. And fucking Richard. All he could think about was how my ambitions made him look in front of his friends.

"You're not serious, are you?" Richard asked me, waving his glass in my face.

"Well, no, I guess not. It was just a passing thing I said. I mean sometimes I *do* wish I'd finished—"

"But what about our life here? Look at all I've given you. And your daughter needs you. And I need you to be by my side. Running the house, taking care of things around here."

As if I were talking about leaving the country. I nodded and gulped down my pride, stifled my dream.

I understood then that I couldn't really trust anyone other than Sally. We had actually met at the college—she'd been taking a women's studies course in her spare time, just as a dalliance, but her husband, Bruce, had been secure enough to allow her that freedom.

She stopped going after she had Jack. And even though she could talk a good game of women's lib with me, there she was, Bruce by her side and Jack swaddled on the couch in his blanket, cutting the corners off her husband's PB&Js.

I quickly learned that in order to keep the peace at home, I needed to watch what I said out loud, watch how I behaved. I needed—no, Richard needed—me to conform to the rest of the group, behave the way the other women in the neighborhood behaved: as if completely and utterly fulfilled by motherhood and marriage. Compliant to their husband's wishes. Or at least appearing to be.

17

KIRA

Jack is waiting for me outside as promised, his back propped against the building. All lean muscle and lightly molded hair, his carved profile a silhouette against the night. Electricity zaps over me: I'm finally getting him alone.

"Thank *god*." He lets out a draggy sigh.

"Sorry, ran into Katie in the ladies' room."

"Shall we?" He gestures toward Dusty's, whose signage flickers in the distance.

Other than the music throbbing from inside the bowling alley, the parking lot is pin-drop quiet, so our footsteps clap in time as we walk across the black asphalt.

"That was *such* a freak show," Jack says.

"Totally. Jesus. Thanks for rescuing me."

"We both left this town for good reason. And I'm so glad. Melanie doesn't see it that way, though. She still likes it, in fact, and misses home, but not me." Jack shakes his head like a horse on a lead.

The mention of Melanie—and not in glowing terms—pricks my attention. "Do you mean she doesn't like Baltimore?" My voice creaks with excitement, so I clear my throat, try again. "Like, do you think she wants to move back?" I ask, this time leveling my tone.

Jack exhales, blowing his dark bangs skyward. "I dunno. It can be so tough with Aiden. Sometimes *I* even think it might be easier, because my parents could help. Not Melanie's—they moved to Houston, and anyway, they're useless—but Mom and Dad are great with him."

"I get it." I don't; I can't imagine what Jack's life is like.

"But then I come back and am assaulted by *this* scene"—Jack hitches his head toward the Oil Bowl—"and I could never. Those guys are just the same as they were in high school. Maybe even worse. But Melanie could. Sometimes it's like she never left here. Like she hasn't grown out of a certain mindset. Like she'd rather be back here with her old friends than living our new life in Baltimore."

He sidesteps a gash in the pavement, grazes me with an elbow. Heat trickles up my arm. Sounds like all is not well with Melanie and Jack; I can't stop the delight zinging through my veins at this news. I know it's terrible of me. I should just want my friend to be happy, but dammit, there's a stubborn part of me that thinks Jack was meant to be mine, not Melanie's, if only my life hadn't veered off course in high school. Of course, I'm not at all sure the feeling is mutual.

"So she's not happy there?" I force my voice to remain neutral while pressing deeper into the blister.

Another shake of the head. "She's—it's . . . whew. It's fine. It's complicated. It's . . . whatever. Let's talk about something else?"

A ping of shame arrows through my chest. But Jack, ever affable, turns to me and grins. "Let's talk about more urgent matters, such as, did Granny Foster give you what you came here for?"

A sigh billows out of me. "No. Not yet. Dodged me all night. Made some excuse about not feeling well."

"She looked great to me." Jack lifts his eyebrows.

"Right? Hard to tell if it's all an act, but she promises she's going to hand it over tomorrow. Whatever *it* is. I did press her, but she would only tell me that it's something Mom wrote." A sudden tightening in my stomach. For the past few hours I've pushed that thought aside: what Gran might have of Mom's.

What secret she's been keeping from me all this time.

"Like a letter?"

"That's what I'm thinking, but I have no clue. She wouldn't say another word; it's like she was scared of that creepy Hilda listening in. So strange."

"Well, you'll find out tomorrow, I guess. Shall we?"

We've reached the door to Dusty's, and Jack opens it, placing his hand, once again, on the small of my back, an ember sparking against my skin. The air is tinged with cigarette smoke and the floor is tacky with spilled cheap beer. An old-timey cigarette machine glows in the far corner next to a sign displaying the rules: **No fussin', no cussin', no wrastlin', no hastlin'**.

Jack guides us to a booth near the front. The black leather cushion squeaks beneath me as I plop down.

"Lone Star sound good?" Jack asks, still standing.

I nod. Dusty's is the kind of place that serves only cheap beer and well drinks, so it's not like we have champagne choices.

He glides toward the bar and I swallow a burning lump in my throat as I watch his backside, the way his pockets hang off his perfect butt. I can't believe I get the gift of this alone time with him. Scanning the bar, I search for faces I might recognize, but it seems to be an older, hard-drinking cowboy and cowgirl type of clientele. The men's faces are crinkled like pecans, the women's hair teased into beehives. Patsy Cline's "Walking After Midnight" oozes out of the jukebox; a lone couple two-steps across the makeshift dance floor.

Jack returns with a pair of bottles that are dripping with water and ice flecks from the cooler behind the bar.

"To good old Longview!" He tilts his beer to mine.

"Hear! Hear!" I take a long pull, the cold beer refrigerating my nasal passages.

"So tell me more about what happened at Gran's." Jack's brown eyes shimmer in the bar's low lights.

"There's really nothing more to add, but I do have something else to show you." I slide my cell from my bag, scroll until I find the texts. My hands quake as I reread them.

You're making a very big mistake. You'll be sorry.

And then the shaky, haunting footage of the Walters's Farm. Bile scorches the back of my throat just looking at it again.

"As soon as I landed in Dallas, I started getting these creepy-ass texts. From an anonymous number."

"Seriously?"

"Yep."

"And did you respond to them?"

The skin on my face burns. "Yeah, I mean just the one time. I didn't know what to do. I thought maybe they had the wrong number? Was that stupid? Should I have just—"

"Lemme see." Jack cuts me off, holds out his hand.

His eyes frost over with concern as he reads at them. I watch his Adam's apple bob up and down as he takes a slow swig of beer. He glances around the room as if the sender of the texts is lurking somewhere in the bar.

"What the *fuck*?" His voice is nearly a whisper; he pinches the space between his brows. "I don't *know* for sure if it matters that you responded, I just read somewhere that you're supposed to ignore texts from strange numbers because of hacking. But this seems like something different altogether."

The label on my beer bottle is a shredded pile of wet paper; my fingernails have been clawing at the bottle, a stupid nervous habit I picked up from Dad years ago.

"Who the hell do you think sent these?" I ask.

He shakes his head back and forth, his eyes still dancing over the screen on my cell. He points to the text with the footage from The Farm. "This one is so . . ." He makes a face like he's just swallowed bitter medicine.

"I know. And you know The Farm was where Mom was on her last night, right? Before she died. Jesus, Jack, why *am* I even here?"

His eyes are still intense as his fingers fidget over the screen. He slides it back to me. "Hopefully it's just someone fucking with you. But why?"

"Hell if I know. I googled how to trace an anonymous text, but everything I read said that if it's from a burner phone—and I'm assuming whoever sent these wouldn't be stupid enough to use their actual cell—then sometimes you can't trace the number."

He reaches across the table, cups his warm hands around mine. If hands could melt like butter, that's what mine would currently be doing. I freeze in place, not wanting to break physical contact.

"I don't know about this tech stuff," he says, shaking his head. "But . . . just be careful this weekend. I mean, I'll be with you, but you know what I mean."

"Thanks. And thanks for being freaked out on my behalf. You're the only one—" Tears strangle my throat. "The only one who's ever believed me about Mom, the only one who didn't make me feel like I was crazy."

My mind spins back to the night Dad found her. Jack entering my darkened bedroom, slipping under the covers with me. The torn edge of my R.E.M. *Green* poster fluttering above us on the wall as the air vent hit it. Jack holding my body, which was shuddering with shock. And later, sitting in the bed of the creek for what felt like endless afternoons as I dissected every angle of Mom's death to him. Jack nodding. Listening. Being there for me when no one else was.

I had lost my soul mate, the one person who understood me the most, and Jack was the only one who was able to grasp that then.

At the time, I wasn't even actively thinking about who might have killed Mom, I was just bone certain that she hadn't killed herself, was sure it must have been someone who had it out for her. Jack indulged all my rages, absorbed all my grief, before Gran whisked me away to boarding school.

Since then, though, it's something I've obsessed over, of course. Mom could be flirty without knowing she was being flirty. She could've caught the ire of one of the neighborhood women. Or men. And then, of course, there's Dad. A pit grows inside my stomach anytime that thought slinks near. But it's always there, lurking under the surface.

Dad's temper, especially when I hit my teens, was no secret. When I was little, though, Dad was just a benign presence in the house. He'd toss the ball with me in the backyard, hoist me up on his shoulders and carry me through the house, which I adored, but for the most part, he was usually quiet and remote. Focused on work, even at home. Like most of the other fathers were, except for Jack's dad, Bruce, who was more hands-on.

As I got older, Dad's attention was in even shorter supply as he scrambled for new clients and became even more engrossed with work and stressed over money. What little free time he had, he spent with Katie, taking her to the shooting range; they both loved rifles. Dad had always spent lots of weekends out on a hunting lease with his friends, and Katie got hooked on shooting because she was a marksman at the local summer day camp. It was a passion they shared—theirs exclusively.

. . .

I never saw Dad hit Mom, but Katie and I would hear their late-night brawls when they thought Katie and I were asleep. We witnessed their daytime arguments, too, and Dad's barely masked anger. I watched as Mom would flinch at his tirades, secretly wondering if he ever struck her when we weren't around.

And I was privy to Mom's ramblings about Dad in the art shed, usually as she was consumed by a batik she was creating. Not just Dad, but men in general. How controlling they could be. How they thought they could "box us all in, mold us into perfect little ladies," Mom would spew while hotboxing her cigarette, the cherry burning bright orange as she sucked in sharp drags.

But the strange thing was, in the summer leading up to her death, even though Mom was, in hindsight, spiraling some, growing edgier, becoming perhaps what a shrink would call more manic, she also had moments of unbridled glee. The likes of which I hadn't seen since I was a little girl. She'd spend a little more time in the peach-tiled restroom she shared with Dad, taming her wilderness of hair into something almost cherubic. She'd take a hot curling iron the width of a baton and twist her hair with it, and I'd watch as the steam would sizzle off her tight curls. The style not only made her look more glamorous, it also gave her an even more powerful vibe: Medusa sprouting extra heads.

I'd gaze as she'd apply her makeup next, smoothing pearly white eyeshadow over her lids, which made her brown eyes pop even more. A cigarette would be smoldering in the ashtray—she'd have the window cracked so Dad couldn't detect it, and she'd be sure to douse herself and the room with Jean Nate perfume.

As if reading my mind now, Jack says, "We haven't talked about that night in a long time, Kira. Do you want to?"

Pressure builds behind my eyes, and to my horror, tears leak. Jack gives my hands a squeeze and I let the tears fall.

"Yes."

The light in the bar seems dimmer now—though I'm sure it's just the numbing effects of the beer—and Jack's features seem to soften. His face is perfect, sculpted, high cheekbones resting under his deep brown eyes. His lips are both full and tight at the same time and I still remember how it felt kissing him as a teen. Delicious.

"Who do you think did it? Who do you think"—he pauses, dips his head an inch—"killed your mom?"

"I don't know, honestly. But"—my throat catches as I'm about to say this next part—"you know how my dad's temper was."

My vision starts to go fuzzy. I can't believe I've finally said the words out loud. I've wanted to shout them at both Gran and Katie on so many occasions. But I haven't ever been entirely sure myself. But then, why else would Gran have rushed me out of town? Insisted that I was behaving like a lunatic? The whole thing has always reeked of gaslighting and cover-up, and that—even more than Dad's temper—made me suspect she was hiding something. Protecting her dear only child.

"Whoa, Kira."

I sniff back the tears. "I know. I know it sounds crazy." Even though I hate to break contact, I have to pull my hands from his to blot my eyes, which are now streaming. He laces his fingers around his beer bottle, leans back in the booth.

"I mean, it does, but . . ." Jack shrugs.

He doesn't have to finish that statement. Though Dad's rages were normally contained within our four walls, there was that one evening the summer before Mom died when he exploded on her at the Shermans'.

Mom was close with Jack's mom, Sally, who possessed a very centering, wholesome energy. Sally wore her neat auburn hair in a short bob—Dorothy Hamill style—and was always slapping together bologna-and-mustard sandwiches for the kids in the neighborhood.

In her parlor, a row of low bookshelves resting against the wall was filled with books on women's lib, feminism, homesteading, and crafts. Even in our well-manicured suburban neighborhood, Mrs. Sherman always tended to a wild, organic garden in her front lawn, a wide patch of earth that was hemmed in by chicken wire, choked with tendrils of miscellaneous vegetables.

She wore Birkenstocks everywhere—even to Sunday school with a summer dress—and professed the benefits of making homemade yogurt. Jack's father, Bruce Sherman, was similarly wholesome. White bearded even in his thirties, Mr. Sherman was the owner and lead pharmacist at the local drugstore. If a kid in the neighborhood had even so much as twisted an ankle, Mr. Sherman was always generous with Ace bandages and Absorbine Jr.

On summer evenings, my family would trot up the hill to the Shermans' so the adults could drink Sally's homemade margaritas on the rocks—with freshly squeezed lime juice from her lime tree—while the kids swam in the pool.

Our visits there got rarer as Katie and I got older, but on this particular night, Mom insisted that we all go as a family. Looking back, I think she was attempting to glue our shattering family unit back together. Her Hail Mary pass for normality.

I don't know what set Dad off, but I do know Sally served more margaritas than normal, and as I was treading water in the deep end, eyeing the sultry outline of Jack's form as he reclined in a pool chair, I heard Dad's voice snap like a twig.

"Goddammit, Sadie!"

Followed by the sound of his glass shattering against the Shermans' brick house.

Mom stormed inside, slamming the French doors behind her,

and Dad rushed to chase her. He was blocked, though, by Mr. Sherman, who stood still as a statue between Dad and the glass doors.

"Go home, Richard," I heard Mr. Sherman say in a low voice. "Go home and calm down. Get it together."

I averted my gaze from Dad before he turned around, his feet stabbing the Shermans' lawn as he trailed through their yard, letting himself out their chain-link gate.

Soon after, Katie slithered out of the water, toweled herself off. She tugged on her acid-washed denim cutoffs and—her face as immobile as stone—left the Shermans' backyard, too, presumably to follow Dad home. An unspoken pledge of allegiance to Dad, not Mom.

I stayed moored in the pool, the water beginning to feel like Jell-O against my legs, my muscles exhausted from the adrenaline spike.

A moment later, Mom emerged from the house in her red bikini, a fresh margarita dangling from her hand. Her eyes were puffy from crying, but other than that, she looked her usual dazzling self as the pumpkin-like summer sun caressed her long hair with golden light.

Sally remained inside the house. I could glimpse her through the kitchen window, stirring the Crock-Pot of queso that she'd been preparing for our supper and shifting ground beef around in a skillet of onions and bell peppers for the tacos.

Jack was still seated in his lounge chair; I hadn't turned to face him since Dad's explosion. I was too embarrassed.

After he swept the shards of Dad's glass into a dustpan, Mr. Sherman took a seat at the edge of the pool near the shallow end in his teal swim trunks, making small doughnuts in the water with his ankles. Everyone, it seemed, was trying to steer everything back to normal, to gloss over Dad's ugly display.

When Mom stepped out, I noticed Mr. Sherman's eyes lingering over her body for a beat too long. He then patted the spot next to him, inviting her to have a seat, which she promptly accepted. Watching her sway from the French doors over to Bruce made me think that she belonged on an album cover. She was missing only the high heels and a cigarette.

She sunk down next to Bruce, her throaty voice squealing over the cool temperature of the water, and I watched as he rubbed her back for the next few moments, seemingly consoling her. They spoke in hushed tones; I couldn't make out the conversation, but it seemed intimate, warm. It made me wish—and not for the first time—that Mom could be with someone like Mr. Sherman instead of Dad. Someone she could confide in. Someone who acted like a sensitive, mature adult and not a hotheaded child.

I take another sip of beer, which has warmed and tastes like metal in my mouth. "I don't know. I don't know what to think. I just feel like my family totally brushed me off. I mean, my own grandmother sent me away. Why would she do that if they weren't all hiding something?" That tire screech has crept back into my voice. I sound like I did when I was fifteen.

Jack rubs his beer bottle between his flattened palms, looking like the Boy Scout he used to be, trying to start a fire with sticks. "I don't blame you for feeling that way. Your gut has always told you that your mom didn't kill herself, so I think you have to listen to that. Not that you aren't. I mean, it's why you're back here. And it sounds like your gran finally admits that she agrees with you."

I feel a warm beam of light in my chest as I sit here, validated once again by Jack.

"It's just so weird. Dad has been dead for eight years. If Gran *had* been hiding something, something that would implicate him, she could've shared it with me after his death. And not have waited eight goddamn years to tell me she doesn't think I'm crazy, to let me know she has something of Mom's."

"I totally agree. It's so strange after all this time for her to come out with it."

I empty the last of my beer down my throat. Jack copies me, angling his bottle so dramatically high that it looks like he's trying to drain every lingering drop.

"I'm gonna get us another round."

He leaves me stranded, alone with my thoughts. As he approaches the bar, I see a woman planted on a barstool near the entrance. Her hair is whipped into the beehive style that is popular here, but when she turns around, her eyes bore into me.

It's Bertie. Genevieve's mom. A smirk plays on her slick red lips as she lasers her gaze over me. How long has she been here? How much has she witnessed? Did she see Jack cupping his hands over mine?

My stomach curdles with shame, though I've done nothing wrong. She's far enough away that I can pretend I don't recognize her—but I'm fairly certain she knows I've clocked her—so I wrench my eyes off her, pick up my cell as if responding to a text.

Out of the corner of my eye, I detect movement, and when I sneak another look, she's scooping her keys up from the bar and slinging her brown leather bag over her shoulder. She bangs out the front door as if in haste; I wonder if she's off to report to Genevieve the salacious news of spotting Jack and me together. She could've even snapped a pic of us with her cell phone, Jack's head tilted toward mine, my hands nesting under his. Where they belong.

18

KIRA

Jack lopes back from the bar with drinks. Beers again, but between his index fingers and thumbs he's clasping tiny glasses that clink against the amber-colored bottles.

He places the loot on the table. Liquid, pale gold and shimmering, swims in the shot glasses with lime wedges resting on the rims.

"Seriously? Tequila?" I raise my eyebrows at him, grinning.

"When in Texas," he says. "Hate the salt part, hope you don't mind I skipped it. And we need something to take the edge off of what's going on."

"Cheers to that," I say, lifting my glass to his.

In tandem, we shoot the tequila, taking it in with one gulp. It surfs down my throat, pleasantly searing, and I swear I can feel it moving through my veins, warming me. Then we suck the limes, which makes my mouth pucker.

Jack wipes his delectable lips with the back of his hand. "Whooo!"

He sets his glass down.

"So . . . we were talking about . . ." Jack's eyes sweep over me. I can't tell if he's flirting or just trying to be as kind and gentle as possible, but it's all I can do not to lean toward him, grab the back of his head, and start kissing him.

"My dad, my gran. My fucked-up family, I guess." A thought turns over in my head. The tequila has loosened something inside me and I'm no longer filtering. "But if it *was* Dad who killed Mom—and that's such a horrid thought—but if it *was* him, who is sending these texts to me now? And why?"

Jack sucks in a long breath. "I don't know. And I'm not trying to freak you out, but like I said, you need to be careful this weekend. And I certainly wouldn't ever be alone."

The pit of dread in my gut expands again.

His phone chimes and zigzags over the table.

He picks it up and his fingers flutter across the screen.

"It's work. A patient of mine just coded." His eyes darken. "Damn. So young. Thirty-seven. Sorry," he says, and slides his phone farther away from him.

"No, I'm sorry. I can't imagine . . ."

Jack rakes a hand through his hair. "It's okay. I know it's going to sound horrible to say I'm used to it, but I am. Except when they're this young and I've met the wife and kids. But we've done so many surgeries on him, all long shots, so this isn't exactly a shocker."

Now I'm the one who wants to take his hands in mine, but I resist.

He slings his beer back and I do the same.

"So, anyway, I was just saying, you really should be careful this weekend. Hopefully it's just someone messing with you. But if not, then clearly someone knew you were coming back to town and doesn't want you here."

My head spins. I think of Randall at the bowling alley and what he said to me: *I heard you were coming in from LA for this . . . Don't look so spooked! I live here. Word gets around.*

So basically everyone in town knows I'm back. But something about the thought of Randall slithers up my throat, making it constrict.

"What else do you know about Randall? You said you'd explain later."

Jack makes an O with his mouth. "You don't think—"

"No, I don't think it's him." My voice sounds just this side of sloppy. "I don't know what to think. I mean, he did say he knew I was coming in for this. But so does everyone else. And why in the hell would he care?"

Jack is still and silent for a moment too long. He bites his bottom lip as if carefully considering what to say next. "Look, I don't *think* you need to worry about him, in terms of this. I was just warning you to stay away from him. That's all."

I detect an edge to his voice, a flare of jealousy over Randall again. It makes my heartbeat thready and fast.

I lean back in the booth, fix my eyes on Jack. "Tell me the dirt," I say in a playful tone. I think back to Randall growing up. To his house that was on the very edge of our neighborhood, the most modest home in the neighborhood; the grass bleached yellow and thinning, like lettuce gone bad; the buckled sidewalk choked with weeds. His mom, Cassie, did everything she could for him, but she was a single parent—his dad had run off years before—and she worked full-time as a cashier at the local grocery store.

Even in elementary school, Randall was labeled a bad boy, a child with behavior problems. Mainly, he was just hyper in class and today he would most likely get a script for ADHD, but back then, all the teachers just cast him in the role of problem child.

When we were in the third grade, on the first day of class, he stole my box of crayons from my desk while everyone was at recess. I didn't realize that he had taken them when I raised my hand to get Mrs. Clark's attention, to let her know they were missing.

She walked the aisles, one by one, and spotted my box on Randall's desk. He had scribbled my name out with black crayon. My cheeks flamed and I felt sick to my stomach as she humiliated him in front of the whole class. I knew he had only swiped them because he was most likely too poor to afford a box of his own.

The problem child label stuck; Randall went from just acting out in class to more mischievous behavior, as it normally goes with a kid who's been labeled as bad. He hurt small animals—the bird that Jack was nursing, for one example, pelting it with a rock until Jack came upon the scene and rescued it. He was also always lighting stuff on fire in the woods just outside the neighborhood and trying to bully the younger kids into getting involved with his hijinks. One Halloween morning, he egged all the front doors of the homes on our block. And when he hit his adolescence, he became meaner, saying shit to all of us, and once yanking Katie's hair because he had flirted with her and she hadn't flirted back.

Deep down, I always felt a little bad for him, but as he got older, I started to despise him. Jack was the only one who was ever nice to him. But even then, as we entered high school and Randall fell in with a rougher crowd, Jack, too, began to distance himself.

Sitting across from me now, Jack fidgets in the booth.

"Well, do tell," I say.

"There's been talk about him beating up his wife. Ex-wife, I mean. Custody troubles with their kid. Rumors of Randall writing hot checks. Forgery. That kind of thing. I mean, are you honestly surprised?"

No. No, I'm not. "No, guess not." I was just hopeful that the new Randall, the sort-of-hot Randall at the bowling alley, might have grown out of that stuff, evolved. And I don't want to be thinking that he has anything to do with the creepy-ass texts. But Genevieve also confirmed that he's bad news, so it's not just Jack's jealousy or protectiveness or whatever it is.

"You probably don't know this, but back in the day, he was always in and out of people's houses during the day while they were at work."

"What?" I practically shout.

Jack nods. "He bragged to me about it once. Remember the burglaries?"

I do. There was an odd string of burglaries in our neighborhood the summer before Mom died. Houses were broken into; only small things were taken. A Rolex watch but nothing else. A portable television. From our house, Mom was missing a pair of diamond stud earrings—her favorite pair, ones she left resting on the bathroom counter. We weren't even sure it was the neighborhood thief that was to blame, so when the cops came knocking door to door, Mom didn't mention it. She wasn't entirely sure she hadn't misplaced them, and she told me not to say a word about it to anyone, because she thought Dad would lose his shit if they were gone.

"I do remember! You think that was him?"

Jack lifts his shoulders into a shrug.

"That's so fucking creepy, Jack!"

"Yep, I know. That's why I'm warning you to steer clear of him this weekend. Especially since he seemed pretty interested in you back at the bowling alley. Just sayin'."

I'm simultaneously freaked out about Randall and delighted at the prospect that Jack might be jealous over his attention to me. He leans his head in near, inches his steepled hands closer to mine. Again, I want to press my lips against his and make out with him, right here in the bar. My stomach is doing jumping jacks as he continues to lock his cocoa-brown eyes on mine, a shiver sizzling up my back.

A buzzing sound interrupts my salacious thoughts. Between us, Jack's cell snakes across the table again.

"Sorry, Jesus," he says, holding my gaze a second longer before clasping his phone.

His brows scrunch together and he lets out a jagged sigh.

"Work again?"

"No, it's Mom. Aiden is, um, melting down." Jack frantically texts as he talks. "I'm so sorry but I need to run over there."

When he looks up again, his eyes are shining, as if he's on the verge of tears.

"Of course. Do we need to just call it a night?" I ask, my stomach sinking at the thought.

"No. I can usually calm him down quickly. I'd ask Melanie to go, but . . ." He lets his statement linger in the air. "Shouldn't be too long; you know it's only, like, five minutes away."

"Totally! Go!"

Jack stands, and before he flits off, he kisses the top of my head; it's as if someone has poured hot oil on my crown. My insides melt and the room swims around me. I hear Hank Williams warble from the jukebox, but I'm so swoony that it sounds like he's singing from a different room. I take another swallow of beer, then twist my neck to watch Jack leave.

Just before he reaches the door, it flies open and Chad and Ethan, as well as two other guys from high school, Dustin and Peter, gust through the entrance.

Jack takes a step back, giving them space to enter. He briefly chats with them before jerking his head in my direction and exiting.

The loud, jovial quartet make their way toward me, and I decide to stand, not wanting to invite them to sit at the booth Jack and I were sharing.

Ethan reaches me first, and the others, thankfully, careen over to the bar.

He arches his eyebrows at me and grins as if to suggest Jack and I are involved.

"Havin' a good time?"

I punch his well-toned bicep. "Ha, funny."

"Sorry to intrude. Seriously, I am. But Melanie told us this is where the real party is." He draws me into a hug.

Interesting. So Melanie might be bothered by the fact that Jack and I are hanging out solo after all and wanted to bust up our alone time.

"If you call this a party," I say, fanning my hand around the room with an open palm, gesturing to the weathered older crowd, "then yeah."

It's such a balm to finally be in Ethan's beaming, easygoing presence. His aqua-blue eyes twinkle in the dim lighting of the bar. His interactions with me have always felt like safe flirtations. He never creeps me out; he makes me feel seen and less like the outcast single that I am.

"Katie was so surprised when she found out you were coming in for this." He fixes me with a stare. "I mean, I was, too. Who the hell wants to come back *here*?" Ethan chuckles, always adept at keeping things light. He clamps a hand on my shoulder. "Go easy on your sister, Kira. Believe it or not, she's been quite emotional since she heard you were coming back."

"Ha!" I sputter. "Could've fooled me. She's acting her usual—"

"Yeah, yeah, I get it. But you and I both know that's her bag. Playing it cool when she's really roiling inside. She hasn't even said anything about it to me; I can just tell." He sweeps a hand over his torso. "Body language and all."

I cackle at this. He's always been the defuser. Always been the one to bring Katie's fever-pitch rages down to a calming flat line.

"I mean Jesus, girl, you haven't been home in years! Not that I blame you. But why now?"

The room starts to sway at this question. I haven't said anything to Katie yet about Gran's revelation; I want to see exactly what Gran has of Mom's. And also, I don't want my sister preemptively talking me out of things. She's always been so dug in to the family position that Mom died by suicide, I didn't want the extra drama of Katie's wrath messing with what I might finally find out.

"Oh, I don't know. To see my old friends!" I say too brightly. Ethan dips his head toward mine; he knows I'm being a wiseass.

"Yeaaah, like Jack, right?" He winks at me, claps a palm against my arm.

My face turns into a space heater. God, is it *still* that obvious to everyone?

"No judgement. He *is* a total hottie."

"You're funny." My lips crack into a wide grin despite my embarrassment. "Hey," I say softly, "I've missed you."

He grabs my hand, gives it a squeeze. "I've missed you, too, Kira." His face grows serious as he says it. "How've you been?"

My heart squeezes and burning tears mist my eyes. I blink them away. "Fine. Good. I mean, nothing to report. My life is dull. I go to work. I meet my friends for dinner. I go back to work. That's the gist of it."

He rakes his hand over his jaw, nodding. "I know it was roughest on you, out of everyone. I know how close you were to Sadie."

To hear her name on his tongue makes the room sway again. I had forgotten that it was not just me, but nearly every other kid as well, who referred to my mom as Sadie versus calling her "your mom." As if she were beyond the status of motherhood; as if she were some other entity. Sadie.

In the way that Jack was there for me that night, Ethan was there for Katie. She went through a lot of guys in high school, but she and Ethan were dating when Mom died, and I think that's the thing that glued them together, that bonded them into eventual marriage.

Katie had been out that night. With her girlfriends. I'm shaky on the details; that was the least important thing to me when everything went down.

I was home long before Mom died. Before she ever made it back to the house from The Farm. My curfew was earlier than Katie's. I had to be home by ten, but she could stay out 'til midnight. Dad found Mom just past eleven.

I've often asked myself, how could Mom kill herself, in the shed, when she knew I was just steps away, inside my room, asleep? That's one of the reasons I never bought the suicide story. No *way* she would do that. Not to me. No freaking way.

But you didn't hear a struggle, did you? Katie used to toss back in my face when I would present that argument to her, her face contorted by anguish.

No, I had not. But that doesn't mean there wasn't one. I've always been a deep sleeper, and our house was brick, making it practically soundproof.

Mom's always been on the verge of ruining our lives and now she's actually finally done it. When are you going to wake up, Kira? Mom wasn't this innocent thing you think she was.

"So, just a heads-up," Ethan says, breaking my reverie. "Katie will be here soon. With Gina and Melanie. She texted me that she had to make some stop first—whatever that means; maybe they're going through the daquiri drive-through like we used to in high school?—but just thought you should know. And just to warn you, Katie's pretty soused. They all are."

Ethan is far too kind to say it out loud, but he's basically telling me to get lost, warning me that things could get nasty. With Katie, or Melanie, or hell, even Gina.

"Duly noted." I let out a pent-up sigh. My evening with Jack is over. As soon as he gets back, I'll ask him to drop me at Gran's. I don't want to stick around for any twisted drama. "Seriously, thanks. I'll split soon."

Ethan gives me a quick nod, but then raises his palm over my shoulder and collects a beer from Chad.

"Hey, girl!" Chad says, eyes blinking over me.

I've despised him since grade school. He's the worst kind of southern prep. All entitlement and family money and the ickiest frat boy traits. Pawing. Leering. The first to crack a joke at someone he deems lesser than himself. A nightmare. But now, glancing at his fat paunch and receding hairline, I feel the slightest twinge of pity for him. According to Meredith, who has, again, kept tabs on this crew far more than I have—from the safe distance of her laptop in England via social media—Chad and Genevieve's marriage has been a shitshow from the word go.

Genevieve clinging to him, tracking his every move. Chad moving out of the house at one point to live in their garage apartment. Chad and Genevieve dragging each other in public, fueled by alcohol and resentment and Genevieve's insistence that they get married way too young. And, predictably, Genevieve using the baby-as-a-Band-Aid fix just as Chad was trying to really leave her.

According to Meredith, Genevieve flushed her birth control pills down the pisser and, in a last gasp to retain Chad as her husband, went all buck-wild sexual with him. Splurging on lingerie, working out overtime with her trainer, even watching "How to do a lap dance for your husband" videos, and initiating sex with Chad every night. Of course, he ate it all up.

One month later she was pregnant with their first in what she deemed "the best accident that ever happened to us!"

"Hi, Chad," I say flatly.

"Thanks for comin' in!" Chad chirps, as if I came to town just for him.

"Sure," I say, because I don't know what else to say.

"You're lookin' good. Big city treatin' you okay?" he asks with that grating tone the men around here sometime use, one of both faux concern and righteousness, as if they know best about everything.

"Yeah, it's great."

More claps on the shoulder. Brandon and Steve. Chad's wingmen.

"Seems like you've gotten too big for us," Brandon says with a sloppy grin on his face. "You never come back to see us."

"Yeah, Kira, you gotten too fancy for us, huh?" Steve piles on.

I actually think they're flirting with me, but it's so pathetic and I don't know how to respond. I catch Ethan's eye and he dips his head in embarrassment.

"No, not at all. I just don't have much reason to come back," I say with too much grit in my voice. They all know it's true. Mom is gone and so is Dad.

"We're just messin' with you, sister," Brandon says. Of the three, he's the most attractive, tall and rangy with dark curly hair. But swathed inside a polo shirt and khakis, he holds little appeal to me. Plus, he's Katie's snarky friend Gina's husband.

"Yeah, don't get all serious, now," Chad says, his voice slippery with booze.

Steve is married, too, but I can't recall her name just now. Heather or Jennifer or something. She's not from here; they met at college, and that's why I can't register her name. Steve is balding and short, with a choirboy's round face. He looks innocent but is the dirtiest one of all of them. Always cracking filthy jokes, and in elementary school, he got caught with a crinkled copy of his father's *Playboy* magazine at recess.

My cell buzzes from inside my bag and I claw around for it, leaping at the chance to get away from these guys. I walk a few steps away to check my phone.

A text from Jack.

En Route. Aiden's better now.

Thank *god*.

So good to hear, I type back.

I don't want to turn around and re-engage, so I stay facing the entrance of the bar, scanning the door for Jack to appear.

The smoke is so heavy now, a layer of cotton churning above my head, making my eyes water.

The door bangs open and Katie, Melanie, and Gina pour inside.

Fuck.

Katie meets my eyes, flashes a diabolical smirk at me that makes my temples feel as if they're being squeezed.

A throaty laugh blankets the room, coming from Melanie as she staggers our way. Ethan wasn't kidding: these three are trashed.

Katie and Gina follow in her wake, both snickering into their hands.

With a sickly feeling, I wonder if I am the joke.

Melanie's eyes dance over my face as she speaks. "Soooo, having fun?"

I feel a pinch in my stomach. "Yeah! It's been nice." I opt for neutral language. "I'm so sorry about Aiden's meltdown—"

"Pshhh," Melanie bats the space between us with her hand. "Happens alllll the time. And *Jack*. Jack is handling it. Haven't you heard? He's the besssst."

Her words are stretched out like rubber bands but also have a bite to them. She takes her exquisitely manicured hand, flips a cascade of hair over her shoulder. "He's always *Super Dad*! I know, I know I'm lucky . . . But, sorry it busted up y'all's"—she makes air quotes with her talons—"reunion." Her eyes narrow with that one word, boring into me.

Katie tugs at Melanie's sleeve. "Melanie—"

"What?" Melanie spews back at her.

The front door flings open again and Jack enters, his hairline sweaty, his eyes darting over to us, taking in the scene.

"And there he is!!" Melanie slur-shouts.

Jack approaches us, his face tensing.

"Well?" Melanie asks. "He okay?"

Jack stares at the floor, nods.

"Hey, everyone!" Melanie cackles. "It's father of the year! Yeaaah! His wife, well, she had too much to drink! But not Jack! Perfect Jack was ready to swoop in and fix things as usual!"

Her dark eyes glint with scorn, basting Jack from head to toe. I wonder how much she's had to drink, and if she's popped another one of Mommy's little helpers.

Jack throws his head back, sighs deeply.

Behind a ring-laden hand, Gina snickers. I glance at Katie, who has her back to me, all her attention now on Ethan, who shoots me a look over her shoulder, his mouth a thin line.

My insides twist; I want to get out of here. I lean toward Jack. "Do you mind giving me a lift to Gran's? Kind of need to get back."

"'Course not."

If Melanie heard me ask, she's not showing it. She's now shoulder to shoulder with Gina, the pair of them cackling. The music from the jukebox seems louder; everything seems to pitch higher, as if their arrival has summoned a rowdier frequency.

"Isn't that right, Jack?" she snorts. "You're always—"

Jack clears his throat. "I'm giving Kira a ride home and then I'm coming back for *you*."

"Pssshhh . . . ummmm . . . no?" she taunts. "Boy, bye."

Gina erupts again into guffaws.

"If I don't cut her off, she'll be miserable tomorrow, and even more of a handful," Jack says to me under his breath, as if he's afraid of looking like a party pooper in front of me, like he needs to explain anything at all about his horrible wife.

"Back in twenty," he says to Melanie, each word coming out as a punch, before guiding me out of Dusty's with his hand, once again, on the small of my back.

19

KIRA

Inside the lush quiet of the SUV, my ears ring from the din of the bar. Jack slouches in the driver's seat, twirling the key ring around his index finger, his jaw clenching and unclenching. The fluorescent light in the parking lot streams through the windshield, making his coal-brown hair glisten, and in the closed-in space, his familiar scent—tangy, citrusy, woodsy—fills the car.

I want to cross the transom of the console between us, reach my hand over, and stroke the length of his tensing, carved jawline.

"Sorry things took a turn in there," I say.

"Me, too." He exhales, flops his head on the headrest. "I don't know what's going on with her. I mean, I do, but she won't do anything about it. I've pleaded with her to go to therapy. Even offered to go to freaking *couples* therapy, but—let's just say, things haven't worked out the way I thought they would."

My insides alight. Again, I know I shouldn't be giddy about their problems—it's so awful of me—but I can't help it.

"I'm just so sorry. It all seems very stressful," I offer weakly. And despite my nervousness, I reach over and place my hand on top of his. His leg is practically vibrating underneath our palms. I turn to him, hoping he'll shift in his seat toward me, too. Maybe even lean over, place his lips on mine.

But he keeps staring forward at the row of parked cars. I give his hand a squeeze, then retrieve my own. I don't want to overstep.

"Thank you for understanding," he says, his voice low. "It *is* stressful with Aiden. That's why I wish she would talk to someone, but she's so stubborn." His Adam's apple bobs as he swallows, as if he's fighting back tears.

My hands twist in my lap; I don't know what else to say.

Jack sighs and presses the round ignition button, starting the SUV.

"Let's get you home and let's stay focused on the real reason we're here." He turns to me, eyes creasing into a smile. He places his hand on the gear shift, slides into reverse. "And that's you finally finding out what really happened to Sadie."

As we coast down the highway toward Gran's, his cell buzzes in the cup holder between us, sounding like a fly trapped inside a screened window. At the next red light, he glances down at it.

"It's Melanie."

I tense in my seat. "Need to get it?"

He just shakes his head. "Not in the mood to hear it right now."

He taps his fingers on the steering wheel, turns down the blacktop that leads us to Gran's.

When we arrive at her house, he inches the car into the drive.

"You can just drop me here."

"You sure?"

"Yep." I don't want her peering at us through a window or, worse, floating out into the driveway again to greet me. "Thanks for dropping me off; I know you need to get back."

A ragged breath whistles through his teeth. "Don't want to, but need to, yes."

A thrill shudders through me; he doesn't want to get back to Melanie. Doesn't want to take her call. He wants to stay with me. And I, of course, could sit in this cozy space with him for hours.

Talking, or doing other things, the thought of which makes my breath catch. I don't want him to leave; I don't want our night to end.

"We'll pick you up on the way out to The Farm tomorrow. Text ya first."

"Thanks, Jack," I say. "For everything." I pat his shoulder like a puppy's head.

I climb out of my seat and shut the door. He lowers his window, calls out to me, "And, Kira, don't leave her house without getting what you've come for."

"I promise I won't," I say, then head up the drive into the syrupy humid night.

As he pulls out, his headlights swing over Gran's rolling lawn. I glance back over my shoulder at him and wave good night. He flashes a bright smile before rolling up the tinted windows and driving off.

After being in the chilled rental car, the balmy night makes my clothes stick to my skin like a deflating balloon.

My head is still swimming from the cheap beer and tequila shot, my heartbeat jittery from the flirting.

Crickets chirp all around me in the dewy grass as I walk up the drive, my leather sandals slapping against the concrete.

I smooth down my hair, tug on my shirt to make sure my cleavage is no longer exposed like it was at the bar. We didn't even touch, but I smell him on my clothes—salty and sharp—and I'm hoping the fresh air will lift if off before I reach Granny's house.

A branch snaps behind me; I whip my head around, my breath shaky and shallow. I spy a squirrel leaping off a low-lying limb of the mountainous pecan tree and exhale. I grew up here; I know every bump of this driveway, but after living in the city for so long, where there is no true night, being back in East Texas feels like being pitched into a dark and empty galaxy.

Still, the nearest neighbor is a football field away, and it is Friday night, and I should've taken him up on his offer to drop me at the top of the drive, closer to the house.

The drive crests up and I climb it, my legs woozy from the adrenaline spike. I'm to the edge of the front lawn when I see it—the words so large and glowing white on the dark grass that they almost look like a neon sign. But it's not neon; it's spray paint, five letters, and the word they spell—*WHORE*—causes terror to shred my throat before I let out a scream.

I see movement in front of me and there's her face behind the windowpane—cold and accusatory as ever—sending a chill over me before she yanks the curtain shut again.

20

KIRA

I'm shaking as I thread around to the side of the house, sucking in huge gulps of air. My scream still ringing in my ears, I wonder if Gran heard me. Her bedroom is on the back side of the house, in the far wing, but did she see it? Did she see the word *WHORE* spray-painted on her front lawn?

In my mind's eye, I see Hilda's face again in the window, as pale as the full moon and stark as ever, piercing me. *She* saw it. But when? How long has it been out there? Has Gran seen it?

I wobble to the side door, place my hand on the knob, and twist, but Hilda's already yanking it open, wrenching me inside.

"I hope you didn't wake your grandmother with all that screaming." Her voice is a nasty shout-whisper. "Get in here."

And suddenly, I'm a little girl again, withering under Hilda's smoldering judgement. The chill of the AC stings my skin, so stepping inside the house is like entering a cold cellar.

"Did you see anything by chance?" I ask. "Hear anything?"

But she doesn't answer, doesn't even look at me.

We've made it to the kitchen, and only the range lights are on, splintering shadows across the walls.

"Don't worry. *I'll* clean it up."

Did *she* freaking do it? I certainly wouldn't put it past her.

From across the kitchen, a cell phone dings. She cuts me a look but doesn't budge to retrieve it. She keeps her eyes locked and loaded on mine, a tense stare down.

I buckle and turn away, creeping down the hall toward my bedroom, doing a walk of shame through the dimly lit hallway. Once I enter the room, I shut the door and click the lock behind me.

Moonlight leaks through the thin part in the heavy drapes, pooling at the foot of the bed where I collapse.

My mind swirls with thoughts. *Who the fuck did it?* Melanie? I think of what Ethan said back at the bar—*she had to make some stop first*. But would Katie really let her go through with defacing Gran's lawn? I think of the way they were cackling when they poured into Dusty's. Maybe.

But earlier at the bowling alley, Melanie didn't seem to care that I was headed off to Dusty's with her husband. She *let* him go with me. Maybe she wasn't jealous at first, but I know from how she was acting that something had shifted, that she had become jealous, livid.

And what about Bertie? I saw the look she gave me, a visual *tsk-tsk* as she exited the bar. She could've tipped off Genevieve about my coziness with Jack, his hands resting on top of mine. And from there it would've spread like wildfire, straight to Melanie's ears.

But something tells me that the same person who spray-painted *WHORE* sent the texts, and it seems unlikely that Melanie is behind it all, especially given how looped she was during the car ride from Dallas. Plus, why would she care about Mom's death?

Randall. That's the next face that springs to mind, my brain now a kaleidoscope of who is out to torture me. Even though he grinned back at me as Jack whisked me away, he might've secretly been pissed that our time was cut short. But why would he be threatening me with texts in the first place? Of course, everything Jack told me about him fills me with unease, signals there's a lot I don't know about Randall, even from when we were growing up.

My thoughts are sidelined by the sound of my cell chiming from inside my back pocket. I fish it out.

Dread washes over me.

Why are you still sticking around? You don't belong here. LEAVE.

I want to reach through the phone and strangle this person. As I stare at it, I hear a rustling noise outside. My heart knocking against my breastbone, I walk slowly over to the window and peel back the drapes just enough so I can see outside.

Hilda's on her knees with a silver pail and giant sponge, scrubbing the nasty letters away. Small rivers of milky white paint run down the slope of the lawn, shimmering in the moonlight.

She must feel my eyes on her because she suddenly looks up at me, fixing me with another wicked stare. She's holding the sponge with one hand and I watch as she slips something inside her pocket with her other hand. Her cell maybe? A burner phone?

My god. I've been back in this town for less than six hours and I'm already paranoid. I'm losing it.

Could she really be behind all of this?

I'm not going to know anything until I get the goods from Gran, so while Hilda is still outside, I take this chance to slip down the hallway and snoop in the library.

It's at the rear of the house, so I can't keep an eye on Hilda; I'm just going to look around, see if by some chance I can find it. The room is dark, lit only by a tiny banker's lamp resting on Gran's stately desk in a far corner.

The giant windows look out over the back lawn, the trunks of the pecan trees coal black against the night sky.

My sandals thwack the tiles, so I kick them off, then creep barefoot across the cold ceramic. I gravitate toward Gran's desk, the surface of which is spotless, save for the lamp and a tidy stack of mail. My heart clenches when I see a note, written in Gran's scrawl, that has the details of my stay here. This visit really does mean so much to her.

The first drawer I try, the one in the center of the desk above the chair, glides open. Its inside is as orderly as the top of the desk: rows of pens, paper clips, and a letter opener inside a drawer divider. Other than an errant discarded lozenge wrapper, everything is immaculate.

I move on to the other drawers. The next one rolls out revealing a filing system. Last year's royalty statements, Gran's investments, a file on remodeling ideas. My fingers quickly flick through and freeze when they come to a file labeled "FAMILY."

I slide it out, place it on the desk. It's thin, and as I flip through the pages, my shoulders slump. It's just handwritten notes of our different mailing addresses, birthdays, etc.

Tucking it back in place, I roll the drawer shut. Because it's so heavy, it slams with a thud. *Shit.*

Three drawers left to try. I tug at each of them, but they're locked. Of course they are.

I open the first drawer again, am rifling through the pens for a key, when I hear Hilda's voice, which makes me jump.

"What *exactly* are you doing?" she asks, pail still in hand.

Red-faced and tongue-tied, I start to stammer. "I was looking for something to write on." Now the lie has swollen on my tongue, taken hold, and an indignant tone creeps in. This is my grandmother's house after all. How dare she? "I wanted to leave Gran a nice thank-you note. So if you wouldn't mind, can you show me where the stationery is?"

Hilda's eyes are narrowed gashes on her face. She sets down the pail, though, crosses the room. Goes over to the rolltop and fishes out a sheaf of blank note cards. The kind I know that Gran has always kept handy.

Wordlessly, she places it right in front of me. Stands there as if she's going to watch me write the note. So I grab a pen and a card from the pile, fishtailing around her to head back to my room.

Before I'm even out of the library, a heavy sigh groans out of her; I keep walking.

As I make my way down the hall, my heartbeat is thready in my neck. Those locked drawers. Hilda spying on me. Gran might actually be keeping this a secret from her after all.

I lock my door behind me, peel off my top and jeans, which reek of smoke, and slip into my PJs. Heading to the window, I yank the drapes completely shut before creaking into bed. My charger hangs limp like a worm from the outlet behind me; I jam it into my cell to charge, just so I don't miss the arrival of another creepy text.

Even though I'm lying down, my heart still hammers in my chest and my head still swims from the alcohol. Hilda. I can't shake the feeling that it's her. That she's the one who wants me far away from here. But why? The why is what I intend to find out first thing in the morning, when I confront Gran and get what I've come all this way for.

The cell is already hot in my hands from being plugged into the ancient outlet, which no doubt needs updating. I want to call Jack. Want to tell him about Hilda and the spray paint and this latest text. I should've snapped a pic of the *WHORE* message before Hilda began scrubbing it away, but I was too freaked out to do anything other than try and get inside the house as soon as possible.

It's 12:45 a.m. Way too late to call. And I wouldn't want to stir

Melanie's ire any more than I already have. They're probably in bed together. Maybe even having make-up sex. The thought makes my stomach squirm.

I think, instead, of his warm hands atop mine, of what he said in the closeness of the rental car, about not wanting to leave, either. No, I can't call him now, but I will find a way to talk to him alone in the morning. As soon as I'm able.

21

SADIE

When Katie turned one, I started dropping her off at the mother's day out nursery at our little Presbyterian church. Just a few hours, three mornings a week.

After being told I couldn't go back to school, I grabbed those hours that first week to completely transform the garage into a full-on art studio.

I shoved everything of your father's—the lawn mower and gas can, his golf clubs, his tools—into the storage closet, consequences be damned. I went inside and took the extra stereo system from our bedroom and hooked it up out there, popping in one of my favorite albums, Roberta Flack's *Killing Me Softly*, and cranked it up.

With the tools now off the shelves, I went to work setting up my paint bottles there instead. I lined the shelves with all the different colors, the jewel tones catching the sunlight through the open garage door, and filled Mason jars with water for my brushes.

He could try and keep me at home, but I'd be damned if I'd let him control me.

But because I didn't want him to erupt, I made sure to prepare his favorite for dinner that night, the goddamn rib eye and mashed potatoes. I wore a halter top so that when he pulled into the drive, he would first notice me, then the growing art studio in the garage. I greeted him with a kiss and a martini and Katie on my hip.

He let out a sigh, but then just dropped his head, defeated. A small smile crept across his face, though—as if he was a little proud of my boldness—and I knew I had won that small battle.

A few weeks later, I mail ordered a set of batiking tools from an art store in Chicago. I went to the local five-and-dime and got a set of white cotton sheets and used my slow cooker as a cauldron for the wax.

I was in heaven.

With your sister being looked after those mornings, I could reliably count on that time to create. Even though it was summer, the mornings were still cool enough to be out there, and because we lived on the edge of the circle, the open garage door looked out over the forest.

I'd sit there, sweat tickling my neck, the box fan humming in the background, utterly engrossed in my art. I'd get into a groove where I'd play one cassette or record over and over—that summer it was the Beatles' *Abbey Road*—and I'd work until the last second possible.

Back then I made mostly textiles—bedspreads, window coverings, pillowcases—sticking to the basics and also the safe stuff that would please your father. Though I'd be all alone with no one to bother me, occasionally a neighbor would pass by on foot or in a car and wave. Or stare. I didn't mind. I actually felt proud of being different, in those moments at least, and almost defiant. Willing them to judge me.

Some mornings Sally would come down with a pitcher of iced tea and hang out with me as I worked, sneaking a cigarette (she kept her occasional habit a secret from her husband, too), chatting. She was always so encouraging, so enthusiastic about my skills; it fueled me. She's the one who eventually introduced me to Cissy, the owner of the museum where my show will be held.

Only you, Sally, and Cissy know, of course, that the batiks that will be shown are not just cute textiles. Sally agreed that they would send Richard over the edge if he found out beforehand.

But I digress. The main point of me telling you all this is that one morning, a neighbor—I'll never know who it was and no amount of begging Richard to tell me would make him fess up—called your father at work and commented on how chaotic the garage looked from the street. How messy. And how they had seen me out there in a tank top with my cut-off denim shorts, hauling buckets around, my ass evidently in the air.

That's why your father had the art shed built for me in the backyard. Not to give me "a room of my own," but to further hide me away from the world. Contain me.

Little did he know that the art shed would become my escape hatch.

22

KIRA

I wake to the sound of sawing. My cell, still plugged into the charger, whirs on the nightstand. It's my alarm. I set it last night so I wouldn't sleep too late.

My head feels like it's being clamped tight, like it does from cabin pressure in a descending airplane. I'm hungover. And definitely not used to doing tequila shots.

When I reach my hand from beneath the covers to retrieve my phone, I'm shocked at the chill on my arm. The room is icy, and outside the window, a branch scratches against the glass. A ghostly rhythmic sound. I can hear the wind shrieking through the treetops. The cold front arrived last night after all, and I'm grateful I packed for it.

My cell is still molten from the charger; I yank it from the socket, tug the cord from the base, and dismiss the alarm. It lolls in my hand. Even though I don't want to see it, I open my texts and reread that last message that came in last night:

Why are you still sticking around? You don't belong here. LEAVE.

A sickly feeling roils over me. I want to respond, to tell this person to fuck right off, but Jack's right: I shouldn't engage any more than I already have.

The old mattress grumbles when I drag myself out of bed, crossing the room to peer out the window. The light outside is gray; a white drape of clouds blankets the sky, blotting out the sun. Just overnight, the pecan trees have been stripped bare of their leaves, and looking out over Gran's lawn, I notice every plant shuddering, as if in need of a wool coat. Fall used to be my favorite season in East Texas. Until Sadie's death twenty-four years ago this month. It's almost been a relief living out in LA, where there is no true change of seasons, no turning of the leaves, no frosty gusts of air to remind me of this tragic time of year. Fall was Sadie's favorite, too, obsessed as she was with jewel-red tones and burnt-orange shades.

This will be the first time I've been in East Texas in autumn since her death; a fire poker of emotion edges up the back of my throat, threatening tears. It feels as if the arrival of the cold front was staged, a set direction to cue the organ music, to turn up the dials of emotion on what already is a fraught trip back home. To remind me, in a visceral, time-traveling way, that this is the season of Sadie's death.

A shiver ripples over me. I peel the curtain back more, trying to find a trace of the *WHORE* remnants, but the lawn is pristine, as if it never happened, scrubbed clean like the shower scene in *Silkwood*. It's hard to shake the creeping feeling that Hilda spray-painted it herself, but again, I feel like I'm losing it. Why on Earth would she do such a thing?

But also, why would she be stalking me in the middle of the night, chastising me in the library?

I turn away from the window and fumble through my carry-on

until I find a hoodie, which I tug over my head. From down the hall, I can hear the clink of silverware and smell the narcotic scent of coffee brewing. I unlock the door and make my way down the frigid hall.

23

KIRA

Gran is seated at the long table in the dining room. The space is awash in light; she's dressed in a plush green velvet top, her hair perfectly coiffed, a flattering bright pink lipstick popping on her lips. Her perfume, White Shoulders, tinges the air as she sips a café au lait from a bone china teacup.

"Gran, you look beautiful!" I say. "Where are you going after this?"

She clears her throat, looks puzzled. "Uh, nowhere."

In the silky morning light she looks softer, less edgy. A twinge of sadness sweeps over me as I realize that like last night, she's all dressed up for me. For this breakfast.

The table is laden with the treats of my childhood. Half-moon wedges of cantaloupe rest on a platter drizzled with honey, and a small bowl of Raisin Bran cereal sits at two o'clock at my place setting, directly across from Gran's.

"Sit, dear."

Gran's plate is immaculate.

"You haven't eaten yet?"

"Of course not. I wanted to wait for you. Plus, you know I like to have my coffee first."

"How long have you been in here?" I ask, sitting down in the reed-backed dining chair.

"Half an hour. I didn't want to wake you. I know you had a late night." There's no accusation in her voice, no trace of anger, and she looks up and fixes me with a grinning stare. So Hilda didn't tell her anything and she didn't see *WHORE* spray-painted on her front lawn. Thank god.

An exhale billows out of me. "Sorry I was so late—"

"Don't be. You *should* be having fun at your age, Kira. You don't have enough of it. Your life is . . . well . . ." Gran pauses, takes another pull of her coffee. "It's stalled."

Inside, I flinch; she's right.

"And that's one of the main reasons I'm finally giving you what I've been keeping in secret of your mother's all these years."

Her eyes flit to the door and she stiffens. Hilda pounds into the room and narrows her gaze at me. "How do you take your coffee?"

"Just like Gran's, please."

"And, Hilda, bring on the rest of the food," Gran commands, as if she's irritated at her for interrupting our conversation.

For one nanosecond, I actually feel sorry for Hilda for being talked down to like that by Gran, but then I remember how nasty she was to me last night and the feeling evaporates.

"I'm positively famished," Gran adds dramatically.

I drag the bowl of cereal toward me, spoon a small white mountain of sugar over the top. I haven't eaten Raisin Bran in years, not since I left town for good, but I need the pick-me-up of the sugar rush to machete through this hangover.

Hilda's at my elbow a second later with a piping hot café au lait. It smells like nectar.

"Thanks, Hilda," I say to her back as she shuffles out of the room.

I sip my coffee and let the bowl of cereal sit for now; I don't want to start without Gran. I can hear Hilda in the kitchen wrenching open the oven, dragging out a cookie sheet, then slamming it shut. Now that she's safely out of earshot, I start up with Gran again.

"Gran, what do you have exactly? Of Mom's?"

Her eyes are averted to the window that looks out over the sprawling back lawn. The wind still howls through the trees, shaking the branches of her ancient pecan orchard.

"We'll get to that in a minute," she says dismissively, flapping a hand in front of her. "But, Kira, as I was saying, your life is stalled. And it's been bothering me for a long time. So I'm hoping what I have will help you finally move on."

Gone are the mind games from last night. Gran's face is drawn and serious. As dressed to the nines as she is, with her face to the window, she now looks exhausted, depleted, as if she's finally surrendered to telling me the truth.

The china cup begins to shake in my hands. I feel jittery, like someone just snuck up behind me. I wrap my other hand around the teacup to steady it and take a long, soothing sip. I can see why Gran is addicted to these; it tastes like caffeinated velvet.

From inside my pocket, my cell chimes. It's a text. From Jack.

We'll be by in about an hour!

I quickly tap the heart reaction button and shove my phone back in my pocket. An hour? Shit! That gives me so little time with Gran; I've got to nudge her along.

"And who is that?" Gran purrs. "Jack?"

"Gran!"

"What?! I can't want more for my granddaughter?!"

"You know he's married!"

"And?" Her eyes dance over me.

"And what?"

"And that's not stopping you from acting like he's not!"

Heat streaks up my neck. "I am *not*!"

"Hmph!" She guffaws. "Are, too." She coughs into her armpit, pretending she doesn't want me to hear.

My face is searing now. "Don't change the subject. I want to talk about Mom. You said in your text that you thought I was right about her, about why she died—"

"Shh!" Gran hisses at me. "Not now; not here."

Just like last night in the library, it's clear she doesn't want to discuss this around Hilda.

"After breakfast, we'll go to the library. Just us."

So at least I was right about the location.

"Okay, but Jack's gonna be here in an hour to pick me up to go—" Panic is starting to bloom in my stomach.

"I only have an *hour* left with you?" she says, her voice sounding like a balloon losing helium.

My chest burns with hurt. I do feel bad that it's such a short visit, but she knew this was how it was going to be before I arrived. "Sorry, Gran. I told you last night I didn't even have time for breakfast. I wish I could spend more time with you, but all the events start soon—"

She flaps her hand again. "It's all right," she says, but her jaw is set.

Hilda reenters the room, her forearms laden with platters of food: strips of crispy bacon with grease still sizzling, servings of eggs Benedict oozing with creamy hollandaise sauce and dotted with clumps of fresh crabmeat, and sides of roasted potatoes. My mouth waters at the sight of the offerings, but I'm also dismayed by all the food because Gran had evidently planned for a long lingering affair, and again, I'm dashing that.

Hilda takes her seat next to Gran's, and before she bows her head and makes the cross with her papery index finger, she fixes me with one more icy stare.

24

KIRA

In the full light of the floor-to-ceiling windows in the library, Gran looks even more fragile. She's poised in her armchair like a brittle, aging bird, her thin fingers working the edge of her velvet shirt; she's agitated.

Sitting across from her, I want to go over and hug her, but even more than that, I want the goods. I want her to finally part with what she's promised me. What *did* Mom write? What did she leave behind?

I glance down at my cell; it's 9:35. Jack is due here at ten. I clear my throat; just as I start to ask Gran about Mom, Hilda sweeps through the room again, wielding the glass carafe of coffee. She tops us both off.

"Hilda," Gran says to her without looking her way, "leave us, please. I don't have much time left with my granddaughter."

Hilda's pale moon face turns red, but she shuttles out, latching the heavy double doors behind her.

Gran shakes her head, lets out a long, ragged sigh.

"Finally. Alone," she says, but her eyes dance to the door again before settling on my face. She offers up a tentative smile.

"Gran, I'm not trying to be rude, but Jack's pulling up outside in twenty minutes—"

"Okay, okay," she says, her whole body deflating as she lets out another sigh.

"Well? What *is* it?" I ask.

She shifts in her seat, smooths down the top of her skirt. Her hands twist in her lap. "Could you go over to my rolltop?" She motions toward the desk.

I cross the room. My pulse is jagged in my neck as I approach the desk.

When I reach it, I am assaulted again by the framed photo of Mom, Dad, Katie, and me on Easter Sunday. My throat swells with emotion as I stand before it, up close. As with last night, I take in Mom, her normal shaggy hair pressed straight here and her slender form fitted into a stuffy church dress, the kind she detested. She usually ran around braless in flouncy cotton dresses and it's painful to see her in this picture, offering up this reduced, constricted version of herself for Gran and Dad.

I don't keep photos of Mom out in my apartment. Years ago I made an album of my favorite pictures of her, of us all together, but it would be too agonizing to look at her face every day, like I'm doing right now.

"Open the rolltop." Gran's voice slices through my thoughts. "In the back, you'll find a key."

I never would've found this last night.

I creak it open and reach my hand inside, run it along the back behind a thick set of stationary until it lands on the cool metal.

"Now unlock the top drawer. Under a stack of papers there's an envelope."

I do as I'm told, the key quivering in my sweaty hands. I dig under the papers and find the white envelope, which feels like it contains a small object. If Gran is about to give me one of Mom's old pieces of jewelry, I'm gonna snap.

"Open it," she commands, her voice strong but shaky.

I slit the envelope open. Inside of it, another key.

Gran's certainly gone to great lengths to keep this under wraps.

"Now with that key, open the bottom right drawer. And there you'll find it."

My vision swims as I bend down and fit the key in the lock. I twist it and slide open the drawer. Inside, a white cardboard box, the kind that typing paper comes in. With shaking hands, I retrieve the box from the drawer. It's heavy in my hands as I make my way back to the chair across from Gran.

Her eyes are shining with emotion. "Sit, dear."

Plopping into the chair with the box on my lap, I ask, "What is this, Gran?" as my fingers work to edge the top off.

The lid falls to the floor.

In the box is a thick stack of typing paper. My eyes rove over the first sheet, which looks to be a title page. When I read the words, I gasp.

A LIKEABLE WOMAN

A memoir by Sadie Foster

A memoir? Mom was writing a book? Her story? Goose bumps spread across my arms.

So, in these pages, allegedly, is the key to finally finding out what happened to Mom, to Sadie. I feel like I can barely breathe. I glance up at Gran, who gives me a quick nod as she purses her lips, sucks in a quick breath.

My mind reels back to Sadie's shed and her powder-blue typewriter. I rarely saw her use it, except when she was fitting index cards in the paper slot to type up title cards for her batiks. But a whole memoir? She must've worked on it while I was at school or after I was in bed for the night.

I peel off the top page and see that the next one is titled "Prologue."

I start to read, but Gran practically shouts from her chair: "Don't read it *now,* in front of me! In here!" Her eyes scan frantically around the space. "Take it with you. Read it when you can; just not here, not now."

It's excruciating to have to stop when Mom's voice is literally sitting right here with me. If I had more time, I would protest. I glance at the wall clock and realize Jack will be here in ten. I retrieve the lid from the floor and place it on top of the box. The manuscript practically burns the tops of my thighs.

"She wrote a memoir?"

"Well, she was *writing* one; I'll just leave it at that. It was unfinished . . ." Gran's statement hangs in the air like smoke. Unfinished because her life, too, was unfinished. I feel the room warble around me and tears sting the corners of my eyes.

"And you can tell from reading it that she didn't commit suicide? That someone else was—" My voice is high-pitched and careening around the room.

"Shh!" Gran hisses. "Keep quiet."

"Tell me," I say through clenched teeth.

She nods.

The room warps and shifts again. Anger and old hurt and confusion bubble up inside, threatening to drown me. I can't look at Gran right now, so I stare out the window at the glaring, overcast day, the pale gray light almost blinding.

I try to keep my voice low when I speak, but it comes out like a growl. "Why didn't you tell me this before now? How long have you known?"

I turn to Gran; she sucks in a quick breath, feathers her fingers over her heart.

"You'll see when you read why I *couldn't* tell you before now."

What the hell does that mean? The implication looms large. Gran was holding this secret tight for a reason, and it's most likely the same reason she hushed me up all those years ago and sent me away. She was hiding something. Protecting someone.

"My whole life," I say, my words coming out like jagged spears. "My whole life you have *lied* to me!" I bang my fist down on the wooden end table, causing my teacup to clatter in its saucer.

"Shh—"

"I'm done shutting up!"

"Kira, I'm pleading with you." Gran has a look of pure alarm on her face so I rescind my volume, pitch my voice lower.

"How long have you had this?" I ask, clutching the box to my chest as if someone, possibly Hilda, is going to burst in and snatch it from me.

Another long, uneven sigh from Gran. "After you were gone. I promise it was after you were gone. Your father, as you know, was a wreck. And I was the one who had to clean out your mother's *things*." She says the word *things* as if they were diseased. "And I found this in her art shed, under a pile of sheets. She clearly didn't want anyone to know about it—well, you'll find that out when you read it—so I kept her secret."

Oh, Gran, you sure can play a good role. Gran the virtuous secret keeper. What a load. "That's bullshit. You weren't keeping her secret for *her* best interest. You were protecting—"

"Just read it."

Blood swooshes through my temples. I'm so furious at Gran but also grateful that I finally might have some answers; I don't know how to feel.

"And what about Hilda?"

"What about her?"

"Does she know?"

Gran mops her brow, tucks a lock of silver hair behind her ear, which is adorned with a sparkling red ruby stud.

"Darling, Hilda knows *everything*."

Inside, I seethe. "Then why the two keys and locked drawers? Why all the secrecy? Why are you making us talk in whispers?"

"She knows about it. She knows it exists. And yes, she's probably read it, many years ago, but soon after I discovered it and brought it here, I decided it was best kept under lock and key. And Hilda *doesn't* know that I'm giving it to you now."

"Does Katie know about this?"

"Absolutely not. I told you, your sister and I aren't close." She paused. "And that's why I've designated Hilda as my power of attorney."

"Gran, you can't be serious. Katie is next of kin and capable and right here in town—"

"I don't trust her." Gran barely whispers this.

"Excuse me?"

"I needed someone who is *with* me, who *cares* about me. And you, you are way out in La-La Land, never coming home, never calling—"

"And you wonder *why*?" My voice is growing louder, so I soften it. "I would certainly take on the responsibility of being your power of attorney."

"And executor. I forgot to mention that Hilda is also the executor of my estate."

The air has left the room. I don't care about Gran's fortune, never have. But the fact that Hilda wields this much power over Gran—so much power that she's quaking in her Gucci ballet flats because she's handing over Mom's book to her own granddaughter—is deeply unsettling.

And the mention of Gran's will is also bait. Bait I know she wants me to take, but I'm not falling for it.

"Gran, you said there were two reasons you were finally telling me this," I say, switching the subject off the will. "One, because you want my life to move forward. What's the second reason?"

A pop of sound fills the air. It's my cell. Jack is texting.

Jack: We're just around the corner!

Shit.

K but can you give me ten? I'm just now getting what I need from Gran. Sorry.

Jack: Gotcha. No sweat. I'll double back through Starbucks. Mel needs more help "waking up" anyway.

I tap the thumbs-up reaction and shove my phone back in my pocket.

"Well?" I ask Gran.

She takes a sip of coffee before gently placing the cup back on the saucer.

"Kira. I—I don't know how much longer I have to live. And I couldn't take this to the grave with me."

The room tilts again. "What is going on? Are you sick?"

"I'm eighty-three years old. Most of my friends are dead by now. I'm lucky to have seen this many years. I have a heart condition. Arrhythmia. Failing heart. I could go at any minute. It's unpredictable."

Which likely explains why Gran looks radiant one minute and weak the next. I feel sadness in the pit of my stomach, but also, I don't know if she's bullshitting me or not.

"I'm so sorry, Gran. But can't the doctors do anything?"

"Yes. But I've declined."

"Why?"

"The surgery they would have to do wouldn't even guarantee anything and it also carries its own risks. Big ones—"

"But why? Why wouldn't you fight—"

"For what? Fight for what? I sit here in the big house all day, all night, practically alone. *Except* for Hilda. If it hadn't been for Hilda all these years, then—" She chokes as tears fill her eyes.

I go over to her, hug her, and she clutches me like a crab.

"I'm so sorry, Gran, I had no idea. I—" My throat seizes up with emotion. Guilt. Grief. Confusion. I don't think she's lying anymore. Not about this.

"You couldn't know, you never call—"

"I know, I know." Sobs rack my body and we cling to each other for a moment.

She then releases her grip, sinks back into her chair. With the back of her hand, she flicks away her tears, waves me off. She's never been one for big emotion.

"Sit down, Kira. And don't be sad. I *cannot* and *will not* be caught dead wearing one of those hospital gowns."

We both chuckle.

"I'm letting nature take its course. I've had a good life. For most of it, anyway. Now it's time for you to get on with yours."

Guilt. Confusion. Anger. Sadness. My insides twist with feelings. This is all too much to process, and right before I'm supposed to hop in the car with Jack and Melanie and attend Genevieve's vow renewal bash.

"Thank you, Gran," I say, not knowing what else to say. My time is up. I need to at least pull my hair into a bun and wash my face before Jack arrives. I lean down to Gran again and hug her again. "I promise to come back home as soon as I can."

Wrapping Sadie's book in my arms like I'm cradling a baby, I turn to leave.

"Just a minute." Gran rises and pulls an old canvas Neiman Marcus bag from a cabinet. "Hide the book in this, okay?"

We slip the box in the tote and I kiss Gran on both cheeks, then squeeze her hand before exiting the library.

25

KIRA

We're just a few miles from The Farm. I shift in my seat; my nerves are on overdrive and I can't quit squirming. Not just from what happened at Gran's, but also because we're nearly there.

As we wind around the country road that will shortly take us to Genevieve's drive, the trees begin to thicken, and among the gangly pines, maples explode in bursts of red, their ruby leaves quivering as gusts of wind sweep through.

Sadie's book sits in the canvas tote on the floorboard, nestled against my legs. It's all I can do not to pull it from the bag and start flipping through the pages, but I don't want to become more unraveled than I already am. I need to pull it together for the onslaught of faces at brunch. And also, I want to be by myself when I start reading it.

Jack texted when they pulled in Gran's drive, alerting me that they were there and adding a quick Can't wait to hear everything to his text. I'm dying to get him alone, to tell him everything, starting with the *WHORE* in the yard, followed by the latest icky text, and of course Sadie's book and Gran's health.

I simply replied, It's A LOT.

When I climbed in their SUV, Melanie acknowledged me with a saccharine hello before twisting back forward in her seat.

Her eyes are covered with oversized black sunglasses, and every few moments she sniffs, as if she has allergies or has been crying. She nips at her Starbucks coffee and keeps her face aimed forward, an aura of sullenness radiating off her. I can't tell if it's aimed at me or Jack or both of us.

And right now I don't care. I only care about getting through brunch and back to my room so I can start reading Mom's words.

The Walters's farm is just as I remembered it, but also quite jarringly different. There was once just a modest cabin and acres of untamed land. Now, as Jack crosses the cattle guard (as if they even have any cattle) and pulls through the wrought iron gates emblazoned with their name in scrolling letters (a new addition), the once-wild grounds are now groomed and sculpted. It's gorgeous, something out of a *Southern Living* magazine spread. Winding paths of crushed petal-pink granite curl in and out of various verdant gardens throbbing with candy-colored wildflowers and stately succulents. Lush herbs and willowy grasses sway in the wind.

Encircling the main grounds (as I remember it, and as the creepy text with the grainy footage reminded me) are thick stands of pines so dense the murky light in the forest resembles a permanent dusk.

Set against the dense tree line is a half-moon ring of different structures. The original, rustic cabin still remains. It's been updated, but it looks miniature as it rests in the shadow of Chad and Genevieve's new build, which I glimpsed some years past on Instagram. A sprawling two-story "modern farmhouse," the likes of which have spread across LA, too. The look is boringly all the same to me: snow-white siding, thick and plank-like; the windows trimmed in black; and a matching black tin roof. It's elegant, but literally everywhere. The only feature I love is the deep front porch, covered and old-timey.

People wander in and out of the front door, male and female. Flanking the house on either side is a string of cottages, all built in the farmhouse style, only tinier. I count a dozen, six on either side, as if Chad and Genevieve live at an event center. For all I know, they might have had the cottages erected for this very weekend.

Jack rolls up to the front of the house and a valet swings the driver's door open, palming the key from Jack as effortlessly as soft butter spreading across toast. Clutching my bags, I step out and spy a tall blonde striding toward us. She's dressed in a white turtleneck sweater and tight black jeans that hug her ample hips. Her high-heeled boots pierce the crushed-granite path, and giant gold hoops swing from her hears.

"Hiiiii!" she says, energetic and bubbly. "I'm Bethany, the party planner!"

Melanie offers her a limp wave and quick smile, which dims as soon as she's flashed it.

"Jack and Melanie Sherman," Jack says, thrusting his hand into hers. "And this is—"

"Kira! I've heard *so* much about you!" Bethany beams and I can't decide if she's being sarcastic or not.

"Nice to meet you," I say, shaking her hand just as Jack has done.

"Well, the ladies' brunch is already under way, so let's get you settled so you can join!" she chirps. "So the brunch is in the main cottage"—she motions toward the Walters's old farmhouse, which has been completely renovated and is now all gleaming windows with a new wraparound porch—"and you're in cabin three," she says to me, flagging her hand toward the right side of the house.

"And y'all are in ten," she says to Jack and Melanie, "which is a *little* roomier," she adds as if she's pointing out that I'm single.

"The lock combo is the last four numbers of your cell, and the itinerary for the weekend is in your room! The activities of the day are just for the closest, with everyone joining later for the vows. Enjoy!"

Bethany strides off in the direction of the garden, where a team of men are arranging wooden chairs in the clearing, presumably where the ceremony will take place.

Jack shoots me a wide-eyed, this-place-is-crazy look, before roping an arm around Melanie and steering her toward their cabin.

A sharp blast of wind scissors through me; I zip my puffer jacket up all the way to the neck and head to cabin three, the middle one in the row.

I clomp up the three wooden steps to the dainty covered porch and stab my code in the keypad. It emits a robotic sound and I twist the knob, step inside.

It's small but cozy, with one little light-filled sitting room with a sink and mini kitchen that leads to the bedroom and bath. The bed is sumptuous, covered in a thick, creamy down comforter and fluffy pillows. A cotton waffle robe hangs from a hook on the bathroom door, and a set of white, perfectly rolled towels is nestled neatly on the bed next to a small stack of paper-wrapped artisan soaps. The walls and ceiling are made of cedar and the air smells rich and woodsy.

If I didn't detest Genevieve, this is the kind of place I'd actually beg to stay in for getaways. It's lovely. I wander back into the sun-dappled sitting room. As promised, Bethany has left the itinerary—a document printed on glittery silver paper—on the two-person wooden dining table. Next to it are a vase of white lilies, a tiny bottle of champagne with a hot-pink ribbon cinched around its neck, and a few glass bottles of both flat and sparkling water. The word *Welcome* is spelled out with foil-wrapped dark chocolates. But horror of horrors, a silver tiara with feathers and rhinestones sits atop the table as well. I'm so fucking sure I'm wearing that.

I know I need to get going, but I glance over the schedule:

10:30–11:30: Ladies' Brunch!

MAIN HALL

11:30–12:30: Arts and Crafts! Paint Your Own Wineglass!

MAIN HALL

1:00–2:30: Spa Day! Manis, Pedis, and Facials!

REAR OF MAIN HALL

3:00–5:00: Wine and Cheese Tasting!
Join Us for Sips & Hors D'oeuvres!

IN THE BACK GARDENS

7:00 sharp: Vow Renewal

CLEARING IN THE MAIN GARDEN

Bonfire and Reception Immediately Following!!!

My stomach wrings at the mention of the bonfire. Are they trying to re-create Sadie's final moments on Earth? I screw the lid off one of the bottles of flat water and take a sip. I know I'm just being sensitive. The Walterses held bonfires out here many times before Sadie's death, and I'm sure Chad and Genevieve have only followed in that tradition, but it still makes my head spin.

Ugh, the brunch. I don't want to go; I'm not hungry in the least after the spread at Gran's. I want to sit here and read Sadie's book, but I've got to put in an appearance.

When I arrive at the main hall, a server in a black apron with her hair pulled high in a swinging ponytail opens the glass doors, ushering me inside.

What was once the Walters's living room—a funky space with wood-paneled walls—has been transformed into a gleaming dining hall. The ceiling has been pitched so high it soars and glittering windows line the roofline, pouring in natural light. Like my tiny cabin, this room is made of cedar, giving it a ski lodge feel, replete with a chandelier crafted from antlers hanging over the long wooden dining table.

Everyone is already seated, of course, including Melanie, and all heads swivel in my direction as I enter.

"Kira! You made it!" Genevieve, who is sitting at the head of the table, rises and gives me a shallow hug.

"Hi!" I say weakly to the group.

I'm the only one *not* wearing the tiara. My eyes land on Katie, willing her to stand and embrace me, but she only raises her half-filled glass of mimosa in my direction, flashing me a grin that's laced with sarcasm.

The server leads me to my seat, which, thankfully, is directly across from Courtney's. Katie and Melanie sit a few seats down from her and I'm sandwiched in between Rachel and Gina.

My skin crawls as everyone stares, and I think about the end of last night—all the snickering and cattiness at the bar and, later, the spray paint—and I want to duck under the table and hide.

"Mimosa or Bloody Mary?" the server asks me.

"Mimosa sounds lovely, thanks."

Through the swinging double doors where the server exits, I catch a glimpse of a bright, spacious kitchen. Standing next to the butcher block is Bertie.

The table is decked out in pastel pinks and mint greens: ribbons, balloons, and confetti. Dainty pink cake stands hold cupcakes and gooey quiches, and potted green planters are filled with fresh rosemary plants atop tree-trunk coasters. A stack of blueberry pancakes—half-gone—rests on a ceramic platter, and a large salad bowl filled with dark greens, shaved Parmesan, and red pomegranate seeds is being passed around. Next to our salad plates, shrimp cocktails rest in tiny silver bowls filled with ice.

I'm not interested in any of the food, but a drink sounds like exactly what I need right now.

A chilled mimosa is placed on my coaster and I grasp it, downing half of it in one swallow. The orange juice is freshly squeezed—actually a richly colored orange and not yellow—and it feels like a smile going down the back of my throat.

"So, Kira," says Genevieve, her voice honking like a goose's, "tell us *all* about LA."

I inwardly sigh.

"Yeah I saw that pic you posted on Insta with you and Keanu Reeves! How freaking cool is *that*?" Courtney says, her blond hair swishing.

Here we go.

"For real, girl?" a brunette with giant hair who I don't recognize asks from the end of the table near Genevieve.

I blush. "Yep. But, it's not like we're besties; I just met him at an awards show—"

"An 'awards show'?" Katie pipes up, putting rabbit ears around the words. "It was the *Oscars*." She's beaming at me, which actually makes me melt a little inside.

"Oooooh!" the group squeals.

"Yeah, but it's not all that out there. I mean, it's not like I'm running around with A-listers all the time or anything. My life's not that glamorous," I deflect.

"Hand me another one of those quichey things," Courtney says, and I scoot a cake stand toward her. She pops one in her mouth, chews. "Girl, you've gotta try one of these. Yum! Anyway, you seein' anybody out there?"

At this question, I feel the sting of Melanie's eyes on me. I glance in her direction; her mouth is a straight line. Without her sunglasses, her eyes are puffy and red as if she's been crying.

"No, no one at the moment . . ."

I can't help it; I peek again at Melanie. She smirks and coughs as if she's clearing her throat. Her bitchy friend Gina elbows her under the table and locks her eyes on me as well.

Courtney makes a frowny face. "Sorry, girl, but I'm sure you'll find *someone* soon!" She's the least toxic friend here, but my god, she really is still so oblivious, saying that like finding someone, getting hitched, is the only end game in life.

"Who's ready for Paints and Sips?" Genevieve trills, clapping her hands together. "After another round of drinks, I say we hit it!"

"And what exactly are we painting again?" Courtney asks.

"Wineglasses! Like, to commemorate the weekend. Or whatever you want. I thought it would be *so* fun," Genevieve says, eyes alight with glee.

The waitress enters the room, bearing a silver tray full of fresh mimosas and Bloody Marys.

"I actually need to shower, freshen up. So I might skip and see y'all at the spa thingy," I say.

"Late night, huh?" Genevieve asks, and the table practically trembles with nervous laughter. This time, I don't dare look at Melanie. "Just kidding, girl, we all had one."

"I'm just still kinda jet-lagged, might need to rest a sec—"

"*No* worries!" Genevieve says, but her inflection drips with disappointment.

"Aww, Kira," Katie purrs from her seat, "you'd be so good at it!"

She's tipsy, but just like with the Oscars comment, she's seemingly trying to be nice to me. I think.

"I actually haven't painted in a really long time," I admit, bowing my face toward my plate, sadness coloring my voice.

"Really?" Katie asks. Her face is pinched with concern. "But it's all you ever used to do—"

"Pssshh." I slice my hand through the air, trying to sound casual. This is an intimate conversation, one I need to have with Katie alone. I actually *do* want to get her alone this weekend, to tell her about Gran. I can't believe she doesn't know Gran is dying. I'm not sure, though, that I want to tell her about Sadie's book. Not just yet, anyways. I need to read it myself first, then see what I'm comfortable sharing with her.

My thoughts are interrupted by Courtney, her voice floating to me from across the table. "Is it weird being back here?" Her nose crinkles at the question, as if she can't imagine the horror of what happened all those years ago.

The room falls quiet. I open my mouth, close it. Take a sec to consider how to answer her with all these eyes on me.

I go for honesty, but bland honesty, keeping things close to the vest. "Kind of, I mean, there's still so much I don't know."

An audible sigh snakes out of Katie and I flick my gaze to hers in time to catch her rolling her eyes. I've been right to keep my trap shut with her about Mom so far.

I also feel the tug of a stare from Genevieve, but I when glance her way, her eyes are downcast, avoiding mine.

Another long pause of silence. Then the brunette I don't know starts in on more small talk and I'm grateful, keeping my mouth closed until I can get out of this room.

Back in the cabin, the wind whistles against the windowpane, making a sound like a teakettle beginning to boil. Breathing in, I clasp the box and peel off the lid. Blood whooshes in my ears, but I grab a stack of pages and begin to read.

26

A LIKEABLE WOMAN

A memoir by Sadie Foster

PROLOGUE

I know you're supposed to start books at the beginning and not in the middle, but the middle is where I'm at right now.

I began this years ago—fourteen, to be exact—while you were still growing inside of me, my wild weed even then. My lower back cramped in constant pain during that last month of pregnancy; only the flower-printed caftan allowed my body to breathe. But I didn't care. I already loved you and ached to meet you.

I'd sit in the mornings at the white wooden table in the corner of my art shed and write longhand, my scrawl curvy and jagged across the yellow legal pad. The small fan in the window whirred, swatting at the thick summer heat—not really cooling the space—but still, I enjoyed being out there, all alone with my thoughts while your father was at work and your sister was at the church nursery.

I'm parked at the same desk now, but this afternoon I'm typing on the powder-blue Remington I bought myself earlier this spring for my birthday. Richard lifted an eyebrow when I peeled off the vinyl casing and showed it to him, as if he were worried I was going to try and train to work outside the house as a secretary or something.

"The hell is that for?" he asked, rattling the ice around in his glass of scotch.

"So I can type up nice labels for the museum show."

It wasn't a lie, exactly; after years, I finally have enough batiks for a show, and Cissy at the museum has promised me one. But I could've had them typed up anywhere.

I bought the Remington—which I've named Gertrude, after Gertrude Stein—because I want to do this right. Not that I even know what *right* means, but at least now I've read a lot more books than when I was just starting this.

At the very minimum, I'll go back to the beginning, put all this in order, type it all up. I might change your name—all the names, actually—and adopt a pseudonym, something that sounds sophisticated and not tawdry like my own name. Maybe I'll use initials. But I don't know; this is a memoir, maybe I should just put it all out there, names and all.

My earliest longhand pages were furtive like diary entries. Then, as you grew into a scabby-kneed toddler, I thought I'd try my hand at writing a children's story.

I've always been writing to you, I realize now, though I won't let you read this until you're much older, of course. And I hope when you do, it will help you, that it will be a guide of sorts; I hope it will be a guide to many young women.

I set it aside for years, but now I know what I want to tell you. To not settle, to not bargain for less, for starters. I want so much more for you than I've allowed for myself.

You're like me, Kira; I've known that since you were a little girl, and I've wanted to nurture that part of you because I know how quickly the world can rush in to try and snuff that part of you out.

We see things the same and that's why I've always been able to be myself with you. You can't imagine how much that means to me, but I'm worried I've put too much on you, I've shared too much. But please know that my problems aren't your problems.

I know you've given up nights out with your friends to hang out with me in the shed and help me, and I know it's because you like being in here, but also because you worry about me. And I'm sorry for that. You're my daughter and you're not responsible for me. I just need you to know that. But the biggest thing I want you to hear from me is not to let the world come in between who you are already and who you're continually trying to become.

I'm also writing this because something has been happening recently and I need to get it down. To process it. Writing does that for me, and I can't really talk to anyone else about it, even Sally, and I tell Sally nearly everything. I can't even tell you about it. Not now, not until you read this.

Richard, of course, can't know about any of this—not yet, anyway—so each day after I write, I make sure to stash the newly typed pages in a cardboard box I keep hidden underneath the tangle of cotton sheets for my batiks.

I'm hoping by the time this gets published, I'll be gone. That's the plan, anyway. I can't stomach your father's temper any longer than I have to.

I never even thought I could write a book, but here I am with a ream of typing paper resting beside me, the hum of the typewriter motor a calming buzz through my bones.

I come out here, too, in the middle of the night, startling the night birds as I walk past the willow tree. But when I can't sleep, which happens more and more these days, typing my thoughts out seems to help to settle me. My stomach has always churned; I've always been classified by doctors as "nervous," but my nerves are even more on edge these days with not only fear but excitement.

Some of this, I realize, will sound amateurish and read more like diary entries and ramblings—well, like how I talk to you in the shed—but I'm hoping a publisher will help me out with that, make it into something readable.

But here's what's been happening. It started a few months ago, just after Mike and his loudmouthed wife, Bertie, moved to town.

Mike sneaking a glance at me across a crowded lawn. Me seeking out Mike's company—for just a word or two—when everyone else isn't paying attention.

But just the other night at our dinner party, Mike made a pass at me. Nothing has happened between us yet, but a warming sensation in my solar plexus tells me that it will. And even though he didn't see us then, I'm afraid that your father is catching on.

27

KIRA

My mouth is dry as powder; my whole body is shaking.

Sadie. Mom. It's like she's just in the next room, speaking to me. I take another sip of the water and my mind reels.

I can't believe she was writing a book. In secret. To me. To guide me. I think of all the times I wished so badly she was still alive—in difficult moments, in crossroads moments—so I could ask her what to do. Now I have her words, speaking to me. I can't believe that's what she was really using that typewriter for.

And I can't believe she maybe had something going on with Mike Walters. Bertie's husband; Genevieve's father.

The weight of it all presses down on me and I can't quit trembling. Grief is a scar tissue and mine's just been ripped open in a way that it never has before. Tears are flooding and all I can think of is Mom. *What if you hadn't died? What happened to you?* I want to shout.

I am absolutely going to find out.

And I'm also shaken by the fact that she felt guilty about making me her confidante. I would give up nights out with Meredith and Genevieve and the crew to stay in the shed with her, especially during the summer before she died, when we were getting ready for her show at the museum. And yes, I did it because I sometimes worried about her and knew she wanted me to stay, to listen to her, to hang out with her.

But also, I loved being in there with her. It wasn't just that Sadie felt like she could drop her guard with me; I felt the same with her. And I don't mean I told her all my teenage troubles, but I felt like I was truly myself just being around her, making art.

Going to keg parties with the others—especially if I knew Jack wasn't going to be there—held little interest for me.

I wish I could tell her now that I would do it all over again.

I rise to my feet and stride around the tiny cabin, churning through the small space. The bedside clock reads 12:30 p.m. The spa thingy starts in just half an hour. How can I be expected to go to that when I have these pages to read? I grab the stack I've pulled out of the box and straighten the pages against the surface of the coffee table. My cell bulges in my pocket; I take it out, tap out a text to Jack.

I need to talk to you.

This is all too much to bear alone, and I'm not ready yet to share it with anyone else, especially Katie. Interesting how Mom was writing the book to *me* and not to her. Interesting, but hardly surprising. No, I can't share it with her just yet. Not 'til I find out what else is in these pages.

I drag a bottle of sparkling water off the dining table and twist the tin lid off it, cracking the seal. After a long glug, I plop down and continue reading.

I check the time on my cell. It's 12:58. Fuck. I need to get going. I've made it through two more chapters and I'm even more shaken. My insides are dancing and adrenaline pings through my blood.

Mom was definitely seeing Mike behind everyone's backs—or so it seems from the first chapter. The two of them flirting heavily at a dinner party at our house. I remember the remnants of those get-togethers. The stench of cigarette smoke hanging in the living room, the pile of dishes in the sink the next morning.

And maybe their fling didn't stay a secret. Maybe Bertie knew exactly what was going on, like Mom was afraid of. And Dad. Maybe Dad was onto them, and . . . maybe he was furious . . . I can't even follow through with the next thought.

But maybe that's why Bertie's behaving with me the way she is; because she knew about Mike and Mom. I have to keep reading to find out how far they took it.

I know Mike and Bertie are divorced now. I believe—based on what I gleaned from Facebook at some point—that Mike is in Florida with a new, younger wife. But surely he's going to be here tonight, attending his daughter's vow renewal.

And the next chapter. Which was all about Grandad's temper (before this visit, I never knew that, never heard that) and Gran subtly warning Mom about Dad. I knew, of course, all about Dad's nasty temper but not that Mom was actively afraid of it. What else happened that I didn't know about?

I read the last few lines again and my stomach roils.

But still. If things don't get better money wise, and if I don't keep myself in line, keep my desire in check, I worry about what he's capable of. About what he'll do next.

Jack's not replying. I know he's roped into some event with the guys, so I gather up the pages I've already devoured, turn them facedown on the coffee table, and head to the bathroom to freshen up before going back to the Main Hall for manis and pedis.

28

KIRA

The room where we're all getting manis and pedis is spacious; the air is tinged with too much lavender essential oil, and floor-to-ceiling windows splash light across the blond plank floors. A group of eight of us are arranged in a circle, feet soaking in wooden basins of warm water made silky by sea salts.

I picture this as a place where Genevieve routinely does yoga, no doubt with a personal instructor. As with the brunch, I was late to this activity, and when I entered the space, Bethany jetted toward me with a rack of nail polishes to choose from.

"We're all doing a crazy color for our toes, since nobody other than our husbands will see them!" Genevieve chirped from across the room. "I mean—" She stuttered, as if catching her mistake in uttering the word *husbands*. "I picked the one called Midnight Eggplant and I think it would look super cute on you!"

I plucked it from the rack and selected a berry-colored shade for my fingernails.

The room humming with chatter, I settled into the empty chair next to the entrance. I glanced at Katie, but she hid her face behind an issue of *Us Weekly*. She's now avoiding me, but I'm not going to apologize for anything, especially for still wanting to know what happened to Mom.

Because of the setup and how we're all spaced out, there's less pressure to talk, so I grab a copy of *People* and feel my body start to go slack for what must be the first time since I initially got Genevieve's invite back in LA. The nail tech takes my right foot in her hand and massages it deeply with both her thumbs; I can't remember the last time I've been pampered like this. As with the yoga classes I dropped years ago, I certainly never indulge in anything that resembles self-care. Part of it's the money. My salary covers the basics, but not too much else, and I'm not about to dip into Gran's funds.

As I sit here, though, with my foot being kneaded, another thought surfs through, one that comes unbidden from time to time that I do my best to ignore: What's holding me back from living my life in a full and joyful way has to do with Mom, because hers was cut so short.

This realization is always lingering somewhere in the periphery, but I'm usually able to drown it out. I don't like wasting time with self-examination; I never went to see a therapist after Mom died. It all honestly just seems pointless. Nothing is going to bring her back.

But being here in East Texas has made the thought resurface in a loud, clattering way. Gran telling me my life is stalled, me admitting to Katie that I don't pick up a paintbrush anymore. Me, the only single person at this shindig.

I suck in a deep breath, roll my shoulders back, and flick through the pages of the magazine, trying to scan for something that will take my mind off my current, heavy line of thinking. I land on a piece about Tori Spelling's on-again, off-again divorce and am a few lines in when my cell summons me. The volume is too loud, so the ping pierces the room from inside my bag.

As if she knows it's her husband texting me, Melanie cuts a nasty stare my way. Face blushing, I bend down and retrieve it.

Jack: Meet at the pond?

I want to, of course. I figure the mani-pedi will last another half hour, tops. After this wraps up, I'll ditch the facials, pleading that I need a shower, which I still do.

Me: I can be there in thirty-ish?

Jack: Perfect. Remember the way?

Me: Yes.

Jack: I'm dove hunting. Kill me now.

I click the ha-ha reaction and drop the phone in my bag. My face still searing with embarrassment, I bite down my grin when I look up and see that Melanie is still glaring at me.

The nail tech pats my feet dry and produces a pair of flip-flops for me to wear. She slides a small portable table over and dips my hands in a warm bowl of water. After soaking them for a few minutes, she starts shaping my cuticles with a wooden instrument, filing my nails. She then begins working on my hands, massaging my fingers one by one with oil. Again, I exhale and feel my body beginning to relax. By the time she's applying the cranberry-colored polish, I'm nearly in a Zen state. And though a facial following this actually sounds nice, meeting with Jack sounds nicer.

After my hands have been slipped into a little machine that dries the nails quickly, I stand and go over to Genevieve, hoping to keep my announcement between us.

"Hey," I say as her hands are still in the dryer. "I'm gonna miss the facial. I *still* need to shower," I say, pointing to my hair that's pulled up in a jaw clip. "But I'll be there for cocktails."

She blinks at me, as if trying to read me. For a split second, I wonder if she's onto me, but how could she possibly be? "That's totally fine. I get it!" she says too loudly, causing the others to take notice.

I slip out the door before anyone else has a chance to comment.

29

KIRA

I head back to my cabin to make a show of actually going there. Once in the bathroom, I freshen up, applying lipstick and straightening up my messy bun.

Peering out the window, I make sure the coast is clear before stepping out. There are two main trails to the pond that I can recall. One runs along the back of the row of cabins where mine is, and another snakes along the backside of the other set of cabins. I remember it being about a ten-minute walk, past where the gardens now stand, over a path that weaves through the woods.

I climb down the steps and quickly wind around to the back of the cabin. I walk briskly, wanting to get into the cover of the forest so no one spots me. It's still so cold out that my breath is a white cloud in front of my face. My freshly manicured hands are freezing; I jam them in my coat pockets, cursing myself for not packing gloves.

I'm in the woods now, the trees rising on either side of me like walls. My footsteps crunch along the orange carpet of pine needles, releasing their heady smell with each step. I take a deep breath, inhale the scent that reminds me so much of the fragrance of the eucalyptus trees in Southern California. Overcast daylight sputters through the tops of the pines, giving the forest an ethereal feeling.

How many walks through the woods around our house did I take with Sadie? Too many to count. Sadie bending down to collect pine cones in her wicker basket, then pine straw, and also leaves. This is what got me started with collaging. We would collect the crunchy fall foliage, then take our loot back to the shed, where she would let me do my thing with a plastic jar of Elmer's glue, spreading it across the poster board as I saw fit. Next, I would scatter the pine needles across the board, then fasten the leaves on top. Sadie would dip a brush in orange paint and help me smear strokes in an artful way across the paper. Fresh tears threaten to form at the memory of being with her in the woods.

Overhead, the pines begin to mix with other native trees, and the brittle leaves of a sheltering sycamore clatter in the wind; I rub the tip of my nose, trying to warm it. I'm sad, too, I realize, that I'm not painting anymore. I feel a deep pang to get back to that meditative state of creating that I enjoyed with Sadie, then later at school. The woods are talking to me, telling me that I've left an essential part of myself behind.

I keep walking. The path in front of me hooks to the right, and in the distance, through a thick tunnel of trees, I can just begin to make out the clearing that holds the two ponds. I still have a ways to go, and a shiver bolts through me: I realize I'm now in the same spot where the shaky, eerie footage was taken, which the anonymous texter sent to me. Who would do that? Who is texting me? Again, I think of who has access to The Farm, and of course, Bertie springs to mind.

Another gust of wind rips through the tunnel, making the forest quiver all around me, and I want to race to the end of the path, escape this spot as quickly as a I can, but I slow my breath, steady myself. I don't want to look like a fool in front of Jack.

The wind rushes around my face, causing my eyes to water, and the ground is now a pelt of golden-yellow leaves, stripped from ancient oaks that nearly hug the stand of pines.

The clearing, once a green blur, now comes into sharper focus as I approach the edge of the forest. If the rest of the Walters's grounds have been manicured into modern perfection, this back section is still the same untamed, wild landscape I remember from my youth: all weeds and blackberry vines creating a fortress around the murky fishing pond.

I spy Jack standing on the high ridge between the two ponds, his dark hair glossy and luscious even from this distance. When he sees me, he smiles and waves me over. As I get closer, my heart leaps. He's picture-perfect, as if he's just stepped out of the pages of a J. Crew catalog, wearing a cream-colored turtleneck sweater underneath a heavy red-plaid jacket, his jeans tucked into a pair of wellies. He looks right at home as he stands on the rust-red path with an oar in one hand, beaming at me. Blood courses in my ears as I ascend the ridge, walk toward him.

"Hey!" he says.

"Hey!" I reply dumbly.

This feels like a date, like a rendezvous, and I sweep my gaze around the perimeter of the clearing to make sure we're alone. We are; it's just us and a family of mallards paddling near the reeds in the swampy fishing pond.

"Finally," Jack says. And I don't know if he means that I've finally arrived or that we're finally alone, so I don't respond.

"Thanks for meeting up," I say. "It's been . . . an interesting twelve hours since we've seen each other, to say the least."

"I want to hear everything. And it's been interesting for me, too," he says, gesturing to his wellies.

"Yeah, look at you!"

"I mean, dove hunting? For real? These guys are stereotypical southern frat males."

"You shoot any?" I ask.

He shakes his head. "You know me, I just can't," he says, and it makes me remember the wounded bird he nursed back to life.

"Of course."

"I mean, I pretended to aim, but, nah, not my bag. But I must say, it's kind of nice being out here." He looks to the pond, to the woods. "And by here, I mean this pond, away from the fray."

"A-greed."

"Well, shall we?" Jack points his head toward a pair of canoes—seemingly the same barn-red ones from high school—that are perched on the steep banks of the clear blue swimming pond.

"Really? You seriously want to take those out? I don't know how much time we have and—"

"Aww, c'mon. We'll be quick, I promise. And when's the last time you've gone canoeing?"

I kayaked once in the ocean near Malibu, but other than strolling around the gloomy lake in Echo Park, I haven't been near a body of water in I don't know how long.

"High school, probably? Probably the last time I was here, actually."

Jack grins and makes his way over to one of the canoes. I trail him.

A pair of sun-bleached oars rests under the metal seats of the canoe Jack noses into the water. He holds on to the tip of it and I climb in. Once I'm seated, Jack hops in after me and the boat rocks a little before he shoves us off the red clay shore, takes his place at the rear. I slide the heavy oar from beneath my seat, but Jack's already paddling, thrusting the canoe farther toward the middle of the pond. I dig the oar into the water, and in just a few minutes my biceps start to burn.

We reach the center and stop rowing. I bring the paddle back into the canoe and inadvertently sling water across my lap; it's icy cold.

I turn around in my seat so I can face Jack. His eyes are scrunched from facing the glare of the sun, which is still hidden behind a veil of clouds, but it pulses white, like a fluorescent moon.

"So," he says, his face now serious, "tell me."

"Whew." I blow my bangs skyward. "Where shall I start? Shall I start with the fact that after you dropped me at Gran's, I happened upon the word *WHORE* spray-painted on the front yard? Or, should I start with Gran's dismal diagnosis? Or the fact that her housekeeper is batshit?"

"Wait, what?" His voice clatters off the surface of the pond.

"Yes and yes. And yes. At least the batshit housekeeper scrubbed the lettering off before Gran could see it."

"Jesus Christ! I *knew* I should've dropped you off closer to the house. Texting is one thing, but someone actually going over to your gran's property?"

Fear climbs up my throat. I had wanted Jack to reassure me, not freak me out even more. I pull my cell from my pocket, show him the latest text, the one that arrived last night before I passed out:

Why are you still sticking around? You don't belong here. LEAVE.

Jack shakes his head, scratches his jawline. "I'm so sorry. It's maddening that we don't know who's sending this."

I swallow the rough lump that's lodged in my throat, nod.

"And what's this about your gran?"

I sigh and tell him all I know. Then ask him his medical advice.

"Yes, arrhythmia and heart failure can be serious, and even"—he pauses a beat before he says this next part—"in some cases, fatal. I'm surprised she's not seeking treatment. But seriously, at her age, I can't say I blame her. Heart surgeries are no gimme. I'm so sorry."

Because of the strong wind, gentle waves lap against the canoe. The water smells marshy, earthy—smells like home—and I feel another pang of sadness and guilt over Gran, for staying away all these years.

"Thank you. I'm sad. And feel bad I never come home." I fight the tears that are threatening to erupt and change the subject. "But I haven't even told you the biggest thing."

"What is it?" he asks, his voice small and soft.

"Mom was writing a book. A book for me to read one day. A memoir, the story of her life and art, but also, like, a guide for me. I don't even really know *what* it is; I just started reading it a little while ago in my room. But this was the secret Gran said my mom had been keeping, and what Gran has kept from me all these years. And like she said in her texts, the book has things in there—things I haven't read yet—that made Gran believe Mom *didn't* kill herself. That she was murdered."

The canoe seesaws side to side a little in the lapping waves—the wind is picking up—and my teeth start to chatter from the cold and my jeans, which are damp from the oar. I blow into my hands, rub them together. I packed a scarf in my bag but couldn't find it this morning; I must have left it at Gran's. My muscles ache from shivering, so I stretch, raise my arms above my head. And when I do, the bottom of my sweater creeps up, exposing my abs.

Jack's eyes drift to my stomach, intense and staring; a hot flash courses over me before the wind knifes me again, an icicle across my belly. I cross my arms over myself and begin to quake again.

"Jesus, you're trembling," Jack says, leaning toward me. He pulls my hands into his, warms them for a moment.

Like last night, a flicker of electricity courses through me with my hands in his. "Thanks."

Jack just watches me.

"I've only read the first few chapters," I say, not wanting to go into the details just yet, wanting to keep Sadie's story to myself a little bit longer. "So I need to read more as soon as I can to find out what Gran is talking about."

"*Whyyy*," he asks, his tone indignant, "would she wait so long to give this to you?" His hands release mine and fly up around his ears, a physical question mark.

"That's exactly what I asked her. She told me that when I read it, I'd understand. So, again, I think she's been covering up or covering for someone all these years."

Jack's cocoa eyes dance over my face. "I can't imagine what you're feeling."

A blade of wind slices over the pond, making my whole body quake.

"Come here," Jack says, opening his flannel jacket.

We lean into each other, and I let him envelop me, wrapping me in the jacket, in his arms. I feel like I've just stepped out into direct sunlight from a darkened, refrigerated movie theater. My head nestles against his neck and my heart beats staccato against my breastbone. Jack keeps holding me and I move my cheek up to his.

"You have to read the rest of it as soon as possible. Like before tonight, so we can know . . ." His breath is hot in my ear.

"I know," I say gently, my voice a whisper.

Our body heat is now a furnace; I want to move my lips across his face until I find his. But I just sit, afraid to break the moment and, honestly, scared to make more of a move than I already have.

In the distance, a loud snap jolts us both out of the embrace. It sounds like someone walking through the woods, stepping on a branch. We both jerk our heads in the direction of the sound, which is coming from the forest, near the trail that Jack took to get here. Squinting, I can't tell if it's a trick of the light, but I feel like I can see a closing up of the woods, like footprints in the sand being filled up by the ocean. A gap that was once there has sealed up, as if someone has turned and walked the other way. But I can't be sure.

Did Melanie follow him here?

I don't dare ask him that, but that's sure as hell what I'm thinking, especially after the way she looked at me when my phone dinged in the mani-pedi session. Shit.

Jack's face is chiseled with concern, but he says, "God, we scare easily, don't we?" He's smiling now. "Probably just a bobcat. I mean, not that those aren't scary, but you know what I mean."

I wish it *were* a bobcat; my stomach needles with tension.

"We should probably get back." I check my cell; it's 2:40. Drinks are in just twenty minutes. "I have a cocktail thingy."

"Me, too. Bourbon tasting. Now *that* I can handle."

After I scramble out of the canoe, Jack tugs it back against the shore. I don't necessarily want to walk back alone, but there's no way in hell we should walk together.

"I'm thinking we need to go back the way we came—like, on separate trails, just in case . . . that wasn't a bobcat?"

Jack sighs. "I seriously don't want you alone anymore this weekend."

I think of Melanie, though, her eyes shooting me daggers as the nail tech brushed petal-pink polish on her fingernails.

"I'll be fine, I promise. It's not that far, and I'll text you when I get back."

He fixes me with those eyes, then nods. "Okay. But just . . . be aware."

30

KIRA

I'm almost back to the main grounds; my thighs are on fire and my armpits sting with sweat. I've never walked so fast in all my life; I really *do* need a shower now.

After we parted, I watched Jack stride around the pond toward the far trail, then made my way back to the feathery forest line, stepping back inside the green-and-yellow tree tunnel.

My heartbeat thundered in my ears as my boots pounded on the crispy leaves; I was anxious to get back to my cabin, worried that it had indeed been Melanie who was spying on us.

The row of little cabins comes into view now, and as I step outside the tree line, a sheet of blustery wind nearly shears me in half. It might not be such a bad idea to have a bonfire tonight, after all; it's positively freezing.

As I reach the perimeter of the gardens, I spot Genevieve making her way from the center—where the ceremony will be held—back to the main house. She must hear my boots on the crushed-granite path because she looks up.

"Hiiii!" she shouts cheerily at me, waving as she continues hurriedly along her course.

I smile and wave back, wrapping my coat around me even tighter.

I reach the cabin and climb the little wooden steps. Punch the code into the keypad, wait the nanosecond it takes for the mechanical lock to unlatch. Every cell of my body is anticipating the warmth from the cozy sitting room, but instead, when I walk in, a sharp breeze sweeps through the room, sending the neat stack of pages I'd read of Sadie's book sailing off the coffee table.

Something isn't right.

The window in the sitting room, the very window I sat by and listened to the gusting wind whistle against, is now open. Not all the way, just cracked about the length of a hand, but open nonetheless when it was definitely closed before I left.

My breath is too fast and I creep into the tiny bedroom, make sure it's empty, then do a sweep of the bathroom, yanking back the shower curtain like I'm in a horror film. Empty, too. Everything—my bags, the bed—looks undisturbed. Exhaling, I walk back into the sitting room and close the window, checking that it's locked this time.

Then I go over to the pile of papers on the floor, gather them up.

Something isn't right here, either.

I had just read Sadie's Prologue and first two chapters, set those facedown on the table, and left the rest in the box, but the pile of papers on the floor is thicker. Goes all the way through chapter four.

What the hell? Someone has been here rifling through Sadie's book while I was out canoeing with Jack. My first thought for some reason is Katie. Did she by chance stop by to see me, then find me gone? And feel comfortable enough to punch in the last four of my cell, let herself in? Did she discover Sadie's book?

Hands shaking, I type out a quick text to her.

Did you come over to my cabin?

Three dots bounce in the text window, indicating she's typing back.

No. I got a facial like everyone else. And am actually still here, gabbing, enjoying myself

A few seconds pass. Then she types, Why?

I believe her and I don't know how to reply without sounding crazy, and also without giving away that I was gone, with Jack. And clearly, she's still pissed. Mom is so obviously still a no-fly zone for her; no way am I going to tell her what's running through my head right now.

I just thought I heard someone outside while I was in the shower, thought it might be you. See you soon! 😊

She only replies, K.

Shit. It's got to be someone who knows my number, or at least the code, which could actually be anyone here. Genevieve, Bethany, whoever. But why? I zip up my coat and bolt out the front door, boots pounding down the stairs.

There's no one in sight. I walk to the side of the cabin, go over to the window that was opened, and scan the ground. Who am I, Nancy freaking Drew, searching for footprints? Out of the corner of my eye, I see a figure moving at the rear of the cabin; I race around to glimpse the back of a tall, stout woman in a black coat, heading down the path at a fast clip, away from the pond and toward the rear of the main house. She's a good ways off but I know exactly who it is.

Bertie.

And before I even think about it, I call out to her. "Mrs. Walters!" I shout, my voice barreling toward her, carried by the wind.

She freezes, twists around.

Shields her eyes with a gloved hand and squints at me. After a second, she drops her hand and starts walking toward me. I take to the path to meet her.

"Yes?" she asks, as if I'm bothering her. "What is it?"

Was *she* the one in my cabin?

"Someone's been in my cabin!"

She looks at me like I'm crazy. "What?"

"I went on a quick walk," I lie, "and when I came back, the window was open—and it wasn't before—and some of my stuff was strewn about. Well, some paper."

As I'm talking, Bertie tilts her head to one side like a dog does when it seems to be trying to puzzle something out. Her mouth is almost taking the shape of a smile, but a worried smile; she thinks I'm mental.

"It could be housekeeping?" she says, but it comes out as a question. "But don't worry about it, Kira. We're all friends here!" She slaps her gloved hand on my shoulder, barks out a laugh as if to say I'm being silly.

I kind of *do* sound a tad crazy. Maybe the window had been cracked and I just hadn't noticed? Maybe I grabbed more pages from Sadie's book than I remember? Or perhaps the wind picked those up, mixing them with the other pages. I don't *think* that's what happened, but Bertie's reaction definitely lets me know that I don't want to go around and ask anybody else. I just need to let it go and watch myself, like Jack said.

"Sorry, I am running around like a chicken with my head cut off; I've got too much to do. Are you all right, dear? I need to dash."

"Yes, of course. Sorry."

"See you later!" Bertie says, then turns and heads back down the path.

After a few paces, though, she pauses, swivels around, puts her hand to her forehead. "Oh, I forgot. I *was* looking for your earlier. Genevieve said you were taking a shower." Her eyes rove over my messy bun, disapproval streaking over me. "But I knocked and knocked."

She fishes around in her giant handbag, retrieves a red scarf. *My* red scarf, the one I forgot back at Gran's.

"Your grandmother's housekeeper stopped by a little while ago to bring you this. Said you left it behind and your gran was insistent that you have it."

My blood turns cold.

Hilda.

Wow. I bet *she* nosed her way inside my cabin. I bet she sneakily found out which one was mine. Maybe from Bethany.

I reach out, take the scarf from Bertie, who has noticed my odd expression.

"Are you *all right*?" she asks for the second time in a span of mere minutes.

I wedge a smile onto my lips, nod. "Yes, sorry, just can't believe she came all the way out here to bring me this old thing! Well, thanks! See you soon!" Face burning, I turn and head back to my room.

31

KIRA

With the window now firmly shut and the heater roaring, the air inside my cabin feels as warm as a campfire, but I can't stop shivering.

Hilda. I can't believe she drove all the way out here to deliver me a scarf. I toss it on the love seat. I mean, I can see Gran ordering her to do that, but I wouldn't put it past Hilda to have hidden the scarf from me in the first place so she had an excuse to come out here. I can feel her icy presence in my cabin now, lurking around, reading as much as she could of Mom's book, before she split so she wouldn't get caught. She probably sweet-talked Bethany into letting her in, or even figured out the code herself. She does have my cell. It's not the first time I've felt like she could even be the one sending me the texts.

Gran's revelation that Hilda is the executor of her will—and, I'm sure, a benefactor as well—means creepy Hilda has a lot to lose if our family secrets are exposed in Mom's book.

If it *is* her, and she wants to threaten me, stop me from snooping around, especially now that I have the book, and she read Mom's book herself, then I need to rethink keeping all this from Katie. Gran might be in danger; I don't know what Hilda's up to, and anyway, my sister needs to know about both Gran's diagnosis and Sadie's book. And soon. Hilda could be hastening Gran's decline.

But what if it was Bertie in here snooping around? She said she knocked and knocked; what if she let herself in? She'd certainly have the passcode, too, control freak that she is. I'm sure she has the entire guest list's contact info in her grubby little hands.

Or could it have been Genevieve? Who so breezily greeted me from the garden as I passed by.

My stomach lurches as I walk over to the tiny kitchen, tear open a mini package of cashews that I saved from the plane. I toss a handful in my mouth, chew.

Of course, there's another possibility altogether: Melanie.

She definitely clocked me texting with Jack. And if that was indeed her watching us from the woods, she would've had time to race back here, creep around. Or maybe she even came here first, wanting to see what I was up to, and discovered I was gone.

I don't have much time before the cocktail party starts, but screw it. I'll just be late to that, too.

I need to find out what exactly is in this book.

32

SADIE

Something strange happened today and I can't seem to shake it. It's nighttime now; you and your sister are asleep, and your father is in the den watching television.

I crept out here to type this, to get it out of my head, to get it down on paper.

Sweat trickles down my back. It's still hot out; the night hasn't cooled us off yet. We had a brief rain shower this afternoon, which made the air even more cloying and heavy than it normally is.

The window is open, the fan is whirring, but even over the *shh* of the blades turning, I can hear the cicadas croaking in the woods, sounding like a million maracas being shaken all at once.

It's one of the things I really love about the neighborhood, that our circle is hemmed in by a forest. That we're just a bike ride away from downtown, but we're also in our own enclave, which usually reminds me of my childhood, of being out in nature, but this afternoon, when I biked back from the pharmacy, I wished that we lived in a neighborhood that was more populated. Safety in numbers and all.

I'm probably just being paranoid. That's what your father would tell me and that's one of the reasons I didn't even mention it to him. And also, my brain's been a bit fuzzier these days.

I've been taking more of the pills lately. After the dinner party and what happened with Mike—our almost kiss—my body and mind have been consumed with adrenaline, drenched in desire, and anticipating the upcoming gallery show has set my nerves on edge, too. And also, there's your father's temper, worsening by the minute.

So I've been taking a little more—popping one in the daytime as well as my usual one at night—and I'm foggier, but the pills do help settle my racing brain. But now I've run out. I took my last one after lunch today and there's still four days to go until the new month, until I can get a refill.

So earlier this afternoon, I hopped on my bike and pedaled downtown to the pharmacy. I have the Volkswagen Beetle, of course, but when it's warm out, I like the exercise. It, too, calms me. I opened the door and the bell clanged against the glass.

I exhaled when I spotted Bruce behind the counter; I was hoping to catch him and not some other pharmacist who would likely turn me away empty-handed.

"Sadie!" he greeted me, flashing a smile.

The store was all but empty, just an older lady in the greeting cards section, plucking through the selection.

"Bruce!" I said as I approached the counter.

I've always found him attractive, with his white shock of hair and beard, his backlit brown eyes that are almost caramel colored. Of course, I'd never entertain thoughts about him; Sally is my best friend and I'd never do anything to hurt her. And they seem solidly happy together. One of those couples that finishes each other's thoughts, radiating an ease with one another when they're together. I'm jealous of that; I've never had that with your father.

But I have always appreciated Bruce's warmth toward me, his unthreatening flirtiness. It feels benevolent, and unlike the rest of the men in the neighborhood whom I catch ogling me, who sometimes utter inappropriate things to me when they've tied one on, Bruce feels safe.

"What can I do for you today?"

I fanned myself, plucked my sweat-soaked T from my sticky chest. "I actually need a refill," I said, trying to keep my voice level.

I slid the empty bottle toward him.

He studied the label for a sec, then switched his attention to his monitor, his fingers pecking at the keyboard.

He squinted his eyes. "Your next script isn't due until next week. First of July." He looked up at me, expectantly, as if awaiting an explanation.

"Yeah, I know, but silly me, I spilled the last few on the bathroom floor the other night. After I'd taken a shower, so they got all mushy from the water I dripped," I lied. "So I flushed 'em."

I know it was just nerves, but the room started to feel warm, closed in, so I kept plucking at my shirt. Bruce's eyes flitted to my breasts for a quick second.

"Ah, well, of course. I understand."

I wasn't at all sure that he was buying my story, but relief poured over me.

"I can refill the missing ones for you, but I'll have to take those out of next month's prescription. And you'll have to come back for the new script next week. Or I can bring them down to the house or you can grab them next time you swing by. Whatever's easiest."

I didn't want him coming to the house and drawing any attention to my new habit in front of Richard. "I'll just grab them next time I'm up there with Sally. Which is, like, every day," I said cheerfully.

Bruce has always taken care of us—bandaging up kids in the neighborhood, ringing the doctor in the middle of the night for antibiotics when you were boiling with fever from strep. I leaned across the counter, gave him a quick peck on the cheek. Something we do as friends, and that Sally and Richard do as well.

"Thanks! I gotta run. Start dinner and all that!"

I pedaled away with the new orange bottle rolling around in my short's pocket.

When I got back to the house, I dismounted, walking the bike through the back gate like I always do. Inky black storm clouds were swollen in the sky, threatening rain, so I leaned the bike against the backside of the house and walked through the squashy grass to the patio.

Then I stopped in my tracks.

The sliding glass door was open. I never leave it open.

Taking quiet, tentative steps, I crept inside. My heart started banging in my chest and I couldn't help it, I called out for you, for Katie, for your father, even though I knew none of y'all were home, my voice pealing through the house and then dying in the empty rooms I was sweeping through.

I yanked open closet doors, peeled back shower curtains, but I was alone. Hmph.

The pill I'd taken after my hurried lunch of a turkey-and-tomato sandwich had hit me an hour before I left for the pharmacy, giving the afternoon a honey-tinged calm, so it was *possible* that in my haze I had pedaled off without closing it. But I doubt it. That's just not like me. I may not be type A, but I am a bit OCD when it comes to things like switching off the lights, locking the house. I think it's because I grew up so modestly and my parents trained me to do those things to save on the light bill, to make sure no one broke in.

But I can't be sure. I'd been in the shed, measuring the batiks for the show. Even though the show isn't for another three-plus months—at the end of October—Cissy wants those measurements soon so she can plot out how much wall space to give me. After jotting down the figures in pencil on an index card, I went inside to take a sip of iced tea before leaving. The Valium increases my thirst and I feel like I can't drink enough after I've taken one.

I set my empty tea glass in the kitchen sink, flipped off the kitchen lights, and left through the front door, locking it. Because the kitchen is right next to the breakfast room, where the sliding glass door is, I would've noticed it ajar, don't you think?

I don't know who could've been in the house, who could've gotten through the front door, which was still locked when I got home. The latch on the back door locks only from the inside, impossible to pick from the outside. But maybe I left it unlatched? I also checked all the windows and they were locked.

It must've been me, being spaced-out, leaving in too much of a hurry without double-checking. It must have been, right? Except I really don't think so.

33

KIRA

The pages rest next to me on the love seat. I take a moment to process all that I've just read.

The back door being open; someone messing with Mom.

Mom needing more pills to calm her nerves.

And, of course, her almost kissing Mike.

I remember being at a neighborhood party and meeting Genevieve for the first time. It was already as if she and her mom were celebrities; upon their arrival, the party became less about a neighborhood toddler's third birthday and more about the Walters's entrance to Longview.

Rachel and Courtney were instantly magnetized by Genevieve, taken in by her wardrobe, plucked, no doubt, straight from the Galleria in Dallas—a Guess shirt with matching shorts and the very latest Swatch. On her other wrist, a silver James Avery charm bracelet loaded down like a Christmas tree.

I remember Bertie coming over to our circle and that loud cloud of perfume that accompanied her. How overbearing she seemed, how brash.

I don't recall meeting Mike that day, but I did eventually, at other parties. I never knew something was going on between him and my mom. I'm hoping to find out more.

Right now, I feel mostly sad that Mom had feelings for this person, and then that was cut short, too.

A finger of sunlight finally slices through the cloud cover, seeping across the wooden floor. The shadow of leaves dances in the honey-colored strip; I could sit here for the rest of the day, reading Sadie's words, but it's 3:45.

The cocktail party is from three to five and I'm already late and need to go. I take the already devoured pages and carefully tuck them under the box this time, closing the lid on the rest. I want to read more, but I also really want to talk to Katie. At the very least, I need to tell her about Hilda and about Gran's decline.

Hair still unwashed, I straighten my bun in the mirror, swipe some lipstick across my lips. This will have to do for now. There's a two-hour break after drinks—to give Genevieve time to get dolled up to perfection, no doubt—and I can shower then. And read more.

The happy hour is in the rear of the house, in another patch of gardens. I take the back way, snaking along the path that Bertie was on earlier. What little sunlight had crept out before has now retreated again behind the tight armor of clouds. At least the wind has died down for the moment; the only sound I hear as I walk is the crunch of crushed granite underneath my boots.

I round the house and see that the gathering is in full swing. Right off the back of the main house is a patio paved with white limestone. A plush flower garden rims the patio and a trio of space heaters—the kind used at fancy restaurants—glows orange against the bitter gray sky.

Bethany is parked behind a table lined with wine bottles, and an attractive brunette in a white shirt with black slacks pours refills. Everyone is clumped underneath the warmers, their chatter peppering the air, and as I approach, Genevieve clocks me.

"Kira! Well, you missed the official tasting," she says, too loud for my liking, "but have a glass!"

She's miffed, I can tell, and she eyes my still-unwashed locks. Heads turn my way, but no one else greets me. They keep their noses in their drinks like I'm an unwelcome presence.

Did Melanie see me with her husband and then tell everyone? Or did someone else? Genevieve? Bertie?

I get the sense that I'm in trouble somehow. Or are they just mad that I'm late again?

I press a tight smile on my face and make my way to the wine table.

"Well!" Bethany trills. But even charming Bethany sounds sarcastic to my ears. I'm probably just being paranoid. "What can Sheila pour for you?"

"We have a nice buttery white," Sheila says warmly, "some reds—oh, and this marvelous rosé."

"Rosé sounds nice!" I say, wanting to somehow capture her for the rest of the evening, make her hang out with me.

The sparkling wine is cotton-candy pink and tastes like spun sugar as it fizzes on my tongue. It's delicious, the alcohol soothing as it goes down, warming my frigid body.

My eyes land on Katie. My view is partially obstructed by Gina, who is holding forth with her. I can't stand to be alone one second longer and I am bursting to talk to her.

When I approach her and Gina, though, Gina keeps rambling, not giving the usual courtesy of pausing to acknowledge me. And to my horror, Katie gives me a blank stare, holds up an index finger as if to say, *Wait your turn. You're not as important as whatever Gina is blabbing on about.*

Hurt pierces me. We haven't seen each other in years, and Gina freaking lives here. They see each other all the time. And goddammit, I have things to tell her.

But my pride won't let me just stand here, withering under their rudeness.

I turn away, head back toward the wine table. Before I reach it, though, Rachel, to my surprise, steps away from the group and greets me.

"How's it going?" she asks. Her already dark eyes are lined in charcoal, giving them a brooding, almost goth edge. Twisting her wineglass between her thumb and forefinger, she seems fidgety.

"Fine," I reply. I've always walked on eggshells around her because she's always so incredibly bitchy.

A jagged sigh whistles out of her. "I'm just ready for tonight. For the real party. I've had *enough* of this parade today. It's just too much"—she motions with her hands like she's tossing a salad—"*togetherness*."

A snort escapes me. "Agreed."

"Well, you've been hiding all day. Smart girl."

"I honestly haven't—I've just been—"

She holds up a slender hand. "Look, I get it. I hang out with Courtney on the regular, but I honestly detest Genevieve and the rest of them now that we're adults. I mean, not your sister or anything, but the rest are just so . . . ugh."

I'm liking her more by the second.

And feel like I can risk asking her about Mike.

"Hey, speaking of Genevieve, do you think her dad's gonna be here tonight?"

A beat of silence.

"Umm, that's random," she says, her face twisting into a mask of bewilderment.

Shit. I've misread my audience.

"I know. I guess I'm just obsessed with other people's parents, since mine are gone?"

She lifts her glass to her lips, takes a long pull. Lets out a sigh. "Oh my god, of course. Sorry. Of course. I just haven't thought of him in *years*, so it seemed totally rando for you to wonder about him. And I don't know if he's coming."

I hope I covered my tracks, am about to reply, when I feel the dagger of Melanie's gaze on me. My face reddens; I hide in my wineglass, downing the rest of it. She must've seen me and Jack together, or heard that we were.

Whatever. I can't worry about that right now. I still want to get to Katie, and Gina is now chatting with Genevieve, so I unlatch myself from Rachel, swerve around the group to try and reach her.

As if she can sense my oncoming presence, though, she starts moving in the other direction, beelining for the back door, most likely to use the ladies' room.

I want to follow her, but Melanie beats me to it, trailing in Katie's wake.

It's not in my head: my sister is clearly avoiding me.

I pause at the wine bar, accept another glass from Sheila, and graze on hors d'oeuvres—figs wrapped in a thin sheet of prosciutto, miniature skewers of charred beef glazed with teriyaki—and wait out the minutes until this soiree is over.

On the way back, I take the longer route, passing in front of the main house and walking along the winding path through the gardens. In the distance, on the far side of the garden, I can see the men gathered around a wooden stand for their bourbon tasting.

Jack's back is turned to me, not that I'd wave to him right now and draw attention to us any more than we already have, but even just seeing his back, that red flannel jacket that I was snuggled up in earlier, makes me swoon.

The bonfire is adjacent, now completely built, looking like a wooden skyscraper. It stands behind the altar where Genevieve and Chad will perform their renewal. To the left of the altar, just beyond the edge of the gardens, the men who were building the bonfire earlier are erecting a white event tent. It's massive, and they are tying down the plastic doors to metal stakes, wheeling in more space heaters.

As I head back to my cabin, I draw a little closer to the bourbon tasting, trying to pass by unnoticed, but gasp when I see him, stepping apart from the group, lifting his chin at me in greeting. His gloved hands are wrapped around a chubby glass of bourbon and his blond hair is elegantly swept to one side.

Randall.

When my eyes meet his, he smiles.

My blood chills.

I quickly look away, walk even faster back to my cabin.

For some reason, I didn't think he would be invited to today's events; I thought, as Bethany explained, that it was just for the inner circle.

And now I'm wondering not only if he was in our house that day but also if he was in my cabin earlier, rifling around.

34

KIRA

Back in the cabin, I toss off my jacket, then rub my hands together to warm them. I'm shaking, I realize, and it's not just from the cold.

Randall.

And the way he stepped away from the crowd to get my attention.

I wonder again—not only if he's the one who crept into our house that day, spooking Sadie, but also if he's the one who broke in here, *and* if he's the one sending me those texts.

If so, why?

I can't make sense of it. Yes, I know he was devious back then, and according to both Jack and Genevieve, he's still devious, but was he actually capable of harming anyone? And why Sadie?

The wine is making me feel light-headed. I don't usually drink during the day; it makes me too hammered. I plop down on the sofa again, knead my temples.

I'm going to read more, now that there's some time before I have to shower, before I need to make myself presentable for the actual reason we're all gathered here.

35

SADIE

I want you to know my story. Not just the little bit I share with you in the shed—which I appreciate more than you'll ever know—but who I am. Who I really am. Not who I am in front of your dad, Gran, or even Katie. And not who I pretend to be in front of the neighborhood women, but who I was before and who I'm going to be again.

Life does this to you; it whittles your form down like a burnished river rock until your course is set and you can't change it anymore. But I can't have that for you. I can't have that for me, either.

I am Sadie. Born of Sarah and James. Sadie Christie was my name until I took your father's and became his property. Your grandparents were kindly people; they would've loved you and Katie. I'm sad they died before y'all were born, but I'm glad they're not here to see me married to an unkind man, to witness the direction I have taken.

Don't feel sorry for me. I will transform again and I will leave your father. I will have my art show, your father's reaction to it be damned. (I will get this book published, and I will get the hell out of this town as soon as I'm able. When I find a publisher, I'm hoping the money will be enough for me to start over where I've always wanted to live: New York. And maybe even with Mike by my side.)

You'll have your grandmother's money, so I'm not worried about you girls in that way, but I don't want you to squeeze yourself into a tiny box like I have.

I have been born and reborn many times and I will be reborn again.

I've found freedom, at first with the medicine—which I promise I'll take less of once the show is over—the medicine that helped me get over the deaths of your grandparents, and later I became reborn again when I had Katie, when I had you, when I became a mother. Vital and strong, with a clear purpose.

And I was as free as a young child.

Mother, as you know, was a librarian in the small town I grew up in. I took you to the library once—it's just a twenty-minute drive—but it was so painful for me to be back inside there that I never took you back.

From the time I was a small child, I spent hot summers there with Mom, on the floor next to her desk, flipping through books. The library is quaint and ancient, with white chalk walls and a beautiful round stained glass window that used to beam rainbow-colored light through the room.

I was obsessed with books on botany, scanning the glossy pages of plants with my index finger, begging Mom to read the words aloud to me, to teach me all about them. I guess that's why my batiks are all about nature: as an only child, my whole world was the outdoors, what Stevie Wonder calls "The Secret Life of Plants."

In our backyard, which was humble and fenced in with chain link, I'd sit in the grass and play with ladybugs and dirt worms, speaking to them as if they were my friends. I lived in a world of my own making, a world of rich imagination. The same kind of world I've tried to re-create for you. I hope that I have.

I've always made art, in one form or another, and when it was time to go to college, I had my sights set on going to an art school in New York. That's where all the action was. But my parents were of very modest means—your grandpa was the manager of a general store; I'm not sure you ever knew that since it's so hard to talk about them without getting choked up—and they simply could not afford to send me out of state.

So I enrolled at the local community college. Our plan was for me to stay a few years, get a great GPA, and then apply for scholarships. I absolutely loved college; I loved learning and soaked everything up like a sponge. And found my true love—batiking—in my first studio art class.

It was in the top floor of the art department—a large, drafty room lined with windows—and my teacher was Dr. Parsons, originally from New Orleans. He was worldly, had studied and taught Latin, painting, and also philosophy. And the studio was charmingly in disarray with defunct, unused art supplies that he'd gathered over the years and stored in the studio. An old kiln that was no longer operational, rickety easels in need of repair. Stacks of canvas and battered frames he'd scored at estate sales.

He was older, his long hair graying and fingers stained from nicotine, and often left the windows open, even in deep winter, so he could chain-smoke as he lectured.

The course was geared around two-dimensional painting, but Dr. Parsons was big on experimenting, on following your muse. And one day, in the corner of the studio, under a blanket of tarps, I found a discarded set of batiking tools.

I was immediately intrigued by the cantings, the long wooden instruments with the metal mouths. Ours at home are made of stainless steel, but the ones in the studio were from Indonesia and made from copper. I also loved the wooden stamping blocks and the idea of using wax as a relief against the dye, the skill of guiding the wax across the sheet—which is difficult—dyeing it, then removing the wax to reveal the design. You have to have mastery to batik, but so much of it is also free thought, which I especially love.

I asked Dr. Parsons if I could use the tools, research batiking, make it the focal point of my study. And, of course, he was game.

The vibrant colors, the ancient art, appealed to me and gave me voice, gave me a fresh new medium to work with. It distinguished me, I believe, and still does.

At first I limited my batiks to home decorations—bedspreads, curtains, pillowcases—but as Dr. Parsons pushed me, I began to incorporate themes into my art, pulling from my other favorite courses—philosophy and women's studies. Joseph Campbell's books on mythology and the feminine divine opened my eyes to a world beyond the Judeo-Christian mindset and I was able to study various goddesses and relate them to my work. Lampetia, Greek goddess, bringer of the light, was my favorite to work with early on. Then I studied them all.

And now I feel like I'm in my renaissance with batiks, incorporating the feminine divine as well as the natural world in my pieces, like *Scarab Beetle*, the one I'm most proud of, the creature that, in Ancient Egyptian times, represented metamorphosis, something I'm always in the process of doing. My art connects the personal with the broader. And I'm proud of that.

But back to college. In my sophomore year, in the spring, when the thicket of white jasmine bloomed along our chain link, coating the air with the headiest scent, my world was shattered. Mom and Dad were taken away from me. Killed in that car wreck, driving at night, coming back from the movie theater.

With me that morning at the breakfast table, gone forever that evening.

Kira, I became a shell of myself. My whole world plunged into blackness. I could barely force myself to eat, and if it hadn't been for our neighbor Mrs. Bridges bringing me pans of gooey casseroles every other day, I don't know if I would've made it.

Since I was an only child, Mom and Dad were my whole world. And then they vanished.

Our family doctor started me on the Valium then. I think he was scared I'd take my own life; I'm not entirely sure he was wrong. The medicine saved me from the depths of sorrow, dulling the sharpest knife points of grief, so that I could at least function.

Right before Mom and Dad died, my grades were sky-high, and I had a hefty recommendation from Dr. Parsons; I was just starting to apply for scholarships at colleges in New York when the accident happened. After they were taken from me, I just couldn't muster the will anymore. And also, there were the practical things that suddenly needed my attention, like paying the mortgage on our small bungalow. Mom and Dad had saved some—for retirement and a little for my college—so I was able to make the payments at first, but I knew if I took all that money and left for New York, I'd run out, and possibly never have another solid place to call home.

I finished out the spring semester. Dr. Parsons let me slide on a lot of coursework, as did my other professors. And then I just sort of hung around that summer, mainly in the school library. I couldn't face being alone at home for long stretches of time.

It was there that I met Sally. She was taking a women's studies course over the summer semester. Not toward a degree or anything, just as a dalliance. She was already married to Bruce, already living in their three-bedroom brick ranch that we've all spent so much time at, but she wasn't yet a mother and wanted something to do with her time.

We started having coffee at a little café after her class let out, and bonded. She was learning all about women's lib and would recommend books for me to check out from the library. Our conversations were stimulating, thought-provoking, and I would eventually go even further with my self-taught studies of feminism, my obsession with it growing in intensity with each book I read.

One day Sally invited me to a backyard barbeque at their place; that's the night I met your father.

He was soft-spoken and shy at first. And handsome, so handsome, with deep brown eyes and his strong jaw. I was instantly taken with him. He was also an only child and a bit socially awkward, just like me, and we spent the evening tucked into a corner of the yard, mostly away from all the others.

He told me that his mom loved books and that he used to be bookish, too. He knew about some famous painters, and that impressed me.

I honestly didn't know what else to do with my life at that moment, so I started doing what Sally and all her other friends were doing, going on double dates with your father and other couples, going to the movies, standing around people's backyards while the women—some already wives like Sally—would haul out Tupperware containers full of potato salad, sliced watermelon, and French onion dip, and the men would chomp on cigars while tending the grills.

There were some freewheeling times, nights when we'd all had too many margaritas or martinis and we'd jump in the pool with all our clothes on. But mainly everyone's lives were following the same trajectory; all the women were housewives or were turning into housewives. Marrying early, getting pregnant, starting their families.

And in my grief, I went along with it all; I chose to be around people instead of all alone.

At night, in the bungalow after Richard left, as I lay awake I would tell myself that I would get back to my art, that I would keep the dream of moving to New York alive. But Richard started pressuring me to get married, said his parents were pressuring *him*, told me it would be the best thing for both of us, that he could take care of me, that we could buy a new build in Sally's neighborhood, be around all our friends.

I held out as long as I could, but I vividly remember the day I decided to go along with it, do what everyone else was doing, and cave to Richard's insistence. I went to a bridal shower for a friend—Laura Jenkins. The room felt too hot and stuffy, the women too heavily perfumed, the cake icing burning the back of my throat. I was thinking, *This isn't the life I wanted.* I felt like I was going to suffocate. But Sally was at my elbow, saying in my ear, "You're next, I bet!" and something in me gave way that day. I went along with it.

I squeezed myself into chiffon dresses, into Sunday brunches, into decorating my new house: into being likeable by all those around me. Your father, your gran, the women in our neighborhood. By my own doing, I narrowed down my world to fit into this one.

I still longed to be bohemian, to live in Greenwich Village, to go to an artists' salon where we'd talk deep into the night about painting, about women's rights, about things that mattered. But that part of me had to lie dormant for a while.

I lost myself, Kira, for years, muted the voices in my head, silenced my muse, all in the name of acceptance.

If I can impart one thing to you it's this: Don't be like me, don't be a likeable woman.

36

KIRA

My vision is blurred with tears. I started crying about halfway through reading—when I got to the part where Grandma and Grandpa died—and haven't stopped since.

As before, I feel like Sadie is in the next room over, talking to me, her voice in my head, louder and more alive than ever. This is too much to process. My stomach spins; I stand and move to the mini-kitchen, set some water to boil for a cup of tea.

Mom was stunted, too. Just like me. In such a bigger way than I ever imagined. She never told me about her art class and Dr. Parsons, about her dream to live and make art in New York. I'm gutted for her all over again.

And furious with Dad for blunting her existence in this way. And for possibly doing much worse.

With so many pages still left to read, I'm certain I haven't gotten to the part that Gran was keeping secret from me all these years.

But one thing is still clear to me: Mom did not kill herself. This is not the voice of a woman who was ready to hang it up.

I will transform again.

The teakettle shrieks. I pour myself a full mug, dunk in a sachet of Earl Grey, and leave it to steep.

I've got one hour left before the vow renewal; I need to pull myself together and start getting ready.

I step into the bathroom and twist the faucet in the shower, turning it to scalding.

As the hot water thrums over me, more tears come. I let them all stream out as a cloud of steam drifts overhead, turning the room into a hothouse.

I turn off the water, rake back the shower curtain, and freeze.

A noise, like the zipping sound of the mechanical lock at the front door, makes my heart jump in my throat.

Still completely naked and drenched, I slowly step out of the shower, tug a towel down from the wall hook, and wrap it around myself. I don't want to make a sound, but also, I can't help myself; adrenaline is spiking through my veins.

"Katie?!" I yell out, hoping like hell that somehow it's her.

I'm met with silence. Then the sound of the door closing.

I don't know whether I should trust that the person is truly gone. I stand in place, dripping on the tile floor for a second, before inching open the bathroom door.

The sitting room is empty.

I make it to the door in two strides, yank it open, and peer around. Not a soul in sight. But I can't dash out in the cold to make sure dressed only in a towel.

I race to the windows, look out each one. Nothing.

I knew it wasn't all in my head. That's confirmed when my eye catches something white just inside the front door, off to the side.

A sealed envelope.

Hands fumbling together, I tear it open.

It's only two brief sentences, neatly typed, but it sets my blood on fire.

You're a whore.
Just like your mother.

I drop the letter like it's covered in anthrax, back away from it. I want to call Jack, tell him what just happened, but I know I can't. Especially not if Melanie was the one who saw us in the woods, and maybe the one who wrote this letter.

My mind somersaults as different faces appear like visions, taunting me.

Melanie. Randall. Bertie. Hilda.

Who the fuck is fucking with me?

My muscles begin to ache from quaking with fear; I can't believe someone had the audacity to break in here while I was showering. To leave this.

I'm terrified, but I'm also trembling with rage.

Mom was no whore and neither am I.

Whoever killed her thought she was. I will avenge her name.

37

SADIE

It's midnight; the night birds are trilling in the willow tree and my sundress is soaked with sweat from the heat and my desire.

It happened. Mike and I finally kissed last night at the neighborhood Fourth of July party.

I waited until the whole house was sound asleep before creeping out here tonight, moving barefoot across the dewy grass to write these lines.

I can't believe it, can't believe his lips grazed mine at last, and oh my, it was more delicious than I could have ever imagined.

I can't stop shivering from the memory of it. I'm now on my third cigarette, the cherry burning orange against the darkness. I've only lit a candle, so I'm typing by candlelight, as if wanting to keep this secret as sacred as possible.

I haven't even popped my evening pill yet. I wanted to get this down while it was fresh, savor every second of it before numbing myself out for the night.

It happened when everyone—including you, your father and Katie—had all gathered in the front of the house, where the grills were set up. Everyone was drinking, their voices growing louder, and grazing on hot dogs before the fireworks were set to explode in the darkening sky.

I decided before it was over that I'd wander off, down a trail through the woods at the side of the house. Nobody was paying me any mind. Your father was yakking it up with some of our friends—always angling for new business—so he didn't notice me slip away.

I sometimes like to do that, wander away from him at parties when he's not paying me any mind but expects me to remain in his periphery—the trophy wife lying in wait to refresh his drink, rush to laugh at one of his flat jokes. And when he *does* notice I've wandered off, he gets quite flustered, and that gives me a little thrill. Makes me feel like I have some power. *You don't own me.*

So, head swoony from a few margaritas on the rocks, I traipsed away from the crowd, sandaled feet padding along the ruddy forest floor. It had been a while since I'd had a proper walk in the woods, and with the nearly full moon making the trees almost shine, it was electrifying, inspiring, and I began to think of a new batik I'd like to create.

About twenty feet into the woods, the moon slid out from behind a finger of pines overhead; I paused to gaze at it, taking a mental photograph so I could later recapture it on a cloth sheet.

Even though the moon shone above, the trail itself was dark, so when I heard footsteps, glimpsed a figure headed toward me, it startled me, made my skin prick. I figured it was your father coming to chastise me, but as the figure drew closer, I saw that it was Mike.

Alone.

As my heart started fluttering in my chest, I twisted the hem of my dress—the white summer one patterned with red poppies.

"Sadie," he said.

"Mike," I said back, playfully.

"Sadie." His eyes twinkling in the moonlight, he brushed my hair away from my face with the back of his hand, leaned down, and kissed me.

My stomach twitches thinking about it. His mouth on mine,

his fingers running through my hair. The pop of fireworks beginning to go off above us.

It was quick, a fleeting moment, but it felt like both the first time I'd ever been kissed and also as if we'd kissed a thousand times before.

Before he turned to head back, he passed me a torn sheet of paper with his telephone number on it.

"You can call me, you know. Let it ring once. Hang up. Then I'll wait a while and hit call return."

And just when my chest pinched with worry, thinking that he was too smooth and probably a serial cheater, he rushed in and said, "I've never done this before."

I folded the paper, wrapping my fist around it, and watched as he walked back to the party.

38

KIRA

I'm dressed, my hair is flat ironed; I'm standing in front of the bathroom mirror, penciling my lids with dark brown eyeliner, forcing myself to use more than I normally do.

In the reflection, I give myself a once-over. In my deep red turtleneck sweater and black leggings with boots, I'm looking as good as I can, honestly as good as I've looked in years. I twist a pair of Sadie's emerald studs into my earlobes—one of the few pieces of her jewelry I kept—and swipe my lips with the shade that Katie gave me last night.

I'm thinking about Mom and the kiss she shared with Mike, wondering again if he's going to be here tonight. Rachel wasn't much help; I hope she keeps her trap shut about me asking about him.

Surely he would attend his only daughter's vow renewal. But he wasn't there last night, so maybe when he left Bertie and Longview, he *really* left. But I'm hoping he's here. There's so much I need to know.

I step into the sitting room. Outside the window, people stream by, heading to the garden for the big event.

It starts in ten minutes. I could leave now, mix with the others, but I'm going to sneak in one last chapter.

39

SADIE

It happened again. Someone was in the house while I was gone.

A few days after Mike and I kissed, I decided, in the afternoon, to take a bike ride to the museum. I know I must be driving Cissy crazy with my anticipation and excitement, but I wanted to drop in, just chat with her.

Every time I walk through the museum doors, my skin tingles with goose bumps. It's a beautiful space, all white walls and natural light splashing in through the floor-to-ceiling windows in a corner of a historical building downtown.

As Cissy and I chatted, I imagined my show, how the evening would unfold, with a mixture of excitement and trepidation. Sally has offered to make hors d'oeuvres trays, and Bruce has agreed to pour the wine.

I've already picked out my dress—a chic little black number, but I'm going to fasten feathers to it, and beads, make it my own.

I hope the whole neighborhood will be there, especially Mike. But what throbs at the base of my skull is thinking about your father and how he'll react to my pieces. They're so unlike anything he's seen me create and they are so outside the box, I know he'll be furious with me for potentially embarrassing him and for keeping it a secret. But my need to show my art to the world outweighs the fallout from however he's going to react.

I thanked Cissy again and pedaled along the cobblestone streets of downtown, the tires running over the pocked roads, sending a soothing bounce through my bones.

But once I got back home, my sunny day turned stormy the moment I entered the house.

I passed through the living room, headed into the dining room so I could go out the back patio door and on to the shed, but when I reached our breakfast table, my feet stuttered into place.

There, on the wooden table, lay my pack of Merit Menthol 100s.

As you know, I *never* leave those lying out—you're the only one who knows I smoke—so my breath caught in my throat at the sight of them.

I always leave them in the shed, underneath a tarp in the corner of the room.

My first thought was Richard. Had he snuck home from the office and rooted through the shed until he found them? Had he smelled smoke on me sometime and gone snooping?

With hairs standing up on the back of my neck, I headed to the sliding glass door.

Like last time, it was unlocked. But this time, it was completely closed.

Had I forgotten to lock it again? I had taken one of my pills with lunch, so possibly, but I don't think so. And I sure as hell didn't leave my cigarettes out in plain sight.

I stepped into the yard, glanced around. Nothing seemed amiss. I continued on to the shed. Opened the door. I gazed around the room; everything was in its place—well, as much as my art stuff is ever in place, because it's usually a disaster zone—but all was where it normally is.

I dreaded going back in the house. I wanted to hop on my bike and pedal off again, try to outrun my racing brain, but I needed to hide my smokes, so I went back inside to retrieve them.

And decided to call Mike. For the first time.

I let it ring the one time, then waited as he'd instructed, my back leaning against the kitchen wall next to the phone, my heart pounding in my throat.

I stared at the pack of cigarettes as if it were a hand grenade waiting to detonate.

A few minutes later, when the phone finally rang, it startled me so much I nearly dropped it while picking it up.

Mike sounded out of breath; he told me he'd been jogging around our neighborhood, that he does that every day. Where was Bertie? I asked.

Out shopping, as usual, he said.

We made a plan to meet the next afternoon in the woods that encircle our neighborhood, down by the creek, where no one usually is.

Bertie, he said, had a luncheon to go to, and I knew Richard would be at work. Mike told me he was glad I'd called, but got off the phone suddenly when his daughter walked in the room.

I went to the bathroom and quartered one of the Valiums; my body was a blender of feelings—anticipation, excitement, and also dread over the cigarettes.

The fact that my secret was laid out bare on the breakfast table felt like a taunt, a threat of sorts. And my mind circled back to Richard.

Either I'm losing it or maybe he's watching me more closely than I thought.

40

KIRA

It's a few minutes before the ceremony, and when I step outside my cabin, the sun is drooping behind the jagged tree line, staining the sky terra-cotta. The view is breathtaking; I'm sure this is exactly how Genevieve intended it to be: stunning and spectacular, with her marriage as the star of the show.

Genevieve. I think back to what I just read, to Mike rushing off the phone with Mom because his daughter stepped into the room. Did Genevieve hear the two of them talking?

Beneath the sunset, the guests are gathered in the garden, most of them already seated, facing the stage that Chad and Genevieve will soon stand on. Rope lights are strung over the chairs like tiny twinkling stars; a string quartet plays a crisp sonata beneath a stand of oaks.

Pale green ribbons are lashed to the backs of the chairs and the stage is festooned with lush, tropical flowers—magenta hibiscus, a starburst of orange and purple orchids, and waxy red birds-of-paradise.

Bethany stands at the side of the crowd, acting as an usher, and when she sees me, she flags me with her hands toward the third row from the stage. There's one open seat near the middle of the row, so I take it.

Seated right in front of me are Jack and Melanie.

Jack's wearing a dark suit that looks like a Tom Ford, and Melanie's in a little black dress with thigh-high leather boots. Jack's black hair is glistening with light product, his arm slung around the back of Melanie's chair, his head cocked toward hers. If I didn't know better, I would think they're a perfect couple, without a care in the world. Still, my stomach sinks a little at the sight of their intimacy, even if it is just for show.

All the women, it seems, are in dresses except for me. Once again, I feel out of step, like I don't belong, like I stick out. But I didn't want to wear one and freeze my ass off.

I scan the aisles for Katie and spot Ethan at the far end of my row, with Katie tucked under his armpit. He flashes me a smile when he sees me looking at him. Katie turns and smiles at me, too, but her jaw is set, her face tense.

The string quartet's music continues sawing through the air and I'm shivering, despite my warm clothes and the heaters glowing all around us. It's positively frigid out; I'm glad the rest of the evening will take place inside the giant white tent that's glowing from the inside like a hot-air balloon at night.

As if she can sense me behind her, Melanie glances over her shoulder. Her eyes, fringed in long fake lashes, give me a once-over, taking in my lack of dress, my boots and leggings and sweater, before trailing up to meet my gaze.

She fixes me with a smirk.

Is she smirking because Jack's got his arm around her, his head tilted toward hers?

Or because she broke into my cabin and left that note?

Either way, that grin smacks of some kind of victory, which makes my skin crawl.

When Melanie turns back around, I scan the crowd for Mike. I glimpse the top of Bertie's updo in the front row. She's sitting in the aisle seat, of course, but I can't make out who else is in that row. Surely if Mike's here, that's where he'll be.

A brisk wind ripples over the crowd, lifting everyone's hair, causing a communal shiver. The music from the quartet dies down, momentarily stops. A silent pause as the wind relaxes, then they go into a strident number and all heads turn toward the back.

Genevieve begins strolling up the aisle. She's stunning, decked out in a strapless forest-green satin dress. Her tits are nearly bursting from the top and her waistline is pinched, as if she's wearing a corset, which she probably is. The shit we women do in order to look perfect.

Her dark hair is pristine, with gentle curls, and a diamond choker hugs her neck. She looks radiant, but I wince at how cold and uncomfortable she must feel.

What I'm really consumed with is who is on her arm, walking alongside her.

Mike.

He looks much older now—of course he does; I haven't laid eyes on him in over twenty years. His once-deep brown hair and beard are now turning silver, but he has the same hooded, kind eyes that Sadie wrote about. He's still attractive in that understated yet distinguished way she described. I feel a pang of sorrow arrow through me as I watch him guide Genevieve up the aisle, the corners of his eyes crinkling into a smile.

That's who Mom was in love with, a love that never had a chance to fully blossom.

With the towering bonfire looming in the distance behind the shade, I feel Mom's presence here, now more than ever.

You're a whore.

Just like your mother.

Bile creeps up the back of my throat as I think about those

words, that threat. Whoever killed her must have found out about her and Mike. And now they're threatening me, too.

If it was Dad who murdered Mom, then who is threatening *me* now?

Clearly someone who doesn't want me to find that out.

Hilda?

And if it was someone else entirely—say, Bertie—they would have a very good reason to be threatening me now.

Another tidal wave of cold air blasts us, slicing through my thoughts.

Mike delivers Genevieve to the altar.

She hikes up the hem of her dress and climbs the steps in stilettos.

Chad mounts the stage from a set of stairs on the side and takes her by the hand. In his tux, with his hair slicked back, he could actually pass for handsome.

They stand there gazing into each other's eyes, holding hands, her face looking up at his as if he holds all the answers to the universe.

The music quiets down again and a tall man in a gray suit and cowboy boots joins them on the stage. Probably a justice of the peace.

I'm hearing the words he's saying, the glowing things he's spouting about marriage and about this couple in particular, but I'm only half listening. I couldn't care less; I can't stop my mind from spinning about Mom and wondering who in the crowd here tonight might be my anonymous texter, if it's not Hilda.

Genevieve speaks next, her voice coming out mousy and squeaky—that baby doll thing she puts on whenever males are around—and I catch some of her words. "We've made it through so much together: challenges, ups and downs, and here we are. Still together."

Next, Chad is saying similar things, his voice booming in the chilled fall air, promising to love her forever. Barf.

They kiss, a long, lingering smooch with her hands laced behind his neck, before he lifts her up, carries her off the stage while the crowd whoops.

The sun is now fully behind the trees; the sky has turned from bright orange to a pale pink and is just beginning to purple.

Bethany appears on the stage.

"Thank you, everyone, for being here!" she says with so much glee I feel like her face is going to crack from smiling so hard. She's probably just relieved that most of the weekend is behind her. "Let's head to the white tent for dinner, drinks, and dancing! After a few hours, we'll light the bonfire and gather 'round with drinks; we plan to go well into the night! Congrats, Gen and Chad!"

The guests all clap and rise together. My row shuffles toward the aisle, and I pick my way across the crushed pink-granite path, trying to catch up to Katie. But she's walking ahead of Ethan so briskly I can't catch her, no doubt beelining for the drinks table.

I feel a hand tug on mine. I twist around; it's Jack.

"Hey," he says, dropping my hand.

"I have so much to tell you."

He jerks his head toward the front of the stage and we head that way as the crowd churns past us down the aisle.

"Melanie darted off for a cocktail. Spill it."

I take in a deep breath, exhale, look around, make sure no one is close enough to listen in.

"This is going to sound crazy, but when I got back from meeting you at the pond, I realized someone had been in my cabin."

"What?" Jack's chocolate-brown eyes blaze with concern. He digs a hand in his suit pocket, which makes him look like even more of a model.

"Yep. The window was cracked—it had been shut; it's so cold

out there's no way I left it open—and the pages of Sadie's book had been rifled through."

"Kira—"

"And that's not all."

"Another text?"

"No, an actual note. Typed up and left just inside the front door while I was showering. I heard someone coming in and—"

"Kira, what the hell? We need to tell someone—"

"I did, I did. I told Genevieve's mom—well, not about the note, but about someone being in the cabin and opening the window—and you know what she told me?"

He lifts his eyebrows.

"Gran's housekeeper, Hilda, had *just* been out here. Under the guise of dropping off a scarf I forgot."

"So you think *she* broke into your cabin?"

"I don't *know* what to think, but maybe she's part of the reason Gran has kept Sadie's book a secret from me all this time. She doesn't want the truth to come out."

"I was serious when I told you that I don't want you alone this weekend anymore at all."

A prick of shame trickles over me.

"Jack, I'm single. I don't *have* a spouse to be with me every sec and I can't expect you to be so—" I shrug, smooth out my voice, which has a new edge to it. "Sorry. I just don't know what the hell to think."

He leans in an inch, closing the space between us as if he wants to wrap his arms around me. But there are people all around us.

"This is *not* okay. Like I said about someone on your gran's property, a text is one thing, but this is something altogether different. Don't you think we should tell someone else besides just Bertie?

His eyes are level with mine, holding my gaze, oozing warmth, and I feel a rush of gratitude toward him. But something in me says to wait. And watch. If I tell the whole party about this, whoever is behind it is liable to just stop, and then I might never actually find out who murdered Mom. I don't want to draw attention to myself right now. I need to just blend into the woodwork. Use myself as a lure to coax this person out.

"Thank you, Jack. I'll be careful, but I don't want to make a big deal of it just yet. Not unless something else crazy happens. And I still have more to read in the book, but—" My throat catches; I'm not sure I want to share this next part, but I can't stop myself. I have to tell somebody, and Jack's the only person I trust. "Mom, well, she was seeing someone. Someone other than Dad."

My face singes with embarrassment, but Jack just nods slowly, a signal for me to continue. I lean in, whisper the rest in his ear.

"Mike. Bertie's husband; Genevieve's dad."

"Whoa," he says, but with no trace of judgement.

"I know. Can't believe he's here tonight. I mean, I can, but, Jack, I have to talk to him."

His face darkens. "Just, I don't know, be careful when you do? You don't know what is what and who is who."

"I know. I need to finish the book, and I will tonight. I have to figure this out. I'm actually going back to the cabin now for a sec. Mom wrote that she felt like she was being watched, like someone had been in the house, and I thought about what you said about Randall."

Jack's eyes go wide. "She did?"

"Yes."

The sky is the color of a bruise, navy and dark purple, but the path to the cabins is dimly lit by pole lights. Still, I feel shaky and don't necessarily want to go back there alone.

"Want to walk down there with me for a sec?"

"I do, but . . ." He hitches his chin toward the tent.

I spin around and see Melanie standing at the entrance, freshly manicured hand wrapped tightly around a highball glass, her eyes fuming at the sight of us talking.

"Got it. Seriously, I'll be fine. See you in a minute." I turn to leave. Jack puts a hand on my arm.

"I'm sorry—"

"Don't be. Look, it's right there," I say, motioning to my cabin that's only fifty feet away. "If it makes you feel any better, you can watch me from the tent."

"Ha! Deal."

"I'll be back in a sec," I say, and start walking away, snaking through the few clumps of people still gathered in the aisle.

I reach the end of the rows of chairs when I hear my name.

"Kira!"

Randall steps out from behind a couple. He's dressed in a black suit, no tie, with the top button of his crisp white shirt undone. His hair is shaped with product and his green eyes flit over me. Like last night, it's clearly registering with me that he's hot, but there's something unnerving about him, a current running through him that still leaves me ill at ease. Plus all those rumors. And again I wonder, was he the one stalking Sadie and is he the one stalking me now?

"Hi," I say, with a little chill in my voice.

"You heading over?" He motions toward the white tent, which sways slightly in the breeze.

"Yes. Just meeting my sister first," I lie, unsure of what else to say but wanting to leave him with the impression that I'm not going back to my cabin all alone.

"Good, I've been wanting to talk to you."

He's close enough that I can smell his cologne on his skin. It's not unpleasant, a woodsy odor, and his eyes dance over mine. My belly clenches at the way he's looking at me. I feel at once repulsed and attracted to him; I don't know what to make of it all, so I stay quiet.

When I don't acknowledge what he just said, he adds, "Okay! I'll see ya there. Want me to grab you a glass of wine, or something even stronger, maybe?" He's flirting with me, or attempting to, but like last night, I'm conflicted, my mind swirling. He's attractive, and he's paying me attention, but there's definitely something a little off about him, a little too keyed up, and right now I need to race through the rest of Sadie's story.

"Um, sure. See you soon," I say, and march toward my cabin before I say any more.

41

SADIE

I know this sounds foolhardy, but I think I'm already falling for Mike. Like, in love.

We met today, as planned. I brought a picnic blanket and a basket filled with cheese wedges, grapes, and a bottle of wine, and we met in the clearing in the woods where the babbling brook forks south before joining up with the larger creek that runs through downtown.

No one in the neighborhood takes advantage of these woods; I'm the only freak out here who hikes them regularly. Everybody else's idea of the outdoors entails dousing their identical rectangular lawns of water-thirsty St. Augustine grass, which always feels like plastic underfoot to me.

You girls used to traipse through the woods with me when you were little, and I'm sure some of the neighborhood kids still like to play out there sometimes, but where we were going, you have to cross over a thick bramble of wild blackberry bushes; I knew we'd be safe there from prying eyes.

Well, I thought we would.

Mike was wearing a long-sleeved linen button-down shirt with a few buttons open. His tanned, toned chest peeked out and I quivered when I saw him sitting cross-legged on the rust-red bank, smiling at me, taking me in as I moved toward him.

On the thin blanket, we kissed for what felt like hours, then I laid my head in his lap as he stroked my tangled mane, frizzed from the humidity.

"You have the most beautiful hair, Sadie," he said, twisting a lock of it next to my ear.

"And you have the most beautiful hands."

And he does. I told him they were painter's hands, or a poet's hands, his fingers long but not too long, refined and graceful, yet manly at the same time.

He asked me all kinds of questions about my work, my process; I felt an opening in my chest that I've not experienced before. Never has a man treated me so much like an equal, like someone worthy of being listened to and even learned from.

I asked a few probing questions about his marriage, got a little insight. They met when they were young. Yes, he was in love with her at first, but that dimmed quickly, though not before they accidentally got pregnant. And he's too good of a man to walk out on someone. Well, he was in the early days, when their daughter was very young, but now he's yearning to get away, just like me.

"So, as I told you," he said, winding my hair around his fingers, his voice as smooth as a cello, "I don't normally do this sort of thing. But I'm so taken with you."

The opening in my chest felt like someone was pouring hot oil into it, then my whole body oozed with warmth, until he opened his mouth again.

"Do you do this sort of thing? Have you done this before?" he asked.

I winced internally. I know my reputation in the neighborhood is that I'm loud and wild and free, but surely the men don't think I sleep around? Or do they? Despite my discomfort, I brushed it off.

"No, of course not. Never before today."

We spent another half hour talking, kissing, sipping the wine and nibbling on the snacks before it was time to say goodbye.

He took a different way out than I did, and when I burst from the woods, I felt like I was walking on air.

But as I headed closer to the house, my sandaled feet smacking against the hot pavement, I had the most unsettling sensation that I was being watched. Birds clattered in the trees behind me when I whipped my head around to scope the area, but other than that, I was the only one around, as far as I could make out.

I rounded the corner then and our driveway came into view; Katie was standing there, cramming a bag into the back seat of her red Toyota Corolla, a scowl stamped on her face when she caught sight of me.

My heartbeat threaded in my throat and sweat slicked my arms. Even though she couldn't have seen me with Mike, I felt busted, like she knew about my rendezvous.

"I thought you were at Ethan's this afternoon?" I asked, my voice high and teetering. The picnic basket swung from my hand and the blanket was tucked under my armpit.

She gave them a once-over.

"I was just having a picnic in the forest!"

She rolled her eyes. "Of course you were," she said under her breath, through clenched teeth. "I totally believe you."

"Well, where are you headed now?" My question came out as an apology, like all my exchanges with your sister seem to be.

I'm forever sorry for being a giant embarrassment to her, for just existing at all. The other night I caught her out in the shed, using my typewriter again without asking. Typing up dialogue cards for theater practice, she said. She's in a troupe that practices over the summer. I don't mind that she uses it. The problem is that the drawer to my desk was flung open, my things rifled through. I don't want her coming and going in my shed whenever she pleases and snooping; it's an invasion of privacy. If I barged into her room without asking, she would skewer me. That's why I'm careful to keep this book hidden.

"Mom, I'm staying at Gina's tonight. Jesus. I *was* at Ethan's; we had a fight, and I'm grabbing some stuff." She slammed the backseat door. "Not that you give a shit." Her long, permed brown hair whipped around her face as she rounded the back of the car to reach the driver's side.

I sucked in a quick breath, exhaled. I wasn't busted, but I was grateful when she started the engine and backed out of the driveway, leaving me alone at the house for an hour to collect myself.

42

KIRA

My blood is simmering in my veins. I had forgotten just how horrid Katie could be. Ugh. I can so see her slicing Mom up with those words, belittling her.

She can't continue to avoid me; I'm going to find her right this second.

I step outside the cabin and it's now pitch-dark, the pole lights doing little to illuminate the path to the festivities. Bass music thumps from the white tent, so loud it makes my breastbone vibrate, making it hard to hear sounds immediately around me, making me walk even faster.

I scan the edge of the tent, but Jack's not there keeping an eye out for me after all. Not that I thought he actually would be, but still, a tiny pang of hurt flares within. I take a deep breath; re-center myself. I'm being a child and need to pull it together. Focus on why I'm really back in this emotional swamp.

To learn what happened to Sadie. And now, to find out who's trying to stop me.

I enter the tent and, after the chill of the open air, it feels like stepping inside a toaster oven. I spy Jack at a far corner, in a half-moon circle of guys, chomping on a chubby cigar; they all are. Again, I feel a prick of hurt—as if he shouldn't be enjoying himself, but instead as committed to my mission as I am. I remind myself I'm not thinking clearly. The guy has a special-needs kid, not to mention that *wife*, and deserves to have a moment of carefree fun. When he catches my eye, he flashes me a bemused, get-me-out-of-here expression that makes me feel instantly and altogether better.

I can do this.

Clumps of cocktail tables are scattered throughout the tent. On the tabletops, sprigs of rosemary are twined together with red ribbon, and candles flicker from glass votives, casting warm light across the space. Silver heaters glow every few feet, the dance floor already a tangle, bodies jerking and swaying, and bloodstreams no doubt already coursing with too much alcohol.

That's where I spot Katie. She's dancing with Gina and Melanie and Genevieve. Her hands are in the air, her head is upturned, her eyes shut, and her shiny dark hair shimmies down her back. In this moment she reminds me of Sadie and the way she used to dance, free and oblivious to all those around her. And I can tell from my sister's fluid movements that she's on the other side of tipsy.

I approach an empty cocktail table, thrum my fingers on the white tablecloth, and wait for the song to finish.

The music is so loud, but in my ear, I feel a hot breath, as if someone is panting. From the woodsy smell, I can tell it's Randall.

"Here you are!" he says, parking himself right in front of me, digging an elbow into the table. He, too, looks as if he's one step from soused; in his hand, a tumbler of amber-colored booze. His glittery green eyes dance over me again, in that same jagged way as last night.

"I got you a drink like I said, but damn, girl, you took so long, I drank it." He swirls his cocktail around, takes a pull. "Whatever, just glad you're here now. Like I said, I've been wanting to talk to you."

"Oh yeah?" I'm not sure I'm ready to hear anything he has to say. Especially if it *was* him prowling in our home, and if he's the one who's been sending me those texts.

"Oh yeah." His eager grin flattens and he casts his gaze around the room, pausing on the cluster of men smoking cigars before turning back to me. His boyish face has grown serious, grave. "There's some things I'm not proud of, if you know what I mean. Ways I acted when I was a kid. Like a bully. But I was just a kid!" A laugh barks out of him and his jittery energy sets me on edge.

I want to get away from him. A sharp sense of trepidation lurks over me from just standing near him.

The music dies down and I see Katie cease her dancing, a puppet whose strings have been slackened by its master. Whatever Randall has to say can wait until others are around us; I feel vulnerable and leery of him.

"Sorry, can you give me a sec?"

He narrows his eyes at me, tosses his hands in the air, opens his mouth, but I don't wait to hear whatever it is he needs to say.

ABBA's "Dancing Queen" blasts through the speakers next and a disco ball hanging from the tent spins splintered light over the space. Katie is heading toward the bar, alone, and I walk as fast as I can to catch her.

"Another vodka tonic, please," she says, smiling at the bartender, a pert twentysomething with a bleached-blond ponytail.

"Hey!" I say, as brightly as I can.

Katie's perfect-featured face twitches when she sees that it's me.

"Hey," she says, coolly.

"We. Need. To. Talk," I tell her, pausing after each word, so she knows I mean business.

"Not right now we don't," she says, accepting the cocktail the bartender slides her way. Her voice is sludgy, her eyes cloudy. Great. I'm definitely getting drunk Katie, which can be ugly. "Don't you ever just want to party? To cut loose?" she asks, slinging her drink in front of her, gesturing toward the pulsing dance floor.

I shrink a little inside. She's always accused me of being too serious, too sensitive, especially after Mom died, and she knows this will shut me down.

But I won't let it. I throw back my shoulders, pitch my voice louder.

"You've been avoiding me all weekend. Why? We *have* to talk, Katie."

She rolls her eyes, crosses her arms in front of her. "If this is about Mom, and I know it is, the answer is *no*."

Heat creeps over my skin. She's discounting me like she did all those years ago. "It *is* about Mom—"

"Well, I don't want to hear it." She snorts, a stupid grin playing on her face.

"Let me finish. And about Gran."

"What about Gran?" Irritation skims her face, and her eyebrows knit together. She's impatient with me, I can tell. She just wants to join her friends again on the dance floor.

"She is *dying*," I say, as melodramatically as I can. "And I'm worried about her. And worried about Hilda and what role she might have in all of it."

Another snort. "Are you serious? Hilda? Kira, darling, I think you've been in La-La Land for too long. Are you sure you're an office manager and not in the writer's room for *Days of Our Lives*?"

Her daggers have always stung, and this one does a little, but she's going to have to listen to me.

"She has a heart condition and doesn't know how much time she has left."

"Again, you're being super dramatic. And I know about Gran's heart. Ethan's best friends with her cardiologist, hello? She's got a while, Kira."

This is a gut punch. Is Katie really this cold? Doesn't she care about Gran? Or did Gran play me, and her condition isn't as dire as she would have me believe?

"And what's this about Hilda?"

I was all ready to tell her my theory about Hilda possibly being the one who busted into my cabin, messed with Mom's book, but I suddenly feel protective over Mom and don't want to tell her that just yet.

"Nothing." I bat the air in front of me. "But, Katie, Mom—"

"I *don't* want to talk about her!" she practically shouts.

From the nearby corner where the cigar-smoking men are gathered, Ethan raises his eyebrows at me. I shrug back.

"Well I *do*!" I shout back. "I need to finally figure out what happened to her; it's holding me back—"

Katie narrows her eyes at me, inches her face closer to mine, as if she's challenging me. "Jesus fucking Christ, Kira! We all know what *happened* to Mom! She offed herself! And we're better off without her!"

If I were a slapper I'd smack her clear across her smug face right now.

"And yeah, you need to move on! She killed herself; you vanished, Kira; and you seriously only think of yourself! You took off and left me and I had to deal with everything from Dad to Gran and all the bullshit here. You have *no* idea what that felt like. You think you're the only one with problems?"

I stand there stock-still and tongue-tied, unable to defend myself against her lashing.

"Ethan and I are two months behind on our mortgage! His business is in the toilet and my kids are a hot mess express, and you roll into town and want to dredge up Mom again and how it's still messing with you? You're pathetic!"

The sunny bartender catches my eye, looks down in obvious embarrassment. Or pity, maybe. She begins sweeping crumbs off the tablecloth, busying herself, but pauses to ask, "Get you anything?" as if she is trying to save me.

"Glass of red, please."

Katie's eyes are searing into me, a mix of hurt and anger. And a familiar look of guilt, one that goes back to our teenage years, because she knows she's just stabbed me and feels bad and is stunned by her own nastiness. But she doesn't relent.

When she leans in even farther, I can smell the tang of lime and booze on her breath. "Mom *ruined* our lives. Don't you get that? She was an embarrassment when she was alive; she was an embarrassment in front of Dad. You just, you don't know that half of it! Of what she did!"

My peripheral vision swims and it feels as if the fabric walls of the tent are contracting around us. What exactly did Katie know about Mom? And did she read her book while she was creeping around in the shed? Was she onto Mom and Mike? Katie was always a daddy's girl; my skin grows clammy with a thought that comes unbidden. Oh my god, was it *her*? Would she be capable? And is she the one fucking with me now?

"You hated her," I say flatly. "She knew it, I knew it."

A sharp sting across my cheek. She's slapped me. It happened so fast that no one other than the once-cheery bartender saw it. She's now walking away from her post, from us, under the guise of emptying the wastebasket.

"Fuck you, Kira. Mom wasn't all there," she spits, pointing her fingers to her temple like she's aiming a gun. "She was a lot more off than you realized. You just always worshipped her and were blind to how she ruined Dad, was breaking our family apart. She killed herself, full stop. Now leave. Me. Alone."

She twists on her sharp high heels and tromps away, toward Ethan and the semicircle of men standing under a cloudy swirl from their cigars.

Fresh tears burn my eyes and my head is whirling. I don't want to cry in front of everyone, and I need to process what just happened, so I clasp my glass of wine and snake out of the far corner of the tent, in the opposite direction from Randall, and race back to the cabin.

43

KIRA

Cold wind stings my skin as soon as I step out from the roasting tent. I'm speed-walking, desperate to be alone, as the tears are now gushing.

The wind shrieks through the trees; it's really howling now, but I can still hear the footsteps crunching behind me. I'm about halfway to my cabin, and though my heart slams against my breastbone, I don't want to turn around to see who it might be.

"Kira!" A voice like warm honey carries in the breeze.

I turn, bat the tears from my face.

Jack closes the gap between us, anchors me in a strong hug.

"I saw what happened, Katie slapping you."

My head nods really fast of its own accord, a defense mechanism to keep more tears from springing up.

"Yeah, we pretty much had it out. One of those torch-the-earth fights. God, she can be such a bitch. And," I add, my voice trembling, "she despised Mom. I just don't know what to think; like, I'm questioning *everything*."

"Whoa, are you suggesting that she had something to do with Sadie's death?"

The wind sweeps along the path again, biting cold. Every brittle leaf still hanging on for dear life clatters in the trees and it almost sounds like a rushing river.

"I know it seems crazy, and I probably *am* being crazy, but there's some stuff in the book that's unsettling. And there's some things about my sister you don't know. It's a long story, but ever since Katie hit puberty, she had it out for Mom. She's always been daddy's little girl, ashamed of Mom, and she just told me there are things that I don't know happened."

Jack looks down at the crushed pink-granite path between us. "Jesus, Kira."

"I know! I know it's nuts, I know I sound nuts, but I honestly don't know what the hell to think. And there are about half a dozen chapters left to read, so I'm going in there now. I need a breather."

"I'll walk you."

"It's okay, really—"

"C'mon, it's, like, right there."

We walk in silence the rest of the way, cold air nipping at our bare faces, our arms tucked around our torsos.

We reach the front steps of the cabin. "Wanna come in?"

Jack looks from the tent to me. "I do, but—"

I hold my hands up. "No, I totally get it. I don't want to piss off any more people tonight," I say with a rough laugh, and I mean it.

I punch in my code, unlatch the door. "But hang on, that letter. Lemme grab it."

Jack steps up onto the porch.

I retrieve it from the coffee table, bring it out to him.

His eyes go wide with alarm when he reads it.

You're a whore.
Just like your mother.

He shakes his head, takes out his cell, aims the camera lens at it. The flash goes off, popping silver light over the porch as he takes a few different shots.

"What are you doing?"

"Like I said, texts are one thing, but this is another. I want to have a backup of it just in case we need it later. Not trying to alarm you even more than you already are, but . . . Also, set it aside, there might be fingerprints or something?" He chuckles. "I sound so stupid about all this, like a gumshoe detective or something, but . . ." He shrugs, looks at me with a boyish smile that turns my insides to drawn butter.

I lean in to hug him. "Thank you. Seriously."

His lips graze my neck just before we hug and I can't tell if that were purposeful or not but I kiss his cheek. Fuck it. He stands there, holding me close, so close I can feel his hip bones against mine, feel him stiffen. I never want to let go. He unlatches an arm, strokes the side of my face.

"I can't believe what all you're going through. But we *will* figure this out, dammit. Listen, don't stay in here too long; come back to the party. I gotta head that way."

The hug is now fully released and it's as if steam is coming off my body, but the cold is already wrapping itself around me; I feel like I've just stepped out of a jacuzzi into the cold air.

"Of course. You know I'll be talking to Mike next."

Jack sighs. "I know. But like I said before, be careful. Please."

He gives me a quick peck on the cheek before dashing off. Which tells me he didn't mind me kissing him, and that maybe his lips on my neck weren't an accident.

My face flushes and I step back into the warm cabin, closing and locking the door behind me this time.

44

SADIE

Mike and I made love. I'm blushing typing this, but like I said earlier, you won't be reading this until you're much older, and I hope I've raised you not to feel shame about lovemaking.

And also, I have to type this out. My whole body is buzzing with excitement; I can barely breathe, can hardly contain it, and I cannot utter a word of this to anybody else. Not Sally, nor any of the other ladies. No one.

I'm smoking my third cigarette of the evening. Or early morning, I should say. It's two a.m. The sky outside is navy, but the clouds look electric, supercharged by the full moon glowing overhead.

It's late July and I haven't written a chapter for a while, mainly because there hasn't been much to write about. But oh my, tonight there is.

I'm taking full, stinging drags, not fretting if your father will catch a whiff of smoke or not. He's passed out drunk—as is his norm these days, even on weeknights—so he's not a threat. At least not right now.

For this moment, I want to live in the glowing cocoon of the memory Mike and I made tonight.

After last time, when I felt like I was being watched while walking home from our picnic, and after coming upon Katie in the drive, I wanted to meet after dark, away from whoever might be spying on me. If anyone really is.

So I called him today. Made the plan.

He brought a wool blanket and spread it out by the creek. We talked for nearly an hour, his voice lulling, the sound of the gurgling water soothing. Tangled clumps of wild honeysuckle stamped the air around us and the whole scene felt storybook magical. He then traced his fingers all over me, and in the bath of that moonlight, I straddled him, hiking up my dress, bucking against his hips.

We weren't quiet then. Our bodies became one—arching, writhing, heaving against each other—until I heard my name being shouted from his lips. I covered his mouth with mine and we rolled over, collapsing on the thick, scratchy blanket.

"I love you," I said to him, and he trampled right on top of my words with his own: "I love you, too."

Saying it out loud felt as natural as swimming in a warm ocean, with gentle rocking waves bobbing you upward, holding you above the water.

Because neither one of us wants to desert our children, we've agreed to carry on in secret but are making plans to be together as soon as possible, most likely waiting until y'all are out of school, on your own. If I can hold out that long. I'm not at all sure I can.

This is how it's supposed to feel, Kira, when you're with someone you love. Safe, natural, organic, and real. No games, no bullshit. No abuse, verbal or otherwise. When you find your person, your body knows. Your mind knows. And your heart *always* knows, even if you've been conditioned to ignore it.

So don't.

Don't settle.

Don't settle for money. For sex. For a man to lie next to at night and dangle off your arm. For anyone who doesn't fill you up like this.

You deserve the sacred, and I hope you find it in life a lot sooner than I have.

But know that I finally have and I'm not turning my back on myself and my desires any longer. No matter what the cost. Even if I have to hide my love and joy for the time being.

45

KIRA

My mouth is dry; my head is swimming.

It feels, again, like Mom is just in the next room, talking to me. Because that's how everything feels with Jack: safe, organic, natural, and real. It's like my heart knows and has since we were kids. But he's married and we've never even gotten past first base, so is it all one-sided?

A stubborn part of me doesn't think so, remembering how he felt against me just now out on the porch. It does feel so right with him.

But more importantly, what's racing through my head after reading the latest chapter is this:

Mom really fell hard for Mike. She was in love with him, and it seems as if he was just as smitten with her.

A few months later, she was murdered.

Someone, it seems, knew about that. Someone found out.

You're a whore.

Just like your mother.

I have to go and find him right now, have to talk to him.

First, I lift the remaining pages from the box, fan through them. The stack is thin. There aren't that many chapters left.

Just one more, then I'll go find Mike.

46

SADIE

Today was strange. A two-pill day, for sure, and yet the effects of my evening dose have still done nothing to calm my nerves, soothe the unease I feel.

Sally called me this morning. Said there'd been a burglary at their home last night when they were all asleep. Bruce was the one who noticed, as he walked from the bedroom to the kitchen to set the coffee on, that their television was missing; only the black cables were left, dangling against the wall like a dog's tongue.

She called the police to report it. But since we live in such a safe neighborhood, the Shermans, like most, leave their back and side doors unlocked.

Of course, I immediately thought of the recent times when I felt like there'd been somebody in our house, and wondered if it was the same person or robber, but I bit my tongue and didn't mention it to Sally. Mainly because I still don't know if all that was in my head, and I don't want to sound crazy.

But just before I sat down to my lunch of leftover king ranch chicken casserole, Sally called again. Apparently, the Walters's home had been burglarized in the middle of the night, too. Bertie called Sally all in a tizzy, telling her that Mike's Rolex—a wedding gift from Bertie's father—was missing and that a back window had been open when they woke up, the curtains fluttering in the breeze.

I almost told Sally everything just then, but instead I crept around from room to room taking inventory.

And that's when I noticed that my diamond studs were missing. My favorite thing I own besides my batiking tools. Because I wear them so often, I always leave them on the bathroom counter in a porcelain dish that was my mother's, but they're gone.

Counting the days back in my mind, I knew I'd worn them last at the Peters's happy hour, over a week ago. But probably not since.

By the time I woke up this morning, the sliding patio door was ajar; your father was out there with a mug of coffee in one hand, garden hose in the other, watering the tiny flower bed that Granny Foster insisted we put in this past spring.

"Your yard looks disastrous, Richard," she'd seethed at him one day when she dropped by.

She was talking to him, but it was me she was staring at. To shut her up, I went to the nursery and bought a row of pink geraniums and tucked them in the soil.

So I don't know if that's how the thief got in or not. If one of us left it unlatched last night.

When you pedaled up to the house on your bike late this afternoon, your cheeks blazing with the summer heat, I, of course, broke down and told you about the missing earrings, careful not to mention the other times. I didn't want to frighten you, but I knew you'd keep it hush-hush and I wanted to probe you to see if, by chance, you knew if your sister had taken them.

She's always been liberal about borrowing my things without asking—a cami top that she yanks from the hanger, returning it to me in a wad on the closet floor. My high heels, since we wear the same size. My lipstick.

But no. You shook your head, didn't think she had them. You didn't think she'd actually be that brazen and take something so precious to me. Ha! I'm not so sure about that, but my frame deflated when you said that, because you would probably know. Unlike me, she lets you come and go freely in her room, and you see her out sometimes on weekend nights, when she'd most likely be wearing them.

The sense of dread I'm feeling now is making me so ill that I might just pop another pill. Because if it wasn't Katie, it was someone else, probably the same person who's been in here before.

I don't want to tell the police. Richard would tan my hide—even though it's not my fault—because those earrings cost him a fortune, right after we got married. He'd blame me for leaving them out in plain sight. He'd yell. Or worse.

47

KIRA

Blasts of wind rattle the windows; I nearly jump at the sound of it. I eye the deadbolt, making sure it's still locked—it is—but even so, I can't shake the creeping feeling that whoever was lurking in our home all those years ago is here tonight.

Who was in our house, violating our sacred space? Obviously it wasn't just in Sadie's head, not with the missing earrings. She'd never just casually misplace those. *Had* Katie taken them, perhaps out of spite, and just kept them stashed away?

Or, like Jack said last night, was it Randall? Could he have been behind the string of burglaries, including our house? And if he was, then why the snooping the other times that Sadie mentioned before? It's all too creepy.

There's some things I'm not proud of . . . Ways I acted when I was a kid.

Was he about to spill it all to me moments ago? At least I have this critical piece of information, this insight from Sadie's book, so I can know what I'm walking into with him.

The path leading to the tent seems even darker now. The wind, howling and bitter, causes the inky outline of trees to buck and twist; the cold makes my teeth chatter.

I'm walking so fast that my thighs are searing, my lungs

burning. I'm nearly there, just a few steps away, when I hear my cell ding, feel it vibrate from inside my sequined crossbody evening bag.

Coming to a halt, I slide it out, swipe the notification.

It's another anonymous text. Two simple words, but reading them makes my teeth rattle even harder.

Watching you.

I look up, peer into the tent, scan the faces in the crowd. In the corner where the men are still gathered, I see Randall. His back is turned to me; his blond hair catches the light of the chandeliers. Is he on his cell, texting? I can't tell from here.

Jack, once again, is in the group of men, a tumbler of whiskey in his hand. He's listening to something Chad is saying—all the men are. I'm sure he doesn't notice me staring.

Another text lands on top of the last one.

You just don't get it, do you? Keep this up and you'll end up just like her.

What in the actual fuck. Whoever is sending this is literally watching me right now.

From across the way, I feel the sting of her eyes on me and swivel in that direction. Melanie, once again, is locked on me, busting me watching Jack. Her jaw is set and her eyes ablaze, with either anger or mirth—hard to tell with her—and after a second, she turns to the group of girls around her, a group that includes Katie, and tosses red wine down her throat.

Did she send the text? Does she know that Jack followed me to my cabin? Again, I wonder if she's been the one threatening me all along. I gaze at the group—all of them decked out in chic dresses and knee- and thigh-high boots, and now Katie glares at me. She sears me with a stare, then raises her highball of vodka tonic to me as if in an evil toast.

I think again about the missing earrings, about Katie's open disdain for Mom, and shudder with the newly formed suspicion that she's behind all this—the creepy texts, the mind games—and that she did something to make Sadie disappear.

When she spiraled after Mom's death all those years ago, I chalked it up to grief. To her feeling regret for treating Mom so ruthlessly. But now I'm seeing that troubled period in her life in a new and menacing light.

She was out that night, allegedly, 'til midnight. Dad found Mom at eleven. I was home by ten, my curfew, but went straight to bed, drowsy from the few Keystone Lights I'd swilled that night in the Taco Bell parking lot with my friends.

Could Katie have beaten Dad home? Was she there, in secret, lying in wait for Mom that night? Knowing Mom and Dad were heading to the Walters's farm for a bonfire, knowing things were becoming increasingly explosive between them?

I'm not saying she planned it, but what if she wanted to punish Mom somehow and it got out of hand? Or if she knew everything about Mike and actually planned it? Mom's official cause of death was labeled an overdose of her Valium; the bottle was uncapped and pills strewn along the floor.

I've always contended that someone could've crushed the pills, put them in a drink that Mom unwittingly drank, but everyone told me I was insane.

And I feel insane right now, harboring these dark thoughts about my sister that make my chest ache like someone is squeezing it too tightly. Kool & the Gang's "Celebrate" comes on; the group of girls rushes to hit the dance floor.

I use this chance to go over to the table that holds their drinks and their handbags. I peer around, make sure no one is watching me, then slip my hand inside Melanie's Louis Vuitton clutch. Sweat stings my armpits as I rifle through. I feel her phone. Or a burner cell, which is what I was hoping to find.

I slide it out, and it's her cell; I recognize the gold case from the car ride from Dallas. Just in case she has an app or something that can scramble her number, make it anonymous, I swipe the screen. There's no password prompt so, quickly scanning the room to make sure I'm still not being watched, I tap on her messages icon.

A flood of names appears. Jack. Sally, Jack's mom. Gina. I click on Gina and find a reply from her that says, "Crazy much?" sent earlier in the day, around the time of our brunch. Probably talking about me. Those bitches.

As I'm scrolling through the numbers, looking for mine, I feel a pair of eyes on me and almost drop the phone.

Katie has stopped dancing and is looking at me, eyes narrowed, as if she's trying to suss out what I'm doing. I stare her down, trying to put out the vibe that nothing is amiss, that *she's* crazy. Even though I'm holding Melanie's phone, standing next to Melanie's handbag. She shakes her head and continues dancing; I slip the phone back in the bag, not wanting to get busted.

My number would've been her most recent text, anyway, and it wasn't there.

That doesn't mean she's not using a burner phone, stashed someplace else. In a jacket, in her bra, in the top of her boot like a gun in a Western.

There's a lull in the music and then lush violin music pours out of the speakers, the opening notes of Etta James's "At Last."

Chad turns from his audience of guys and strides across the dance floor, reaching his hand out for Genevieve.

The lights dim all around the tent and a spotlight shines on Chad and Genevieve as he spins and twirls her around the dance floor. She looks resplendent, and as he dips her, it's by some miracle of gravity and boob tape that her breasts don't crest over the top of her green satin dress.

But my eyes don't stay on her chest; they rove over the semicircle that has formed around the glowing couple, the crowd's faces barely lit in the shadows.

And then I spot him. In a tuxedo, beaming with pride at his daughter.

Mike.

Right next to him is a petite blonde who, like me, has a more natural look. Her pale hair straight and simple, her little black dress elegant but not at all showy. Demure, youngish looking. The opposite of Bertie, who stands at the other end of the semicircle in a loud sequined pantsuit, her eyes misting with tears, a hand over her mouth.

I pick my way through the crowd until I'm just a few bodies away from Mike.

Studying him again, I can see why Sadie was drawn to him. His eyes shine with love for Genevieve, and he and his new wife seem out of place in this tent of bravado and garishness.

When the song ends, I go to him, the veins in my neck pulsing with adrenaline.

"Hi, Mike!" I say in an overly familiar tone that I hadn't planned on using.

He smiles but cocks his head as if trying to place me.

"I know you probably don't recognize me; it's been years. Twenty-four to be exact. I'm Kira."

His eyes scuttle as if he's trying to remember my name. It's such a rare one, and I'm certain Mom spoke of me to him, but his eyes are still searching, trying to remember.

"I'm Sadie's daughter."

At that, his whole face shifts and he jerks his head back like I'd just slapped him.

The weight of her name hangs between us.

His wife grins up at him nervously, stirs her cocktail glass with a stiff red straw. If she's aware of who Mom was, she's not showing it.

"Ah, Kira, of course," Mike says, recovering. He reaches out for my hand, cups it in his, which is warm and dry. "It *has* been forever."

His eyes flit to his wife. "Carole, this is Kira, one of Genevieve's oldest friends." He looks at me purposefully, as if to say, *Let's not discuss your mother in front of my new wife.*

"Hi!" I say, beaming at her like a loon.

"Nice to meet you," she says, smiling. "Please excuse me; I'm dying to use the ladies' room. Be right back!"

Relief floods over me, but also nervousness. I am completely unprepared for this conversation.

"Can we talk?" I say, motioning with my head to the far side of the tent, where fewer people are gathered.

He nods, holds out his arm for me to go ahead of him.

I'm hoping that with the couple's dance wrapping up, another slow song playing, and folks filing onto the floor with their partners, Genevieve won't notice me talking to her father.

Out of earshot, under the cozy glow of the heating lamp, my tongue feels like dead weight in my mouth; I'm not even sure how to start.

Mike seems equally tense, hands shoved in his pockets, his eyes trained toward the ground.

I clear my throat. "I know you were involved with my mother." I can hear my muffled heartbeat swimming in my ears.

He glances up at me, palms the side of his beard, shakes his head.

"Mike, Sadie was secretly writing a book when she died. And I'm finally reading it," I blurt out without thinking about it. "She wrote a lot about you, so you don't have to deny it."

A grimace grips his face, but then he gives a sharp nod.

"I'm not here to question you about that or to talk about it. But she obviously loved you and trusted you. She showed you her true self; it seems like you knew her better than anyone else, from what I've read."

His face softens, his hooded eyes glinting in the shadowy light. Another quick nod, as if he's afraid to speak.

"And what I want to know from you is this—do you think my mother was capable of taking her own life?"

Mike drops his gaze again, shifts his weight from foot to foot. He exhales a sigh, looks around as if he's making sure nobody can hear us.

"No, no way."

My throat constricts with emotion; I feel like my turtleneck is suddenly too tight, like it's choking me. After all this time, to have someone believe what I've always known in my gut to be true makes me instantly tear up.

"Really?" I ask, but the word comes out garbled, the knot in my throat expanding.

"Yes. It never sat well with me; I never bought that." He shakes his head as if he's just eaten something bitter. "She was happy, we were happy, and we were planning the rest of our lives together, but then . . ."

He doesn't finish; he doesn't have to. My eyes blur, the tears now raining down my cheeks. I flick them away with the back of my hand.

He blows out another sigh. "She was excited; she was making plans." His eyes rove over my face, taking me in. "And as sad as I was, I can't imagine what you've been through." He places a hand on my shoulder. His voice is measured, considerate, and again, I can see why Sadie fell for him.

I nod, yank a tissue from my bag, blot at my face, my nose.

"Can you tell me, did my father know? Did your wife know?"

He scans the room once more, dips his head slightly forward, and I turn to see. His wife is clear across the room by the bar, holding up her highball glass and shaking it, pointing to it as if to see if he wants a refill. He nods at her.

"We felt like they were most likely onto us." Mike scratches the back of his neck, winces. "And your mother, well, she was increasingly worried that someone was watching her. Told me about her things being gone through. So . . ." He shrugs, looks over my shoulder.

Carole is mere steps away, an eager smile on her sunny face.

"Thank you," I say to him and he pulls me into a hug, pats my back in a fatherly, pep talk kind of way.

"Ahh, much better!" Carole chirps behind me.

I blot my face with the tissue again, wad it in my hand to hide it. "Yay! So glad you got some relief! Great event, by the way. And good to see you again, Mr. Walters! You must be *so* proud of Genevieve."

"I sure am. Thanks, kiddo. Good to see you, too!"

Feeling like my body is on fire, I find the nearest exit to the tent, step out into the frosty night, and wrap my arms around myself as if I can hold in all the emotions that are swirling inside. But something nags at my back. When I twist around, I see Bertie, hands on her hips, glaring at me from across the dance floor.

48

KIRA

Bertie's look chills me. I pivot, but can still feel her eyes spearing me from across the way.

I think of the latest texts—*Watching you. You just don't get it, do you? Keep this up and you'll end up just like her*—and Bertie walking away from my cabin at a fast clip after someone was in there, rifling through Sadie's pages.

I think of her downplaying my fear around it all: *Don't worry about it, Kira. We're all friends here!* And dread quicksilvers over me.

I think about what Mike said, that he felt like Dad and Bertie were onto him and Sadie. Maybe *she* was Sadie's watcher? I doubt she's a thief, but it's interesting that only small things were taken, like Mike's Rolex watch. I'm sure she didn't break into the Shermans' house, though. My thoughts, again, are spiraling.

But if she knew about Mom and Mike, what does that mean? What could she have done, and what could she still be doing?

I'm dying to talk to Jack, to tell him everything Mike just shared and my latest theory about Bertie, but now another slow song, Foreigner's, "I Want to Know What Love Is" seeps out of the speakers and I watch as Melanie drags him by the hand to the dance floor to join all the other couples.

When she sees me staring, she clasps the back of Jack's head, puts her mouth against his ear. Then levels a wicked stare at me.

I spin around and stumble from the tent into the prickly, cold field. I feel rootless, alone, like I'm the only single person here.

The porch lights from the cabin wink in the distance, calling me. There's only one thing left to do: go back and finish Sadie's story.

I take a step, but freeze when I feel a hand on my arm.

A smile is smeared on Genevieve's face and she's out of breath, probably from dancing. "Hey! Where ya going? Aren't you having fun?"

I suck in a breath, prepare my lie. "Of course! It's great! I just wanted to go freshen up for a sec. Be right back!"

"Okay. Just wanted to check on you." Her voice is loose with alcohol and drips with condescension. "You sure you're okay?"

"Positive." I should just end it there, but I can't help it; the words shoot out of me. "Why wouldn't I be?" I ask, daring her to say what's really on her mind.

Behind her, the tent swells in the wind. Her eyes skim over my face, searching. "I saw you talking to my dad?" She says this as if it were a question.

Great.

"Umm . . . yeah. I bumped into him; we were just making small talk. Mainly he was gushing about how proud he is of you." My nerves are splintering as we speak.

"Seemed more than just small talk?" she says, her words again taking the shape of an insidious question. "I mean, did you even know him that well back then?"

What is she getting at? More importantly, what does she know? I have to be careful here, watch what I say.

"I guess I met him a few times at neighborhood stuff and when I was at your house. He didn't even recognize me at first. So yeah, again, it was small talk."

Her green dress is shiny with the lights from the tent dancing over it. She should be in there, whooping it up. Why is she out here interrogating me?

"Cut the shit, Kira. My mom told me years ago that your . . . *mother*"—she says the word with the same disdain that makes *mother* sound like code for *whore*—"was always after my dad."

Motherfucker.

Is that what she really thinks? And is that what Bertie told her? Or is she fishing for more?

I don't say a word; I want to wait her out.

"Don't act like you don't know what I'm talking about; don't act like it wasn't obvious."

I want to spit in her face. Instead, I say, "I wish I knew what you were talking about. Sorry, Genevieve. Can I go now?"

She heaves a huge sigh, which fogs over me. "Fine. I'm only saying this for your own good: Maybe leave the past alone? Like, if you were talking to my dad about your mother, maybe check that?"

She places her hand on my arm again, a sign of pity. "I just want you to have fun tonight. Loosen up. Enjoy yourself.

She jerks her head toward the tent. "Jack sure as hell is."

Before I can respond, she retracts her hand, swivels around, marches back inside the tent.

My breathing jittery, I take in a few stinging, chilly gulps of air to try and steady myself.

What just happened? Was she warning me?

This whole time I've been thinking about Bertie. Bertie watching me all weekend. Making comments. Bertie near my cabin.

Mike telling me that he thought Bertie knew about him and Mom.

Bertie *could* be the one texting me, threatening me, but it hits me like a fist to my stomach: Bertie couldn't have been the one to kill Mom because she was right here that night. On her own land.

My mind spins back to the night Mom died. I had been out with Rachel, Courtney, and Meredith.

Where was Genevieve that night?

I never considered it before now, because why would I? But she wasn't with us.

My brain racing, I start back to the cabin.

Genevieve is the most likely person who could've sent me that creepy footage from here. And I remember passing by her, too, earlier today when someone was in my cabin, going through Sadie's book.

I also think of what Mom wrote, about Mike getting off the phone with her quickly because his daughter had walked into the room.

But if Genevieve killed Mom, why on Earth would she invite me back here? To taunt me?

Looking at the stack of logs waiting to become a bonfire, I shudder at the thought that this could also be some ritual echoing Sadie's death. Is Genevieve playing some twisted game with me?

I keep walking, the cold pricking my face, but stop when I hear my name being called out.

"Kira! Is that you?" a rich male voice calls out.

I turn around and come face-to-face with Bruce Sherman, Jack's dad. He's in a crisp dark suit, same white hair and beard. Everything trimmed and fresh and glistening, as if he's just stepped from a steaming shower. He looks the same, only a bit heavier. My heart melts at the sight of him.

"Bruce!" I walk toward him 'til I reach him at the edge of the tent.

He smiles Jack's gleaming smile and wraps me in a hug, clapping me on the back, his scent of Irish Spring soap and pipe tobacco so comforting. He always liked his pipes.

"I was hoping I would see you tonight!" His caramel-colored eyes twinkle in the low lighting.

"I thought you'd be home with Aiden! I know he requires a lot of attention."

"Yes." A quick shake of the head, eyes downcast. "Jack certainly has his hands full. But he zonked out early and I wanted to come join in on the fun."

His voice is so soothing, his presence so calming, that I have to shake back the tears that are threatening to roll.

"So is this what has finally brought you back home?" He angles his head to one side, a note of concern in his voice.

"'Fraid so. I just—"

"You don't have to explain. I don't blame you for staying gone all this time. What you've been through, what you went through, is . . . a lot, Kira. But Sally and I have missed you! She would love to see you."

"I would love to see her, too, but we leave at dawn tomorrow."

"I know, Jack told me."

"You must be *so* very proud of him."

We both turn to find him in the crowd. I spy the top of his luscious hair on the dance floor; he's still slow-dancing with his wife. She must feel us both staring because she looks our way and narrows her eyes; now it's my turn to shoot her a smug look.

"Am I the only one who thinks you two belong together?" Bruce's voice comes out as warm as a crackling campfire, and he keeps staring straight ahead at Jack, as if he just let that slip out.

I can't believe he said that out loud. I look at him and when he faces me, he's grinning. "It's true. A father knows these kinds of things."

I'm tongue-tied, don't know how to respond, but I can feel the loneliness that gripped me only moments ago beginning to lessen its hold.

So I'm not the only one who thinks this.

Interesting.

"Don't be embarrassed. It's just that my boy deserves the best. And I always thought you guys would end up together."

Wow, he just tossed Melanie under the bus and backed up over her.

"Well, he's with Melanie," I say, startled by my own bravado.

"That he is." Another quick shake of his head.

Impulsively, I want to ask him the same question I posed to Mike—if he thinks Sadie was capable of killing herself—but something stops me. He was the one who doled out her pills. Not that I'm blaming him, but there may be some guilt or regret. I don't want this to get weird, don't want to ruin the moment.

"Bruce!" calls out an older man I don't recognize with a beer in his hand, and he starts to lumber over. I want more time with Jack's dad, but this man's eyes are swimming with excitement, like he's just spotted a celebrity.

Before he can reach us, before I get trapped into talking to someone who could hold us hostage all night, I reach up, give Bruce another hug. "I'll be back. Just going to freshen up."

"I'll be here until Sally calls me home!" His cheeks are rosy from the wind and I again feel that tug of emotion toward him, this benevolent father figure from my past. Fresh tears now—these impossible to stop—sting my eyes, and I wave to him and turn away before I fall to pieces.

I head back to the trail that leads to the cabin; I smell cigarette smoke and hear a throaty laugh.

Rachel.

She's standing about ten feet away, under a crepe myrtle tree, her skinny hand gripping the smooth bark while clutching a cell in her other hand.

"It's pretty over-the-top but at least it's open bar," she spouts to whoever she's talking to.

I walk right up to her, stare at her until she ends the call.

"Wanna smoke?" she offers, digging in her bag as if searching for the pack.

"Nah, I don't smoke. But thanks."

"Sure thing." She tugs a sharp drag off hers, exhaling and spraying me with smoke. "Some shindig, huh? Really glad I'm crashing out here."

"Yeah. Hey, I know this is another random question but, do you by chance remember the night when my mom died? Do you know where Genevieve was?"

She lifts her chin, blows out another puff, this time aiming the stream away from me, looks at me with puzzled eyes. "Umm. Why?"

Shit. I have no good reason to offer. "Do you think she was out here? At the party? I just think it's a little tone-deaf to throw a bash like this and invite me back. It's so much like Mom's last night, ya know? Maybe I'm just being overly sensitive."

She turns her head sideways, as if she's trying to get a good read on me. "Look, I can't imagine the shit you went through. Seriously. But are you really out here thinking about all that still?"

At least I've distracted her. "Yes."

"So, I can't remember. Fuck, that was so long ago. But Gen was probably out with Chad, ya know? 'Member how she used to bail on us so they could screw in the back of his Bronco?"

I nod. "Okay. Thanks so much. And could you not mention to anyone that I've asked? Everyone here thinks I'm batshit crazy as it is."

She cackles, sucks in another drag. "Yes, they do. But fuck 'em. And of course, you have my word."

I pull her into a quick hug, walk away as quickly as I can.

The cold is still bitter, but my body is coated in sweat as I practically sprint back to my cabin.

49

SADIE

I'm finally doing it. I'm leaving your father.

For the first time, I'm really afraid of him.

He must know about me and Mike; in fact, he's probably the one watching me, probably saw us in the woods that day, but his ego won't go there. He's likely scared of what I'll say, that I *am* in love with Mike, that I'm *not* in love with *him* anymore.

Sure, he's lost his temper on me, way too many times, and I've been frightened, but this is the first time I've truly been terrified for my life.

Last night we went to a dinner party at the Walters's. A back-yard barbecue.

Under the string of rope lights in the far corner of their yard, Mike and I stole a few minutes together, drinking margaritas. Laughing. And yes, my laugh can be loud and abrasive, but I was doing my best to keep things nonchalant. The alcohol wasn't helping, though.

It was just the briefest of encounters, but when Tammy Wynette's "Stand By Your Man" came on over the radio, I couldn't help it. I kicked off my sandals and started swaying to the music, my feet bare in the grass.

Mike's eyes never left me and from across the lawn. I saw your father staring at us—eyes singeing me—before he slammed his drink down on the card table, rattling the bowls of chips and salsa.

No one else noticed, thank god, because the music was loud, but I knew I'd be in for it when we got home. And I was right.

"Don't you make a mockery of me, Sadie," he seethed, red-faced, with a string of saliva spewing from his lips. I actually felt a pinch of pity for him just then, this man who knows his whole life is unraveling before him. Busted business, wife in love with someone else, but more than that, I was trembling, dodging him, trying to weave my way around him in our kitchen so I could lock myself in the bedroom, let him sleep it off on the sofa. Deal with him in the morning.

First, a slap across my face. Not the first slap ever, but it landed on my jawbone, red-hot pain searing up my face. And when I tried to step around him, he wrapped his hands around my throat.

At first I was too stunned to think. He'd never gone this far before. Then, when I tried to pry his fingers off my neck, he squeezed harder, until I kneed his nuts with as much as force as I could manage. He released his hands, then, and groaned, crouching down. I'm thinking all the booze he'd consumed gave me a leg up. I raced to the bedroom, locked the door, then shoved our love seat in front of it just to be safe.

He didn't try to enter, but I stayed up all night, anyway, just in case.

In the buttery morning light, I peered at my reflection in the bathroom mirror as a cigarette smoldered in the ashtray (I could hear your father snoring from the living room, so I decided to sneak a smoke) and saw myself for what I was: a battered woman.

Streaks of red lining my neck where his hands had been, my cheek purpled by his blow. Me allowing myself to repeat the same pattern of abuse that Granny Foster had no doubt endured from her Richard.

I sponged skin-colored concealer over my neck, selected a sheer scarf to wear, stubbed out my cigarette, and resolved to get away as soon as possible.

50

KIRA

Oh my god. It was Dad. It had to be.

I knew back then that his temper had gotten out of hand—I'd heard enough yelling through our wood-paneled walls to suss that out—and knew from reading Sadie's words earlier that it was bad, but nothing like this.

He had actually tried to choke her, to smother the life out of her.

Obviously he knew about her and Mike and couldn't handle it.

The cabin walls feel too close, like they're squeezing me in; I feel like I can't catch my breath. I tug at my turtleneck, wanting to shed the whole sweater, but instead I step out on the porch, let the icy fall air cool me.

In the distance, flames start to flicker from the bonfire. Soon the drunken crowd will spill from the tent and bask in its glow. It's so much like Sadie's final night I can't even believe it's about to happen.

I go back inside, lock the door behind me.

If only Mom had gotten away from Dad sooner. I wonder what made her stay for another few months. I know that leaving is easier said than done, but dammit, if she had just left, I would still have her.

I retrieve my cell from my bag and stab out a text to Gran:

We need to talk.

Call me.

51

SADIE

Even though it's nearly midnight, my dress is soaked with sweat. It's late August, and this is one of those nights when the heat doesn't break—an unrelenting fever that pursues us even into dream time.

I could go inside, join y'all in the house, where the air-conditioning is pumping, but I *have* to get this down. The inside of my brain is a mess; I still can't believe what happened today.

It's Tuesday and your father was at work today, as usual, and you girls were off with friends, enjoying the bottomless last days of summer.

I was home alone.

Ever since my earrings went missing, I've been extra careful to double-check the locks when leaving the house and today was no different. I went for a long, meandering bike ride, cycling to an older neighborhood in town where the trees are so thick that riding on the streets at noon can feel like it's dusk, and the older homes hold so much character—leftover relics from the early twentieth-century oil boom—that I almost feel like I'm in a different town altogether.

My mind was whirling with thoughts—about Mike, about your father, and biking always cuts through the sludge.

After your father tried to kill me—well, there is no delicate way to put it—I considered leaving the very next morning.

But when you came out of your room, hair matted with sleep, wearing your R.E.M. concert T-shirt and asking for a waffle, I froze.

I couldn't just up and abandon you and your sister and vanish. I need to plan. Let you know somehow. Make it work.

And, predictably, your father, when he came to in midmorning, eased up behind me in the kitchen, roped his arms around me.

"Don't you fucking touch me," I whispered, so that you girls wouldn't hear, then jerked him off me with my shoulders.

He skulked away.

Later that evening, after his first cocktail, he apologized. Said it would never happen again. Tears wobbled in his eyes.

I don't believe him, of course; it fucking will happen again. It's just a matter of when. I'm going to stay out of his line of sight until I get my ducks in a row. Get the gallery show behind me. Figure out if Mike will, indeed, run away with me, even though he's said, like me, that he'd rather wait until his daughter is out of the house.

I need to talk to him, tell him what happened with your father. Hash out a strategy.

And in the meantime, I've pulled your grandaddy's derringer out of the gun safe and put it into the top drawer of my nightstand. I won't kill him, of course, but I also won't hesitate to shoot him in the arm, blast through his leg, if he so much as lunges at me again.

I'm hoping it won't come to that. I'm hoping I'll be gone soon, far away from his rage.

I pushed myself hard today on the bike ride, taking a steep hill I'd normally skip. It's so precipitous—probably the highest point in Longview—and I usually avoid it, or at the very least hop off the bike and walk it up alongside me.

But today I needed to feel the burn in my legs, needed to dull the edges of anxiety—my lunchtime pill wasn't cutting it—so I pushed and pushed and panting, sweating, actually crested to the top. Up on the ridge, hot wind blasted me from all sides, and I felt victorious, strong.

I then sped down the hill, lifting my feet off the pedals, sticking my legs out like a little kid, and squealed until I reached the bottom and my tires slowed.

Exhilarated, I headed home. I was drenched when I reached the front drive, thirsty for a frosty glass of iced tea, so I laid the bike down on the lawn and unlocked the front door.

Instantly, I could feel that the house was off. A gust of wind ripped through it when I entered, which made no sense. I crept through the sunken living room, then through the door that leads to the dining room, and saw that the back patio door was wide open.

Headed to our fence, a male figure.

"Hey!" I shouted out, even though I was shaking. My body was spiking with adrenaline, which made my mouth taste of metal, leaving me even thirstier than before.

The figure stopped.

Then I got scared. I didn't recognize him from the back, but when he finally turned around, I saw that it was Randall, the little bully from down the way.

I say *little* because I've known him since he was a young boy and he's your age, but he's not little at all anymore. He's tall and rangy and wiry and could've taken me on if he had wanted.

I thought of the gun in the nightstand, but it was too far away.

"What do you think you're doing?" I screeched at him, furious that he'd invaded our home like that, had probably been the perp all along. And probably had hocked my diamond studs.

Our eyes met; his were sad. There was no other word for it. He held his palms up, as if I *were* holding him at gunpoint, and I could see his fingers trembling.

And in that moment, I jutted my chin toward the gate, motioned for him to get lost.

Kira, I let him go. And I haven't turned him in. That kid has had enough problems. His mom, Cassie, is the only single mother in the neighborhood and she works her fingers to the quick trying to keep a roof over their heads. One night when he was little, she came to the front door and asked if she could borrow a few eggs for a cake she was baking, said the supermarket was closed. But I instinctively knew that there was no cake, that she was more than likely just trying to put something in their stomachs until payday.

I've always wanted to adopt him—not really, but take him in, clean him up, give him some nicer clothes. So, as foolish as this may sound, I took pity on him and let him go.

And I must say, even though he looked caught and frightened, I was a little afraid of him, especially given his neighborhood reputation. It was like turning over your wallet and jewelry to a mugger without putting up a fight.

And then, poof, he was gone, vanished through the side gate, which clanged behind him.

I searched the whole house; nothing else was missing, which at first came as relief, but then the question hovered over my mind like a rain cloud all day—if he wasn't here today to steal something, why had he been in my house? Maybe my bursting through the front door interrupted the robbery; maybe that's why he was fleeing out the back.

But what explains those other times? My pack of smokes on the dining table, the sliding glass door pulled open? Is he—and not Richard—the one who's been watching me? If, indeed, someone *has* been watching me.

And if so, why?

52

KIRA

The pages lie limp across my lap. I'm unable to budge, even as my heartbeat jitters double time.

So Jack was right. It was Randall. He was the one in our house. And Mom let him go. Which I can totally see her doing; her kind heart was too naive for her own good.

But I'm with Mom in wondering if he was also the one watching her. Why the hell would he be doing that?

My cell sits silently next to me on the love seat. No word from Gran yet.

And if it *was* Randall lurking, snooping on Mom all that time, then it wasn't Dad or Bertie or Genevieve or even Katie. Or maybe the stalking was all in Mom's head. Only one thing seems certain—Randall stole the earrings and came back for more.

I honestly don't know what to think.

Was he about to confess all that to me? Or was he about to do something more twisted, more sinister, and that's why Jack, and even Genevieve, have been warning me off of him?

Suddenly I feel stupid for being in here all alone, cut off from everyone.

I clasp my cell, fingers flying over the screen as I pound out a text to Jack, even though I'm not sure he'll hear the notification with all that's going on.

You were right. Holy shit, Randall had been in our house.

Leaving the cabin now. See you at the bonfire?

I straighten the pages together, tuck them back inside the box. There's only one chapter left, but it's a long one. I could sit here and read it now—finish, and be done with Sadie's story—but that thought makes me feel extremely sad. I don't want her and this version of her, talking to me across time, to end. And also, even though I'm safely locked inside this cabin, I need to get going while everyone else is milling about outside, moving from the tent to the bonfire.

I stash my cell back in my bag, head outside.

The bonfire is really sparking now, neon-orange embers spewing from the top like lava. Even with the roaring fire, though, the path between here and there is dark, empty.

Another idea takes hold. Instead of walking that way, I'm going to circle back on the lesser-known path that runs behind the house and then forks over to the clearing where the bonfire is.

Randall knows which cabin is mine—he spotted me heading there during the men's cocktail hour—and I don't want him lingering, lying in wait for me on the way.

And also, I feel compelled to take Sadie's last walk. She burst into the woods, jetting away from the bonfire on that cloudless October night, taking this same route to get away from Dad.

I think of the latest texts, especially the one that warns: Watching you.

If Randall is indeed watching me, I decide to try and throw him off my trail. I start on the path toward the tent, then duck into the forest line. Night birds flutter in the treetops and my heart rate is even speedier than it was in the cabin, my breath quick and sharp.

I thread through the tangle of trees and brambles until I'm directly behind my cabin. Then, as quickly but as quietly as possible, I take the narrow walkway behind the row of cabins, a thin horse trail, really, my feet numbing from the cold.

The farther I get from the tent and bonfire, with their din of noise, the louder the crunch of granite sounds under my boots. Pops and clicks. Another blast of wind groans through the trees, lifting my air, causing me to shiver.

I join up with the trail again, and as I creep behind the main house, with light pouring from its generous windows, I pick up the pace. In case there's someone in there, I don't want them to see me loitering back here.

The curve of the trail arcs away from the house, deeper into the forest. I follow it, my breath and footsteps finding a steady staccato rhythm. Fully away from the lights of the house and still only halfway to the bonfire, the woods are completely dark now, the cotton ball quilt of clouds overhead dousing out the moonlight. My heartbeat is jagged in my neck and I suddenly feel stupid for coming this way. It's so much longer than I remember from when I was a teen. But I try to think of Sadie, storming away from the bonfire that night, trampling along this same path until she reached the old farmhouse, lifting the keys from the kitchen counter, driving the car home without Dad.

Had he hit her before they left for the party? Was this it for her? Her turning point? The moment she decided that, no matter what, she was leaving him?

Everyone at the party said they'd fought that night, their argument hanging out in front of them all like filthy laundry.

Had she told him she was done? Were those her final words? Is that the reason he chased her home—hitching a ride from a neighbor—and killed her?

Had Mom gone out to the shed, hoping to pack some things before leaving, and that's when he stopped her? For good?

My throat tightens with emotion, but my reverie is disrupted by a loud snap. I freeze at the sound, my feet jerking to a stop.

Silence. The only sound is the wind whistling through the trees. I can now see the top of the bonfire, fully alight but wavy in the sharp breeze. I keep walking, picking up the pace.

Another sound; my eyes land on a dark figure sliding from the tree line in front of me. My heartbeat is now drilling in the back of my throat and I can't even find my voice to scream.

The figure hurries toward me, tall, looming. I want to turn and run, try and make it back to the main house, but I'm closer to the bonfire and don't know what to do, so I stand still, mired in panic.

"Kira!" The sound of his voice suffocates my own with dread.

It's Randall.

He was the one watching me.

And he was probably the one watching Sadie.

"What the fuck do you want?" I shout, my voice ripping out of me, raw and terror struck.

"Shh, shh—" He holds his palms up, just like he did when Sadie caught him. "Calm down. I just want to talk to you. I've been trying to talk to you all weekend. There's something I need to tell you—"

His eyes, skittering as usual, and his voice, edged with that same manic tone, set off alarms in my chest.

My scream fills the night air, loud and animal sounding in my ears.

I can still hear the thump of bass from the tent, can imagine that I'm too far away from the bonfire to be heard, the trees around me so thick that the sound of my voice dies in the forest like in a padded room.

And then he's on me, cupping a rough hand over my mouth, shushing me again, over and over.

"If you will just be quiet and *listen* to me—there's something you need to know."

Part of me wants to hear him out, see what he has to say, but I'm scared shitless right now and need to get the hell away from him.

I try to twist out of his reach, but he's strong—Sadie was right to be afraid of him—and my struggle only causes his hold to increase. I yelp a scream through his fingers, but it comes out muffled.

"I'm not gonna hurt you. Believe me, that's the last thing I want to do here. Just—shh, shh—just listen to me for a second." He sounds drunk, his words blurring together.

I attempt to steady myself, try to take in a breath but it's hard with his coarse hand blocking my windpipe. I consider biting him, am about to when I hear another voice, shouting from the distance.

"Get your goddamn hands off of her!"

It's Jack, his voice loud and sonorous and authoritative.

"Fuck," Randall mutters. "Fuck, fuck, fuck."

He loosens his grip on me.

Jack is running now, full speed toward us.

He grabs Randall by the shoulder, spins him around, punches him square in the face.

Randall bends over, clasping his jaw.

"Stay the hell away from her, man," Jack says, stepping over to me, pulling me into his side, as if I'm all his.

Randall stands, narrows his green eyes, which are dilated, at Jack. He looks furious, but also afraid. He spits at the ground, turns around, and shuffles back toward the bonfire.

Jack takes me in his arms fully, wrapping me tightly in a hold.

"You okay?"

I feel so safe with him, I don't want to ever move.

"Yes, thank you. But how did you know?"

"I saw your text a little while ago and was expecting you, and then I thought I heard you yelling, but wasn't sure, so I followed the sound."

"Thank god you did."

"Yes. He's such a bastard, but I truly didn't think he was capable of hurting you. Now I'm not so sure. What was in your mom's book about him?"

Teeth clattering from the adrenaline letdown and the icy air, I tell Jack all about Sadie's story.

"What the fuck? I mean, I knew about the burglaries because he bragged to me, knew he was in and out of people's houses during the day that summer. But your mom actually caught him? He *never* told me that. And she felt like he was also watching her?"

"She was completely confused. She really thought it was Dad, and maybe also Katie, but then she busted Randall red-handed and didn't know what to think anymore."

The air is tinged with smoke from the bonfire, and we can hear the din of voices rising in pitch; everyone must be gathered over there by now.

"Let's get you back to the cabin," Jack says, roping his arm around me, guiding me away from the bonfire.

"You sure?"

"Positive. You need a breather. So do I, if I'm honest."

"But what about—"

"Don't worry about Melanie." Her name rolls off his tongue distastefully. "She's too lit by now to care if I'm around or not, really just wants to cut loose with her friends. It's how she gets."

"A breather does sound nice right about now."

We walk, and as we do, the dark woods actually seem pleasant with Jack by my side, less menacing. Our breath clouds white in front of our faces, and my arm is laced through his, our feet walking together in time.

"I spoke with Mike," I say.

"Yeah, I saw you. How'd it go?"

"Well, he doesn't think Sadie killed herself, either. Let me know that they were very much in love, had big plans for the future, and that the suicide explanation never sat well with him."

"Oh god, Kira, I'm so sorry. I can only imagine that makes the loss hurt all the more."

"Yes, and Mike also said he thought Bertie and Dad were onto them."

Our feet crunch the granite as we round the back of the main house, warm light oozing from the windows, and we hurry along.

"And then I had this super weird interaction with Genevieve, where she was drilling me about talking to Mike. And I realized, Bertie couldn't have killed Mom. But if Genevieve knew about Mom and her dad? But . . . I think she was with Chad that night? I know you think I sound insane."

"No, you don't."

"But, anyway, it's the third-to-last chapter that's really got me," I say.

"Yeah?"

"Yeah. Dad tried to choke Mom one night."

"Kira—" He almost whispers my name, sounds like he's struggling to fight back tears.

"I know, I know. I mean, I knew—well, hell, we all knew—how bad their fights could be, how nasty his temper was, and while I've suspected it might be Dad who killed her, to actually read about his violence toward her is gut-wrenching. And also makes me convinced it's him."

We reach the cabin, where I jab in the code.

Stepping inside, Jack sheds his overcoat, hanging it on the back of the dining chair, rakes his fingers through his hair, pacing. "Got anything to drink?"

I cross the room to the mini fridge, pluck out an airplane-size bottle. I unwind the foil, pop the cork. Champagne fizzes from the top and I dump some into two glasses.

"Feels weird to be drinking bubbly while discussing *this*," I say, palming Jack a flute.

He dips his head, taps his glass against mine. "Well, here's to figuring this all out once and for all."

"I'll drink to that," I say, swallowing about half the glass, letting the bubbles spark in the back of my throat.

Jack stretches his form across the love seat, pats the empty space next to him for me to join him.

"I'm so sorry about your dad." His face is tense, and again, I sense that he's holding back tears. "But there's something else that's nagging at me. Your father has been dead for several years, so he can't be the one threatening you now, right?"

Being this close to Jack in the closed-up cabin with the heat roaring is dizzying. I can smell his skin—tangy, citrusy—and even though he just raced through the woods and got into a scuffle with Randall, every lock of his dark hair is in place. It's hard to think clearly with him sitting next to me.

"I've thought about that, too. I don't know. Obviously there's someone who doesn't want the truth of that to come out. Hilda, as I mentioned before, or even Katie. I know I shouldn't be sharing this, but she blurted out that she and Ethan are two months behind on their mortgage, that his business is in shambles. So if Gran is close to dying, then either Hilda or Katie might not want some long-buried truth coming out, mucking things up when they are both close to inheritance."

"Yeah, I hear you, but there's something else still bugging me.

About Randall. If your mom caught him red-handed, maybe he was worried that she'd turn him in, that she'd tell?"

My mouth turns sour thinking of this. It never even occurred to me. Yes, Sadie busting him gave him motive to kill her. Also, he did just basically attack me. It's probably been him this whole time, texting, breaking in here just like he did at our house, leaving that nasty note.

"I didn't think of that, but you could be right."

Jack tips the rest of the champagne down his throat, sets the glass on the table. I do the same.

"But Dad. Something tells me it was him; he was at his boiling point."

I fish my cell from my bag, stare at the blank screen.

"I really need to talk to Gran. I texted her, but she's not answering. And if it *is* Hilda who's onto me and threatening me, I need to get in touch—"

"Well, fuck it, let's go over there!" Jack rises from the love seat, rubs his hands together.

"What do you mean? Like, *now*?"

"Yes!"

"Can we really just leave?"

"Yeah, if Melanie misses me, maybe I can tell her that Mom needed help with Aiden again, especially since Dad is here and she's all alone. And no one will have to know we're together."

What he doesn't say, but what I'm sure he means without actually even realizing it, is that no one at the party will miss me. I'm not entirely sure that's accurate, though. Those latest texts seep back into my brain. But right now, I don't care. The alcohol through my veins and the warmth of being so close to him, the chance to have even more alone time with him, it all mutes my edges, turns me into putty.

He lifts his overcoat from the chair and while he's slipping into it, I glance back at the coffee table.

There's still that final chapter to read, but it will have to wait. Truth is, I can't bear to read it, don't want her story to end, but as soon as we get back, I will force myself.

Right now, I need answers from Gran. It's high time for her to stop withholding—to share everything she knows with me, once and for all. Before it's too late.

53

KIRA

"I can't believe it's only been, like, twenty-four hours," Jack says, guiding us over the blacktop road to Gran's, "and all this shit has already happened."

The forest coasts beside us, sooty and jagged.

Hot air purrs from the floor heater, toasting our legs and, once again, I never want this alone time with Jack to end.

"I know, my head is swimming," I say.

The tires of the SUV kiss Granny's drive as Jack steers up the hill and toward her house. Cloaked in darkness, it looks even more menacing than it did last night. At least some lights were left on for me then.

Jack kills the engine and we sit at the top of the drive for a minute.

It's ten p.m. and Gran is most likely already asleep. But peering into the house through the parted curtains, I see blue-and-white lights strobe in the den. The television. Hilda is probably still up, watching god knows what.

"Let's do this," I say, opening my door.

We enter through the portico again, on the side of the house and I press the glowing doorbell.

After a few moments, Hilda scowls through the glass, then yanks open the door.

"Do you have any idea what time it is?" she hisses through her teeth. "You're going to wake your grandmother up." Her voice is a dagger until she notices Jack standing a few feet away from me. She quickly recovers, softening a bit. "It's too cold to be out there; come in," she orders us.

Once inside, Jack looks at me, lifts an eyebrow as if to say, *This bitch is crazy.*

A cackle sneaks around my cupped hand; Hilda glowers at me.

She leads us to the kitchen. Like last night, it's lit only by range lights, casting scissored shadows across the room.

"I thought you were at the party," she says to me, arms crossing her chest. She's wearing a plum-colored robe over her pajamas and I'm sure she's furious with me for catching her in this intimate state, with Jack here to witness.

"I need to talk to Gran."

A stiff shake of her head. "She's *sleeping.* I told you that."

"Please, it's important," I hit back, emboldened because Jack is with me. His presence gives me clout; she can be only so mean in front of him.

Her mouth sours, her eyes sharpening into thin lines. "You've already put her through so much this weekend, and you know she's not feeling well—"

"If you could just kindly wake her, I promise Kira and I won't take much time." Jack's voice pours out of him, oozing charm.

Hilda's hands churn in twisted balls at her stomach. She's a fortress, but even *she* can't stand a chance against Jack, his soft eyes batting at her like she's a thing worthy of his gaze. "And you and I can have a cup of tea while Kira chats with her grandmother," Jack adds, honest to god winking at Hilda.

"Oh, forgive me, I didn't even offer you something to drink." The back of Hilda's hand flies to her forehead, her sour mouth beginning to form into a smile. "Tea, you said?"

"That would be fantastic."

She doesn't offer me anything, just sails around the kitchen wielding the silver teakettle. After she fills it at the tap, she plonks it on the stovetop, twisting on the gas.

"While this boils, why don't you come with me to her room, Kira? I don't want her to have to go far."

I mouth *Thank you* to Jack, who dips his chin at me before I vanish down the gloomy hall behind Hilda.

"You could have called or something," she whispers, admonishing me when we're just out of earshot.

My insides scald with annoyance, but I don't take the bait.

When we arrive at Gran's closed door, I can smell traces of her White Shoulders perfume.

Hilda raps her knuckles against the door a few times before easing it open. She steps in, closes it nearly shut again behind her, leaving me adrift in the hallway.

I hear a lamp switch on, then snatches of Hilda's voice: "I tried to tell her, but she wouldn't listen—"

"Well, for god's sake, let her in! She's leaving in the morning and I didn't think I'd ever see her again."

Hilda's footsteps pound on Gran's carpet like dumbbells, angry, percussive, toward the door.

She swishes past me. "Don't keep her long," she spits over her angular shoulder before moving down the darkened hallway and fading from sight.

54

KIRA

"Come in, Kira." Gran's voice filters through the half-open door.

The room feels cavernous and shadowy—a master suite the size of a living room. The only light on is Gran's glass globe lamp, which spills a gilded circle across the side of the bed.

"Here, sit," she says, motioning to the tufted armchair adjacent to her side of the bed.

I creak across the carpet, which is worn, the trail of it leading to Gran's bed almost shiny in places, I'm sure from Hilda's endless march in and out with coffee, tea, medication, and the like.

"What is this all about? And why aren't you still at the party?" Gran's face is only half-lit by the lamp, causing her cheekbones to look gaunt, drawn.

She's in pajamas, a matching violet-colored silk number, with a robe sashed around her. She shifts in bed, digs an elbow into one of her sumptuous pillows. Her face is washed clean of makeup and her silver hair is pulled back with a headband.

"Hilda mentioned that *Jack* is with you." A devious smile blooms across her face. "How very clever of you. I am *so* hoping you keep in better touch with him."

I nestle into the cushy armchair, tuck my legs beneath me.

"Gran, I've read all of Mom's book except for the final chapter. And I wanted to hear it from you. Who do you think killed her?"

She sucks in a delicate breath, her thin chest heaving as she does. Her gaze falls to the corner of the bed, eyes averted down. Her head is tilted forward, a Madame Alexander doll in repose.

"Isn't it obvious?" Her voice is husky and then her eyes find mine.

"Dad," I state, as if it's obvious and not a question.

She slowly nods, chews the edge of her thumbnail.

"Did he admit it to you?" I ask.

"No, but he didn't have to." Gran crosses her arms in front of her, as if she's protecting herself from my questions.

Heat licks up my neck. Anger. "What does that mean, exactly?"

"After her death, he was different. He was grieving, yes, but also, edgy, paranoid. Neurotic. Not innocent acting. And then one night"—Gran gives her head a brisk shake, as if she's trying to shoo away a mosquito—"he came to me."

Her mouth clamps shut; she gazes at the corner of the bed again. The air between us is as thick as cream and I'm afraid to break the silence, terrified she'll never spit out the rest if I utter a word. I stare across the room into the pools of shadows, trying to give her some space to speak.

"He came to me about a week after it happened." Her voice is brittle, fragile, a piece of cut glass that will shatter under too much pressure. "Late one night. You were here, in your room," she says, flinging a hand in that general direction, "and you were asleep. I would've been, too, but I couldn't sleep at all that first month."

She begins rocking slightly back and forth, as if that will ease the words out. "He was in a state, pacing around the room. Drunk. But maybe also high on something else. Jittery. I sent Hilda away to her room and made him sit down with me in the kitchen to talk.

Even though he was already drunk, I poured up a few cans of beer, hoping that would help. He wouldn't open up to me, not really, but he asked me then: If they came for him, could our family lawyer could get him out of it if needed?"

A shiver trickles up the back of my neck; the temperature in the room feels as if it's dropped twenty degrees.

"And I didn't have to ask him what 'it' meant." Gran works her hands in her lap as if she's applying her rose-scented lotion to them. "I mean, I *did* ask him if he had done it, but he wouldn't say anything else. He left soon after and we never spoke of it again."

My neck is now scorching with fury. "Why didn't you report him? And why didn't you tell me?"

Gran flinches and I realize that my voice is raised. "Kira, he didn't come out and admit it, so a part of me was hoping that he *didn't* do it. That he figured he might become a suspect because they always think it's the husband. I *still* don't know for sure. But then I read your mother's book . . ." Her eyes trail off to the corner of the bed again.

I raise my voice higher. "Your son murdered my mother! She deserved at least some justice, and you allowed me to believe all these years that I was crazy, that she killed herself! You ruined my life. How could you *do* this to me?" Hot tears stab my eyes. "You knew what was in that book!"

Her glacial blue eyes lock onto mine. "Enough ruin had rained down on our family and"—her hands are balled into tiny fists beside her hips—"it wasn't going to bring her back."

"I can't fucking believe this. You covered up for him, all to protect the family name?"

"Kira," she hisses, her face flaring with ire, "you don't understand. Forgive me for how this is going to sound, but you don't have children. So you can't imagine the position I was in. How could a mother turn on her son? I was worried he was guilty. But I didn't really believe it until I read the book a few months later. And by then, everything was all—"

"Sewn up, washed away, made whole again?" I'm shaking as I rage at her.

"My husband had it in him—that volatility—and I suspected Richard did, too, but I didn't know it had gotten that bad," she says, her gaze far away again as if she's not even aware of my anger anymore, as if she's talking to herself. "It wasn't all his fault. He saw a bad marriage between his father and me, saw your grandfather do things to me that no child should see, and I didn't protect him from that."

She's rocking back and forth again, clutching her gut as if she's going to be ill. Her speech is becoming more rapid; for a moment, I'm worried about giving her a heart attack. "Why did I allow that man to be his role model?" she mutters to herself, aloud but barely audible.

Even as anger scalds the inside of my skull, the sight of Gran sitting across from me, seemingly frail and diminished, softens something. And she's right about one thing: turning Dad in wouldn't have brought Mom back.

She opens her mouth, then closes it. Opens it again.

"I know you'll never forgive me." Her voice creaks out of her and she locks her blue eyes on me again. This time, they blur with tears. "But at least I've finally told you. I could not take this to my grave."

I want to close the space between us, go over and hug her into me, but I'm barely able to catch my breath.

I want to tell her that someone is threatening me now, ask her who that might be, but I press my lips together, force myself to keep quiet. She is a broken woman, and as horrible as it is that she kept this from me all these years, I don't want to rattle her any more than I already have tonight. Without the armor of her expensive clothes and heavy makeup, she looks like a husk of her usual self, a specter of the steely Granny Foster I've always known. And at least, at last, she has finally given me the truth.

And if it *is* Hilda who is throwing up this smoke screen, I *will* find out. I won't let that bitch get away with whatever she thinks she's getting away with. I'm grateful that Jack is with her, that she's not a phantom on the other side of the wall, making both Gran and me uneasy, unable to speak freely.

Flattening my palms against the seat cushion, I rise from the armchair, step over to Gran, and bend down to hug her. She grips my back with her skeletal hands, her slight frame shaking with sobs. I have never seen Gran cry before, so I'm equally moved and baffled, a strange, painful current coursing through me.

"Go and live your life now, Kira. And spend some of my damn money," she cracks, finally springing back to her old self. "I love you."

I squeeze her as tightly as I can without breaking her. I want to shake her for keeping this from me for so long, but I'm also overcome by the fact that I will likely never lay eyes on her again. This is it.

"I do forgive you, Gran. And I love you, too."

Her hand trails down my arm, grabs my hand. Gives it a few squeezes. We stare at each other for another thick moment, and then I turn to leave, my limbs trembling as if not sturdy enough to hold me up.

55

KIRA

We coast slowly down the driveway, and through the window, the stoic pecan trees, naked in their fall state, bid me goodbye, one by one.

I turn and glimpse Gran's estate a final time, the windows blank and lightless once again. Fresh tears wobble in my eyes.

After I left her, I found Jack sitting on a barstool in the kitchen, sipping his mug of tea with Hilda, who had transformed herself from an ice queen into a ruddy-faced conversationalist. She did manage to shoot me a disapproving parting stare before Jack and I left.

"Well, how did it go with Hilda?"

"Ha." Jack grins. "She regaled me with stories of the motherland."

"Yes, I'm familiar with those."

"But do you know about the time she went swimming in a fjord—not a lake, mind you, but a fjord—in the dead of winter?"

"Umm, no, but I'm sure she swam naked and then caught a wild boar afterward and roasted it in her own smokehouse."

"And the muesli? She tell you about the muesli?"

"You're funny. Seriously, you're such a gent for bringing me there, keeping her company and away from Gran and me so we could talk."

We're zipping over the blacktop road again, passing through a thick tunnel of trees. The car is toasty now and Jack's delicious scent fills the space.

"So, how did it go?" His voice is no longer light; it's quiet and heavy.

"It was Dad. I'm positive. Gran told me she thought so, too, and especially after she read Mom's book. And Dad apparently came to her one night, asking if the family lawyer could get him out of it if need be."

"Whew." Jack glances at me. "He actually *said* that?"

"Yup. Gran didn't know if it meant he actually did it or if he was just paranoid they'd suspect him because he's the spouse. But yeah."

More trees swim past us; I feel dizzy taking all these curves, reliving the conversation with Gran, which basically confirmed everything I've always known.

Except now it's real, a knot that must be untied.

"Kira." Jack's voice is a balm in my ear. "I'm so, so very sorry."

As he says this, he reaches over and places a hand on my thigh, holds it there.

I don't move. I don't say anything; I'm not going to puncture this moment.

Through the blur of town—city lights streaking past us along with strip malls and midsize chain restaurants—we drive until we reach the farm-to-market road that leads us back to The Farm.

His hand is a hot coal on my thigh, searing through my leggings.

"What are you gonna do?" he asks, staring straight ahead at the country road.

"I have no idea. I mean, Dad's dead. But I can't just leave the truth buried. Everyone needs to know that Mom didn't kill herself, that she wasn't 'off,' as Katie suggested to me earlier."

"Yeah, of course. And we still need to figure out who the hell is threatening you. And why."

"I think it's obvious; it's either Hilda or Katie."

Saying Katie's name makes my stomach bunch up.

"And then there's Randall. And Genevieve."

I flinch, remembering his coarse hand over my mouth.

I'm not sure what to make of that, not sure what to make of any of it. Katie, Hilda, Hilda, Katie, Bertie, Randall. Their names swirl around my brain as if it's a blender.

The pressure point of Jack's hand on my thigh snaps me back. But all I can think about is Dad. Dad wrapping his angry hands around Mom's neck. Dad yelling at her, probably shaming her, in front of everyone as the Walters's bonfire licked the darkness around them. Mom streaming through the forest to find the keys, to get away from him, to leave him forever. Her solo drive home in her burnt-orange fox coat, face probably bloated with tears, windows down even in the cold, Mom taking in singeing drags off her cigarette.

My mind is a kaleidoscope, seeing the past finally play out.

Mom entering her shed, most likely to grab her batiks and then head inside to pack a bag. If she had made it out of the shed, she would've stopped by my room, planted a kiss on my cheek, left me asleep, telling herself she would call me later, from somewhere safe.

Mom in the shed, frantically rolling her batiks, sweeping the room for anything else she might take. Her book, for one. No way she'd leave that behind for Dad to read.

The sound of tires in the drive, the clap of a door slamming shut, the car sputtering away.

A light flicks on in the kitchen. Does she notice? Dad grabbing her pills, crushing them with the side of a butter knife, sifting them into a glass of champagne, something tart that could mask the bitterness. A conciliatory drink.

Does Mom accept it? Stifle her plans for the moment because she's terrified of him? He's drunk; she knows he'll pass out soon, and at least he's not aggressing toward her.

"Kira." Jack's easing the SUV over to the side of the road.

There's an empty field next to a tree line with a long dirt driveway and a cabin in the far distance. The moon is still sealed behind the cloud cover, but in this open terrain, the sky is backlit, trapped moonlight glowing behind it the way sunlight looks when you're under the surface of the ocean.

He puts the car into park, shifts in his seat so he's facing me.

"I thought you could use a few minutes before heading back into the party." His eyes, crinkled with worry, dance across my face.

His hand is still on me. I don't want to move, but I slightly twist in my seat so I'm facing him, too. His hand stays put. I look down at it.

"Yes, I really do need a moment."

"Want to talk more . . . or just . . ." His voice is low, husky.

Or just what? Sit here with you touching me? Yes.

"It's almost like this huge relief. Finally knowing," I say, a rough sigh edging out of me. I feel limp, depleted suddenly. "I always knew she didn't kill herself. And in the back of my mind, I always thought it might be Dad, but to *know* it is another feeling altogether. I feel weightless and free and also like I have a giant boulder sitting on my chest."

Jack squirms in his seat, his free hand tugging at his collar. He probably doesn't know what to say to me. *Hey, you just found out that your father killed your mother! Is that weird or what?*

I drop my head against the headrest, let my whole body go slack.

It was Dad, it was Dad, it was Dad.

I both can and can't believe it. I *do* believe it, but it's a massive thought to carry in my head.

Through the windshield, the weave of clouds scrapes the sky, idly rolling overhead.

I'm aware of Jack's fingers, still poised on my leg, his steady breath not far from my face.

He reaches over, strokes my cheek, and I wince because it feels like I've been stung by static electricity.

I think of the detritus of my life—my dried-up paintbrushes languishing away in the top of my closet, my tiny apartment with only one bedside table, my lonely little life, the way in which, since Sadie's death, I've always kept myself on the sidelines. And then I hear Sadie's words, clearly, a startling rush into my mind.

Don't be like me, don't be a likeable woman.

And also:

When you find your person, your body knows. Your mind knows. And your heart always *knows even if you've been conditioned to ignore it.*

So don't.

And then I hear Bruce, earlier tonight, asking if he's the only one who thinks Jack and I should've wound up together.

I think of Melanie and what a bitch she is.

We fly out in the morning. When will I ever see him again? This is it; this is my moment. He's given me every sign, and I haven't gone for it. I'm going for it now.

I take Jack's hand from my cheek, kiss it.

He stirs in his seat, sighs.

I nibble on the tip of his finger, then lean over the console, bring my face to his. His eyes search mine, but before he can speak, I place my lips on his, kiss him.

He pulls his head back, looks down between us. Shame simmers over me and I'm mad at myself. What line have I just crossed?

But his palm is still on my thigh, torching my skin through my clothes.

I climb over the console and on top of him.

Through his pants, I feel him.

"What are we doing?" he asks, but his voice is breathless, his eyes closed.

His hands rub up and down my sides and I don't care what we're doing. I don't care about Melanie, about what's right or wrong, I just want to be with him. I peel my sweater off; I'm straddling him, topless other than my bra.

"Oh," he says, a gentle thrust from his hips.

His lips scorch my neck, planting dry kisses over it, tracing my jugular with his perfect mouth.

And I'm grinding against him. "I want this, Jack. I want you." My voice sounds disembodied, like it's not even my own, but saying it frees me up in a way that I've never felt, so I reach my hands behind me, unclasp my bra.

The vents blow heat against my bare back; Jack's breath is rapid, his eyes level with my breasts.

"Kira," he moans, and soon his mouth is on them, tender and electrifying and I'm reaching for the top of his pants, fiddling with the button.

He pauses. "I'm married," he says as I edge down the top of his boxers.

"I don't care." My voice is raspy with desire.

It's as if I've freed him, too, because his tongue is hungry on my breasts, his hands yanking down his boxers.

Before he enters me, he breathily asks, "You sure?"

"Yes."

He slides his hands to my leggings, tugs them off. Runs his fingers along me, touching me.

I've never been touched like this, so hot, so sensual, so intensely perfect that it feels as though I'm leaving my body; then he's in me and we're rocking against each other, the engine causing the seats to hum, Jack's mouth and hands all over me, my name in his mouth like a pained thing.

Afterward, I collapse on top of him, both of us spent.

My head rests in the crook of his neck and his fingers slowly stroke my hair, the other arm wrapped solidly around the small of my back, pressing me to him.

"Umm, wow," he says.

"Yeah," I answer. "Wow." I pull back, stare at him.

"That was, like, over thirty years in the making," he jokes, his face crimping into a smile.

I don't know what to say, so I don't say anything.

"We shouldn't let so much time pass," he says. "Clearly."

He holds my gaze. A flicker of hope lights within me. Does that mean . . . he wants to keep seeing me? But I'm not about to ruin this perfect moment by asking, so I repeat his word back to him. "Clearly," I say, my mouth cracking into a wide grin.

We ride the rest of the way to The Farm in satisfied silence. When the SUV rumbles over the cattle guard crossing, the towering bonfire blazes into view.

Jack nestles the SUV into the same parking space as before. I don't ask if he's heard from Melanie; I don't care, but I do suggest we take different paths back to the party.

My cabin is just steps away and I don't want us to get busted being together.

"You sure?" he asks, taking my hand.

"Yeah. I'm gonna go finish Mom's book."

"Well, text me when you're headed back to the party so I can at least meet you halfway on the trail, and deck Randall again if I need to."

My insides bristle at the mention of his name, but honestly nothing can wrench me from this state of euphoria. "Deal," I say.

Jack walks me to the edge of the tree line near the rear of my cabin. From the bonfire, we can hear music pulsing, voices clanking. Around us, trees twitch in the wind. He pulls me in for one more kiss.

"See you soon."

I watch as he disappears down the trail, his wiry figure silhouetted against the licking flames.

56

KIRA

The inside of the cabin feels like sunshine after the dark of the forest.

I practically float through it, my body buzzing, unable to still itself after being with Jack.

The air smells sugary sweet, the remnants of our champagne still puddled in the bottoms of the flutes. And I smell Jack on me—tangerine and woodsy and warm.

My skin hums with heat, as if I'm glowing from within, and I realize I am. This is the most alive I've felt since Mom's death.

I realize I've been holding myself back, carrying survivor's guilt. It's not just that I didn't know for sure what happened to Mom—though that's a huge part of what's kept me at a standstill—it's that I've paused my own life because Sadie's was cut short.

She didn't want that. She wanted me to have this, to live fully.

With her book, I finally have permission to.

I cross the room, open the mini fridge. There's a single bottle of white in there—a sauvignon blanc. I unscrew it, empty it into a glass. I settle into the love seat, think of what just happened with Jack, and tug a lock of hair around my finger.

He paused at first; *I'm married*, he reminded us both, but then continued to go through with it. From what he's said, his marriage to Melanie is on the rocks, and I know what we had was real. The room eddies around me, expanding with my daydreams of getting to be with him. Really with him.

The wine is tart on my tongue; I slide the glass away. I don't want to dull this feeling at all. But regardless of what happens with Jack—whether he'll actually leave Melanie, whether we'll actually see each other again—it felt good what I just did. Making that bold choice, likeable or not, doing something that just feels right for me for once.

Gran is not wrong: my life has been stunted and it's time I start living it.

I wedge a pillow behind me, drag the box of Sadie's book toward me.

My phone rattles inside my bag, dinging and vibrating, causing the purse to scuttle along the hardwood.

I've read only the first line of Mom's last chapter; I set the pages aside to get it.

It's Gran.

57

KIRA

"Kira?" She says my name as if she's nervous.

"Hi, Gran."

"There's something else I thought of, one last thing you need to know." Her voice is gravelly, as if she's just woken up.

"What is it?" My heartbeat thrums in my neck.

"Your father swore me to secrecy on this, and I forgot all about it until after you left."

"Go on." My breathing feels tight.

"Your sister was there that night when he got home."

My vision goes murky; I blink hard a few times to clear it, rub my eyes.

"What? What do you mean? What are you saying exactly?"

A draggy sigh on the other end. "When your father got home that night, he saw your sister leaving, driving away with Ethan."

"That's impossible—she didn't get home until midnight."

But I know it's entirely possible. I've wondered as much myself about Katie, about her whereabouts.

"Don't get all worked up. I just thought you should know."

"But why would Dad ask you to keep this a secret? Especially if there's nothing to get out of sorts about?" I ask, my voice now very worked up.

Another ragged sigh. "It wouldn't have looked very good, now, would it? Better to just stick to the story of her midnight curfew. Your father said that Katie claimed she didn't even know your mother had come back home. She *was* in the shed, after all."

It's entirely plausible. Mom probably went straight to the shed as I've theorized, and Katie did like to use our house as a make-out spot when Mom and Dad were gone. Why did I have to be in my room, asleep, during all this?

But Gran obviously feels compelled to share this with me now. There must be a good and pressing reason.

"But Gran, do you think . . . Are you suggesting . . . ?"

"No. No, I'm not. That's not what I'm saying at all. I think we both know it was"—she pauses—"Richard." Her voice wavers on his name, like she's choking back tears. "But . . . ?" She says the word like it's a question, one she leaves dangling in the air, open to interpretation.

"But what?

"Nothing," she says quickly.

"This is obviously bothering you or you wouldn't call me in the middle of the night to talk about it."

She clicks her tongue; I can picture her deliberating whether to continue.

"All I'm saying is that you're aware your sister could be trouble," she says at last. "I had to bail her out a time or two, and you know how relentless she was with your mother. She saw herself as your father's guard dog. So . . ."

Bile climbs up the back of my throat. All of that is true. Katie was wretched to Mom, overprotective of Dad. And most importantly, Katie *was* there and never thought to tell me about it. Maybe it was all innocent, maybe she honestly didn't know Mom was back home, but why the hell keep that from *me*? The cops are one thing, but I'm her sister. My stomach clenches. I thought I had it all figured out, that it was definitely Dad who killed Mom, but *was it*?

Now I don't know what to think. It sounds like Gran doesn't, either, even if she's saying otherwise.

"Take good care, Kira." Her smoky voice fills my ear before cutting the line.

I sit with my cell clasped between my hands, as if in prayer, as if I'm praying for an answer. Maybe this final chapter will settle it, but no matter what, Katie needs to start telling the truth.

58

SADIE

It's three in the morning. I can't believe I'm still up, but there's no chance of sleeping tonight.

I'm in a daze, in shock over what happened tonight; my mind is still reeling.

What *did* actually happen?

I can still smell the lake on my skin, still feel his lips on mine, abrupt and startling.

The ashtray is wedged full of cigarette butts and I'm sipping on the strong stuff—a short tumbler of your father's bourbon, which I normally never touch—trying to still my nerves.

We all went to the Fieldings' lake house tonight for their annual end-of-the-summer swim party. Of course, no one ever swims except you teens.

The adults grill steaks and drink on the back lawn that rolls down to the lake while you all swim in the glittering pool in the side yard. It's the last big party in September, the last gasp of summer, and usually it's a fun time.

But your father was in a mood before we even left the house. Tipsy and barely speaking a word to any of us. Grumpy. Tense.

I couldn't wait to get out of there, to get away from him and be in the refuge of other people. To see Mike.

I know I said I was leaving Richard; I am. I think part of him knows and that's why he behaved the way he did tonight.

You and Katie filed from the car and joined the rest of the teens by the pool while I trailed a few steps behind your father.

Everyone thinks August is the hottest month in Texas, but they're wrong. It's September. The sun has baked the parched earth all summer and heat radiates up from it. Even the wind is hot, Saharan.

The Fieldings' pool always looks so refreshing, the water a sparkling turquoise in the late afternoon sun; I wished I could jump in the water with you kids, have a normal, carefree time.

I also wished I had made your father leave after his second martini. He put on a jovial face for the crowd, but when I passed by him on the way to get my dinner plate, he grabbed me by the upper arm, yanked me into him. Hissed in my ear, "You better be on your best behavior tonight."

I scanned the crowd and, sure enough, people were gawking at us. He released his grip, no doubt embarrassed to be caught manhandling me like that.

I hadn't even had the chance to speak to Mike yet—so I hadn't even given him a reason to be angry with me—but after so many drinks, he never has been able to control himself.

Bertie has been all over Mike, as if she knows she needs to keep him on a short leash. Away from me. On the way back from the bathroom, I passed her on the patio and she just shook her head, dropped her gaze downward, and shouldered past me as if I were contagious.

I spent most of the evening chatting with Sally and some of the other women, all of us swatting mosquitoes off our bare ankles and fanning the sweat from our faces with paper plates.

After Mike and I stole a few glances at each other, an irrational part of me became angry at him for not storming across the party, declaring his love for me, and whisking me away once and for all.

We've talked more about leaving together, but he's stalling a little bit. Of course, his spouse doesn't physically abuse him like mine does, so his need to leave isn't as urgent, but I know he wants to. When we're together, not only can we not keep our hands off each other, we also talk, really talk, for as long as our rendezvous lasts. He's promised me we'll leave soon. He keeps saying after Christmas. I just hope I can hold out until then.

But with your father eagle eyeing me and Bertie muzzling Mike, we didn't get the chance to talk tonight. And now Mike's not answering my calls; that's one of the things that's troubling me the most.

Was he the one who saw us in the lake?

As the sun glided behind the pines—streaking the sky in bright pinks—the party seemed to kick up a notch. All you kids were still in the pool, the boys cannonballing into the water, no doubt buzzed on stolen beers, and someone cranked the stereo up, so the soused adults started dancing, our conversations growing louder as we competed with the music.

Mike was moored in a clump of men, but I caught his eye, motioned for him to meet me at the water's edge.

I picked my way across the lawn, a boggy breeze lifting the hem of my yellow sundress.

Waves lapped against the dock and I stood there, waiting, sipping a watery margarita—impossible to keep the ice from melting—and watched the sky turn to night. Over the water, stars appeared, lancing the deep purple sky, transfixing me. I actually forgot all about Mike for a second and just gazed, dreaming of a new batik I'd like to create. Something with the night, the stars, the foamy waves.

"Saaaadie!" A woman's voice tumbled toward me, sounding hoarse and festive with alcohol.

Monica Styles, the most free-spirited one of all of us. I mean, I consider myself the most free-spirited and the most liberated, but after enough margaritas, Monica loves to let her hair down. And usually, some articles of clothing. I love her.

"I wanna go skinny-dipping!" she said to me, loud enough for all to hear. "But I don't have any takers. They are all such prudes. C'mon, Sadie, go with me?"

I scanned the crowd for Mike, who was still with the men, his arms crossed in front of his chest, head tilted to the side as if he were really giving a shit about what any of them were saying while leaving me stranded on my own. That irrationally angry part of me surged up again; just then, I peeled off my dress and followed a very naked Monica down to the dock.

"Yes! I knew I could count on you!"

She was still being so loud, her voice bouncing off the surface of the water, but I didn't care at that point who saw us. I wanted to piss off your father after he had yanked me by the arm in front of everyone, and I wanted to show Mike that I was sick of waiting on him. Mostly, though, I wanted Bertie to see.

Monica dove in first, her figure-eight form vanishing in the dark lake before emerging, squealing like a teenager.

I stood on the rickety dock and dove in next, swimming underwater as long as my lungs would let me. The water was as warm as a bath and felt like velvet against my skin. I haven't been skinny-dipping in years and forgot how good and freeing it feels.

I swam back to Monica and we treaded water near the shallow end, the tips of our toes touching the silty bottom.

"C'mon, you wimps!" Monica shouted at our friends on the lawn.

The women giggled nervously and went back to their chatter, but a few of the men seemed to actually consider joining us. Not Richard, though; he would never. He just stood there, jaw squared, squinting at me, his mouth working a half-used cigar.

After a few more pleas from Monica, her husband, Frank—who's as freewheeling as she is—and their friend Tony, recently divorced, lumbered down to the dock and shed their clothes before jumping in. They brought us icy cans of Coors Light; the coldness of the beer going down coupled with the warm lake produced such a heady feeling.

Swimming had felt so good after I dove in, like a release, so after I finished my beer, I crunched up the can, tossed it on the shore.

I caught Mike's eye and raised my chin, a secret invitation for him to join me. He grinned back, his eyes tracing my upper torso, lingering on me as I bobbed in the water, a look of longing in his eyes. He glanced around at everyone, though, gnawing on his lower lip. He looked at me then—his hooded eyes filled with sadness—and shrugged, as if to say, *How in the hell can I possibly do that?*

I threw my hands up, shrugging, too, to say, *Figure it out*.

Bertie stood a few feet away from him, but her head was turned in the other direction. Mike looked at me then, pointed to his watch and raised both palms, signaling that he'd sneak down in ten minutes.

I put my feet against the marshy shore and pushed off, taking long strokes, the loudness of the party dying out the farther I swam.

I thought about swimming out into the open water, but boats zip by so fast it can be unpredictable, so I paddled to the left, farther into the cove.

When I got far enough away from the Fieldings' to be out of sight, I flipped over and started doing the backstroke, my favorite.

The cove began to narrow so that I was near the shoreline, but it seemed that no other lake houses were occupied, that I was all alone, and so I stopped and just floated on my back, letting the gentle waves rock me. I gazed up into the sky again—more stars had appeared and it was majestic watching them wink at me while I floated.

After a few moments, I went into the breaststroke, really pushing my body hard until I reached an empty dock. Out of breath, I rested my forearms on the slippery wood and thought more about leaving your father and whether I could really hold out for Mike's timeline of Christmas. Whether he was truly going to grow the balls to leave Bertie.

Then, behind me, I heard paddling, a body lapping through the water, and smiled, thinking it was Mike.

It was so dark in the lake I couldn't make him out at first, but my whole body eased, thrilled at the idea that we could steal this moment together.

Then the swimmer got closer; I could tell it wasn't Mike.

It was Bruce, swimming right for me.

I gripped the dock with my fingers, resting my back against it.

Had he stripped down, too, like Frank and Tony? It would be so unlike him that I couldn't believe it. Of course, I could only see him from the top of his chest up, couldn't tell if he had his swim trunks on or not.

He swam right up to me, so that there was only a foot between us.

"Nice night, isn't it?" he asked, grinning at me.

It wasn't that I was unhappy to see Bruce; I absolutely adore him, as you know, but I didn't know how Sally or your father would feel about us out there together like that, me naked, and Bruce also, quite possibly.

As if reading my thoughts, he said, "Don't worry, no one saw me get in the water." He pointed to the shoreline. "There's a little walking path and I slipped away from the party without anyone seeing. I just wanted to check on you."

My head swam and I felt a little woozy from the margaritas and the beer—and also the swimming—but told myself to relax and be flattered that he was concerned about me.

"I know I've had a little to drink, but I *am* a damn good swimmer," I joked.

Bruce's eyes crimped into a smile, and he kept treading in place in front of me, his hands making wide circles in the water.

"It's not that, Sadie. I've seen you in our pool enough times to know how well you swim." He cocked his head. "I saw Richard grab you. I saw how rough he was with you," he said, looking at my arm. "And I wanted to see if you're okay."

Tears built behind my eyes and I felt a surge of emotion toward Bruce then. He had such concern in his voice that I felt loved and cared for, as corny as that sounds. I couldn't believe he'd swum all the way out here to see about me, in secret, so that it wouldn't look funny.

"Thank you, Bruce," I said, my voice cracking with emotion. "I'm, I—"

He paddled right up to me then, so that our noses were just inches apart. And then he roped one arm up on the dock and pulled me into him.

"It's okay, Sadie, it's okay, you're going to be okay; I promise you." His words were rapid, but soft, in my ear.

And at first, I still felt comforted, but then the fact of my nakedness shot into my awareness like a rocket. Here was Bruce, holding me to him, my bare chest smashed into his. When my leg grazed his, I could tell he was nude, too.

This wasn't right. This was very, very wrong, but before I could say anything, he pulled me in even closer and wrapped his other arm around my neck so that he was holding us both up. He lowered his head and kissed me, pecking me at first, but then probing my lips with his tongue, running his hand through my hair.

"Ah, Sadie," he moaned.

My whole body jerked back, my mouth clamping shut.

What the fuck was happening? I thought he was consoling me, my dear old friend worried about my well-being, my marriage, but no. Shock shook my whole body and I froze.

"Bruce, this isn't right; we shouldn't be doing this." I put my palms on his chest, pushed him away, but it was like pushing against a wall.

Why wasn't he moving?

His eyes darted over me with something like hurt in them.

He grabbed me again, tried to kiss me some more.

"Bruce, no!" I shouted, thinking of Sally. Thinking of Mike. Thinking of me. I wanted no part of this.

He snorted. "What? Everyone else can get a piece but me?"

The lake swam around me. I couldn't believe that he was saying this. I opened my mouth to protest, but couldn't find my voice. Did everyone know about Mike? I've never cheated on your father with anyone else before; what was Bruce saying? Is that what all the men think of me? That I'm some piece of meat?

My mouth was dry, so dry it almost hurt breathing in, but I wrestled away from him, slipping under his arm and swimming away as fast as I could.

"Sadie," he called out after me, his voice mean, demeaning, "it wouldn't be smart for you to tell anyone what just happened."

It was when I was about twenty feet away from Bruce that I heard it, a snapping sound. My head whipped in the direction of the noise, which was coming from the shore, and then I saw it, a dark figure standing on the walking path.

I wanted to dive under the water then and never come up. Who was it, and what had they just witnessed? It seemed like the shape of a man, but I couldn't be sure. My mind went to your father, and then to Mike, and then back and forth and back and forth between the two of them.

When I made it to the Fieldings' dock, my chest tight, my lungs on fire, and my muscles limp, I slithered up the ladder and found my dress on the dock, quickly slipping it on before heading to the lawn.

Everyone was carrying on as usual, their voices even brighter and louder than before from the booze. I glanced around for Mike but didn't see him. Your father, however, was lying in wait for me, standing apart on his own, and when our eyes met, he motioned with a quick jerk of his hand for me to come over.

It could've been him on the trail—he certainly walks faster than I swim—but where was Mike?

"We're leaving. Get the girls," he seethed in my ear when I approached him.

He circled around the side yard, lumbering toward the car as I approached the pool area. You were sitting cross-legged near the deep end, chatting with friends, while your sister was entangled with Ethan, leaning her back into his chest, his arms crossed over her in a protective hold.

She skewered me with her eyes when I got into her field of vision, then skewered me further when I told her it was time to go.

"I'm not going anywhere."

I was rattled and in no mood to argue, so I shrugged and left the Feildings' party with you by my side.

When I opened the passenger-side door, the stench of alcohol poured out. No telling how much your father had had to drink. I shouldn't have let him drive, but there was no way I was going to say a word.

"You disgust me," he said under his breath before you climbed in the back.

On the drive home, he white-knuckled the steering wheel the entire way, taking the curves of the lake roads like a maniac.

"Richard, stop it," I begged, but he kept flooring it.

When we got home, I stuck close to you. I don't know if you noticed, but you were my last line of defense in front of your father. I even went into your room with you, tucked you in as if you were a child, biding my time, knowing it would be only a little while before he passed out.

When the house grew quiet, I crept out, saw Richard blacked out in our bed.

My whole body felt like a wash rag being twisted, like the life was being wrung out of me. Remembering what happened with Bruce, I shuddered. Would Sally find out? I would absolutely die. And what gave Bruce the idea he could do that? That I was interested in him? *Everyone else can get a piece but me?* What does everybody think of me? Did I in some way invite him to hit on me? Did he think that my stripping down and going skinny-dipping was some sort of sign that I was open to his come-on?

I tiptoed into the bathroom, opened my bottle of pills, shook one out, and swallowed it.

Then I picked up the wall phone in the kitchen and traveled as far as the curling cord would allow.

I tried Mike. They had to be home by then.

I did our secret code—one ring, then hung up—but he didn't call back.

I waited an hour and tried again. Still, no call.

I tried one last time at one a.m. and nothing.

So I'm now in the shed, my stomach sick with worry, wondering what's going to happen to me, if anything. Maybe no one saw me and Bruce. Maybe I imagined someone watching us, but no, there was someone there. It could've been your father, easily. *You disgust me.* Or he could've just been mad that I swam in the nude.

I did catch Mike's eye, motioned for him to join me. He led me to think he'd be down to the water in ten, so maybe he, like Bruce, followed the path to find me instead of diving in for all to see. And instead of finding me in the water waiting for him, he found me intertwined with Bruce. I can't imagine what that might have looked like, to Mike or to your father.

But it must've been Mike. He always calls me back. Always.

59

KIRA

My hands are shaking as I stuff the last pages back into the box.

Mom's story is over, and instead of feeling like I have some closure—like I did moments before I read this final bit—I'm now more puzzled than ever.

I feel sick, like I've eaten too much candy—jumpy, jittery, and nauseated.

That Mom had to feel that shame rocks me to the core.

And that Bruce was the one who made her feel that way—what the actual fuck?

Then for him to have the nerve to act like he cared about seeing me tonight.

I always thought he was so good, so pure, the paternal counterpoint to Dad's nastiness. The picture of stability, wholesomeness.

I hate that he violated her like that, that he made her feel that way.

And Mike. Had he told the other men that he was seeing Mom? It doesn't feel like that's the case, especially because he was so tight-lipped about it when I first approached him.

But Bruce's words slither back into my brain. *Everyone can get a piece except for me?*

Mike obviously didn't want anyone to know, though, and I just don't get the sense that he bragged to the other men about conquering Mom, but what do I know?

Perhaps Bruce is just a letch, a chauvinist pig who interpreted Mom's openness and innocence as an invitation to trespass.

Or, if Bertie had been onto Mike and Mom, she might have spread it around the neighborhood, but I suspect she's the kind of person who wouldn't have wanted that attention and shame brought on her, on her family.

But who I'm really wondering about is Mike. Why didn't he call Mom back that night? And also, was he the one on the shoreline, the one who saw Mom with Bruce?

I remember that party at the Fieldings'. Jack was there that night and we flirted by the pool as we sipped stolen beers in red Solo cups. I remember Dad making us leave in a hurry—which I was pissed about—his jaw squared and tense as he mashed on the gas, speeding with anger through the swampy night.

I never knew why.

Only that two weeks later, Mom was dead.

I know I'm supposed to text Jack before I head back to the bonfire, but I don't want to just yet.

I've confided in him, told him nearly everything that's in Sadie's book, but this . . . this I can't tell him and it's filling me with dread, making me ill at ease. I feel like I've swallowed something that's expanding in the back of my throat. I've always been so open with Jack; I feel strange about keeping it from him, but there's just no way I can go there. *Hey, Jack, as it turns out, your dad's a total douche and he tried to force himself on Sadie.*

No. I'm going to keep that part to myself.

I unscrew a bottle of sparkling water, take a long sip, letting the bubbles cut through the spongy feeling in my throat.

I need to find Mike before he leaves for the night, need to see what else I can get him to tell me.

60

KIRA

From my porch, the bonfire glows, illuminating the path so that there are only a few puddles of darkness between me and the party.

I still don't want to text Jack, still need to digest what I just read, so I stuff my hands in my pockets, walk quickly down the path.

In front of the bonfire, a makeshift dance floor has been made from an oblong pool of crushed pink granite.

The rows of chairs from earlier have been rearranged into smaller clumps of pairs and trios, little disks of drink tables resting next to them.

Everyone who isn't dancing, though, is standing around the fire, warming themselves and drinking, faces shining from the flames, cocktail glasses twinkling in the blaze.

Curls of smoke thread skyward, and the air is tinged with the rosemary scent of burning pine. Again, I think of Sadie and how eerily similar her last night was to this one.

Did she ever get the chance to speak to Mike again?

Surely he called.

And surely she talked to him that final night. It's probably why she and Dad were arguing so ferociously. I suspect, again, that she might have told Dad she was leaving, and maybe leaving with Mike, and that's why everything ended the way it did.

I stop when I reach the outer ring of the party. Katie is grinding on the dance floor to Missy Elliott, hands on her bent knees, ass pumping in the air. Melanie and Genevieve and all the girls cheer her on, hooting and clapping.

I want to stride over to her, yank her off the floor by her ropy hair, but I'll deal with her next. For now, I need to find Mike.

Jack is with the same constellation of guys, shots in their hands, the pretty bartender refilling their glasses with bourbon. His hair is still mussed from the sex and a spasm of warmth shudders through me, remembering us together, me on top of him, him saying afterward that we shouldn't let so much time pass before we see each other again.

I watch as he tosses back another shot, wipes those velvet lips with the back of his hand. He seems to be genuinely enjoying himself now, cutting loose. Seems I'm not the only one with a little pep in my step from our decades-in-the-making release.

I pick my way over to the cocktail table, freeze when I spot Bruce there, his broad back turned to me.

I don't want to see or talk to him for the rest of the night.

I peer around the bonfire and spot Mike on the opposite end, standing off to the side alone, nursing a green bottle of beer. Practically jogging, I weave along the edge of the crowd until I reach him.

"Mike!" I call out, my voice edging out of me more frantically than I'd intended.

He starts, his shoulders hiking up as he spins toward me.

When he realizes that it's me, he cocks his head to one side as if to ask, *You again?*

"I have some more questions," I blurt out.

Mike nods, gestures for me to follow him. He circles around to the back of the roaring fire where we walk to the edge of the forest. Even twenty feet away from the fire is far enough to plunge us into the cold again. Wind needles my face, causing my eyes to water. From where we're standing, no one can see us, so I jump right in.

"I just finished Mom's book."

He stares at me, his Bambi eyes looking sad.

"And the last thing she wrote about was this party." My voice is shaky. "Do you remember the Fieldings' lake party? The one in late September?"

"Of course."

Mike, like me, has probably clung to every last memory of Mom in those final weeks.

"Well, she wrote about how she went skinny-dipping." I pause, search his face for recognition.

He quickly nods, looks down at the ground between us.

"Mike, she tried to call you later that night, using y'all's special code."

He lifts his beer to his mouth, takes a pull. Beside us, the fire crackles and hisses.

"And you never called her back. Why not?" My question has a stab to it and Mike actually flinches.

He grips the beer, picks at the metallic label with his thumbnail. "She asked me the same thing. The next day."

"And?"

"I never got the call. We were some of the last people at the party—actually, because Genevieve insisted on staying—and I honestly had too much to drink after your mom left. So as soon as I hit my back door, I was out."

"Did she tell you why she needed to talk?" I want to guard Sadie's privacy. If she didn't tell Mike what happened with her and Bruce, I'm not going to be the one to spill the beans.

Mike sucks in a huge breath of air, tosses his head back and exhales toward the sky. "Yes," he says wearily.

A mixture of relief and also anticipation twists through me. Relief that Mom got to talk to him again, clear things up, but anticipation because I'm about to ask if he was the one on the shoreline.

"Was it you, then? Did you see her in the water with Bruce?"

Sorrow flickers again across his eyes. "No, I did not. Because if I had, believe me, Bruce Sherman wouldn't still be in one piece."

So it wasn't Mike who saw them. My eyes begin to burn and water again, but this time, for a different reason. For the millionth time, I'm sad that Mom's time was cut short with this kind and decent man who clearly was in love with her.

"But your mother . . ." he says, his voice cracking. He pauses, takes in another deep breath before continuing, "Wouldn't let me do anything about what had happened. Believe me, I wanted to knock his lights out the second she told me."

I can't help it; I step toward him and hug him. He hugs me back, patting me on my shoulder blades. "Thank you for being so good to her," I say.

"I'm so sorry I couldn't save her."

We unlatch.

"Did she talk about who might have seen them, then?"

"Yes." He stares at me with concern. "Your father."

I bite my lower lip until it stings, nod.

"I'm not saying your father—"

I hold my hand up. "You don't have to defend him. I've accepted that it was probably him—"

"I'm not saying that. I don't know. But those last few weeks . . ." He looks down at the ground again, shakes his head.

"What?"

"Those last few weeks were hell for her."

I wouldn't know because her story ended after that night. My throat stings with emotion, and fresh tears race down my face. I'm not even sure I want to hear any more. But I have to.

"How so?"

"Your father was on her. Watching her every move. We still managed to sneak away during the day, of course, while he was at work, but it's like he was trying to make her more on edge than she already was, like he was trying to sabotage her big night at the museum. To punish her."

"You think he actually thought she was with Mr. Sherman?"

"I don't know. She was worried about how it might've looked to someone from a distance. I kept telling her she was crazy, that it wasn't her fault Bruce pulled that, but it was like an exposed nerve for her, something she kept fixating on."

From the other side of the bonfire, whoops and howls erupt. The pounding beat from House of Pain's "Jump Around" throbs through the air and I can picture the guys jumping, doing a lame white-boy dance while Katie and her flock twerk.

"And that last night out here? Can you tell me more about it?"

"Same thing. Your father was all over her, keeping her on a short leash. Belittling her in front of the rest of the guests. Snapping. And I guess she'd had enough, because the last time I saw her"—Mike shakes his head—"she took off down that trail." He points to the far trail by Jack's cabin.

"And did you—"

"Go after her? Yes. I waited, of course, until I thought no one was looking; I didn't want to make things worse for her. He was already onto us and I didn't want to give him, or my wife, one more reason to snap, but, I waited too long, I guess. By the time I reached the house, where I was sure she was, she was gone. Their car was gone. But I never thought I wouldn't see her again."

Mike tosses his empty beer bottle into the woods, nudges the crushed granite with the toe of his shoe. "I'm sorry you lost her, Kira. She was a magical person, a special person in my life. I've never stopped thinking about her."

My throat is dry and I need a drink. At least I have the answer about that night at the lake. It was Dad, and he tortured Mom until the end.

"Thank you, Mike. You've helped me so much."

He leans in and hugs me again, clapping me on the back.

"Take care."

I turn from him and as I'm heading back to the fire, he yells, "She would've been proud of you."

I feel more tears coming on but I force them back.

I'm on a mission. I'm going straight to the blond bartender, devouring a strong drink, then pulling Katie from the dance floor.

61

KIRA

"What the fuck, Kira?" Katie hisses at me while I wrench her from the dance floor by her elbow.

The sea of writhing guests parts as I lead her away; I feel the prick of stares on us, but keep marching her forward until we reach the far side of the bonfire.

"Jesus, what is it?" She jerks her arm free of my grasp.

Her hair is scruffy and her dress hangs off her in an odd way. Too much grinding.

"You were *there*." The words spew out of me like bitter coffee.

The bonfire is more smoke than fire now, the bottom layer of wood pulsing orange embers. It pops and cracks as a huge tunnel of fumes gushes from the top.

I see recognition in her boozy, watery eyes—she knows exactly what I'm talking about, but still pretends as if she doesn't.

"Where? What the hell are you talking about now?" She's shouting, but over the roar of the fire and the pounding music, only I can make out what she's saying.

"The night that Mom died, you were home."

She scoffs, crosses her arms in front of her.

"Don't bullshit me, Katie. I just got off the phone with Gran and she told me. Everything. She said Dad saw you and Ethan drive away when he arrived home. That Dad made her keep it a secret. What in the actual fuck—"

"I didn't *see* her!" Her voice comes out as a wounded shriek. "I didn't even know she was home. Ethan and I came back to the house after they left to come here," she says, stabbing a pointy fingernail toward the ground. "We were, umm, 'busy'?" She tosses her hands up to make air quotes around the word *busy*.

I can't believe she has the nerve to act haughty to me now, after I've caught her in this lie.

It's not as though I have trouble picturing her making out with Ethan, oblivious to Mom's return. But if that was the case—if she truly had no role in Mom's death—then why keep it a secret?

"How the fuck did you not think to tell me this? Why did you lie about this?"

"You were there, too, you were just asleep! What's the difference? And why are you and Gran talking about me anyway?"

"Because I'm trying to figure out who killed her! And, by the way, you should know that even Gran doesn't trust you. That's why she made Hilda the executor."

"Oh, for fuck's sake! For the thousandth time, nobody killed Mom! Gran is a controlling bitch, but you wouldn't know anything about that. You left. Remember? And for your information, I don't give two fucks about Gran and her will."

Yet another lie. She and Ethan are on the ropes financially and she would definitely be motivated to keep Mom's murder buried.

I remember Katie's slap earlier, remember the stinging words that poured out of her: *We were better off without her.* Walking over here from the cabin earlier, I had actually considered telling her about Mom's book, but not now. No way. Not when she's still acting like a giant bitch, like someone I can't trust. Heat sizzling up my throat, I practically choke the next words out.

"You knew about her, didn't you? Who she was seeing. You were the one spying on her. Making her feel crazy. Did you know that? Did you know you made Mom feel like she was losing it?"

Katie's jaw is trembling. She's raging. She raises her hand to slap me again but stops herself, balls her palm into a fist and grinds it into her other hand like a baseball in a catcher's mitt.

"Mom didn't *need* my help losing it. You sound just fucking like her! Insane! I mean, digging through Melanie's bag? You're losing it. And no, I didn't tell her, but what the fuck, Kira? And what do you mean someone was spying on her?"

"Cut the shit. You knew about Mom and Mike—"

"Everyone did! *Hello?!* Did you see the way Mom acted around him at parties?" Her mouth is pressed into a condescending smirk. "You think Dad was the only one picking up on that? I can't believe you are still so hung up on her. And don't you think I've felt guilty enough? That's why I couldn't tell you. I knew you'd torture me about it forever, how I didn't save Mom. Kira, get a fucking clue when you get a fucking life. Mom was headed full steam toward disaster and there wasn't a damn thing any of us could've done to stop her."

I want to believe her, that she didn't kill Mom, that she just happened to coincidentally be home that night when Mom showed back up. But I still don't understand why she chose to lie about it. Being inside with Ethan is the perfect alibi. Unless, of course, there's more to the story. My instinct still tells me that Dad was the killer, but Katie hated Mom *so* much and wasn't sorry at all she died, so I just don't know what to think.

Then I'm reminded of the texts. If she were involved, and if she's the one trying to stop me from actively digging up the past, then maybe she's the one threatening me now.

I fish my phone from my bag, tap on the screen to awaken it, and select the texts from the anonymous number.

"If Mom wasn't murdered, then how do you explain these?"

Shaking, I thrust my cell at her. My eyes are glued on hers, in search of any flicker, any shred of recognition.

Behind her head, the bonfire sputters and spits, casting a tangerine glow around her already frayed hair. Her eyes squint as she reads the texts.

"Who sent these?" she asks, her face never leaving the screen of my cell. She's avoiding eye contact; I can feel it. I also detect that note of condescension again, like she's implying I'm making all this up.

"I was about to ask you the same."

"You're fucking joking, right? You don't think—" She's yelling.

I yank the phone from her. "I don't know what to think. You've been lying to me all these years, hiding and covering shit up. Do I even know you anymore? Do I know what else you're capable of?" I'm screaming and spitting; I don't have to bother turning to see that all eyes are on us.

Before I know it, Ethan is at my side, prying us apart.

"I'm not sure what's going on here, but I think you've said enough tonight, Kira."

I feel like someone has dumped acid all over me. I always thought Ethan was partial to me, the sane note to Katie's insanity, but here he is, publicly defending her and belittling me, not letting the facts get in the way.

Tears blurring my eyes, I scan the crowd for Jack who's tucked in a far dark corner between the event tent and bonfire. Melanie is at his side, her head twitching as she speaks; they are clearly having words, too.

Ethan draws Katie into him, smooths down the top of her hair with his broad hand. The smirk has reappeared on her face, as if she's won some battle.

"You're one of the biggest reasons I keep my distance, why I stay away from this toxic place. I truly hope I never see you again!" I stagger away from the bonfire without turning to look back at her.

62

KIRA

I walk as far away from Katie and Ethan as possible without exiting the party. I stop when I reach the path that leads to my cabin so that I'm still mingling with the outer rim of the crowd that has hardly thinned.

Nestled under Ethan's arm, Katie picks her way back over to the bar. She makes the sign for the number two, indicating to the blond bartender that she wants a double shot. Most likely for a vodka tonic. Just staring at the two of them sets my blood simmering; I shift so I can see around the throng of bodies to try and find Jack again. I need to talk to him, to tell him about my fight with Katie. I'm desperate for him to console me. I need him.

There he is in that same pool of darkness with Melanie just outside the white tent, but instead of arguing, as they were, his hands are all over her, snaking up and down her bare back, fingers twining through her hair.

A sick feeling swamps my stomach: they're making out. Not just kissing, but full on going at it. Tears bite my eyes again and I feel like I'm going to throw up.

"Smashing couple, aren't they?" I jump at the sound of Randall's voice, then take a step away from him.

"Hey, sorry about earlier. I really am."

I take another step, putting more distance between us. "You're sorry about scaring the shit out of me and putting your hand over my mouth while I tried to scream?" I flick my tears away so he doesn't see them.

Randall throws his head back, exhales. "Yes, but look, you're safe from me here in front of everyone. And there's some things I really need to tell you."

He's right, there are bodies on either side of us. And I'm so mad at Jack right now, having Randall pay me attention doesn't feel so wrong. Still, I keep the distance between us and don't make eye contact.

I nod. "Go on."

"Your mom, she protected me."

"What are you talking about?" I know what he's talking about, of course, but I want to see how much he'll tell me.

"Remember earlier tonight when I told you I'd done some things when I was younger that I'm not proud of?"

I sneak a glance at him. His voice sounds clearer now, sober and steady, and in the flickering light of the bonfire, his eyes almost look like emeralds.

I nod again. I'm still giving him the cold shoulder.

"I broke into y'all's house once, and she busted me. But she never ratted me out. And then when she died, I was so sad. So sad she killed herself, because she was a great lady. That meant a lot to me, what she did, and I never forgot it."

"She didn't kill herself, she was murdered," I blurt out.

"What?"

"Yes, but you're full of shit. You didn't just break in once, you broke another time before that and stole her diamond earrings."

"What are you talking about?"

I face him fully now. His eyes blaze, his head is shaking back and forth; he genuinely looks baffled.

"Don't bullshit me. I know you stole a bunch of stuff in the neighborhood—"

"Whoa," he says, putting his hands up. "I did, but nothing from y'all's place, I promise."

"Were you also spying on her?"

"God no, I swear I was just in there the one time." He threads his fingers through his blond hair, as if he wants to tug it out in frustration. "And she coulda totally called the cops on me, or at least told my mom. And my ass woulda been grass. But after that day, after Sadie caught me, I stopped breaking into houses. I was scared. I promise, I don't know anything about a pair of earrings."

Randall's eyes probe mine, begging for me to believe him. I don't know what to think. He truly does look baffled about the earrings. Sweat beads on his hairline and the air between us is tinged with his clean, woodsy scent. He must have eaten a full meal to be so sober now.

Katie's angry face zooms into my mind again. Along with my theory about how she might've swiped Sadie's earrings just to fuck with her, knowing they were her favorite, knowing that Dad would be furious if he ever found out they were missing. I think of Sadie coming out of the woods that day after being with Mike, then having words with Katie in the driveway. Maybe my theory about Katie being Mom's watcher isn't wrong.

Randall turns his head from me; he now stares ahead at the crowd. I follow his gaze and watch as Jack weaves through the flock of bodies, tearing his way quickly toward us.

"Listen, there's something else I really need to tell you, what I've been wanting to tell you all weekend, but this is not the time."

"What *is* it?" I practically screech. "You had better tell me right fucking now!"

"I can't," he says, backing away. "Come find me later. Please. It's very important."

He hurries into the crowd just before Jack reaches me.

63

KIRA

I'm not ready to face Jack just yet, so I let my eyes trail after Randall. He was definitely running from Jack, doesn't want to get punched again.

But what is he burning to tell me?

Jack is on me now, breathless, the top of his shirt undone.

"What were you doing with him?" He pants, eyes wide with concern.

"What were you doing with *her*?" I practically shout, jerking my head in Melanie's direction. She's resumed her position on the dance floor with Katie and the clique of girls, hands in the air, silky hair flowing down her impeccable back.

"Shh—not so loud," Jack says, taking me by the elbow, inching me away from the party.

I twist myself away from him, cross my arms in front of my chest, eyes blistering his face.

"Hey," he murmurs, reaching for me. I move back.

"Look," he says, digging his hands in his pockets, hanging his head, "she saw us. Emerging from the woods together. After we . . ." He gnaws on his bottom lip, looks up at me with a grin.

The stabbing feeling in my chest begins to soften a little.

"So I had to, you know, kill her suspicions."

"If you're so worried about that, though, why are you standing with me here now?"

"Don't worry about Melanie; she's fucking soused at this point. Couldn't see this far now if she tried."

He steps toward me. This time, I don't inch back. But I'm still furious, reliving the sight of his hands all over her, his mouth on hers, when it had just been on mine.

"That was *hard* to see."

"I know. I'm sorry. Believe me, it was even harder for me to pretend. We haven't even been intimate since Aiden—"

I raise my hand like a flag; I don't want to hear about their sex life or lack thereof. Don't want to imagine more than I've already witnessed.

"Okay, well, can you just forget you had to see that? I'm so sorry." He glances toward the dance floor and we both see Melanie, seemingly lost in song and movement.

"But, Kira, why in the world were you talking to Randall?"

I'm not in the mood to answer him just yet and haven't fully forgiven him, so I bite back with a question of my own. "Is your dad still here?"

"Umm, no, why?" Jack palms his wavy hair. His words come out a bit woozy; I can tell he's definitely tipsy. His smoldering scent of citrus is tinged with whiskey, taking me back to the front seat of his rental.

"Just wanted to say bye before he left," I lie, swallowing down the attack on Bruce that I was about to unleash.

"Aiden," he says softly, "woke up and started having behaviors, so Dad—"

"Yes, of course. I'm sorry."

His dark chocolate eyes are pools of sadness as he drops his gaze to the ground between us. Melanie *is* his wife and if she saw us together, *and* if she was the one who saw us at the pond, then yes, he had to smooth things over with her.

"Wanna go back to your cabin?" he asks.

I feel a tug between my legs; yes, yes, I do. "But are you sure about Melanie?" I glance her way and she's still immersed in dancing, eyes closed, hips swaying as bodies swirl around her.

"Positive. I . . . handled it . . . She's in her own world. Come on; let's go. Talk some more, hang out. While we still have time."

I don't argue.

"Let me go first, though. Give me a few minutes, then come down."

I nod, watch as Jack ducks away from the party and down the dark trail.

64

KIRA

I wait a full five minutes before heading to my cabin, sticking close to the forest line; I don't want to be seen. The air is filmy with smoke from the bonfire, giving the night sky a ghostly feel.

I still can't chuck that image of Jack and Melanie kissing out of my mind, his hands roaming all over her.

When I reach the front porch, Jack steps around from the side.

"Just trying to stay out of sight."

"Of course," I say, jabbing in the key code.

The door unseals with a crack, the wood swelling from the extreme temperature change between indoor and out.

My bladder screams, so I leave Jack in the sitting room, float to the bathroom.

I hear Jack rustling around in the mini kitchen. In the mirror, I study my face. Cheeks rosy from the cold, hair lashed by the wind. I look feral, but not unattractively so. I fumble in my bag for Katie's tube of lipstick, apply a fresh coat.

In the sitting room, Jack is propped on the couch, overcoat and jacket hanging on the back of a chair. The light in here is soft and gauzy from the side table lamp; Jack has opened a pair of beers for us.

His eyes take me in, and he pats the space next to him.

Heart hammering in my throat, I practically sail across the room.

The air in the room is cooking with heat and Jack's delicious scent. I sit next to him, tuck one leg underneath the other.

We clink the necks of our bottles together and sip.

"As much of a freak show as this weekend has been—and I don't mean with you, I mean with that circus," he says, gesturing toward the bonfire, "I kind of wish we were staying longer."

After all the yelling around the campfire, the sudsy beer feels like a balm as it flows down my throat. I take another long sip. Not only because it tastes good, but also because I don't know how to answer Jack without professing my love for him.

He snakes his hand along the back of the love seat, tickles his fingers up the base of my neck. I tremble, draw in a shaky breath. I let his fingers tease my hair while I keep my hands wrapped around the bottle. I want to make him work for it so I can know without a doubt that he wants to be with me, that it wasn't me initiating things, that I didn't throw myself at him earlier.

"Kira." His voice is molasses in my ear. He's slurring even a little more now and I decide that I'm enjoying tipsy Jack.

"Hmm?" I ask.

"Tell me more about what you and Randall were discussing."

I freeze. Face flaming, I feel chastened. But I also suspect that he is jealous of Randall. And I like it.

"Nothing, seriously," I say, not wanting to go there just yet, not wanting to break this spell.

"Sure didn't look like nothing to me." He edges closer to me, his fingers continuing to trace loops at the back of my neck. Leaning in, he kisses me, his hand moving up to stroke my cheek. I'm pinned in place; I never want to leave this spot, my insides unspooling beneath his heat.

I reach over, place my hand on his thigh. At this, his breath grows craggy in my ear. The gauzy light is growing even gauzier, and my whole being buzzes with calm. I've had my fair share to drink tonight, but I think this has more to do with the effect Jack has on me.

He breaks the kiss, drawing his thumb over my lips, leans back, and stares at me like he wants to devour me. I bend his way to kiss him again, but he inches back, keeps circling my lips with his finger.

"So, you think that Randall is all innocent now? I mean, we pretty much *know* it was your father, but, are you just, like, forgiving Randall for attacking you? For breaking into y'all's house that summer?"

I don't understand why he wants to keep talking about it, picking it apart.

"Well, he apologized for earlier."

Jack snorts. "Well, I would hope so!"

"He actually told me a really sweet story about Sadie. I mean, I told you already, I'd read in her book that she caught him breaking in. Well, obviously it meant a lot to him that she never ratted him out. And he assured me that was the one and only time he was in our house. He said he was sad when she died, and that after she busted him, he actually stopped breaking into people's homes. So," I continue, turning to meet his gaze, "I'm thinking he's not all bad, ya know? I mean, he was so much poorer than the rest of us coming up. It couldn't have been easy."

To my ears, my voice sounds just as boozy as Jack's and the room tilts a little behind him. He grabs his beer, slams the rest of it. My mouth is dry, so I lift the bottle to my lips and take another long pull, even though I probably should stop now.

Jack's mouth is hanging open, as though he's waiting for me to say more.

"What?" I ask.

He looks down at his legs, shakes his head.

"You're jealous, aren't you?" I nudge his shoulder.

He lifts his eyebrows. "Well, I'd be lying if I said it didn't bother me that he's paying attention to you, so yeah. Guilty as charged."

It doesn't feel very good, does it? I think, but don't say it out loud.

"But . . ." Jack says, shrugging.

"But what?"

"But it's more than that. He's still such a fucking liar."

"How do you mean?"

"Kira, he wasn't in your house just once. He was the one who stole your Mom's earrings."

The cabin grows still. Like all the air has been sucked out of the room.

Jack's outline grows fuzzy in the lamplight, which feels like it's on a timed dimmer.

I believed Randall when he denied knowing about the earrings. He was pretty convincing. And I still don't believe he knew about them. If he had, I feel like he would've come clean and admitted it to me. No reason to keep it all a secret now, especially since I told him I knew about the other burglaries.

So how *does* Jack know about the earrings?

The room tilts even more.

I guess Randall could've swiped them, bragged to Jack. But that's not sitting right with me.

Sadie never told the cops, never even told Dad. *I* was the only one she ever mentioned the earrings to.

No one else should know.

Unless.

I've been silent for too long, and Jack has picked up on it. Has he realized his slip? Hoping he'll say something to clear all this up, I sit tight, waiting him out.

A quick bark of a laugh escapes his throat. Manic sounding. Out of character for him.

"What?" I ask.

"You were never good at just letting things go, were you?"

My vision starts to blur; I can't believe he's just said that to me.

"How do you know about Mom's earrings?"

"Like I said, you can't ever just let things be. I mean, obviously. Look at why you're here. Digging up all this shit."

I squirm in my seat, shift away from him.

He reaches out, puts his hand around my wrist, as if to hold me in place.

"Do we really have to keep talking about this, or can you just let it go?" His hand squeezes my wrist, but not in a pleasant way.

I try and scoot a bit farther from him, but my thighs feel like Jell-O. I can't be this drunk, can I?

I ask once more how he knows.

He releases my hand, discarding it from his like it's a thing he's disgusted by. "You're ruining this, Kira. You're ruining all of it." He sweeps his arm around the room. "We had something nice, but now . . ."

Blood thunders in my ears, which feel like they've been stuffed with cotton. I suddenly feel overheated, clammy. Like I'm going to be sick. Something is wrong, very wrong, but my brain can't piece it all together. So Jack obviously knew about Mom's earrings, but what does that mean? I can't seem to make myself travel much further from this single, pressing thought, as though following the succeeding logic will lead me over a precipice.

"How? How did you know about them?" My voice sounds faraway, disembodied; I can't bring myself to look at him. I stare straight ahead, eyes focused on the sinewy wood grain of the coffee table.

A deep inhale from Jack, followed by a jagged exhale. He brings his hands together, tenting them over his lap.

"Because, Kira, I was the one who was watching her."

65

KIRA

I feel like I can't breathe, like I can't hold on to a simple breath.

Jack's eyes are burning on me, so I finally turn to face him.

He cocks his head to one side, offers a tiny shrug, as if to say he's sorry. But it's the look in those eyes that makes my stomach shrink into itself, threatening to send me over the precipice. Once velvety brown and comforting, they now dance with menace.

"What are you talking about, Jack?"

I want him to explain all of this, make it go away. Rewind to where we were, not half an hour ago, heading back here for round two.

"I swiped her earrings. I was the one in and out of your house."

My mouth is so dry I almost choke. I'm woozy, don't need more alcohol, but I desperately need liquid, so I take another sip of my beer, which is now half-finished and lukewarm.

I want to move away from him, get to the other side of the room. I begin to stand, but he reaches across my belly, guides me back down to the sofa, his forearm a guardrail over a child on a roller coaster.

"Why, Jack? Why were you watching her? What the fuck do you mean?"

"Because I had to."

My stomach churns, a spin cycle; I feel like I'm going to be sick.

I don't want to hear the rest of what he has to say, but his mouth keeps moving and the cotton ball feeling in my ears grows thicker.

"I don't understand; what do you mean, you *had* to?"

"Not only could you never let things go, but also, you've always been slow on the uptake. Naive. Too trusting."

A quick shake of his head.

"You know, you really are just like her in a lot of ways."

I nod, numbly. "How so? Naive?"

"Yep, that. But also, you're a whore, just like Sadie."

Fuck. I clutch my lurching stomach, my head shaking in confusion, not wanting to believe what I've just heard. I can't . . . Jack wrote me the letter. I feel like I'm going to vomit.

"Sounds familiar, eh?" he snorts.

The light from the lamp now throbs, pulses. The room tilts again and I hold my abdomen tighter, trying desperately to keep myself from being sick.

How is this even happening? How can it be Jack? If he wrote the letter, then, holy shit, he sent the texts. He's the one who's been threatening me. And now here's the edge of the precipice I've been dancing to avoid—I can barely even allow the thought to take root, much less string the words together in my head.

A fire poker of anger bolts through me, awakening my joints. I tear his arm off me, scramble to my feet. Though the floor beneath me tilts like a seesaw, I stand over him, pummel his chest with my fists.

"Hey, hey!" He laughs, wicked and dark.

I slap his face, swiftly, hard. My palm vibrates from the strike.

"Hey, that's enough," he says, not laughing this time. He clamps his strong hands around my forearms, shoves me back onto the love seat.

"You sent me those fucking texts," I scream through clenched teeth.

"Yep." His grip is searing on my arms.

I think of sitting across from Jack at the bar, showing them to him, telling him everything, while he was pretending to console me, acting concerned. Driving me out to Gran's to help me finally find out the truth. Then pulling over in the field. Having heated sex with me in the car.

"The whole weekend you pretended you were helping me. And then you, you even—"

"Fucked you? No, you came on to *me.* Remember? I *reminded* you I was married. Gave you a chance not to take it further. I was hoping you'd rein it in, show me that you're not exactly fucking like her, but you just couldn't help yourself. Because you are. A whore. Just like your mother."

I go to knee him, but he bucks back, grabs my wrists even tighter.

I should be able to fight harder, but my motor skills aren't lining up with the fury inside my brain.

I feel disgusting, filthy, violated.

"My mother was no whore!" I screech so loudly that spit flings from my mouth.

Another demented laugh sputters out of him; he squeezes my wrists so hard I fear they'll snap.

"Yes, she was, and that's why I had to watch her, keep an eye on her. She was always parading around, dressed like a slut, trying to catch the eyes—and god knows what else—of all the other dads. So yeah, I spent that summer watching her. Very, very closely."

I'm fully over the precipice now. Jack murdered Sadie, and everything I thought I knew is wrong, lopsided in the most grotesque of ways.

I eye this vile stranger. Instead of seeing how handsome he is, now I see pure evil, a monster. I recoil, am repulsed. I can't believe he was behind all of this, orchestrating it all, manipulating me.

"You're fucking sick."

"You got that right. Glad you're finally catching on, Kira. Like I said, slow on the uptake." He clicks his tongue. "One thing, though, that's different between you and Sadie. You're putting up much more of a fight than she did. Of course, you've only had about half the amount of Valium—"

"You sonofabitch!" That explains the druggy feeling. He spiked my beer.

"You're starting to feel it, aren't you? Don't worry, I haven't given you enough to kill you. Just enough to make you puke and eventually pass out. Enough so that when I hold the pillow over your face, you'll struggle, try and fight it, but I'll be able to overpower you. And you'll probably get sick in, oh, let's see"—he hikes up the sleeve to his shirt, taps on the face of his watch—"six or seven minutes."

"You killed my mom?" I have to force myself to say it out loud. Dread writhes all over me; I am starting to feel queasy.

"Had to. But I went a little overboard with the drugs. Crushed way too many up in the beer I gave her. She went so quickly, it just felt too easy. Almost unsatisfying."

A thought shoots through me. "But you weren't even around that night. You were at an out-of-town game."

"I never got on the bus. I forged a doctor's note earlier that day about a sprained ankle. And my parents were here at the party that night. It was perfect."

His hands are still clamped over my arms. I try to remain calm, but I need to outrun the effects of the drugs.

"Why? Why did you fucking kill her?"

"Lower your voice, Kira." He digs his nails into my flesh.

A whimper escapes my parched mouth.

"I'll explain everything. It's another reason I didn't knock you out completely. It will actually be fun to go through it all with someone else. I'm quite amazed with myself. Oh, and when you need to get sick, please go to the bathroom. Melanie would *not* appreciate puke on my suit.

"So. Where should I start? Well, let's get one thing clear: by the time I was old enough to know better, I *never* liked your mother. The way she carried herself, the way she pranced in her bikini, the way she made men sit up and take notice of her. I knew, even at thirteen years old, that she was trouble. But when she started banging Genevieve's father—yes, that was me who saw them in the woods that day—I knew she had to be stopped. So I started tracking her every move. Nobody keeps up with their kids in the summer, so I had total freedom. My mother is even more naive than yours, thinks I hung the moon. So I spent a lot of time watching Sadie."

Bile floods the back of my throat. "Jack, I'm going to be sick."

He releases my wrists and I stand up, stagger to the toilet. I vomit up the contents of my stomach—mostly alcohol; I haven't eaten for hours—and pray that I'm getting rid of some of the Valium, too. I rinse my hands in the sink, look around for a weapon, but there's only a plastic squirt bottle of soap and a soft hand towel.

Jack knocks softly on the door. "Don't get any strange ideas. And don't worry, the pills are well into your bloodstream. After fifteen minutes, it doesn't matter if you puke; the medicine is already metabolizing in your system."

If there were a window in here, I'd kick it out, clamber through it, but there's not; the space is minute. No room for one.

I blink at my reflection in the mirror; my face looks like it's expanding and shrinking, expanding and shrinking. I'm definitely unsteady, but not as intoxicated as Jack likely thinks I am. I'm going to play it up a bit. It's the only strategy I can come up with.

I open the door. Glance at the bed. "I actually feel like I'm going to faint. Will you please let me lie down?"

Jack's eyes are scissor sharp on me; he's silently examining me with them, sizing me up.

"Please?" I ask, drawing out the lisp in my *s* so that I sound fucked-up.

His breath is hot on my face. He shoves me to the bed. "Lie there and don't fucking move."

I sink into the bed, roll over on my back. Jack stands over me, then wrenches my legs to the side to make room for him to sit. He grabs my calves just like he did my wrists, holding me in place.

"Your mom wasn't even that interesting to watch. Always smoking. Talking to herself. Painting. Or whatever the hell it was called. It was boring, actually, except for the sex I got to see her having with Genevieve's *father*." He shakes his head. "What pushed me over the edge, though, is that apparently he wasn't enough for her. I knew he wouldn't be. Like I said, she was always parading around in front of all the men in our neighborhood. She got *off* on the attention."

My throat is scorched from vomiting; I have to fight back the urge to puke again.

"But it's when I saw her with Dad that I lost it. I knew a woman like that had to be snuffed out. Before she busted up any more families, ruined more lives."

The room behind Jack spins and twirls. I'm feeling the full effects now. The light from the small ceramic lamp on the bedside table seems to pulse like candlelight. I know the answer, but I have to ask him anyway, hear it from him.

"When did you see them together?"

Another snort. "She was fucking skinny-dipping in the lake. At the Fieldings' lake house. A *family* party."

"Wow, it was *you* who was standing on the shoreline."

At this, Jack jerks his head back in surprise, a small smile spreading across his lips.

"Your dad, he tried to force himself on her—you think you saw something that you didn't. And you *murdered* her for it!" I screech. "She went swimming out into the cove, thinking Mike was going to follow her, but instead your dad swam up and started pushing himself on her, assaulting—"

"That's bullshit! Of course that's what she fucking wrote in that sad little book of hers. But I *saw* them. Saw the top half of her tits in the water, saw her hugging him. Yeah, there might've been some disagreement, but c'mon, she was begging for it. That tramp couldn't get enough. So after that, I made my plan."

His hands go slack on my calves as he's talking, and I consider kicking him, fighting him, but I know I'll be no match, especially with me lying down. I have to keep him talking, keep biding my time until I can figure out what to do.

"And what was your plan, exactly?" I ask, my voice neutral and flat.

"To kill her, obviously. But I knew I'd have to frame it as suicide. So I got ready. I knew she was on Valium—which we had an unlimited supply of in my house—so I started stealing pills from my parents. And I knew about the Walters's party, figured it would be another boozy night for all. And I knew from watching her that Sadie was often in her shed at night, all alone. But I never expected her to show up by herself! It was like a gift! Bam! And she was in such a state that by the time I knocked on the shed door, asking if *you* were around, she was ripe for the picking. When she told me she was sorry but you were asleep, I offered to bring her a beer, listen to her. Easy peasy."

I feel ill, an immersive sickness that makes me feel as though

I've left my body and am watching it from the other side of the room. I see Sadie opening the shed door, being surprised—but pleasantly so—that it's Jack. The innocence of him—polite, affable, charming—asking after me, then asking her what's wrong, and would she like to talk about it. Sadie, my sweet mom, falling into his trap.

Sadie on the floor a half hour later, dead.

Tears begin to leak from my eyes; I let them slide down both cheeks without wiping them away. I don't want to draw attention to my emotions. I want Jack to keep talking, keep letting his guard down.

"She actually told me about your father hitting her, abusing her, can you believe it?" A smile creeps across his face.

I nod.

"That's how *desperate* and sad and pathetic she was. Unloading all of that on a teenager. But she was truly all over the place. I have no doubt she would've eventually told me about how she was banging Mike, too, but like I said, I made the mix too strong and it was lights-out."

I close my eyes. I can't look at him one second longer.

"You don't have to kill me, too, Jack. You don't need to do this. Seriously, no one needs to know. Nothing will bring Sadie back now," I say softly. "But if you kill me, you might get caught, and that won't be good for anyone, especially little Aiden."

I pry my eyes open, study his face.

A twitch of sadness crosses his brow. Am I reaching him?

"As sick as this sounds, I love you, Jack, and I care about you." I actually feel like I'm leaving my body for real as I say this next part. "And I kind of understand why you did it. I know how Mom could be. And now that I know the truth, I can let it go. Never come back to this place. Start my life over in California. I love you, and no matter what you say, I know you love me, too. So let me sleep, and let's just forget this whole thing ever happened. I could never prove it, anyway. And I honestly don't have the energy to even try. Go back to Melanie, go take care of that beautiful little boy who needs you."

I reach for his hand and he lets me take it. Hope springs in my chest. Is this actually working? I give his hand a squeeze; he whistles out a sigh and his back slumps, his body relaxing.

66

KIRA

I'm still holding Jack's hand, which feels heavy, clammy. I give it another squeeze. This time, he squeezes back.

"You're right about one thing."

"Yeah?"

"Aiden needs me. And that's why I've made sure I won't get caught. I'm not going to kill you—I mean, yes, technically, I am—but you're going to kill yourself. Just like your mom."

He squeezes my hand harder. Too hard. I don't dare to budge; I'm too gripped with terror.

"I didn't want to kill you, Kira, I really didn't. I thought the past was in the past. But *of course* I had to come here when you called to tell me what your gran said. I tried my best to scare you away, to shut you down, but you were so insistent and kept digging. And when you told me about that book, well, I had to hear what was in it. Even though I knew *I* wouldn't be implicated, I wanted to see what conclusion you would come to. Hoped it would clearly point to someone else. Which it did; your drunk father—ugh, sorry, Kira, you lost out big-time in the parental department. But then you had to keep digging and picking. And then, when I saw you talking to Randall, well, I had to know what all he told you."

"Why did you steal the earrings? It's not like you needed the money, like Randall did."

"Oh, that? That was just to fuck with her. To further screw with her already screwy mind, no pun intended."

"Does Randall know?"

"What? That I offed her?"

I inwardly flinch at his casualness.

I nod.

"God no. I wouldn't ever be that stupid. But let's just say he knows other things."

"You still don't have to kill me, Jack. I promise I won't—"

"Bullshit." His hand pulses around my wrist; the pain makes my eyes water. "I can't risk that. Like you said, Aiden needs me."

"Jack, please—"

"Shut up and let me finish. Also, it's just all too perfect. You killing yourself here, where your mother spent some of her last hours. And you doing it in the same fashion she did, by overdosing. Don't worry, you won't suffer. In just about ten more minutes, you'll be fully out and won't feel a thing. And I'll inject more Valium into your bloodstream so that there's no question whatsoever about your death."

As terror washes over me, I make a final plan. I hope I won't be as knocked out as he thinks I will—but I'll pretend like I am—and when he moves to put the pillow over me, I can catch him by surprise and attack him as best I can. It's my only out.

"But what about the texts on my phone? I showed them to Katie. Surely someone will catch on—"

"I planned for that. That's why the burner phone they're sent from is now planted in the next room. In your luggage. Kira, no one will have trouble believing you're cuckoo." As he says this, he points to his temple, tracing a circle. "That you went crazy over your mom's death, and that coming back here is what finally pushed you over the brink."

Motherfucker.

"So it will look like you sent the texts to yourself."

"But what about Hilda? She saw with her own eyes the spray paint, the 'whore' message in the yard."

Jack laughs that maniacal laugh again. My blood chills.

"Yeah, I took care of that, too, when I drove you to Gran's. You didn't really think we were talking about muesli, did you? I explained that you spray-painted it, that you had me drive you home from the bar because you forgot something, but then made me wait at the foot of the drive. I told her I saw you doing something strange in the yard and asked her about it."

I hate both of them so much right now.

"And she was all too eager to believe it was you. I asked her to keep it hush-hush, told her you weren't mentally stable, even offered to toss her a buck, but she wouldn't hear of it. The old bat was gleeful to hear how nuts you are. Man, you really are from one extra-fucked-up family."

I can't believe I've been so blind. I hate myself for believing in Jack for so many years, beginning with him climbing in my bed to console me right after Sadie died. Right after he killed her. But it's not my fault. He's too good, too smooth, too conniving. I want to get this over with, want to fight while I'm still halfway here.

"Jack," I ask, slurring his name. "I'm fading. Can you give me something to reverse this? Please, I'll never . . ." I let my hand go slack in his, shut my eyes, go silent.

He releases my hand. Taps on the side of my face with his fingers. Pries my eyelid open. Then I hear the sound of the pillow, sliding across the bed. Before I can react, it's over my face, tight, blotting out everything around me.

67

KIRA

I'm struggling to breathe. I can't believe I'm gonna die in here like this.

I start to flail, trying to kick, but he just pushes down harder.

But then stops; there's a loud knocking at the door.

"What the fuck?"

He releases the pressure of the pillow.

The banging continues.

"Fuck."

The sound of a male voice.

"Open the door."

Randall.

"Fuck, fuck, fuck." Jack's voice is panicked.

Jack slides the pillow from my face, holds an index finger to his lips. "Not a fucking word."

He takes a few steps from me toward the bedroom door. I try to sit up, but beneath me, the mattress creaks.

Jack spins around. "Don't you fucking dare."

I sink back down.

He turns back toward the bedroom door.

The knocking amps up, now a frantic, hammering sound.

"Umm, we're kinda busy in here, if you know what I mean," Jack shouts.

The knocking stops.

My heart is pulsating in my throat, and even if this is going to get me killed, I scream as loud as I can, "Help me!"

"You dirty bitch," Jack growls, underneath his breath.

No more knocking. Shit.

Jack walks toward me. I sink farther into the mattress, bracing for the worst.

He wrenches the pillow from the bed, holds it over my head again.

With all my might, I kick; I'm too slow. He lurches back. Then surges forward, shoving the pillow so tightly over my face I feel like I'm choking.

My heartbeat is now thundering in my ears. This is it.

Then a noise like a gunshot, loud and clear.

Jack releases the pillow and I gasp for air, coughing and choking on my own spit.

The window in the bedroom is shattered, and I watch as Randall climbs through it.

"What the fuck is going on in here?" Randall shouts.

A guffaw rips through Jack's body. "What's it look like?" He gestures to me lying in bed.

"I heard Kira scream."

Jack rushes toward him, takes a swing.

"Fuck!" Randall says, bringing his hands to his nose, now trickling blood.

"Stay the fuck out of this, man, I'm warning you," Jack says.

Randall's eyes flit to mine; he raises his eyebrows as though to ask me what is going on. My eyes go wide, to signal danger.

"She's onto you, isn't she?" Randall says. "She's figured you out. That you're not the golden boy everyone thinks you are."

"Shut the fuck up, dude," Jack says.

"Did he tell you, Kira? About the bird?"

Jack lunges for Randall, tackling him, knocking him into the wall.

Randall yells, "He was the one who hit the bird with the slingshot. He was always abusing animals. Told everyone it was me."

The room rotates as if time is unfolding in slow motion. Fucking Jack. Pretending to nurse a wounded bird.

"He blackmailed me my whole childhood. Because I stole something and he found out about it. I didn't have any money to eat, so I had to. He never let me forget. Forced me to break into people's homes—including his own—and steal more stuff. It was all a big—"

Jack has wrestled him to the ground and is now pummeling his face with his fist.

"What are you gonna do, kill me?" Randall yells.

"You were attacking Kira here, so yeah, I'm defending her."

The blows continue, and with each one, Randall groans.

I can't let this happen. I sit up in bed, as quietly as I can. Jack is totally absorbed in taking Randall out.

I glance around for something, anything. The lamp. I slip the plug from the wall, grasp the lamp by its neck. It's small but made of glazed ceramic and has some heft to it.

I slip off the bed, lamp clutched in my hand by my side, and creep over to Jack.

His back his to me, his body fully over Randall, whose face is already a pulp of blood and bruises.

I'm unsteady on my feet and feel like I could pass out, but I keep walking, tiptoeing as quietly as possible.

Randall knees Jack in the groin, causing him to collapse forward for a moment, before rearing back and clasping his hands around Randall's throat.

I think of Sadie, dying in her shed, her life cut tragically short by this psychopath. I think of Jack, toying with me, having sex with me, doing shots with his buddies after. He wasn't celebrating our lovemaking; he was celebrating the fact that I was finally willing to let it go, to believe it was my dad who killed Sadie. He was letting his guard down, basking in his victory.

My hands are quaking; the lamp nearly slips through my palms because they're oiled with sweat, but I raise it as high up over my head as possible before crashing it down on Jack's skull.

It connects with a thud. Jack's body goes limp across Randall's legs.

68

KIRA

ONE YEAR LATER

The afternoon sky is bright blue and sunny. Only a few bleached-white clouds are suspended in the sky, like hand towels hanging to dry. Crisp, starched. A quintessential California sky in early autumn.

We exit the car and the hem of my sundress swishes over my thighs. I press the remote, locking the car, and we wait for the light to change before crossing the busy street.

I'm nervous, but it's an electric kind of nervous, a giddy, sparking energy that crackles through me.

Outside, a small line has formed. I scan the faces to see if I can spot theirs, but they must be running late.

We walk to the front of the line; I pause for a second before going in.

"You ready?" Randall asks, his smile gleaming in the California sunlight.

I nod. He cups the small of my back, tugs open the door.

Even though we've been in this space a few times before now, measuring, speaking to the curator, my eyes still brim with tears when I see them, hanging together on the far wall, side by side.

Randall pulls me into him.

As it turns out, he's got a masterful eye, an organic feel for art, and is a very savvy manager.

And more importantly, he's a wonderful partner. A loving, devoted, true-blue person.

It kills me what was said about him back home before the truth came out: that Jack was the real psycho.

And the later gossip about Randall abusing his wife, forging checks, was also false. He was another victim of the small-town rumor mill. I hate that he had to live under that cloud for so long.

After I bashed the base of Jack's skull with the lamp, Randall slid out from under him. He knelt, placed two fingers on Jack's neck, looked up at me, and shook his head.

No pulse.

Jack was dead; I had just killed him.

Randall dug his cell from his pocket, dialed 911.

My vision was cloudy, my stomach still sick from the pills, but adrenaline spiked, kept me alert. That and the bag of pretzels Randall found for me in the kitchen.

While we waited, he held a clean washcloth to his wounds—not wanting to clean himself up so much that he didn't look like he had been attacked—just enough to stunt the bleeding. There was so much blood.

"You had to do it," he told me over and over.

And even though I knew it to be true, I was still shaken; I had just taken someone else's life.

In Jack's suit pockets, the police discovered the syringe, the rest of the Valium he was planning to dose me with, along with a suicide note he had written for me.

Bastard.

I stayed in Longview for a few more days to answer questions from the police, and while I was in town, Randall bought me dinner.

Over plates of spaghetti, he told me more about how Jack had bullied and tormented him as a boy and teen. Jack was the real menace, as it turns out. And once he noticed Jack and I were together that weekend, he kept trying to find a way to tell me, even if he was worried I'd never believe him.

He was even the one, he explained, who had been in the woods, watching Jack and me at the pond that day, keeping close tabs on me for my safety.

The sunshine drenches the gallery, splashing light against the wall. Before the crowd comes in, I want just a few more minutes with these pieces. I cross the room, stepping right in front of them, and more tears form.

The three batiks Sadie was going to feature at her own show in Longview—and the ones I've kept all these years—are now hanging in front of me, almost glowing from the sunlight.

MAGNOLIA TEARS

CADDO LAKE

SCARAB BEETLE

A square card sits to the right of each, explaining Sadie's process and the story behind it.

I've realized why I never wanted to hang them in my apartment until this moment—it's because somewhere in my subconscious, I knew that wasn't their home. Their home is here, in an art gallery. What Sadie created them for.

"It's incredible. I'm so proud of you," Randall says, smiling.

He loves Sadie's pieces, but he's talking about mine, which hangs right next to the batiks.

After I returned home to LA, I started dabbling again with mixed-media, like my work in college. I never went back to my day job.

Randall and I had long, meandering phone dates, and before long, he took a trip out here and never left.

I had enough money from Gran's trust to rent us a tiny bungalow in Santa Monica, ten blocks from the ocean. Randall took a job in computer sales, but spent so much time encouraging me with my art—taking me around to galleries, introducing me to the owners—that we soon decided to join forces and do this together full-time.

Gran passed six months ago.

I found out from Katie.

Her heart finally gave out, but she went peacefully, in her sleep.

Katie and Ethan took me in during my final days in Longview, while I was wrapping things up with the police, and that was the beginning of the repair of our relationship, but I've never gone back since then, even for Gran's funeral.

She apologized a thousand times—still does—but I apologized over and over, too. I mean, I accused her of killing our mother.

"I don't deserve you, Kira," she said to me one morning over breakfast, when it was just the two of us eating scrambled eggs in their sunny dining room.

I punched her softly in the arm. "No, you don't. But guess what? You're stuck with me."

After I returned to LA, Katie kept me abreast of everything. Like what happened to Melanie. Even though her life detonated after Jack was killed and the truth of him murdering Sadie came out, she did get her wish to move back to Longview. She needs all the help she can get with Aiden, and even though Bruce is a total letch, she needs the support that he and Sally can give.

She's also apparently gotten sober. According to Katie, even though Melanie didn't know her husband was a murderer, life with him had been fraught—he was controlling, a perfectionist, and it drove her to drink. She kept her troubled marriage to herself—wanting to keep the image of a perfect marriage intact—only telling friends back home once Jack was gone.

Now the door chimes and I hear their giggles before I see them. My nieces come scrambling over to me; I feel like a celebrity.

I scoop them up in a three-way hug and then Katie comes over, places her arm around me. She takes in a deep breath as she looks at Mom's work and mine, together on the wall.

Katie, of course, has seen Mom's art before, but never mine.

I'm nervous.

The girls bolt from me, racing toward the hors d'oeuvre table.

Katie unwinds her arm from around me, moves an inch closer to the wall.

"Kira, it's perfect." She turns to me and her eyes shine with tears.

She lifts a finger, reads the title card.

A LIKEABLE WOMAN

ACKNOWLEDGMENTS

Writing and publishing a novel truly takes a village and I'm so lucky to be working with one of the most supportive and brilliant teams out there. My gratitude is due to many.

To Victoria Sanders, tireless champion and incredible friend, your unwavering faith in me is a shelter in the storm, and means the absolute world to me. Thank you for everything you've done, and everything you continue to do.

To Benee Knauer, book goddess and dearest friend, thank you for jumping into the trenches with me on this one as we hammered out every plotline and character arc, talking endlessly every day. You're a lifeline and I'm beyond grateful for you. And to Renny and Silvio, I love you guys!

Massive thanks as well to the rest of the amazing team at VSA—to Bernadette Baker-Baughman, Diane Dickendsheid, and Christine Kelder—I cannot thank you enough for all you do to keep things rolling on my behalf. Your diligence and good cheer and overall tremendous support make my job so much easier.

To Jen Monroe, my incredibly brilliant and wondrous editor, I'm so very grateful we're on this journey together and I can't thank you enough for pushing me at every turn to make this book as compelling as it could possibly be. I'm so grateful for your wit, charm, and also razor-sharp edits and guiding hand! Also, huge thanks to the fabulous Candice Coote for your insightful notes and helpful feedback and for keeping everything always running extremely smoothly!

To my acquiring editor, Danielle Perez, I'm so very grateful for the way in which you said yes to *A Likeable Woman* with such enthusiasm. I cannot thank you enough for everything, and for our early conversations about the book.

To the entire dream team at Berkley, thank you for being such an incredibly warm and fantastically creative publishing home. All my gratitude as well to Ivan Held, Craig Burke, Jeanne-Marie Hudson, Claire Zion, and Christine Ball. I'm so unbelievably fortunate to get to work with all of you!

Huge thanks to Loren Jaggers, my rockstar publicist. I can't believe we're on our third book together! Also massive thanks to the wonderful Chelsea Pascoe and Hannah Engler. I'm so thrilled to be working together. Enormous thanks to Bridget O'Toole, digital marketer extraordinaire

A huge thanks is also due to my amazing film/TV agent, Hilary Zaitz-Michael at WME, for working miracles.

And to the incandescent Rebecca Cutter, thanks for being so lovely, always.

To my dear friend, Josh Sabarra, there are no words sufficient enough to capture my gratitude for all your endless support, treasured friendship, and insanely stellar publicity dreaminess. I love you.

My writing career would not exist without the support of my family, and I must first thank my best friend: my mom, Liz Hinkle, who continues to inspire every novel I write, but especially this one. So much of your spirit and art inspired Sadie's story, and thanks for letting me make you my muse.

To my sister Beth, who always says the right thing at the right time to pull me out of the bell jar, I love you. And to my sister Susie, for your endless faith in me and for telling me to knock it off when I'm overthinking things, I love you!

To Amy, my first reader and first responder and my best friend since we were three, I'm so lucky you're my BFF and don't know what right thing I did in a past life to deserve you.

To my sweet father, Charles, I love you so very much and can't thank you enough for always cheering me on and cheering loudly and proudly. You're the man!

Huge thanks as well to my brother-in-law Paul (especially for the recent boat tour) and my amazing nephews, Xavier and Logan. Also big thanks to Joni, Courtney, Buddy, Marc, Kip, and Mac.

Thanks also to my husband's family, Jake and Stephanie, Amanda and Matt, Pam and Kevin, and especially Martha and Larry Lutringer.

Thanks to my extended family, Delena and Rex, Keegan, Jessica, Noah, and Trevor, T-pa and Feeney. Huge thanks to Slade for all the pep talks over the years.

A giant thanks as always to my East Coast family, beginning with Dorthaan Kirk. I am so very grateful for our friendship and for your unending belief in me! Special thanks also to April, Yolie, Iris, and all the Grands. Big thanks to my Houston family, Charlotte, Shan, Kia, Bailey and Akyla. And I'm forever indebted to Rahsaan Roland Kirk, my forever muse.

Massive thanks to my wonderful friends Kim and Chris and Elliot; Shannon and Drew Crawford; Sarah King; Lauren, Lori, Jackie, David, and Clara Ward (seriously, David, thank you for the Jell-O and all the pre-orders and for a lifetime of friendship!); Bo and Laura Elder; Tanya Manning Yarde; David Hess; Mark and Da; Betty and Felice; Lew Aldridge; Sara Zaske; Cody Daigle-Orians; Alex Giannini (thanks for having me back at StoryFest!); Bob Drinkwater; Carole Geffen; Dave and Joyce Dormady; Ron Shelton and Lolita Davidovich; Kellie Davis; George and Fran Ramsey;

Patricia Tippie and Henry—whom I miss dearly; Terri Whetstone; Adam and Colette Dorn; Stanley Smith and Mee-Mee Wong; Guy and Jeska Forsyth; Sumai and Hannibal Lokumbe. Special thanks as well to the Dallas crew: Amy, Missy, Ginny, Kristi, and Renee, thanks for always being there!

To Carmen Costello, I miss you more than words but you were right here with me as I drafted these pages, whispering in my ear. So much of you is in Sadie and just hell yes to our enduring, timeless friendship that will never die.

Many thanks as well to Tanda Tashjian, and Li, Bob, Don and Sharon Zhang. Also much gratitude to Kayla, Kristen, Erica, Lynne, Shelley, Kelsey, and Marissa. A huge heartfelt thanks to Laura. I seriously don't have the words to thank you enough for all you do.

Huge thanks to Annabelle Garza.

To the warm and supportive crime fiction community, especially Riley Sager, Jen Dornan-Fish, Eliza Jane Brazier (I'd die without our chats), Samantha Downing, P. J. Vernon, Kellye Garret, Chandler Baker, Vanessa Lillie, Zoje Stage, Amina Akhtar, Andi Bartz, Jeneva Rose, Megan Collins, Robyn Harding, Kaira Rouda, Ed Aymar, Cate Ray, Rachel Harrison, Hank Phillipi Ryan, Ashley Winstead, Kimberly Belle, Jeneva Rose, Mary Kubica, Nikki Dolson, Don Bentley, Tessa Wegert, Hannah Mary McKinnon, Liz Alterman, Debbie Babitt, Wanda Morris, Heather Gudenkauf, Amy Suite Clark, David Bell, Sharon Doering, Karen Dionne, Catherine McKenzie, Alma Katsu, and Liv Constantine.

All my love to Cathy Fast Horse and Ed "El Po" Chacon-Lontin; I'll bring the margaritas, just name the time and place.

To the legendary Joe Landsdale, I'm so happy that we've met.

A big thank-you to John Searles, for shouting out about *My Summer Darlings* on the *Today Show*!

I must say a special thanks to these early readers and crime fiction partners in crime: Laurie Elizabeth Flynn, your notes and our calls were everything; thank you and Jesse Q. Sutanto for reading early and letting me into your unlikeable female authors' coven. Huge thanks to my forever CP and dear friend, Katie Gutierrez, who always has my back and jumps in and reads at the drop of the hat, overnight; looking forward to more book touring and wine slamming with you! And to the exquisite Samantha Bailey, thanks for reading early and for your wonderful friendship; I love you more.

The writing community in Austin is solid gold. Giant thanks are due to my writing friends here, starting with my work wife, Marit Weisenberg, as well as Amanda Eyre Ward, my incredible friend Suzy Spencer, the amazing Gabino Iglesias (I'm happy to get stuck in an airport with you anytime), Stacey Swann, Kathy Blackwell, and Mary Helen Specht.

To Owen Egerton, I could not do without our chats, your pep talks, and the cocktail/plotting sessions. You rock.

Special thanks as well to Hillery Hugg, Beth Sample, Alyssa Harad, Maya Perez, Stacy Muszynski, Carolyn Cohagan, Felix Morgan, Meghan Paulk, Michelle Cullen, Alyssa Harad, Dalia Azim, Nick and Jordan Wade, Michael and Stephanie Noll, Becka Oliver, the Writers' League of Texas, and the LLL. Huge thanks also to the Texas Book Festival and Lois Kim, Susanna Auby, and Matthew Patin.

Enormous thanks to the phenomenal Amy Gentry, whose brilliance blows my mind on an hourly basis. Let's have pancakes then cocktails more often.

Massive thanks to Molly Odintz of Crime Reads. I'm so happy you're back in town and that we get to hang all the time. Thanks so much for your incredible support and friendship.

Huge gratitude as well to the incredible Stacia Campbell, Roxanne Pilat, Elia Esparza, and the entire Cabin 20. Massive thanks to Luis Alberto Urrea, who saved my writing life years ago by inviting me into the Cabin. Also big thanks to Kassandra Montag and Clare Empson.

Thanks as well to the fabulous Arielle and David Henry Sterry (aka The Book Doctors).

And an enormous thanks to all the wonderful booksellers, bookstagrammers, and librarians who truly keep books alive, with a special shout-out to Sally, John, and Mckenna at Murder By The Book; Barbara Peters and The Poisoned Pen; Scott Montgomery at BookPeople; Charley Rejsek at BookPeople; Amanda at Barnes & Noble at the Grove; as well as Pamela Klinger-Horn, Maxwell Gregory, Mary O'Malley, and also the good folks at Book Soup and also Lark & Owl. Huge thanks as well to Carol Ann Tack at Merrick Public Library.

Bookstagrammers are truly the lifeblood of social media, and I must thank Gare, Dennis, Jordy, Kori, Kate Rock, Lauren, Tracee, Carey, Ashley Kritzer, Abby with Crime by the Book, Carrie, Jamie, Stephanie, Laura, and Amy. Also special thanks to Marcy, Christina, and Tonya Cornish.

Saving the best for last, all my thanks goes to my incredible husband, Chuck, for being such a supportive partner, plot collaborator, and the best dad ever. EVER. I love you more than I can ever say.

And finally, to my sweet, hilarious, big-hearted boy, Johnny, let's go walking through the woods!